THE FINAL CUT

Love didn't surrender to hate, it merely tolerated it like a sister emotion.

She'd bathe and rest here for a while, and then she'd move on. Tomorrow she had off, and she'd use the day to find a more permanent place to stay. Somewhere Lucian wouldn't be able to find her, because as much as she insisted this was how she wanted things, her heart was of a whole different opinion.

She didn't trust herself not to go running to him the first time life got complicated. If he knew where she was and knew how to find her, it would only take a matter of visits for her to give in. She was too vulnerable, and hiding herself away was a safeguard she needed until she could trust herself to be strong.

She needed to maintain distance or he would eventually wear her down. That was something she couldn't allow. She *needed* to be *done* with Lucian for her own good.

COMING HOME

lydia michaels

BERKLEY BOOKS, NEW YORK

THE BERKLEY PUBLISHING GROUP
Published by the Penguin Group
Penguin Group (USA) LLC
375 Hudson Street, New York, New York 10014

USA • Canada • UK • Ireland • Australia • New Zealand • India • South Africa • China

penguin.com

A Penguin Random House Company

This book is an original publication of The Berkley Publishing Group.

Copyright © 2014 by Lydia Michaels.
Penguin supports copyright. Copyright fuels creativity, encourages diverse voices,
promotes free speech, and creates a vibrant culture. Thank you for buying an authorized
edition of this book and for complying with copyright laws by not reproducing, scanning,
or distributing any part of it in any form without permission. You are supporting writers
and allowing Penguin to continue to publish books for every reader.

BERKLEY® is a registered trademark of Penguin Group (USA).
The "B" design is a trademark of Penguin Group (USA).

Library of Congress Cataloging-in-Publication Data

Michaels, Lydia.
Coming home / Lydia Michaels.
pages ; cm.—(The surrender trilogy ; 3)
ISBN 978-0-425-27508-5 (softcover)—ISBN 978-0-698-62612-2 (ebook)
I. Title.
PS3613.I34439C66 2014
813'.6--dc23
2014017706

PUBLISHING HISTORY
InterMix eBook edition / January 2014
Berkley trade paperback edition / December 2014

PRINTED IN THE UNITED STATES OF AMERICA

10 9 8 7 6 5 4 3 2

Cover design by Rita Frangie.
Photo © Mikhail hoboton Popov/Shutterstock.
Interior text design by Kristin del Rosario.

To Mr. Dubois, Mrs. Muska, and Ms. Dailey.

Ha.

PART NINE

scout

one
. . . . .

SHAM SACRIFICE
An offer of material, which is made at no risk

THE burst of pollen hit Scout's nose like a feather laced with pepper. No, she couldn't sneeze. If she sneezed, she'd get glassy-eyed and look as if she were crying when she certainly had *not* been crying. As a matter of fact, she hadn't cried for days. After what was likely the most trying five days of her life, Scout made a vow to never cry again. Tears were useless and, frankly, a big pain in her girlie ass.

As she shifted to the shade out of the warm May sun, her pale pink dress shirt was a light cover to her skin. Her heavy gray wool slacks, however, were not. Coming directly from work and living out of a small bag for the past week hadn't left her much choice in the wardrobe department. Pavement smacked beneath her Nikes along the busy Folsom sidewalks with each determined stride.

For five long days, Scout contemplated her predicament. She'd always aimed to be something more than homeless, but tolerated her circumstances all the same. Now, however, things had changed. There was no way she was going back to where she'd started.

Her memory was an endless revolving door of strife, covered in a bleary haze, smothering the prettier things in this world. Scout never had pretty things. Well, that wasn't true. Lucian gave her many pretty things. He also *gave her away.*

The pain hadn't subsided. It was very real and seething angrily inside of her. Scout simply made a decision to channel that anger into something worthwhile. And that was what today was all about, something worthwhile.

She was worthwhile. So worthwhile, it was possible to put aside the hurt and the sting of his betrayal to do something for herself.

For twenty-three years she had struggled to survive. At age four she was diving in dumpsters for the smallest scrap of salvageable food. At age seven she'd been scavenging while other girls her age played house and learned their ABCs. Scout never played house, because she didn't know the first thing about living in a home. And she never learned her ABCs, because her mother, the only person Scout ever had to look up to, didn't know how to teach her.

Pearl wasn't a typical mother either. She never baked cookies, sang lullabies, or kissed scraped knees. Rather, she cooked crack, mumbled ramblings of a stoned soul, and gave her body to men who funded her next high. Scout was likely seven by the time she realized if you gave certain things to men, they'd give you almost anything in return; yet she never wanted to go down that same degrading road.

Scout wanted to *be* somebody. Her needs were more basic. She wanted four walls and a roof to call home. She wanted a key for her own front door. She wanted a job, and she wanted money for food and heat, and clothing thick enough to keep her warm even in the coldest blizzard.

Now she was halfway there. She had a job working at Clemons Market. It wasn't a spectacular place to work, but she liked it. The people treated her nice. And her boss, even though he sometimes gave her the creeps, was tolerable.

Her last boss expected much, much more. *He* expected her

heart. The son of a bitch got it too. Scout was still dealing with that emotional fallout.

Lucian Patras was likely a name she'd always know. He was a person quite difficult to forget. She tried. Lord knew she tried, but he was inside her, like a tattoo inked deep into her flesh. She couldn't wash him away no matter how much she wanted to.

Scout finally admitted that he'd used her, and with that shameful admission came some much-needed clarity. She could use him too.

She required a plan. Lucian had taught her many things. He taught her how to make love. He taught her how to socialize with aristocrats. He taught her how to play chess. And he taught her that she was more than a lost cause. However, he also taught her what it feels like to be truly fucked over.

She learned the agony of a broken heart, the torment of betrayal, and the misery of knowing the one person she wanted was the one she could never have. Her intimate relationship with Lucian was over.

One didn't have to be literate to read between the lines. She was given a chance to see behind the scenes as to how men of wealth play the game. She might not know how to count very well or be able to read heavy books, but Scout was not a stupid person. And she was a survivor.

Business was business, and so long as she kept the intimacy at bay, she could do what she needed to do. Scout's abbreviated taste of high society left nothing but a bitter taste in her mouth, and it was time to change the game.

Rounding the corner, Scout brushed her moist palms down the coarse wool covering her thighs. She could do this. She'd thought long and hard about what she wanted and nothing, not even the infamous Lucian Patras, would get in her way.

The revolving door of Patras Industries reflected the bright rays of sun peeking through the high-rise buildings across the

street. Scout's sneakers moved silently over the polished marble of
the lobby floors, and her thumb pressed with purpose into the
smooth button of the elevator.

After keying in the floor, she waited, her empty belly doing a
row of summersaults having nothing to do with the rise of the lift,
and everything to do with coming face-to-face with her past and
finally having the balls to go after her future.

Cheeks puffed as she forced out a shaky breath, her clammy
palms brushing over her blouse. "Your terms, Scout. Don't take
any shit," she whispered as the elevator eased to a stop.

The door chimed softly as it opened, and she stepped onto
smooth burgundy carpet. She looked nothing like she had the last
time she was there. Her polished Mary Janes were humbled down
to rubber-soled, serviceable shoes. Absent was the lace that once
adorned her legs. This was not a mission of seduction, but an exercise in influence.

Same as before, she arrived at the reception desk with a deep
hunger burning in her belly, but this hunger was something much
more potent than any form of lust. This was a hunger for well-
deserved recompense. No need to pretty herself up to get what she
came for, what she deserved.

It might've taken her five days to figure out, but she finally
understood. She held all the power. She was no longer an outsider.
She'd been on the other side of the looking glass and realized she
very well could stand on her own two feet. It was only a matter of
declaring her intentions and not backing down. It was time to do
for *her*.

"May I help you?" Seth, Lucian's personal assistant, greeted.
He clearly didn't recognize her, and why would he? She'd only
met Seth once, several months ago. She'd been dressed to the
nines and ready to seduce his boss. Without makeup she looked
like a child. Her hair was pulled into a no-nonsense ponytail, and
her Clemons uniform was anything but flattering. She'd also

dropped well over ten pounds, which on a small frame like hers was not a welcome loss.

"I'd like to speak to Mr. Patras."

His eyes narrowed with rejection before he voiced his reply. "You need an appointment to meet with Mr. Patras."

"I'm sure I do not." Insecurities rattled her confidence, but she kept her chin up and remained polite. She had every right to be there. Convincing herself of such was step one. "Please tell him Evelyn Keats is here to speak with him."

Seth's eyes bulged. "Ms. Keats, I'm sorry. I didn't recognize you. Let me tell Mr. Patras you're here."

That's right!

He pressed a button on the intercom, and a tight shiver pinched her heart at the sound of Lucian's voice. "Yes?"

"Mr. Patras, Ms. Keats is here—"

It shouldn't have been possible to get from his desk to the door in such a short span of time, but the door to Lucian's office whipped open and his muscular frame filled the doorway, stress marring his expression and exhaustion weighing in his eyes.

Lips parted in obvious surprise, he stilled. "Evelyn." His voice was a mere rasp of the self-assured baritone he usually spoke with.

She nodded. "I came to talk—"

"Come into my office."

Her lips twitched as he cut off her request. She wouldn't let him obtain the upper hand. This was *her* show. She was there for a reason, and she couldn't let her heart distract her. That foolish organ had caused enough problems.

Aiming for poise, she nodded and carefully stepped past him. The office door shut with a sharp snick. Her mind replayed the first time they'd met. Lucian had stood like a giant, a thin veneer of control, masked in immeasurable power, seething behind her then, and he reminded her of the same giant now. Her sneakered feet quickly stepped away.

When he faced her, she saw he was still speechless, his eyes scanning her from head to toe. "I need to talk to you," she said quickly.

"Where have you been?" he asked, his gaze filled with bewilderment as it traveled back and forth from her feet to her face.

"That's not your concern."

"Evelyn." He leveled her with a look that said he wasn't in the mood for games. Neither was she.

There was no way she'd tell him she'd actually returned to sleeping on the streets, using her bag as a pillow, a playground for shelter, and a McDonald's for facilities. He'd see it as a weakness, and she couldn't stomach his pity. Her pitiful circumstances were only temporary and tonight she'd be in a bed once more, so long as she stuck to her plan and didn't let him intimidate or bully her.

Steeling herself, she met his gaze. "Lucian, I came to talk about other issues, not where I'm living."

"You haven't been at the shelter."

She pursed her lips. "No doubt you had your minions checking every crevice of the city for me. I'm a lot more resourceful than you give me credit for."

His brow softened as though her words wounded him. "Did you expect me *not* to look for you? I told you I'd find you."

"I expected nothing less. Luckily, your search can stop now that I've come to you."

He stepped forward and she moved back. "Don't." Her hand shot out in warning. Regrettably, her request didn't come out as confident as she would've liked.

The hand reaching for her stilled and detoured to fork through his hair, tension clear on his face. He looked ragged, but still devastatingly handsome. The shadow on his tanned jaw should have looked sloppy, but only added another layer of sexy to his distinguished presence. His blue dress shirt had a white collar. Paired with the paisley red tie and black suit vest, he looked quite the tycoon.

"How long are you planning on keeping your distance, Evelyn? You're killing me. I've been going crazy since you ran off. I can't continue like this."

"And whose fault is that, Lucian?" she snapped, instantly regretting the show of emotion. *Keep it together, Keats.*

"I can't fix it if you refuse to let me—"

"There is no fixing it, Lucian! You used me and betrayed me."

"Bullshit!" he snapped. "I love you." His feet swiftly carried him across the office, incidentally boxing her into a corner. "I fucking love you, Evelyn. He had me at his mercy. *He* set the conditions."

He, being Parker, her once-dear friend turned Judas. Scout's understanding of their agreement was still foggy. Lucian had apparently been looking for her during a blizzard last winter and ran into Parker. After begging Parker to tell him where she was hiding, Lucian agreed to give her away for a month, with Parker driving some kind of bargain. Nope, still didn't compute. They were both guilty.

"And *you* agreed to his terms," she hissed. Fury at the injustice she'd been the victim of bloomed inside her, fresh and scorching. "I'm not here to talk about that. I don't care about your pitiful excuses. What's done is done. Either we discuss what I came here to discuss or I leave."

His gaze searched her face, likely hunting for some validation that she wasn't bluffing. Eyes that read opponents and colleagues with ease homed in on every visible strength and weakness she allowed him to see. Her jaw locked in determination.

"Go ahead and try to push me, Lucian. I'll be out that door so fast your head will spin."

He stepped back. *Good.* "What did you want to talk about?"

She glanced at the leather chair across from his desk. "May we sit?"

His dark eyes followed her gaze and he waved his hand in theatrical invitation. Irritation was evident in the set of his mouth and narrowed stare. Probably because Lucian was a man who didn't easily relinquish control. "By all means."

She sidestepped him, careful not to get too close, and he slowly returned to the seat behind his desk, his assessing gaze never leaving her. Her slight form sunk into the smooth leather chair. Her shoulders ached with the effort to remain stiff as she settled deeper into the soft seat. Exhaustion beat at her, threatening her resolve not to appear weak in front of him, but indignation and bruised pride stiffened her spine.

"What did you want to discuss?" he asked again.

This was it. Her entire life had been about survival, and now she wanted to survive in a more desirable way. She didn't need a billionaire to do that. She did, however, need a foundation to find her footing. Lucian could provide that foundation. While he may look at a woman like her and see someone vulnerable and in need of coddling, he was wrong. She didn't need someone to hold her hand. She simply needed a push, and then she'd manage on her own.

Taking a breath of courage, she said, "I want a loan."

His brow arched, telling her he hadn't expected such a request. "You're aware there's an account with over two hundred thousand dollars in your name? What could you possibly need that your bank account won't cover?"

That money had never been hers. Her dignity forbade her to touch it. Above all, Scout was practical. Lucian had more money than Midas and could afford to loan her what she was after. However, she was wise enough to know loans came with penalties and interest. Those were necessary stipulations to protect her pride. Unfortunately, Lucian's pride would likely face off with hers, and they were both incredibly stubborn.

"I don't want that money. I won't touch money earned on my back. I'm talking about an actual loan with interest and penalties and—"

He winced, then rolled his eyes. "Watch it, Evelyn. Tell me what you need. I'll give it to you. There's no need for this formal bullshit."

"I need my dignity back," she said succinctly, causing him to come up short. The "bullshit" that made this an official business deal was the only way she'd be able to stomach his help. It was just business. Taking those penalties away made it a favor, and she was done depending on favors from him.

"I see. And how much does one's dignity cost?"

"I'd like thirty-five thousand dollars."

His jaw ticked. "For?"

She met his challenging stare and tightened her lips. That was her business.

He sighed. "Evelyn, when an establishment finances another's endeavors, they're foolish not to question the investment."

"A second ago you were prepared to offer me anything I wanted. I don't see why my intentions should suddenly be an issue. This is just you being nosy. I'm not falling for it. Thirty-five thousand dollars is nothing to you. It's a new beginning for someone like me. Give me the satisfaction of at least believing you know I am capable of taking care of myself. I'm practical and I'm not stupid. Trust me to have a plan and I'll trust you to treat me fairly, like you would any other person asking you to invest in their future."

Those intimidating onyx eyes narrowed. "You're not any other person. Look at it as legal extortion. I have what you want. I'll trade you thirty-five thousand dollars for a bit of information."

Anger bloomed inside of her. Extortion indeed. She would *not* let him run her life. "I'll just go to a bank then," she bluffed.

"With what? You have no social security number, no identification, no birth certificate."

The molars in the back of her mouth clicked together. "I know you have those things. You're trying to manipulate me and, by doing so, only losing more of my respect."

He'd looked into getting her legal documents months ago. For him to be able to place a bank account in her name, he'd have needed to obtain some form of identification for her. Likely, he'd been holding it, too cowardly to hand over the documents before the big trade with Parker. If she had an ID, she could've fled a lot faster. That was Lucian, always the thinker and planner.

"I do," he agreed shamelessly.

"It wouldn't take long for me to go to a federal building and report them stolen. The numbers are on record, Lucian. Hard part's over. All you're doing is wasting my time. To be honest, your pettiness reeks of desperation."

His desk drawer slid open and snapped shut. Papers fluttered to the surface of his desk. He glared at her. "There."

Scout gazed at the documents. A neatly printed card with blue scroll trim filled her vision. Evelyn Scottlynn Keats. Nine digits formed her social security number below the neatly typed name. She was real!

Emotion had her chin trembling. So long she'd waited for such validation of her existence. So many obstacles could be overcome with those simple pieces of paper.

With unsteady fingers, she reached for the documents and stilled when Lucian's firm hand caught her wrist. Her gaze jerked to his.

The respect she held for him was in shreds, but giving her these documents that were rightfully hers mended a bit of the damage. She was gambling with his affections, asking for these things. If he didn't give them to her, he would annihilate any remaining faith she had in his goodness. She hated him for what he'd done, but deep down believed there was good behind the man. If he was so desperate to help her, it would have to be on *her* terms.

Don't deny me, Lucian. Please. She waited him out.

"I'll help you. But our other issues are far from concluded. Eventually we need to talk about what happened."

She glared at him and shook off his hold. "I'll ask that you keep your hands to yourself."

"And I'll ask that you drop the haughty performance you've been affecting since you got here."

Fingers snatching up the papers, Scout quickly removed her body from within his reach. Her brow tightened and her voice was dangerously close to cracking with emotion. "It's not an act. These are *my* papers and I deserve them. You have no right to keep them from me."

"And what of my money? Do you deserve that as well?"

"All I asked for was a loan. You can afford it. Either you help me or I go somewhere else."

"With what credit, Ms. Keats? No bank will sign over that amount of money without a cosigner."

He was likely right. He was also being mean and spiteful on purpose. Two could play that game. "I could always find another wealthy man willing to help me. After all, it was you who taught me *everything* is for sale."

He growled. "Watch yourself, Ms. Keats. I'm in no frame of mind to be pushed."

"Lucian." She took a deep breath. "I'm not forfeiting my morals for money. Even *you* can't afford them. You either agree to my terms and help me with a loan, or I'll figure out another way."

"Another way for what?" he snapped.

She wouldn't give him more information than necessary. She needed to do this for herself and if he knew her plan, he'd try to take over. Lucian was a leader—a very successful one—but she was sick and tired of following the tide. She needed to prove she could do this on her own. "For my future. I have nothing! I want to invest in *me*, since no one else gives a shit, and I need thirty-five thousand dollars to do that."

He stilled, his eyes narrowing, and she saw him weighing her words. Again he reached into his drawer, only this time he removed a heavy blue ledger. Long fingers flipped it open and reached for a pen. His hand swiftly moved over the check, the ballpoint scratching across the dense paper. The tear along each tiny perforation mesmerized her with its slow intent, but at last the slip fell free. He dropped the check in front of her with flourish. "There you go."

Scout stared at the check. The numbers read *$35,000.00*, but she couldn't read the script. She had trouble with anything that wasn't printed in capital letters.

Eyeing him suspiciously, she blinked as he arched a brow. "Take it. It's yours."

Her fingers hesitantly reached for the check. Once closed over the thick paper, she pulled her hands back to her lap. "I'll . . . I'll pay you back."

"I don't care about the money, Evelyn."

"Well, I do. I'll pay you back. Every cent. I'll make payments whenever possible. Once I've paid off the principal, we'll figure out what I owe in interest."

He rolled his eyes. "All right, but here are my conditions."

Her mouth opened. She shook her head, trying to scramble up the right words. "But you already gave it to me."

"I gave you a voucher. A check of that amount has to be cleared through me. What you have is trash unless I approve it when the bank calls."

"Fine," she gritted. "What are your terms?"

"Your payments will be made *in person*. I also require an address of where you're staying. These are simple requests, and any bank would demand a hell of a lot more from you. Be grateful that's all I'm stipulating at the moment."

Her jaw locked against what she wanted to say. He was trying to intimidate her. It wasn't happening. "Fine." He'd have to wait on the address.

"Good."

Several beats passed where neither of them said a word. She glared challengingly back at him, refusing to be bulldozed or bullied. She read Lucian's intentions in his eyes just as he likely read hers. She stood.

"I should be going."

All the intensity left Lucian's face. He shot to his feet. "Can I offer you a ride?"

She laughed. "Do I look stupid?" His expression was wounded. She sighed. "Lucian, I have no doubt the second I walk through that door you'll be on the phone with Dugan or some other underling, insisting they follow me. Can we skip the stalking for a change? I've been through hell and back over the past month. I think I'm entitled to my privacy."

"You know I can't do that."

"Why not?"

"Because I worry."

She shook her head. "How would you feel if someone followed you everywhere?"

"People follow me every day. I'm in the tabloids. I'm on the news. There aren't many places I can hide, Evelyn. You know that."

"And I know you hate it, so how could you intrude on my privacy in the same manner?"

"Because it's *not* the same. You're on your own and I'm only trying to keep an eye out." He suddenly frowned. "Why are you dressed like that?"

She glanced down at her Clemons uniform. Her hand quickly snapped off her name tag, and his eyes narrowed.

"You got a job," he guessed.

"I told you I plan to pay you back. I need money to do that."

"Where are you working? I would've given you your old job back."

"I don't want any ties, beyond this loan, to you or your companies."

His head slowly drew back, and she saw how her words wounded him. "Did what we have mean so little to you?" he asked in a quiet voice.

"Perhaps you should ask yourself that question." She picked up her bag and folded the check, slipping it safely inside the zippered pocket. "I have to go. Please don't have anyone follow me."

She turned and he called her name. "Evelyn."

Her resolve was waning and she had to get out of there. It was so hard seeing him and not touching him. Her heart wanted to run to him, feel his arms around her as she cried about the injustice done to her, but he was the culprit behind all of her heartache.

All she needed to do was think of how he'd betrayed her, and the pain was enough to drop her to her knees, cutting off all urge to step closer.

"Will you continue to pay for Pearl to stay at the rehab?"

His eyes narrowed. "The fact that you can even ask that shows how little you think of me."

What did he expect? He'd completely shocked her when he'd let her go and broken his promise to always protect her. She shrugged.

"Yes, I will continue to pay for your mother."

"Thank you."

He shook his head. "I'm glad to do it."

She remained facing the door, not wanting to look at him anymore. He stepped close but didn't touch her. "For what it's worth, I'm sorry."

"So am I." Quickly opening the door, she fled. Her finger pounded into the elevator button as if she were tapping out Morse code.

SOS. SOS. SOS!

Not until the doors of the elevator closed behind her did she turn and exhale. She did it.

two
·····

BLOCKADE

Using a pawn to obtain shelter from an attack

S COUT pressed through the revolving door and rushed into the busiest part of the sidewalk, hoping to get lost in the crowd, thus losing anyone who might be following her. The sooner she was safe, the sooner she could move on with her plans. She needed a bank.

So long as she stayed in public she wasn't in any danger. Not that she expected one of Lucian's minions to abduct her, but she really wasn't sure what he was capable of at the moment.

Hustling with serpentine movements from crowd to crowd, Scout made her way toward Edison Street, where there was a financial institution. Going directly there would offer shelter. However, it also meant if she was already being trailed, it would give her follower time to catch up and wait her out.

So be it. She wasn't sleeping outside again, and she needed money to rent a place to stay.

The tall white building stood like a grandfather among his offspring. Folsom Liberty & Trust was perhaps the oldest bank in the city and therefore, to her thinking, possessed good credentials.

Pressing through the heavy glass doors, Scout came up short.

The crisp air had a scent unlike anything she'd ever smelled. Was this what money smelled like when there were uncountable sums of it? Were mere mortals allowed in here? Did she need an appointment?

She glanced around nervously. Everyone seemed to know what they were doing. Trying not to look like a bank robber, she stepped aside as another man came through the door. He went to a section delineated with velvet rope.

Another woman leaned on a glass island, filling out a form. To her right was a carpeted area with fancy desks. People spoke in hushed tones much like they did at the library.

Scout's gaze traveled upward. There was a mural of a scale painted on the ceiling. Behind the scale were outlines of numerous men in white wigs. She wondered who they were. Likely, one was Lucian's ancestor.

"Can I help you with something?" a man in a suit asked.

"Um, I . . . do you work here?"

He smiled and the soft creases surrounding his eyes put her at ease. "I do. My name's Michael McGregor. Is there something you needed help with?"

"I wanted to open an account."

He nodded. "Okay, why don't you come have a seat at my desk?"

Following him to the carpeted area, Scout found herself sitting in a curved-back wooden chair. Mr. McGregor shifted to face his computer and typed a few buttons. "What kind of account were you hoping to open today, Ms. . . ."

"Keats. Evelyn Keats."

"Ms. Keats." His smile seemed friendly, but slightly artificial and haughty. Perhaps haughtiness flourished when one spent every day surrounded by money. She really liked the smell of the bank and found it distracting.

"A normal account."

"Checking?" he asked.

"Yes, I'd like to be able to write checks."

"Well, with our checking forgiveness program, you have no minimum balance for the first year. We do require you open the account with at least one hundred dollars, however. There are also no fees for the first twelve months. Does that sound like something you might be interested in?"

Banks charged fees? "Um, yes. Is that what people usually get? I've never had a bank account before."

"Not a problem. Did you bring two forms of identification?"

With shaky hands, she unzipped her bag and pulled out the documents Lucian had given her. "You'll give them back, right?"

"Of course. I just need to make copies." He turned and sifted through the documents. "These are in outstanding shape. Are they new?"

"Yes."

This bit of information seemed to make him examine the documents a bit more closely. He picked up her social security card and typed the number into his computer. She glanced at the people around her. Some looked stressed. Some looked angry. No one at the bank seemed to be happy except the employees. Money was obviously taxing but necessary, and she finally had some, or would, as soon as Lucian cleared the check.

Scout realized they'd likely call him, thereby letting him know where she was. Sighing, she contemplated how to get around being followed.

"Is this your current address?"

She looked at Mr. McGregor. He held her ID card. "Um, can I see it?" He passed it to her.

1900 Gerard Ave., Suite C

Shit. The group of words was one she recognized. It was

Lucian's penthouse. She didn't want him getting her mail and see-ing how she was using his money. *Her* money. "For now, but I'm moving. Will changing the address be an issue?"

"No, just bring in proof of residence and an updated ID."

She nodded. That would take some time, but she'd do it.

"How much were you planning on opening the account with?" he asked as he typed in more of her information.

"Thirty-five thousand dollars."

His fingers stilled over the keyboard. He nodded. "Do you have a check?"

"Yes." With stiff motions, she unfolded Lucian's check and flattened it on the desk. Once the creases were smoothed, she slid it to Mr. McGregor.

Examining it, he gave her a skeptical look. After clearing his throat, he said, "Excuse me for a moment." Standing, he left with her check and ID.

Scout's breath quaked in her lungs as she watched him walk away with her money. He disappeared behind a door, and she waited. Her eyes followed the line of people behind the velvet ropes slowly snaking through the main part of the bank, one cus-tomer after another concluding their business, and Mr. McGregor still hadn't returned.

Finally, after what was likely ten minutes but felt like an eter-nity, the door opened and he came out wearing the same smile he'd approached her with in the beginning. He sat at his desk. "Sorry about that."

Scout wasn't sure what had happened, but when she turned and saw Dugan, Lucian's chauffeur, step through the main doors, she understood. He'd called Lucian. Great. A familiar sense of humiliation prickled her pride. No matter how many times she begged him to leave her be, he simply couldn't. Her jaw tightened. She was supposed to be a goddamn adult.

Mr. McGregor typed in more information, then asked her to

endorse the deposit. The crisp check and a fancy pen slid in front of her. Scout's hands shook as she pulled the slip close.

"Just write my name?"

"Yes. Just sign above the line there."

"In cursive?" She didn't know how to write or read cursive.

"Yes, please."

Her throat was dry as she swallowed and carefully formed her letters, paying extra care to connect them where she could, faking the best script her hand could manage.

Insecurity knit her brow as she slid the check back to him. He only glanced at the signature before sliding it through a device and stamping the back. He then passed her a plastic card.

"This is your debit card. You'll be able to withdraw sums up to three hundred dollars from any automatic teller machine. All you have to do is follow the prompts." He slid a device toward her. "Please select a pin number between four and nine digits. You'll want to pick something you can remember and not share it with anyone."

She carefully typed in 1-9-0-0, Patras's address.

"Would you like any cash back today?"

"Um, could I have three hundred dollars, please?"

"Sure. We normally have to wait for a check to clear, but since Mr. Patras is one of our trustees and offered to come down here himself in order to clear the funds, I don't see a problem."

Her teeth ground together. Was he here? Casually looking around, she caught Dugan's gaze. He nodded once, letting her know that, yes, Lucian was somewhere nearby. *Wonderful.*

"How would you like that?"

Her gaze jerked back to the banker and she forced her expression to soften. "Excuse me?"

"Would hundreds be okay, or did you want smaller bills?"

"Could you give me some smaller bills too? I'd prefer to not have anything larger than a fifty."

Mr. McGregor nodded. "Let me go put this through and I'll be right back with your money."

When he left she shot Dugan a cold look that was more intended for Lucian, but he wasn't making his presence known at the moment. Dugan simply arched a bushy brow. The rest of his granite expression remained unmoved.

Mr. McGregor returned. Some paperwork spewed from the printer and again he asked her to sign after going over some policies with her.

"These are your temporary checks. Will ten be enough? You should receive your personal checks in seven to ten business days."

Scout nodded. She needed to get a place and get her address changed quickly, before the checks went in the mail. Otherwise she'd have no choice but to see Lucian again sooner than she wanted to.

When they finished, she tucked her bank card and checks and the rest of the paperwork safely into her bag and shook Mr. McGregor's proffered hand.

"The remainder of your funds should be available in two business days, Ms. Keats. It was a pleasure doing business with you."

When she reached the door, Dugan was already holding it for her. "Nice to see you again, Ms. Keats."

"Bite me," she grumbled as she exited the bank and came face-to-face with Lucian's sleek black limo. Her shoulders drooped. "Is this really necessary?"

Dugan again arched a brow, but said nothing.

"Is he in there?" she snapped.

"Yes, ma'am."

Huffing, she pivoted without a word, marching away from the limo with no idea where she was heading. As horns began to honk, she turned and found the limousine crawling at a snail's pace beside her, holding up a good deal of city traffic.

"Get in the car, Evelyn," Lucian's voice calmly called from the shadows of the back window.

"Go away, Lucian." Her legs trudged on. When she spotted a one-way street they wouldn't be able to enter, she picked up her pace. The limo continued beside her as she steadily speed walked in that direction.

Voices of aggravated drivers shouted at the limo from the line of traffic. Finally reaching her planned detour, she turned and the limo shot off in the distance. Her walk transitioned into a jog. She needed to get out of there.

Just as she reached the intersection of the next block, the limo slid in front of her, blocking all traffic and causing a driver across the way to slam on his brakes. Horns blared and Lucian's window rolled down.

"Evelyn, you're causing a scene. Get in."

"*You* are causing a scene. Go away." She pivoted, walking east when the sound of a car door opening had her doubling her pace and risking a glance over her shoulder.

Sure enough, Lucian was out and coming after her. Should she run? Surely he wouldn't force her into the car.

"Where's your jacket? It's still chilly out."

She glanced to her left. Lucian strode beside her with an air of casualness she didn't understand. His hands were wedged in his pockets and his expression light. Dugan putted along beside them, continuing to block traffic.

"It's May."

"Still, the low is fifty-eight. You should have a jacket."

She rolled her eyes. "I don't *own* a jacket." This was ridiculous. "Are you just going to have Dugan follow me? He's causing a traffic jam."

He shrugged. "I offered you a ride. If you'd let us drive you where you're going he'd be able to obey the speed limit."

Silently she counted to ten before facing him. He stopped. "Lucian, I know what you're doing."

"I wasn't trying to be secretive."

"This isn't going to work."

"What do you suggest I do then?"

"Leave. Me. Alone."

He smiled sadly, eyes downcast in an expression that was downright inappropriate for a man of his stature. Guilt rode her hard, but pride got her second thoughts under control. He deserved this.

His voice rasped in a hoarse confession. "You see, I can't do that Evelyn. I love you, and without you I'm miserable. Even standing in your shadow is better than not knowing where you are."

Her fingers rubbed her forehead. "Damn it, Lucian . . ."

"Come home with me, baby. Let me feed you and let's talk."

She shook her head. "No."

"Why? You know I'll eventually wear you down."

"Doesn't it mean anything to you that I *don't want* to be worn down? I just want to live my life without being harassed or stalked."

His eyes grew sadder. "But I can't sleep without you in my bed. I can't think, not knowing where you are each day, worrying where you're spending your nights, if you're warm enough or if you've had dinner."

"Those aren't your worries anymore."

"They'll always be my worries, Evelyn. Please, let me at least give you a ride where you need to go."

Her shoulders sagged. She'd worked eight hours that day and didn't have the energy to play hide and seek in a city the size of Folsom. She needed to get away from him, but clearly that wasn't happening tonight.

"Fine." His face lit with a smile. "You can drop me off at the Slumberland Motel."

Happiness morphed to disapproval. "The fucking Slumberland, Evelyn? I don't think so."

She huffed in exasperation. "Then good-bye." Pivoting on her heel, she walked away from him at a quick clip. Her steps faltered as he jerked her to a stop.

"I own the nicest fucking hotel in the city. Stay there. This is ridiculous."

"You're ridiculous! When will you get it? I don't want anything to do with you!"

His lips thinned. "Nothing except my money."

"Fuck you, Lucian. I'll use that money as equity and get a lesser loan from the bank. I'm not stupid. With that as collateral I'll get approved for at least half, and then I'll gladly write you a check and give it all back if it comes with your manipulation or judgment. You know I'm not like that."

"Don't do that. I want you to have the money."

"Then don't make me feel like a user for taking it! It's a loan, not a fucking handout."

A frustrated groan rumbled from his chest as his hands fisted his hair. "Tell me what I can do? I just want a chance to make this right."

"There *is* no *this*! There is no *us*. We are over. The sooner you come to terms with that the better."

"Goddamn it, Evelyn, how can you say that?"

She glared up at him and in a voice far too calm to reflect all the turmoil raging inside of her, she said, "You *gave* me to him, Lucian. You *gave* me away to another man. I trusted you and I trusted him and you *both* betrayed me. I'll never forgive you for that."

"I explained. There was no choice. In time—"

"*No!* There's no amount of time that will take back what you've done. You'll always be the first man who touched me, the first man who loved me, and the first man to royally fuck me over, and I'll never forget that. You can't negotiate your way back into my heart. I won't let you. If you think I'm bluffing, try me. All of my life I've had one cardinal rule: The only person I can trust is myself. I'm the only person I can count on to truly look out for me without ulterior motives. That's what I'm doing now, looking out. I don't need your hotel. I don't need your damn limo to give me a ride. And I don't need you."

He stared at her, a blank expression on his face for a long moment. Finally, he whispered, "But I need you."

Weary, she shut her eyes and shook her head. "You don't need me, Lucian. You're gorgeous, wealthy, and, for the most part, a sweet man. Find someone else to give your heart to. I don't want it."

"Is that what you really want?" he rasped.

No. God, no. The thought of him loving another woman was agonizing. "That's what I need. That's what's for the best."

"And what will you do, Evelyn? Will you find someone else?"

"My mind is so far away from that right now, Lucian, I can't give you an answer."

He visibly swallowed. "Will you be okay? Will you promise to come to me if there's anything you need?"

His words showed he was relenting. That was what she needed, but the pain in her chest was back. "Yes."

"For what it's worth, I'm sorry. I know that means nothing to you right now, but it's the truth."

She looked away. He didn't deserve any sign of forgiveness from her. She lacked even the ability to acknowledge his apology at that moment. Everything was still too fresh, too raw. It had only been a few days since she found out about his betrayal—his and Parker's, the man she loved and the man she thought was her best friend.

She was tired, needed a shower, and wanted to sleep in a bed with blankets. "Will you drive me to the motel?"

He hesitated, but nodded. They walked back to the limo in silence. Scout slid onto the cool leather seat and stared out the window. Lucian climbed in beside her and shut the door.

"Take us to the Slumberland Motel, Dugan," he said, and the limo eased into traffic.

They arrived at the motel ten minutes later, neither of them speaking a word along the way. Dugan parked but didn't get out. Scout sighed. Would they leave or continue this ridiculous trailing?

Her hand reached for the door handle. "Thanks for the ride."

She was yanked back to the center of the bench seat, and Lucian's mouth was suddenly on her. A squeak slipped past her throat as he kissed her hard, his fingers digging into her shoulders. It took everything she had not to melt into him.

He betrayed you!

Her palms shoved at his chest and he drew back. His breath was labored. "This is not the end of us, Evelyn. I don't care what you say. I'm not done with you and you're not done with me."

Scrambling off the seat and out of the limo, Scout slammed the door behind her. Her heart pounded wildly in her chest. Lucian didn't roll down the window or try to come after her. Her shaken expression reflected in the tinted glass, and she felt his eyes on her, staring through the barrier.

Turning, she headed toward the window with a blinking light. By the time she opened the motel's office door, the limo was gliding away. She was shocked to actually see it go and keep going until it disappeared.

Wavering emotions had her hand settling over her empty belly. Disbelief that he'd actually gone was quickly followed by sharp devastation. Lucian never walked away from something he wanted. But what if he no longer truly wanted her? *Careful what you wish for.*

Perhaps this was all part of his next calculated move. Or perhaps this was truly the end of them. Asking for space didn't make it any less painful to bear. She hated him, but missed him all the same. Love didn't surrender to hate, it merely tolerated it like a sister emotion.

She'd bathe and rest here for a while, and then she'd move on. Tomorrow she had off, and she'd use the day to find a more permanent place to stay. Somewhere Lucian wouldn't be able to find her, because as much as she insisted this was how she wanted things, her heart was of a whole different opinion.

She didn't trust herself not to go running to him the first time life got complicated. If he knew where she was and knew how to find her, it would only take a matter of visits for her to give in. She was too vulnerable, and hiding herself away was a safeguard she needed until she could trust herself to be strong.

She needed to maintain distance or he would eventually wear her down. That was something she couldn't allow. She *needed* to be *done* with him for her own good.

three
.....

THE KEY TO HAPPINESS . . .

"*SCOUT? Come on, child. It's getting dark.*"

Scout turned as her mother came out of the house without windows. Boards with swirled graffiti filled each socket, eyes to a home without a soul. Dropping the piece of onion grass she'd been nibbling on, Scout stood, her gaze drawn back to the children across the way.

"*Momma, what's that place there?*"

Her mother righted her clothing and stashed a bag of her medicine in her pocket. "That ain't nothing you gots to be worrying about."

Scout regarded the children running over the blacktop, their laughter floating on the breeze and teasing her in ways she didn't understand. "But why's all them kids there?"

Her mother huffed. "That's a school, baby. Thems is there to learn."

"*Learn what?*"

"*Nothin' you need to know. We different. Now come on.*"

Her small fingers were swallowed in her mother's bony hand as she was pulled down the sidewalk back toward the tracks. Each time she glanced back at the school, her mother tugged her along.

SCOUT frowned as she carefully drew the letter *E*. She'd been practicing her penmanship for over an hour, simply writing and rewriting *EVELYN KEATS* on the tiny notepad she found in the drawer of her motel. A callous formed above her knuckle, and she admired it like the badge of honor it was.

It was three in the morning and she couldn't sleep. She'd rested for a few hours, but awoke restless and hungry. Nothing would be open until the sun rose, and her mind was running wild with things to do. She desperately wanted to write them down in a prioritized list, but the task was more frustrating than productive. She glanced at her shabbily jotted notes.

FINED HOME
FOOD
COTE
CHANJ ~~ADRIS~~ ADRES
TUTHE BRUSH
~~SAMPU~~ SHAMPU
SOAP

Her bones were weak from thinking so hard. Anger rose, and each time she thought to blame someone else for her problems, she reminded herself her predicament was no one's fault but her own.

Not knowing what the day would bring, around five she showered again, using tissue to carefully wrap the remainder of soap, stuffing it into her bag. Her clothes were wrinkled and damp from washing them in the small sink. She didn't want them to get musty, but as the sky pinkened with the first sight of dawn, she grew eager to leave and folded them into her bag anyway.

Her stomach cramped with hunger. She'd taken to stealing dented cans of fruit from the back room of Clemons. It wasn't technically stealing, being that the damaged cans were on their way to the dumpster. Her belly was revolting, and she was growing weaker with each passing hour. Her stomach needed a real meal, and she finally had the money to purchase one.

At seven, she laced up her sneakers and glanced around the room one last time, making sure she hadn't left anything behind. She returned her key to the front desk and headed west, where a small diner was open.

Sidewalks were empty at this hour, aside from a distant silhouette moving along. The bell above the door jingled as she stepped inside. Shiny red stools were lined up along a counter, and there was a pie safe slowly spinning at the end. The snapping scent of bacon brought her hunger pains to the forefront of her mind. Her tired legs climbed onto the stool in the corner, far away from the truckers finding their morning meals. Older couples filled the booths lining the windows.

A waitress with bottled black hair and red lips pressed a napkin in front of her and slid over a grease-stained menu. "Coffee?"

"Yes, please."

A saucer and a mug appeared as the waitress filled it with steaming dark sustenance. The man to her left dropped some money on the counter and left. Scout eyed the paper he'd abandoned.

"You need a minute to decide, hon?"

Her gaze returned to the waitress. "Can I have French toast, please, and a side of bacon?"

"Sure thing." The waitress jotted down the order and, before pinning it to the clips lining the cook window, began clearing the place to her left.

When her hand touched the newspaper Scout asked, "Do you mind if I take that?"

The waitress passed it to her and bustled off with an armful of dirty dishes. Scout self-consciously stared at the inky words scrambled over the pages. The door chimed repeatedly as patrons arrived, and soft chatter filled the small eatery, as did the scent of sizzling meats.

A heavy white plate slid in front of her. The French toast wasn't as thick as the kind they served at Patras, and there were no strawberries, but the dish still earned a jolt of excitement from her empty belly. Sliding the paper aside, she picked up her fork and knife, noting the tiny scratches in the imitation silver, and dug in.

It was irritating not being able to clean her plate, but her stomach was overly sensitive from lack of food. She drank another cup of coffee and asked the waitress to wrap up the rest.

After using the bathroom, she returned to her stool to attempt the paper once more. The morning crowd shifted, newcomers ate, paid, and left, and Scout found she was blinking back tears.

When there was a lull in the crowd, the waitress surprised her by sitting in the stool to her left and cutting into a fresh-baked pie. She sliced two sections into creamy triangles and served them up on small saucers, sliding one directly in front of Scout.

"You look like you could use some pie."

Caught off guard by the generous offering, Scout stared. Her eyes went to the name tag clipped on the waitress's blouse. It started with a *B*.

"Go on. It's on the house."

Instinctively, Scout hesitated. Food was something she was rarely treated to prior to Lucian. She smiled and reached for a fork. The pie melted like a cloud of heaven on her tongue. Chocolate.

The waitress grinned and moaned as she took a bite of her own slice. "Good, right?"

"It's delicious."

"Thanks. I made it this morning. Girl's gotta have chocolate. Best substitute for sex there is."

Scout laughed. "I should have a dozen then."

The waitress snickered. "You having men troubles?"

Scout truly laughed. "Oh, you could say that. The trouble is I don't want one."

The waitress nodded knowingly and bit into another forkful of chocolate heaven. "Don't want one, but your heart says otherwise, I'm guessing."

"I'm not on speaking terms with my heart right now," Scout admitted, scraping up the last bit of whipped chocolate from her plate.

The waitress laughed. "I'm Barbara."

Scout smiled. "Scout."

"You looking for something particular in that paper? Been thumbing through it all morning."

She opened her mouth, but hesitated. "I'm trying to find an apartment."

Barbara glanced at the paper then, with halting progression, reached over and turned a few pages. "The apartment listings are here, hon, under the classifieds." She met Scout's gaze, a curious look in her eyes. Leaning close, she whispered, "Can you read, Scout?"

Swallowing tightly, lips sealed, she shook her head. "Not much."

Barbara scooted closer and nodded. In a soft voice, she said, "Okay, well, here's one that's not too far. It's a one-bedroom loft, rents for eight-fifty a month."

Scout's breath shook on an exhalation as she nodded humbly.

"And this one here's a little less, but that isn't in the greatest section of Folsom. It's an efficiency. You pay utilities and the rent's seven-twenty. Are you looking to be close to a certain area?"

"I work at Clemons Market."

"I know where that is. Let's see . . ." Barbara pulled the paper closer and dragged a painted fingernail down the typed column of listings. "Here we go. This one's around there. Oh, and it rents for only six-fifty. Says it's an efficiency. You pay utilities. There's a number here. You got a phone?"

"My phone broke."

Barbara glanced at the cook window, then reached over the counter, a cordless phone appearing in her hand. "Better let me make the call. My boss gets a bug up his ass whenever I let the customers use the phone."

Scout nodded and Barbara dialed, her fingers drumming over the Formica countertop as she waited. "Yes, hello, I'm calling about the apartment located at twenty-five South Knights Boulevard . . . Mm-hm . . . No, just me . . . Today at two o'clock?" She glanced at Scout for conformation and whispered, "He can show it at two today."

Scout nodded.

"That would be wonderful . . . My name's Scout . . ." She looked to Scout questioningly.

"Keats."

"Keats. Scout Keats, and I'll see you at two. Thank you very much." Barbara clicked off the phone and returned it to the other side of the counter. "There you go, hon."

"Thank you."

"Thank you!" she said in return. "I'm hoping some good karma will pay off tonight when they pull the Powerball."

"Well, I hope you win," Scout said.

"Me too. Mmm! What I could do with a couple hundred thousand."

Scout grinned. "What would you do?"

"Oh, I'd buy this here diner and make it into the cutest little pie place Folsom's ever seen. Get rid of my man and find someone who treats me nice, someone who really appreciates me for me. Maybe buy one of those fancy televisions." She giggled. "Who knows?"

Scout saved her comments. There was no point in letting her jaded opinions of the cost of frivolous luxuries taint this woman's dreams. She hoped Barbara someday had her own pie place. Her pies deserved a good home.

Taking out her money, she counted out a generous tip. "You buy yourself an extra ticket with this."

"Aw, you don't have to do that, hon. That pie was my treat."

"I know. I want to. Take it as a thank-you for helping me find an apartment."

"Well, I hope it's real nice for you."

SCOUT cooled her heels on South Knights Boulevard for twenty minutes waiting for the landlord to show, checking her cheap watch. She paced, hoping he hadn't given the apartment to someone else.

Like a gap-toothed grin, the Boulevard was made up of storefronts separated by cavernous alleys. Clemons was three blocks away, and Patras was over four miles distant. Scout liked the location for its practicality. Number twenty-five was an old building. The bottom floor was an office of some sort. At two thirty, a blue sedan finally pulled along the curb.

"Ms. Keats?" The pudgy older man called as he climbed out of his car.

Scout smiled. "Yes."

He bustled over and held out a hand. "Name's Snyder. You ready to see the apartment?"

Nodding, she followed him down the alley beside an office building. A nondescript brown door was the only interruption in the long brick wall. Mr. Snyder dug out a set of keys and, with a little elbow grease, got the door open.

"I just had new paint and carpets put in."

The new fibers of the gray rug tickled her nose and tempted a sneeze as she followed him up a steep set of stairs. The landlord hunched a little once he made it to the top. The entrance was small.

The ceilings were low. Mr. Snyder was short for a man, but seemed cramped in the squat apartment. Everything was painted a clinical shade of white. There was a small stove on a tiny patch of linoleum and a sink. No counters. The fridge seemed made for dwarves.

Walking across the new carpet, Mr. Snyder opened a cheaply made wooden door, also painted hospital white. "This is the bathroom."

Tiny black and white tiles made up the space. There was a pedestal sink and a claw-foot tub. A dormer took the ceiling space over the tub from seven feet to about five. She wouldn't be taking many showers there.

"Over here's a closet for your clothes." It was more like a pantry.

Her stomach sunk and then propelled somewhere behind her heart. She could afford this place. It wasn't much, but it could actually be hers if she played her cards right.

This was going to be her home. Her *first* home. She could make it her own and fill it with personal touches.

Mr. Snyder's cheeks flushed in a way that spoke of too many heavy meals and not enough light exercise. He ran a hand over his thinning hair. "What do you think? Utilities won't be much here."

Her lungs released a pent-up breath she hadn't realized she'd been holding. It seemed that breath had been held for twenty-three years. "I'll take it."

"Great. All I need is the first and last months' rent. I'll take a check. You can move in today if you'd like. I have the lease here." He handed her a long, yellow slip of paper with a pink carbon copy on the back.

Paperwork.

Taking the paper, she glanced over it. It was a lot of printed writing. For the first time she missed Parker. He always helped her with this sort of thing. "Do you have a pen?"

He handed her a blue pen. "Guess there isn't really a place to write, being there's no furniture. Tell you what. Why don't you just write out your name there at the top of the lease and sign? I already filled in the numbers. I'll do the rest when I get back to my office."

The literary gods must've been smiling on her that day. She carefully wrote her name, then signed the bottom, much like she'd signed her name at the bank. Finding her temporary checks, she pulled one out. She thought about what Lucian's check had looked like.

"The check's for how much?"

"Thirteen total. Then your next check will be due on the first of June. It's a month-to-month lease, but it states you give me sixty days notice of intent to move. Electric's already set up. The bill arrives on the fifteenth of the month. You can pick it up at the insurance office directly downstairs. Once I get the company a copy of the lease, your name will be added to the account. Cable and phone are your responsibility to set up."

Leaning against the stove, Scout drew the numbers *1300.00* in the box on the check and signed her name. Tearing the check from the others, she handed it to him. He frowned. "You forgot the rest, dear."

"Um . . ." She swallowed. "I . . ."

He tilted his head. "You special?"

She bristled. "No, I am *not* special. I . . . I hurt my hand yesterday. Would you mind filling out the rest?" *Dickhead.*

"Oh, my apologies."

She scowled at him as he filled in the rest of the check. He turned and held out his hand. "Well, it was a pleasure doing business with you, Ms. Keats. Oh, before I forget. Here's your key."

Her heart stuttered. *Her key.* She took the small piece of carved metal and squeezed it tight, its jagged edges a welcome pinch of reality in her palm. "Thank you."

After tearing the carbon copy from the lease, Mr. Snyder, her new landlord, handed it to her. "My office address is at the top. I charge a late fee after the fifth, so you want to have your check in the mail well before then. You have any trouble, you call my office."

After a few more instructions, like where to find the breaker box and thermostat, Mr. Snyder left and she stood alone in her apartment. It was surreal.

Scout turned slowly in a circle and took in the space that was now her home. Her cheeks pulled as a grin slowly split her face, and suddenly she was jogging in place doing a happy dance and squealing like a child.

She fell to the stiff carpet in a fit of giggles and held her stomach. "Home," she whispered. "You have a home."

four

·····

INDULGENCES

THE euphoria Scout experienced at having *her own* place to call home was unexpected and definitely welcome. When she finally dragged herself off the floor, she dug out her bank book and carefully wrote:

Transaction	Check	+/-	Balance
L.			$35,000.00
BANC		-$300.00	$34,700.00
HOME	0001	1,300.00	$33,400.00

Tucking the checkbook back in her bag, she looked at her watch. She had two hundred and four dollars and thirty-six cents left after the motel and breakfast. Gazing around her *home*, she considered the necessities she needed.

She stood and opened the fridge. How incredible. The air that touched her hand was cold. She opened the freezer—also cold. Amazing! She ran to the bathroom and turned on the water. Beautiful, clear liquid flowed from the spigot. Cupping her hands, she drank a mouthful, laughing at the purity of the taste. *Running water!* In *her* bathroom!

She flushed the toilet and spun in place. Her fingers flipped the switch as she watched the simple bulb behind the glass flicker with each click. On. Off. On. Off. On. Off.

Her cheeks cramped as her smile refused to abate. Sighing, she turned and faced her living room slash bedroom. Decision made, she swept up her bag, dug out her key, and nearly broke her neck as she rushed down the steps.

Calm down, Keats. You want to be around to enjoy it.

After locking the door, she exited the alley and headed toward Clemons. Her eyes snagged on the people in the insurance office below her apartment. Eventually she'd need to introduce herself to them.

Her job was the perfect distance from her *home*. Every time she thought the word she beamed. She had a home!

A few doors down from Clemons Market was a mattress store. She was getting herself a bed! As she approached the store, she took a deep breath. She'd never bought a big-ticket item, but this was definitely a dream worth pursuing.

Scout pressed the glass door open and stepped into a showroom full of various white mattresses.

"Can I help you find something?"

Scout jumped. Where the hell did that guy come from? He wore a brown suit with a yellow shirt and brown tie. He must work there. "I want to buy a bed."

He smirked, as though they were old friends, which automatically made her uncomfortable. Oh, well. She was getting a bed and this was the only bed store she knew of.

"Well, you came to the right place. Name's Sal. What kind of bed are you looking for?"

"Um, the kind you sleep on. Do you guys deliver?"

"Yes. Thursday's one of our delivery days, so you're in luck if you were hoping to get it today. Will you be shopping for a mattress and box spring as well?"

Yes, mattress, that's what she meant. "What's a box spring?"

"Box spring's the support piece under the mattress." He pointed to the bed closest to them and lifted the plush mattress to show her the box spring. It looked like a mattress, but wasn't cushioned.

"What does it do?"

Salesman Sal's brow creased. "It lifts the mattress, offers more support. You don't want to put a mattress on the frame."

"Frame?"

"The metal support." He pointed to the brown metal beams that raised the mattress and box spring off the ground.

"Oh, yes, I'd also like a box spring." Her days of sleeping low to the ground were over.

"What size were you hoping for?"

"Um, square and a one-person."

He frowned and laughed in a way that was insulting. "Well, they're all square, dear. Let me show you our twins."

"It's just for one person," she explained.

"Right. That's a twin."

Oh.

They walked to the far left of the showroom. Several narrow, one-person beds were lined up on the wall. "This is a good brand, one of our best sellers. Go ahead. Try it out."

Eyeing him skeptically, she looked at the bed. Pockets of white curved up in firm diamond-shaped clouds, neatly sectioned off with ivory stitching. Cautiously, she stepped closer and sat on the edge. It was firm.

"Go ahead. Lay down. Get comfortable."

Her brow tightened and, with shifting movements, she scooted more on the bed. As she eased back, she was very aware of her breasts pressing into her shirt and Sal observing her. It was impossible to get comfortable with him hovering over her. She sat up. Anything was better than the floor.

"How much is it?" she asked.

He looked at the tag she hadn't noticed tacked to the side. "This one's four ninety-nine."

"Four ninety-nine? As in four *hundred* and ninety-nine dollars?" She nearly spit.

"It's a memory foam. You're talking about one hundred and eighty degrees of spring and three hundred and sixty degrees of comfort."

She stepped away from the bed. "I'm looking for something a little more affordable."

Sal stepped to the right. "Well, this here's a notable brand. It's a traditional spring."

She looked for the tag. It was two hundred and ninety-nine dollars. Her stomach sunk. Scowling, she marched down the line, flicking up each tag until she found one that was in her price range. She sat on the edge of the mattress and bounced. This one wasn't cut in with white stuffed diamond shapes, but it had nice blue ticking. It was firm and squeaked as she bounced.

The salesman approached with a regretful expression. "I don't think you want that one, sweetheart. You'll be spending the difference on visits to the chiropractor. That there's a backbreaker."

Lips pursed, she met his gaze challengingly. "Do you make a commission?"

His mouth opened as he gathered his words. "Well, yes, but I'm more concerned with your comfort than making a sale."

"I'm sure you are," she mumbled, standing to examine the box spring. "How much is this?"

He sighed. "That box spring's fifty-five. Can I show you a better model? It's only a little more. I'd hate to see you throw away your money on a mattress you aren't happy with."

Scout faced him. "Sal—it is Sal, isn't it?" He nodded. "Well, Sal, I'm sure the mattress isn't as bad as you say. A man like you wouldn't have shoddy merchandise in his store."

He blustered. "Well, now, I wouldn't call it shoddy—"

"But you'd call it a backbreaker?"

"I only meant there are better—"

"Right. I know what you meant. This mattress will do just fine."

His lips formed a thin line. "Our store has a nonrefundable policy—"

"That's fine. When can I have it delivered?"

His eyes narrowed and he sighed. Lifting the clipboard he held, his pudgy fingers flipped a few pages. "Where's it going?"

"Only a few blocks from here, South Knights Boulevard."

"I have an opening for tonight between five and seven."

She beamed. "Perfect! I'd like to pay now."

She followed a very sulky Sal to the register. Her grand total for her mattress, box spring, and frame was one hundred ninety-four dollars and four cents with tax. She signed the order form carefully. She'd never written her name so much in one day.

"Slide your card," Sal said, gesturing toward the fancy card device on the counter. Luckily, from clerking at Clemons, she was familiar with the device. She swiped her card, and words came up. Lots of words. *Shit.*

"Type in your pin and hit Enter."

Blowing out a calming breath, she typed in the address for Patras. 1-9-0-0.

"You have to hit Enter."

Where was Enter? When she took longer than usual, Sal said, "The green button."

Scout quickly hit the button. "Sorry. I forgot my glasses," she lied.

"Hit Enter again if the amount's okay."

She looked at the screen. $194.04. That was correct. She pressed the green button again and more words appeared as a paper receipt spewed from the register. She'd been a bit concerned the funds wouldn't clear, but it looked as though her money was available. Sal stapled it to her signed receipt and slid it across the counter.

"If you miss the delivery there's a twenty-five-dollar service fee and our next delivery day isn't until Saturday." He certainly wasn't as friendly since he learned he wouldn't be making a living off of her.

Taking the paperwork, she gave him a nice smile. "Thank you very much."

He grumbled a *have a nice day* and she left. Tonight she'd be sleeping on her own bed!

SCOUT was huffing and puffing by the time she made it up the narrow steps of her apartment with her bags. The living space was swamped with other bags and assorted items. She needed to get things put away before her bed arrived.

She was nearing a crash. Her legs ached. Over the past two hours, she hustled her ass off trying to get everything she'd need to make her place a home. She'd visited the general store and found sheets, a pillow, blankets, towels, her very first one-cup coffeepot. Every purchase validated her arrival into the real world.

As her bank account chipped away, she suffered little remorse for her purchases. She still had a ton of money in her account, and these were all items she needed. Although she asked Lucian to loan her thirty-five thousand, her actual plan would cost less. She was smart to ask for a bit more, knowing she needed a home. Well, maybe not *needed*. She'd certainly gone without such luxuries before, but it was time to join the ranks of normal adults.

She'd bought enough from the market to make it through the night. It was more sensible to bring a couple of bags home from work each day. For now, she had enough to keep her busy.

Hoisting her butt off the top step, where she collapsed with an arm full of purchases—she really needed furniture—she began emptying out her loot. The coffeepot was an easy setup, and she used the box as a trash can for now. Stacking all her linens in the corner with her pillow, she carried her toiletries to the bathroom.

As the apartment dimmed, the sun retreating for the day, she dug out her box of light bulbs and searched for an outlet. She'd found a lamp at a secondhand store for four dollars. She frowned once it was plugged in, realizing she had nowhere to put it. Using a large bag, she dumped in the trash from the coffeepot box and, instead, used the box as a makeshift end table.

"That'll have to do for now," she mumbled, admiring her handiwork.

The knock at the door startled her. Carefully walking down the steep, narrow steps, she opened the door a crack. A man in a blue jumpsuit stood with a clipboard. "Evelyn Keats?"

"Yes." *These must be the bed people!*

"I have a delivery for you."

She peeked out the door. The alley was dark. There was another man standing behind her mattress, which was now wrapped in plastic. "Come on in."

She waited anxiously at the top of the stairs as the men maneuvered the mattress up the steps. Good thing she'd opted for the smaller variety. A bigger bed never would've fit.

"Where would you like it?"

She pivoted and considered the space. The bathroom and closet door took up one wall, while the kitchen took up another. The partition from the stairs made up the third, leaving only one choice. "Right there by the window will be fine."

They perched the mattress against the wall and left to get the box spring and frame. In a matter of ten minutes, she was signing for the delivery and saying thank you. Anxiously, she shut the door, locked it tight, and rushed back up the steps. Her feet didn't stop until she propelled herself into the air and crashed on her bed. It smelled new and she liked it.

Smiling, she sighed and rolled off. Making the bed up was a quick task, as she had much experience with such chores from keeping house at Patras. With considerable pride, she placed the pillow at the top. Beautiful.

The blanket was soft pink in the fuzziest material she'd ever felt. Despite all the luxuries she'd experienced while living with Lucian, her own things, purchased with her own money and by her own hands, meant so much more.

It complicated things, seeing Lucian yesterday, but it also felt better stipulating a loan on her conditions. By doing so she'd altered their relationship to a business one. The two hundred thousand he'd left in an account for her was tainted and tied to their intimate past, which was why her pride refused her to touch it.

Breathing out a pleased sigh, she gazed at the roof over her head. It amazed her that she'd already accomplished part one of her plan. Part two would require a bit more research, but she'd talked to some people at the library and they explained a great deal to her as well as gave her some phone numbers they had on hand.

It felt wonderful to take responsibility for herself again. Lucian wasn't opposed to her independence, but as a man who had always been in control, he'd never truly understand what it meant for her to stand on her own two feet.

It wasn't about proving something to him. He was in her past. This was about proving something to herself, creating her own future.

GLANCING at her watch, she noted it was only a little after six. After straightening up some of the mess, she bagged up her trash and walked it to the cans she'd noticed in the alley. Her belly grumbled.

For dinner, she made a can of chicken soup. The pot was a dollar find at the thrift shop. She washed her dishes and tucked everything away neatly in its proper place.

She bathed in her little tub and brushed out her hair. Using the sink, Scout rewashed her uniform by hand and hung her clothes from hangers on the doors. And it was time for bed.

Her feet slipped beneath the soft covers, and she pulled the sheets to her chest. Reaching out, she shut off the light and stared at the ceiling. Home. This was home.

It was a very intangible moment. She was satisfied, yet something was missing. Her mind knew what it was, of course, but had done a wonderful job of not thinking beyond her independence that day. And at night, when the world slept, that was the easiest time to get wrapped up in regrets and swept away by depressing thoughts.

Her conscience fought to hold on to the peace steering her all day, but memories were slowly pulling her down. Sighing into the dark, she stared blindly out the window.

Where is he right now? Who's he with? What's he doing?

She shut the door on such questions and tried thinking about work. Nick was working tomorrow, and he always made her days a bit more entertaining. Nick was young—her age—and funny.

Her eyelids grew heavy, and the slow echo of traffic in the distance soothed her like waves rushing by. Her battle to keep her memories at bay failed the more tired she became.

With a sigh of acceptance, she gave over to the random thoughts playing in her head and found herself back in Lucian's limo after having dinner with Shamus several weeks ago.

"Did you enjoy yourself?" Lucian asked, his fingers making gentle whorls over her stocking-clad knee.

"I always enjoy Jamie," she said.

He grunted, a sound of approval with little censure. "You didn't eat much."

"*I had enough.*"

As Dugan drove, the city slowly rolled by, a tapestry of moonlit blues and shadowed buildings. Her eyes drew away from the window at the sound of the partition going up. She glanced at Lucian. The side of his mouth kicked up, intent clear in his eyes. "*Pull up your skirt.*"

Evelyn laughed silently. As soon as the partition was completely up, she lifted her hips and shimmied her skirt upward, bunching the thin material around her torso. Her stockings were black with zigzag designs sewn in and a blunt strip of lace at the top. She wore no garters. Her pale purple panties showed in a narrow triangle at the apex of her thighs.

Lucian turned his back to the door and eyed her. His elbow rested on the back of the seat as his fingers slowly swirled like a clock gear cranking. The slight telltale motions letting her know gears were turning in his mind. She waited.

"*Are you wet?*"

His words were like the kick of a marble running between them, knocking over little points, rolling up her flesh and plunking into a basket that set her arousal in motion, successfully plumping her sex and causing her channel to contract. "*Yes.*"

"*I want a blow job.*" She shifted and he stilled her with a flick of his fingers in the dim air. "*I want your hands folded behind your back.*"

Nodding, she slid to the floor. Her arms stretched behind her, fingers latching at her back. Lucian made no move to assist her or pull himself out. Leaning forward, she nuzzled his knee with her nose. His lungs drew in an audible breath.

Seeing he didn't plan to help her, she carefully eased up and nudged his suit jacket out of the way. Her lips pulled at his pants until her teeth found his zipper. Carefully, she lowered the catch.

His thighs shifted, the soft leather seating crinkling under his weight. The gentle tug over her hair as he dragged his palm down *the side of her face was welcome. His nonverbal praise filled her belly with warm honey. Turning her gaze on him, she smiled.*

"You're so beautiful, Evelyn," he whispered, voice thick with affection.

His touch disappeared as the echo of his fingers deftly unlatching his belt filled the car. His cock filled his strong fingers, and he pumped slowly. The head was smooth and dark as his fingers gripped his shaft tightly.

She leaned forward and kissed the tip, a dewy pearl of precome anointing her lips. With a final glance at him she bent to her task, taking him deep to the back of her mouth. His cock was big, filling every crevice and stretching her lips wide. She sucked aggressively, bobbing over him. He gathered her hair in a makeshift ponytail and groaned as she worked him over.

She wanted to use her hands, but liked the sense of surrender he elicited by forbidding their involvement. Her head was forced low. Unhinging her jaw, she welcomed him to the back of her throat. Saliva coated him, and soon he was controlling her motions, using her hair as a rein to quickly fuck her mouth.

His hips lifted and his cock pulsed over her tongue. The quick touch of two fingers to the pulse point of her throat was enough of a warning that he was coming. Sealing her lips around his flesh, she sucked deep, milking his release and swallowing every drop.

Once she was sure he was finished, she sucked him clean, offering a final lick up his beautiful shaft and lowering herself back to her heels. He sighed. "Thank you."

Tucking himself away, redoing his belt but not bothering to tuck in his shirt, Lucian watched her in the subdued light of the limo. The gusset of her panties grew weighted with her own arousal as the floor of the car vibrated faintly beneath her knees. Dugan would continue to drive until instructed otherwise.

"Still wet?" Lucian asked.

"Very."

Long fingers caressed his chin and tapped his lips. "I'm debating what to do about that." His comment caused her brow to kink. "You were very chatty with Jamie tonight," he said thoughtfully.

"I like Jamie."

His expression gave nothing away. "What do you like about him?"

She considered Lucian's best friend. He had a disposition that always set her at ease. Although he didn't always make her laugh, he made her smile. He was . . . nice. "He's nice to me."

"He thinks you're beautiful."

Heat tinged the crests of her cheeks and she hoped the soft lighting of the limo disguised her reaction to his confession.

"How does it make you feel, knowing Shamus has seen you come?"

Her blush intensified. Jamie was there the first time she'd ever had an orgasm. It was at Lucian's hand and on his command, when they'd first begun their association. Since then, she'd believed it was an exhibit he'd regretted greatly. She wasn't like his past lovers, she suspected. Once he realized that, he'd been a lot more discreet with his sexual displays while in the company of others. Exhibitionism was fun, but he never again flaunted her as a toy. There was a difference and they both knew it.

"No answer?"

She shrugged. "I don't think about that when I see him."

"Good." He reached for his glass and took a sip, returning it to the sunken coaster by the door. "Do you mind being watched, Evelyn?"

"It depends."

"On?"

"I don't know. It just depends on the situation and who's watching us, I suppose."

"What if I lowered the partition and fucked you."

Oh God. *She shook her head.*

"You wouldn't want Dugan seeing you?"

"No."

Lucian seemed to consider this, but nodded. "Me neither. Is it strangers then?"

She shrugged. There was something titillating about being watched, but knowing she might see her audience again sometimes made her alter her actions. "I guess that's it."

He glanced at his pocket watch. "It's almost eleven. Are you tired?"

"No."

"Good. I want to play. Pull your skirt down and come sit."

She did as he asked. Once she was seated, he brushed his lips over hers in a teasing kiss. Her body was primed and anxious for release. The partition lowered.

"Dugan, take us to Church."

"Yes, sir."

Evelyn frowned. "We're going to church?"

"Different sort of worship . . ."

The car navigated through the upper west side of Folsom, where boutiques and high-end eateries made up the storefronts. Mannequins were placed in provocative positions under aesthetic lighting, wearing the world's finest fashions. The car turned off the main strip and into a slightly seedier commercial district.

They were still in a higher-class section of Folsom. The limo pulled up outside a building with an awning. She stared at the neon sign above the door, unable to read the word. "Is this it?"

"Yes." *Lucian said, shifting and pulling out his wallet. He removed a card and placed his wallet back in his pocket.* "Keep your hand in mine at all times and don't talk to anyone. If someone addresses you, simply nod or shake your head."

The door opened and he slid out. She had questions, but they would have to wait. Once outside of the limo she could hear music pumping from inside the stone walls of the establishment. Was it a club?

"I'll wait at the corner, sir," Dugan said quietly as Lucian took her hand.

He knocked at the black metal door, and a man in a tuxedo answered. Lucian flashed the card he'd taken from his wallet, and the man let him pass. The entrance was dark and loud. A slow, sultry rhythm vibrated the walls from speakers unseen.

"Welcome, Mr. Patras. It's been a while," the man in the tux greeted as Lucian paid the cover.

"Good to see you again, Mr. O'Malley. This is Ms. K. We'd like a seat in the Red Room."

The man nodded and led them through a dim corridor. The accents she could see were nice. Expensive sconces adorned the walls, which were papered in an antiquated black-and-ivory floral print. She wanted to ask if this was a bar, but Lucian instructed her not to talk.

At the mouth of the corridor there was a large room filled with tables dressed in crisp linens. It looked like a number of the functions Lucian had taken her to, except it was dark. They weaved their way to a table in the front of the room, where a stage sat as empty as a shell. Lucian pulled out a chair and she sat, sinking comfortably into the cushioned seat.

"I'll have a brandy and Ms. K. will have a tequila sunrise."

She faced him, her brow arching curiously. Lucian often gave her wine to sample with dinner, but she wasn't much of a drinker being that she got intoxicated rather quickly. A tequila sunrise was the first cocktail she'd ever had. The night she'd first tried it, she drank about eight of them, and Lucian had to practically carry her home.

The other man left and she looked around. Lucian took her hand and rubbed his thumb over her knuckles. "You okay?"

"Yes. What is this place?"

"You'll see."

The other patrons were granted a bit of anonymity by the cleverly placed lighting. Shadows created private pockets of space. On the stage, she could make out the silhouette of what looked to be an old-fashioned button-back settee.

A woman appeared with their drinks. Her outfit was bizarre. Deep purple hues reflected in a velvet jacket. Hook buttons marched up her busty chest in military style. Her breasts were overflowing from the expensive-looking garment, and the back let out in a train reaching to her knees. Her hair was slicked back and appeared blue under the lights, but Evelyn deduced it was blond. A petite top hat perched on her head, and a black lace choker collared her neck. She looked like she'd escaped the Black Hills during the high times of Deadwood.

Evelyn's drink was set before her, its attractive graduating blush deepening like a crimson sunrise. She took a sip. The sweet grenadine countered the burn of tequila.

Lucian scrutinized her. His posture relaxed and the thumb of his other hand rubbed slowly over his glass of brandy. "Good?"

"Mmm, very," she agreed, easing back in her chair.

The song changed, and the lighting amended from blues and reds to pinks and vibrant shades of fuchsia. The music was a cross between contemporary and some form of opera. It was very sultry, with words in some fluid language much prettier than English.

A woman walked onto the stage, dressed in Victorian finery. Her hair was white and pinned in a crown of toppling curls. Her bust overflowed from the tightly cinched whalebone corset. And from her hips flowed a cascade of rich fabrics in shades of corn-flower and gold.

She carried herself gracefully, her motions clearly choreo-graphed with the music as she perched herself on the edge of the settee. Producing a fancy feathered fan from her hip, she fanned herself rapidly. Her expression was tense and upset.

*Suddenly another woman bustled onto the stage. Her cloth-
ing was much more subdued, but nonetheless spectacular. The
hoop-skirt gown was all black and covered even her wrists. She
wore a delicate apron that had impeccable lacework. Upon her
head was a muffin-top white cap. A maid.*

*Lucian's hand tightened on hers. His breath tickled her neck
as he whispered, "Mmm, she doesn't look half as beautiful as you
did in your uniform."*

*Evelyn blushed and quickly turned back to the stage. The
women were playacting, but not speaking. The foreign lyrics of
the opera spoke for them. The mistress in her finery stood and
showed a great deal of duress as her hands swung in animation.
The maid soothed and petted her until she calmed.*

*The mistress sat and cupped her face in her palms as the maid
caressed her shoulders in a comforting manner. The tone of the
music shifted, and slowly, the maid began to undo her mistress's
clothing. The mistress glanced at her curiously and the maid gave
her a subservient bat of her eyes. The mistress nodded and the
maid continued.*

*Lucian's arm rested over Evelyn's shoulder. He passed her
right hand to the hand dangling over her shoulder, locking their
fingers together above her breast. His other hand went to her
knee and rubbed softly over her stocking.*

*The mistress stood and the maid undid her bustle. Her lux-
urious skirt fell in a puddle at her feet and the maid kneeled to
collect the garment; Evelyn gasped. It was a dirty show. Sweeping it away, the maid remained low and stared up at her mistress,
an inquiring set to her eyes.*

*Small hands petted tentatively down plush, lily-white thighs.
The mistress tilted her head in confusion. The maid traced a
finger over her garters and paused just at her mistress's sex. The
mistress jumped and so did Evelyn, as Lucian's hand was suddenly touching her in the same place.*

Evelyn's eyes jerked from the stage to Lucian's hand at her crotch, then to his face. His mouth kicked up in a slow, wicked grin. Leaning forward, he whispered, "It's burlesque. She's going to fuck her naughty maid right here in front of everyone . . . and I'm going to fuck mine."

Understanding dawned with the force of a tidal wave. A full-body quiver rushed through her, and Lucian swept aside her panties and sunk his finger deep between her folds just as her sex contracted in a mini pre-orgasm.

"Mmm, good girl."

Evelyn's knees trembled as his finger slowly fucked her under the linen covering the table. Her eyes swept the room, seeing no one was watching them. Onstage, the mistress was sprawled out on the settee. One vintage slipper fell to the stage as the maid pressed a trail of kisses up her leg.

Lucian's fingers found her clit and rubbed gentle circles over the tiny nub. Evelyn was shaking so fiercely it was a wonder she could remain upright. His teeth scraped up her throat and nibbled on the lobe of her ear. "Come."

Just like that, her body exulted. Quivers rocked her as her sex contracted. Luckily, the intense opera covered the moan that escaped her parted lips. Bodies writhed on stage in time with the pulse of her pussy. Evelyn's vision blurred and she was lifted onto his lap.

Lucian arranged her limbs over his and kept her facing the stage. She braced her palms on the table. A man suddenly appeared onstage and the women sprang apart. The maid was chased off and the man leered at the mistress. Her gown was dragged to the underside of her pert little breasts. The man approached, scooping up a feathered fan and dragging it over the mistress's throat, slowly undoing the hook fastenings of her corset.

Lucian's heated flesh brought Evelyn back to her own circumstances. He was really going to fuck her! Here!

"Shh, shh, shh. Look around. We're not the only ones."

Evelyn's gaze covertly scanned the room. Bodies arched and couples leaned close. She could almost smell the carnality of the space. Church indeed!

He lifted her limbs, and her panties were jerked to the side once more. Fitting himself at the mouth of her sex, he slowly slid her down, forcing her to take all of him or risk exposure. Not that anyone seemed to care what they were doing.

She moaned at the sense of fullness. His fingers dug into her hips, through the fabric of her bunched skirt, as he lifted her and brought her down hard on his cock.

He grunted. The fingers of his other hand gathered her clothing and found her clit. Evelyn's flesh was still sensitive from her recent climax. Her body jerked reflexively in his grip and his hold tightened.

"I'll never forget how you disarmed me that day I found you in my suite, dressed so properly in your little housekeeping uniform. When I thought you were nosing through my belongings I wanted to throttle you, but not nearly as much as I wanted to fuck you. The moment you looked at me with those crystalline blue eyes I was hard. I've never wanted a woman the way I want you, Evelyn."

She was beyond speech. The actors were past performing. A full-out sexcapade was taking place on the stage. Hands groped and toes curled. Evelyn was stuffed full of Lucian's big cock as he continued to direct her motions, making her ride him hard as he whispered into her ear.

His fingers pinched down on her clit, and her sex convulsed. He groaned and moved her faster. His hands slid under her blouse and dragged the lace cups of her bra down. He found her hard nipples and pinched the little tips. His hips rocked into her. Her leg muscles worked to keep her body moving with his.

The actors onstage screamed and grunted with pleasure. It

was a fantasy of the flesh. Peeks of pink folds and blushing breasts swirled before her. Dainty hands caressed lush thighs and painted lips curled in expressions of raw pleasure.

"You're going to come for me one last time, Evelyn. With me. Are you ready?"

He thrust into her, hard. His fingers curved over her breasts in a bruising grip. She moaned long and loud and . . . something hard suddenly crashed into her.

Scout shouted. The fuzzy sense of falling lingered in her sleep-addled mind as she pressed up on her hands and knees. *What the hell?*

She was on the floor, blankets twisted around her feet. Disoriented, she looked around. It was dawn. She was in her new apartment. Her earlier erotic memory must have carried over to her sleep.

Sitting back on her heels, she rubbed her forehead, visions of the night Lucian had taken her to the burlesque show dancing in her head. God, that was an incredible night.

Defeated, she sighed and moaned. The sun wasn't even up and she'd already broken her vow not to think about him. Throwing her head back on her mattress, she drew up her knees where she sat on the floor, and groaned. The problem with having a lover like Lucian Patras was, once he got inside of you, it was impossible to get him out.

five
·····

SNAP

WORK was work. Fridays were always a bit more hectic than other days. Wednesdays were big with the seniors, she'd learned, but on Fridays customers slammed the store with orders for the weekend. Scout barely had a chance to pee all day.

Around one o'clock they had their first lull since morning. She straightened up her register and tidied her drawer. She was just about to tell Nick she was going to take her lunch when the back of her neck prickled. Turning, she spotted Mr. Gerhard coming down her aisle.

"Evelyn, I'd like to speak to you in my office, please."

Her stomach knotted. Her manager, who wasn't much older than her, carried himself as though he were in his fifties. For some reason this guy gave her an oozy feeling—not in a good way.

She nodded and shut her drawer, flicking off her light. Mr. Gerhard had a neatly trimmed mustache and thin lips under there somewhere. His glasses were dated and so thick they made his eyes huge. He always smelled of peppermint and coffee and looked as if he were made of wax.

They entered the glorified storage room that was his office and he gestured for her to take a seat in the metal folding chair. She waited for him to talk.

Sighing, he steepled his fingers and studied her for a long moment. "Ms. Keats, there seems to be a problem with your paperwork."

Oh no. "What's wrong?" It was likely her information. She'd applied for her job at Clemons before Lucian handed over her legal documents. She'd worked a myriad of jobs under false information, never having paid taxes a day in her life.

"Your social security number belongs to a man who died last April."

She pretended surprise. It was all a random selection of digits. She hadn't purposely tried to steal a dead person's identity. "It does?"

"Yes, it does," Mr. Gerhard said with zero amusement.

"I have my card in my bag. Maybe I got the number wrong."

"I'll need to see a copy of your card."

She reached down and produced her identification papers. They were too precious and she'd gone without for far too long to not carry them everywhere with her. Life was unpredictable, and proof of identity was a new freedom she'd never had. She slid the papers across his desk.

He examined the documents carefully. "This is nothing close to what you put down."

"Sorry. I recently moved. I've been doing a lot of paperwork and must've crossed that number with a number for something else."

"I'll have to copy this and send it down to headquarters."

Mr. Gerhard seemed to think he worked for the CIA, not a local supermarket. "Sure. But I'll need the original back."

"Of course." His posture relaxed as he tucked the card away. She didn't like that he was keeping it for even more than a minute. "How are you enjoying your job so far?"

Aside from missing her lunch and starving and being forced to endure this awkward, private conversation? "So far so good."

"Good."

Several beats of time passed in uncomfortable silence. "Any problems I should know of?"

"Umm . . . no."

"Good. Well, I'll let you get back to work. Have you taken lunch yet? I was going to walk down to Little Sicily's if you'd—"

Ew!

"I packed my lunch, but thank you."

He looked regretful. "Perhaps another time."

Not freaking likely, wax man. "Perhaps," she said uncomfortably, probably wearing the most insincere smile to ever exist.

Scout stood and made her way to the door without looking back. When she returned to the main area of the store her appetite vanished. Sighing, she walked back to her register.

"What was that about?" Nick asked from the register beside her. He was folding a receipt in the shape of a football and proceeded to flick it into a basket at the end of his belt. His voice mimicked the sound of a crowd screaming in the distance when it reached its goal.

"Something with my paperwork."

"You look frazzled. He ask you to comb his mustache or something?"

She snorted. "Ew, no! He tried to ask me to lunch though."

Nick laughed, his blue eyes shutting as his head tilted back. He was her age and definitely made the days at Clemons go by faster. "That's great! You too can have a bunch of little farsighted babies with receding hairlines and hairy lips!"

She threw an apple at him someone had left because it was bruised. "Shut up! It's not funny."

"Whatever you say, Mrs. Gerhard."

The rest of the afternoon passed quickly. The rush of customers petered out, and by three o'clock Scout regretted skipping lunch. She'd contemplated eating her sandwich on the sly at her register, but Mr. Gerhard appeared to return her social security card and once more obliterated her appetite.

As she walked the three blocks home, she decided she'd eat and then find the DMV so she could change over her address on her ID. Although she didn't have a driver's license, Nick, from work, told her that was where state IDs came from.

"Scout!"

The sound of her name being shouted so urgently had her jumping. She turned and sucked in a breath. *Parker.*

Her teeth locked down as he jogged across the street after her. She turned and quickly walked toward home. He must have been waiting for her outside of Clemons. He'd helped her apply for her job and was right to assume she wouldn't give it up just because her life derailed—derailed partly because of him.

"Scout, wait!"

"Go away, Parker. I have nothing to say to you."

Her feet slapped against the pavement as she sped up. She didn't want to even look at him.

"I need to talk to you."

"Tough!" She turned the corner and heard him closing on her. Could she just have one day without assholes from her past stalking her every step?

"Please wait."

Saying nothing, she marched on, her lips pursed tightly over her clenched teeth and her eyes narrowed. Parker used to be her best friend, but proved to be nothing but an underhanded schmuck.

"Scout, please—"

Hissing in frustration, she turned on him. *"What could you possibly want?"*

She gasped. Jesus Christ. His face was a hodgepodge of black and blue bruises. There was a gash over his left eye and his jaw was discolored with a smattering of ugly green marks. "What the hell happened to you?"

"Lucian's what happened to me. Scout, don't you see? He isn't safe."

Her lips tightened. She wasn't falling into this pissing match. "Well, he isn't in my life anymore, so you can find another cause." Pivoting, she walked off.

He grabbed her arm, and that was mistake number one. She turned on him and a beast emerged from within her. *"Don't touch me!"*

He flinched and immediately let go of her arm. "I'm sorry," he whispered.

She laughed bitterly. "Sorry? You're sorry? Oh, well, doesn't that just fix everything. How's this, Parker? *Fuck you!*"

"I never meant to hurt you."

She'd had just about enough of men and their crap. "Hurt me? You didn't hurt me. I'm not the one standing here covered in bruises."

"You know what I mean."

She stepped into his space and shoved a finger in his face. "Let me clear something up for you. It takes more than some self-serving asshole to hurt me. If I was hurt, I'd have to care *and I don't*! I don't care about you. I don't care about our past. I don't care about anything you may think I do. Your arrogance is what got you into this mess, so I'm going to do you a favor and tell you your intuition sucks. You don't know me. You don't know anything about the person I am or the things that hold meaning to me. You. Are. *Nothing*. So go play your games with someone who gives a shit."

His shoulders drooped, his expression dejected. "I did it to protect you."

Emotion bit at her throat, and tears burned her eyes.

"Protect me?" she barked. "Since when do I need someone to protect me? I was the one looking out for your dumb ass all those years! You may know how to read and sell stocks, but you don't know shit about surviving. You know and I know this ambitious act you've been putting on is all bullshit. I'm not buying it, and I regret the day I ever trusted anything out of your mouth. Now, leave me alone."

The blood rushed from his battered face. "You don't mean that."

"I mean every word," she growled.

"Scout . . . I love you."

Rage choked her, but she shoved it down. Shutting her eyes, she growled. His proclamation did nothing for his case. It merely irritated her a hundred times more. "Love, Parker? Really? Let me tell you something about love. People write about it because it's harder than any war and greater than any epic. It's vast and cold and empty and usually unrequited. *That's* what love is. It's misery, and if you love me I'm glad, because I'll never love you back and that is exactly what you deserve."

She turned and walked away. He didn't follow. Fuck the DMV. She was going home and if she ventured anywhere it was going to be to a liquor store. When she saw the insurance office below her apartment relief set in. Almost home.

As Scout rounded the alleyway to her apartment door, she came up short. Nerves pinched at the back of her neck as she intruded on two unkempt men passing money and drugs. They jumped at her sudden appearance. Great. They were blocking the few steps separating her from her home, and there was no way she was letting them see this was where she lived.

"You need something, girlie?" the man with a gap in his teeth asked.

"Uh, no. Just made a wrong turn." She turned away to exit the alley.

"Well, now wait a minute. Maybe we can help you find what you're looking for," the other man said.

She kept walking. "No. I'm set."

Gap-tooth skipped alongside her and cut her off before she

could reach the sidewalk. "Pretty thing like you shouldn't be walking around by yourself. Young too. Bet you aren't even eighteen. What do you think, Kev?"

She scowled at the scumbag. This wasn't necessarily a bad section, but there was crime everywhere. It wasn't late, but the alley was narrow and dark. While "Kev" was behind her, Gap-tooth was blocking her escape. Other than anyone who might be visiting the insurance agency beneath her apartment, there wasn't much foot traffic going by.

"If you'll excuse me," she said impatiently.

Gravel crunched behind her and her lungs seized. Fuck.

"Looks about sixteen to me," Kev said.

Gap-tooth's gap was slowly displayed in a lascivious reptilian grin. "She sure does."

His hand lifted and without thought, Scout reacted. Something tired and outraged snapped inside her. Her fist connected with his nose, and he folded like a cheap metal chair. Her knee slammed into his face, and he dropped like a sack of potatoes to the ground. *Goddamn men!*

The other man shouted and grabbed hold of her arms.

A scream high enough to curdle blood ripped from her lungs. *"Don't touch me! Fire! Fire!"*

He shoved her against the brick wall, her hair catching on the rough, porous surface, and she shoved her knee into his crotch. He grunted and she nearly vomited when spit came out of his mouth. "You fucking cunt!"

His grip tightened and she clocked him right in the ear. He howled and grabbed his head, stepping back. She kicked him in the nuts as hard as she could, and he dropped to writhe beside his partner in crime.

"*Hey!* What's going on?"

She turned and a man in a suit was blocking the exit of the alley. She'd kick his ass too!

Her chest heaved as she panted, adrenaline pumping wildly through her veins. Fists clenched in front of her chest, she pivoted, waiting for one of the men to rise. They both were on the ground moaning as she huffed and shook.

"I need a police officer at twenty-three South Knights Boulevard," suit man said into some fancy cell phone.

Instinctively, at the mention of the cops, Scout's gut urged her to run. Having grown up under the circumstances she had, the law didn't usually take kindly to her type, but she'd done nothing wrong and she wasn't that type anymore. She had papers and a home. She'd merely defended herself. It took everything she had not to run and hide.

She grabbed her bag off the ground and quickly left the alley.

"The cops are coming. You can't leave."

"I didn't do anything wrong!" she snapped at Suit Man.

"You have no business being in this alley," he snapped back, like an adult chastising a small child.

"I live here!"

He drew back. "Are you Evelyn?"

Finally, some clarity. She assumed his suit meant he worked in an office. Knowing her name meant he likely worked in the insurance office below her apartment. "Yes. I moved in yesterday. These two assholes were doing some business I inadvertently interrupted, and they wouldn't let me leave."

He paled. "Holy crap. Are you okay? Do you need to sit down? *Ellen!*"

A rotund woman in a purple suit came out the door to the office. "What? I'm on the phone, Elliot."

He scowled at her. "This is Evelyn, the new tenant upstairs. She was just attacked. Take her inside and give her some water and a place to sit until the cops get here. I don't want these two vagrants getting away."

The woman's mouth popped open like a trout. "Oh, dear!

Come along, sweetie. Are you hurt? Do you need anything? Imagine, such a small girl like yourself being accosted. What's happening to this world? I tell you . . ."

She continued to prattle on as she shuffled Scout into the small insurance office and shoved her into a seat. Scout gazed at the ceiling longingly. Home was so close. All she wanted to do was get there. From one of those blue coolers, the woman poured a glass of water and wrapped Scout's fingers around the little plastic cup.

Lights flashed outside and she turned as a uniformed officer stepped out of his car. Through the glass, Scout could see Elliot talking to the policeman. Moments later the men were being pressed over the hood of the squad car and cuffed. Another police car arrived on the scene, no doubt after the officer discovered whatever was in the little baggie the gap-toothed man had been purchasing.

The insurance woman—Scout couldn't remember her name—paced by the window, chattering like a small bird trapped in the large body of a woman. Scout had the distinct impression Elliot was her husband.

The door opened and the officer stepped in. He scanned the room, and when his gaze landed on her she drew back and shrunk in her chair. Cops had never been nice to her. Even as a child, she'd been taught not to trust them because, if caught, they had the power to take her from her mom.

"Evelyn?"

She nodded.

"I'm Officer Ludlow. How are you doing?" His voice and soft expression claimed sympathy, but Scout wasn't falling for it.

She shrugged. "Okay."

He grinned. He had very white teeth that were slightly crooked, but still made a nice smile. "You did quite a number on those guys out there. Did you take self-defense?"

Yes. The course was called *Life and Basic Survival 101*. Scout shook her head, and his expression sobered.

"I know you're pretty shook up. I just need a statement from you, and then you can go."

She didn't like being put into this position. Authority made her nervous. She wanted Lucian, which was odd, being that he held more authority than anyone in Folsom. Or perhaps that was why.

"Hon, do you think you could tell me what happened?"

She wasn't his honey, and the endearment did nothing to open her up. Her voice seemed lodged somewhere deep in the pit of her belly, and her trembling had morphed into a full-body tremor as her adrenaline ebbed.

Scout faced the woman in the office . . . Ellen, she thought. For some reason she was able to speak to the woman. Clearing her throat, she said, "Could you get someone on the phone for me?"

Ellen rushed to her desk. "Sure, sweetie." Her chair creaked as she sat and her manicured fingers grasped the receiver. "What's the number?"

"Um . . . I'm not sure. It's . . ." He would be at work. Patras Industries. But her request wouldn't budge past her lips.

You can do this! You do not *need him!*

Fear had her trembling. If she called him, he'd come. He'd handle everything and get her out of this mess as quickly as possible. Lucian would know exactly how to proceed. But she didn't want to keep running to him whenever she needed help.

Eyeing the cop, she felt the same anxious tremors she'd always suffered when faced with an authority figure. *You're not a child anymore! They can't take you away from your mom.* She thought about Pearl, alone and afraid in rehab. She was doing her part, and this was Scout's.

Swallowing back her request, she glanced at Ellen. "Never mind."

"Are you sure, dear?"

No, but she nodded anyway. When the phone returned to the receiver, Scout faced the officer. "What do you need to know?"

"Why don't you start with what you were doing in the alley?"

"I live upstairs."

"There's a small efficiency above our office," Ellen confirmed. "The landlord notified us yesterday that Evelyn was the new tenant."

The officer jotted down some notes in a little tablet and faced Scout again. "Could you explain what happened from the time you arrived?"

She was fighting with everything she had not to fall apart. Her thoughts were jumbled and her hands wouldn't quit shaking. Swallowing, she kept her focus on the man's badge and explained what had taken place. She told him they'd been making a drug deal, how they tried to corner her, how they grabbed her, and how she just reacted.

"You did a fine job of defending yourself."

She blinked at the admiration, but his praise meant nothing. What was she supposed to do? Let them attack her without fighting back?

Once he took down her information, he thanked her and left. She sat for a few moments just staring at the empty space where the squad car had been.

"Would you like me to walk you to your door, Evelyn?"

Reminded of her surroundings, she blinked up at the man in the suit. What was his name? "No, thank you. I should go."

As she stood, her legs wobbled. She scooped up her belongings and thanked the insurance couple again. Her eyes combed every shadow as she made her way down the alley and quickly unlocked her door. Once she made it inside, she locked everything up tight.

Too stunned to cry, she climbed the stairs, stripped off her clothes, and drew a bath. She did it, and she did it on her own.

• • •

SCOUT typically woke up a little after dawn, but the following morning she was up before the sun had a chance to rise. She jerked upright in bed and made a startled sound as something that sounded like a wrecking ball rattled her walls.

Scrambling out of bed, her foot caught on the cord of her lamp and knocked it onto the ground. "Shit!"

She righted the lamp and turned it on. Her feet turned in a circle as she tried to find her bearings. It was six in the morning. Shuffling to the kitchen, she grabbed a butter knife and her one-cup coffeepot. Not the best weapons, but they would do.

Marching down the dim steps of her apartment, she quietly waited, only to flinch when the banging started again. "Who is it?" she hissed.

"Evelyn?"

She frowned and lowered her weapons. "Lucian?"

"Open the door."

"What are you doing here?"

"Open. The damn. Door."

Sighing, she shifted the knife and coffeepot in her hands and unlocked the door. Pulling it open, she snapped, "Do you have any idea what time it is?"

He wasn't dressed like he usually was outside of the penthouse. He wore dark jeans, a rumpled sweater, and his jaw was unshaven. Shoving his way through the door, she gasped as his arm shot out in front of her. "What the hell is this?"

She glanced at the papers twisted in his fist. "It's a newspaper."

His jaw ticked. "Explain to me why—at five in the morning—I am reading *your* address and description in the criminal reports."

Her mouth opened. "*What?* I told them I didn't do anything wrong!"

"*You were attacked?*" She jumped at the sharpness in his voice. He didn't give her time to reply. "*Why the hell didn't you call me?*"

Her lips firmed. "It had nothing to do with you."

"Your safety has everything to do with me!"

"*Pfft!* Please, Lucian—"

Her words cut off as he crowded her in the tiny entryway. "Do *not* act like your safety has not been my priority since we met. Jesus, Evelyn! What the fuck happened? Are you hurt?"

She blinked at him. He was really upset. "I . . . I handled it." Her voice was smaller than she would have liked.

Lucian forked his fingers through his hair and dropped to the second step of her narrow staircase. His seemed totally distraught. "I want you to depend on me in times of trouble. Why won't you?"

Because she couldn't trust him to always be there. "I'm fine." How had he found her? "Did they put my name in the paper?" That seemed a major violation of her privacy. She wished she could read the article.

"No. They put your description and the location of the attack and stated it happened only a few feet from your residence. Whoever runs the office downstairs must have made a statement to the media, because there's an article on page six of the business section. I've already been to the police. Dugan handled the rest. No more interviews will be given regarding your personal life."

Damn it!

He suddenly looked around the small entryway. "What is this place?"

"It's my home."

His brow kinked. "Since when?"

"A few days ago."

Letting out an aggravated huff, his expression turned defeated. She didn't like seeing him like that. He reached for her hand and she allowed the contact. His fingers ran over the crest of her knuckles. "Tell me what happened," he said with gentle patience.

Scout drew in a deep breath and attempted to set him at ease. "I was heading home from work and as I turned into the alley, I accidentally walked up on two guys making a drug deal."

His eyes narrowed. Under his breath he said, "We won't touch the fact that I didn't know where home was or work currently is. Go on."

She swallowed. "They saw me and when I tried to turn and leave, they wouldn't let me go."

His hands tightened over hers. "Then what happened?" he asked through clenched teeth.

God, he was going to freak. "One guy blocked my way and I punched him in the nose. I put him on the ground, but the other guy grabbed me."

"Motherfucker," Lucian hissed.

"He only tried to . . . but I got him down too. Then Elliot showed up and called the cops."

"Who the fuck is Elliot?"

"He runs the insurance office. We share the building."

Lucian turned like a viper on her. "This man is a friend of yours?"

She rolled her eyes. "I was introduced to him yesterday, and you should be grateful. He called the cops."

"He also gave away enough personal information that I could tell it was you in the paper!" His expression turned sympathetic. "You handled the cops on your own?"

He wasn't asking because he thought her incapable, but more because he knew how much she feared officers of the law. Her smile was shaky, but proud as she nodded. "I did."

"I would have come. All you had to do was call and I would have taken care of everything."

Her gaze lowered to her bare feet. "I know. But this was something I needed to handle for myself. Don't you see, Lucian? I need to start depending on me first. I can't run to you every time life gets hard."

"Why not?"

"Because we aren't together anymore."

His gaze held hers for a long minute. "But you let some stranger help you."

"I didn't ask for his help. I screamed and he showed up."

"You screamed?" he rasped.

"I was scared," she confessed quietly.

"Jesus, Evelyn," he whispered. His lips thinned, as he appeared to battle the impulse to do something. She wasn't sure if that something was kissing her or throttling her. Neither was welcome at the moment. She withdrew her fingers from his tight hold.

Nodding tightly, he stood. "You're changing."

Her head slowly shook. "No, Lucian, my circumstances are. This is who I've always been. You simply covered it up with fancy dresses and jewelry."

"Don't act like all we had was some superficial arrangement. You know it was more than that."

"It was, but now it's over. I have to do for me and I can't do that worrying about you."

"How do you shut it off, the worry?"

I don't. She worried about him constantly; whether he was lonely, sad, taking care of himself. Although Lucian had the world at his fingertips, he only had a small circle of people he could really trust. "I just do."

"I don't know what hurts more," he said. "Worrying about you or knowing you don't worry about me." He laughed without humor. "I'm supposed to be the hard one, Evelyn."

"I was never soft."

His onyx eyes drilled into hers. "You're everything soft, everything gentle. No one said you couldn't be strong too. Why do you assume I can't see your strength?"

She stilled. She didn't know why she thought that, but she did. Since they broke up, she had created a list of faults in their relationship that didn't necessarily mesh with what they shared. Anger toward Parker resurfaced as she contemplated all the negative thoughts he had put in her head. She didn't know what to believe anymore, what was real and what was fabricated by her bruised ego.

"*Do you* see me as strong?"

His brows shot up. "You have as much, if not more, determination than me, Evelyn. It's one of the things I love most about you, but you refuse to believe that. I don't admire weak-willed people. Look at how far you've come . . . Sometimes I worry you're so strong willed you'll actually get to a point that you don't need me. I need you to need me."

And she needed independence. "Lucian . . ." What could she say? They were at an impasse. Aside from all their other issues, they were simply too broken to fix. She'd thought they were too different, but maybe the problem was they were too alike.

She fidgeted, as they both seemed to contemplate the stalemate situation they faced. Shifting her butter knife into her other hand, she held out the coffeepot, her only olive branch. "Would you like to come up? I can make coffee."

Lucian eyed her skeptically, hope clear in his dark eyes. It would only be coffee. She couldn't manage anything more.

Without taking his eyes off her, he withdrew his phone and pressed a button. After a second he said into the phone, "I'll call you when I need a ride."

six

THE CHIPPED TEACUP

SCOUT anxiously glanced back at Lucian as she took the stairs
slowly. His expression was blank, but his eyes moved, observing their surroundings as though he were cataloguing every as-
pect. As her feet reached the landing, she smiled nervously at him.

Once he reached the top she nearly giggled out loud at how
ridiculous he looked in her tiny home. He hunched under the low
ceiling and scanned the area, turning his frown on her.

"Evelyn—"

Rather than stand through a lecture, she went to her little cof-
feemaker, which she was proud to own. He was *not* going to come
in here and shame her with comparisons of his life and hers. Her
home was just fine! "I'll make coffee."

He sighed and went to peek in the bathroom, then the closet.
She set the pot to brew and righted the covers on her bed. No
table or chairs were available as she'd yet to purchase those items.
Luckily the bed was small and likely didn't look inviting to a man
like Lucian. He was not invited there. However, she needed to
offer him a seat.

Flipping her pillow against the wall, she tried to convert the tiny bed into a sort of sofa. "I haven't bought any furniture yet." He stared at her with a look she couldn't interpret. Fisting her hands so as not to fidget, she moved to the small fridge and withdrew the quart of milk. "Coffee should be done soon. You can have a seat if you want."

He slowly crossed the room and sat on her bed. She couldn't expect him to stand when he was nearly as tall as her ceilings. Removing two teacups from the shelf, the ones she purchased at the thrift store in a set of five for twenty cents apiece, Scout noted how small they were. Trifling, compared to the gargantuan tubs people drank coffee out of nowadays, but she liked them.

She took the one that had a chip in the rim, not minding the flaw the way Lucian might. She liked that she'd given these five cups a home when they were a step away from being thrown out like yesterday's trash.

After filling the cups, she handed Lucian one. He was Alice trapped in Wonderland, right about when she got her head stuck in the chimney. Scout giggled. He simply didn't fit in her home. He glanced at the petite teacup, swallowed by his large hand, and chuckled. His eyes met her gaze and they laughed.

"Well . . ." She giggled as she sipped her coffee.

Dark eyes glanced at the delicate scrollwork on his cup and the tiny flowers. "These remind me of a set my grandmother used to have."

"I doubt it. I got them at a thrift shop."

His smile faltered. "Evelyn, how much are you paying for this place?"

"That's none of your business."

"I don't want you living like a pauper."

"Believe it or not, Lucian, to me, this is living like a queen. I can come and go as I please. There's running water that's hot when I want it. I have electricity, a bed, and a place to keep food. I don't need much more."

"I thought when you asked for money you'd use it as a down payment on a condo."

"No. This is it."

She gave him credit. It was clear he wanted to say more about how unacceptable her home was by his standards, but he kept his mouth shut. He scooted over. "Sit down. I want you to tell me again what happened yesterday."

She sighed. "I don't want to talk about that anymore."

"Well, I do. Those men will get theirs, I promise you that."

"Do me a favor, Lucian. Don't make me any more promises."

His lips parted. "Please sit."

She didn't want to sit on her bed with him. That was dangerous. "I'm fine."

"Evelyn, you were attacked less than twenty-four hours ago. Sit down."

Relenting, she huffed and sat on the opposite end of the small mattress. "There. Happy?"

"No, but I'll take that much for now."

She'd invited him into her home, but the sad truth was she was still so very angry with him. "I saw Parker yesterday," she said suddenly, not knowing where the confession came from.

Lucian stilled, his lips an inch from his coffee cup. His jaw ticked and his throat worked under the stubble there. His shoulders slowly lifted as his breathing became labored. He said nothing.

"You did quite a number on his face."

"He deserved a hundred times worse," he snarled.

"And what do you deserve, Lucian? Whom do you answer to?"

He stood and placed his cup on the counter. "Evelyn . . ." He paced. "He touched you," he growled, as if that were reason enough to beat someone until they looked like a rotten piece of fruit.

"Maybe I asked him to."

"Don't," he barked, angrily forking his fingers through his hair.

"Why?" She was poking a surly bear, but couldn't help it. He was confusing her with all his sudden concern for her well-being, and they needed a reality check. "What did you expect? For all I knew you were never coming back. I was on my own."

"I told you I would be back!"

She laughed derisively. "In thirty days, Lucian. What kind of assurance is that? In my book you were gone and never coming back. You threw me away and he wanted me."

He lunged and she backed up, his arms bracing his weight over the mattress. "He had *no right* to lay a finger on you. Now, unless you want me to track him down and completely emasculate him this time, I suggest you stop taunting me."

"Get off of me, Lucian." The words whispered out in a perfectly calm voice altogether contrary to her emotions hidden inside. He glanced down at their position and stood.

"I don't want to ever hear that man's name again."

"That makes two of us." His sharp gaze met hers, weighing the sincerity of her words. "Don't look so smug. My feelings toward you aren't much different."

"But there *is* a difference?"

Her lips twitched. He might as well know. "You were so afraid of losing me you gave me away. Yes, Lucian, there is a difference. If only you'd realized it sooner. I tried to help you understand. What I felt for him could never measure up to what I felt for you."

He blinked, his eyes creasing with regret. "Felt. As in past tense?"

"The feelings I have about you now are too contaminated by anger to work in your favor. The only way I can process what you actually did is to completely sever the future from the past. You're a piece of my past. But that's it."

"That night . . . you said you loved me."

"I was confused," she lied. She should have never asked him up for coffee.

He approached, lowering himself to the floor. His eyes were

tormented as he turned her chin, forcing her to meet his gaze. "I fucked up, Evelyn. I fucked up and I have no idea how to fix it. I can't sleep. I can't eat. I can't concentrate at work. I want you back. Tell me how to fix this and I will. I'll do anything. I love you."

She pulled her chin away and averted her gaze. "You can't."

"That word isn't a part of my vocabulary and it isn't a part of yours."

Her throat worked. "I don't know how to forgive you."

He ducked his head to her lap, his arms wrapping around her hips and pulling her tightly to him. She lifted her hands so as not to touch him.

"I'm sorry. I'm so damn sorry, Evelyn. I go over what happened last winter again and again, and I don't know how else I could have found you. I was scared to death for your safety. I knew the moment I agreed to his terms I'd made a deal with the devil, but there was no way around it. Don't you think I would've done *anything* else if I could've avoided this outcome?"

"You could've told me," she hissed. It took everything she had not to touch him and offer him comfort as he confessed his regrets. She clung to her anger, needing it to keep her grounded. If he'd actually confessed what was really happening, the truth may not have hurt so much.

"I thought you would've agreed to marry me. If you would've agreed to be my wife, all bets were off. I was shocked when you said no."

"Is that the only reason you asked?"

He drew back. "What?"

"Did you only ask me to marry you to get out of the deal with Parker?"

"God, no. I asked you to marry me because I want you to be my wife. I still do, Evelyn."

"You want me to be your wife, yet you sent me away and let another man seduce me."

The muscles in his jaw locked. "You said no."

"Oh. So for the first time in your life you decided to accept defeat without a fight. I thought *can't* wasn't part of your vocabulary."

"You said no over a dozen times," he said with not a little irritation ringing in his voice. "I practically fucking begged and you still rejected me, Evelyn! What more could I have done?"

"Leveled with me. Trusted me to understand. I have to believe, if you'd taken the time to really explain what happened last winter, I would've understood. But you let it go so far, Lucian. I let him kiss me, touch me—"

"No," he snapped. "I'm not going to listen to this."

"Well, I had to endure it! And the whole time, do you know what I kept thinking? What was wrong with me that I wasn't enjoying it? I was so brokenhearted over you abandoning me, I wanted nothing more than to forget, but I couldn't. For two weeks I thought of little more than dying, and then my fake friend showed up and I thought, wow, at least *he* cares. But he still wasn't enough. I hated you for hurting me, and I hated you more because I think you broke me."

"Evelyn, you're not broken. That's love. It makes it impossible to want someone else."

"Well, I don't want to *love* you," she snarled, jumping to her feet and dumping her coffee in the sink.

Lucian turned and slowly lifted himself off the floor and onto the bed. His knees parted as he braced his elbows there and cradled his head. "This is making me crazy."

"I think it's time for you to call Dugan."

He glanced at her, shock and fear warring in his expression. "Don't ask me to leave yet."

"It's getting late, I have work soon, and there really isn't any point in us rehashing things we can't change."

His head shook. "Evelyn, this isn't the end of us. I can't accept that. I won't."

"Your declarations are a little late and hollow. I'm sorry. I won't change my mind."

"What about how happy we were? What about how compatible we are, how well we complement each other? Do you think it's easy to find someone like that, someone who does it *all* for you?"

"I'm not looking for that. I never was. All I want is a home to call my own and my independence." It was getting harder to argue with every passing second, because while her head knew what was best, her heart wanted him more than her next breath.

His brow kinked. "But you were happy."

"I was. But that all changed the minute you left me. For as happy as I was, the sadness of being abandoned by you was great enough to make me never want to love again. Life's hard enough. I choose to live it alone."

"You aren't meant to be alone, Evelyn. None of us are."

She'd heard the theory of coupling a hundred times before, yet her experiences left her heart severed, and she never wanted to chance feeling that way again. "Maybe I'm not like everyone else. I'm a nomad. I can't do things the normal way. I never could. I think"—her chest tightened and she swallowed back the pain—"I think you need to move on as well."

"Fuck that, Evelyn. I don't want anyone else."

"Well, you can't have me." She needed to get away from him. His presence was suddenly too much. "I'm going to take a bath. When I come out I'd appreciate it if you were gone. Please lock the door on your way out."

"You're fucking dismissing me?"

What if this was it? There was really nothing more to say. "I get paid at the end of the month. I'll drop a payment in your office soon after that."

"Consider the loan forgiven."

"You know I can't do that, Lucian. You gave me your word you'd treat the loan as such. No favors. It's business."

"This is absurd."

"This is the reality of it. The sooner you accept it, the better we both will be."

He stood. "You're wrong. Don't forget I was your first, Evelyn. Your first kiss, your first lover, your first true friend. You can't claim to know the outcome with things you've never experienced before. You'll see."

What was there to see? The agony of losing him compared to the joy of having him brought about so much turmoil, she couldn't take the risk again. Her trust had been shattered and she wasn't sure if there was any fixing that. What else could there possibly be to experience? Their time together was over.

They stood silently for a minute. "Well . . ." she said, edging her way to the small bathroom. "Thanks for coming to make sure I was okay, but as you can see, I'm fine. It was scary, but I managed."

Her shoulders shivered as she sensed his hand brushing over the back of her hair, barely making contact. "You could have called me. You can always call. I know you can handle yourself for the most part, but . . ."

"My phone got wet somehow. I took it to the phone place, but they said there was no fixing it."

"When?"

"When it first stopped working."

"Which was when?" he asked again.

She shrugged. "I don't know. It's all a blur."

"You called me when I was in Paris. Service was terrible there. It went right to voice mail, but I called you back shortly after. Was the phone broken then or did you deliberately not answer my call?"

Breath sucked deep into her lungs and she pivoted. "You called me back?"

"Yes, I fucking called you back. I was halfway across the world, cursing myself for leaving. Then there was an issue with the engine when all I wanted to do was get back to you before it was too late and tell you what a jerk I'd been."

He called!

This was exactly why she should've locked herself in the bathroom ten minutes ago. Information like this was detrimental to her cause. "Were you alone?" she rasped, unable to meet his gaze.

"Of course I was alone. I was at my father's. I was miserable here without you and figured, what the fuck, might as well drown in all the screwed-up parts of my life."

She blinked as her throat tightened. "So no one went with you to Europe?"

"Evelyn, why—*motherfucker*—did he say I wasn't alone? That son of a bitch!" He pivoted and she tensed, fearing he'd punch one of her walls and break her tiny apartment. He turned on her. "The phone technician said your cell got wet?"

"Yes, but I never—" She gasped. *Parker! He must have heard it ringing when Lucian called.* "That fucker!"

He came toward her and grasped her shoulders, his expression rigid. "Evelyn, I want you to stay away from him. He's underhanded and he doesn't play by the rules that he wants everyone to believe he does."

"Oh, you don't have to tell me."

"I do." He shook her. "There are things you don't know. There was a woman—"

She jerked out of his grip, her hands going to her ears. "I don't want to hear this!"

"I'm being honest with you. You need to listen. You need to know what kind of person he is. He hired a prostitute who looked just like you and sent her to the penthouse."

"Oh my God." She was going to be sick.

"I didn't touch her. I knew he was behind it. I sent her away, but I think she stole the lease to the apartment I rented for you and I think that's how he found you. The only other person who could've told him was Slade, but Slade didn't know."

"Slade? What does he have to do with any of this?"

Lucian sighed. "Part of the deal was I give Parker a job. He was your friend and I had no problem helping him. It wasn't until he made his other conditions known that I realized my first instinct about him was right. He's a prick. I gave him a job as a bellhop—"

"At Patras? I knew I saw him there!"

"You saw him?"

"Once. At night. I went to visit the girls at the salon."

"Well, he only worked there for a short time. He somehow crossed paths with Slade and Slade found out about our deal. He offered him a job making several times his salary at Patras on the spot."

"What's *wrong* with that guy?"

"Who knows? I stopped trying to figure him out, and I'm in the process of buying out his shares and dissolving our partnership. My point is, Parker Hughes isn't a man you can trust or afford to underestimate. If he comes here, I want you to call the cops or me."

"He doesn't know where I live."

"Nothing remains a secret forever. Just promise me you won't talk to him."

"The bastard broke my phone and lied to me. I want nothing to do with him and told him so yesterday."

It was stupid to be so angry about a phone in light of everything else, but she couldn't forgive him for that additional transgression of honor. When she realized her phone was broken, she was completely cut off from Lucian, and her mind couldn't deal with that. She'd fallen apart all over again and it was Parker's fault. All for what?

"Promise me, Evelyn."

Not a difficult thing to do. "I promise."

He nodded and stepped back. Glancing around, he asked, "Is there anything you need?"

"No."

Lucian swallowed. "Believe it or not, I'm proud of you. Your home's small, but nice. You did this, Evelyn. You."

His praise touched parts of her she'd censored off, and she didn't need him poking her softer sides. Besides, she couldn't take full credit for her independence. She wouldn't be there if not for him. "Thank you."

He stepped closer to the stairs, but hesitated. "I'll have a new phone delivered today—"

"No, Lucian. I can buy my own phone now. I'll get one."

His lips thinned, but he didn't argue with her. "You'll call if you need anything?"

She nodded.

He mimicked the motion. "Lock the doors. I'll talk to your landlord about getting some cameras in that alleyway. I'll contact FPD about those two men and make sure they never bother you again."

She had no doubt. "Good-bye, Lucian."

"I'll see you soon." He turned and headed out down the steps. Before the door clicked behind him, he muttered into his phone to Dugan that he was ready.

She turned and pressed her head into the wall. Her brain was too tired to think.

seven

A PICTURE'S WORTH A THOUSAND PAINS

SCOUT dragged the order across the scanner as the woman in line chatted about the weather. The steady blip of merchandise being tallied had become the symphony of her days over the past few weeks of working at Clemons.

It had been a week since she'd seen or heard from Lucian. He'd gotten the last word and was now giving her space. The evening after he came to her apartment, a package arrived with a new phone. The note attached was simple and to the point. *Now you can call.*

He just couldn't let her get her own damn phone. In a way it pleased her that he'd gone against her wishes because now she had his number again, but it still pissed her off.

She couldn't make sense of her feelings anymore. Space was good, but the more time that passed the more she missed him. Missing him was dangerous, so she embraced his absence like a vaccine, accepting it was part of the healing process. Sooner or later it had to stop grating on her. Did all women feel so irrational? She didn't like it, yet couldn't seem to control her tumultuous emotions.

"Oh, I have a coupon for that, dearie."

"Okay," Scout said as she continued to ring up and bag the order.

She slid a few birthday cards over the scanner, and her hand stilled when she reached for the tabloid crossing the belt. Her brain froze. With numb fingers, she lifted the magazine and stared dumbly at the picture on the front. Lucian wore an expression of disinterest as a woman laughed beside him, her arm looped affectionately through his, her palm pressing into his shoulder.

"The price is on the back, dear. And here's that coupon."

Scout blinked at the woman waiting to be rung out. Nodding, she turned the tabloid and scanned the price. Her numb hands bagged up the order as quickly as possible and, once her line was empty, she shut out her light.

Her feet carried her to the display where all the magazines were exhibited. She quickly found the one with Lucian on the front. Her stomach knotted until she could barely breathe. The woman was stunning, blond, and nothing like Scout.

Running her finger down the words spread all over the cover, she scanned for the name Lucian or Patras, two words she could immediately recognize. She found the name Patras and tracked the sentence following it.

"New whoa-man in . . ." There was a long word that started with a *b*, which she didn't have a shot in hell at sounding out. Shaking her head in frustration, she followed the words until she found a number that was likely the page the article was featured on.

She turned to page four and her knees shook. There were more pictures. Lucian leaning close as Satan's whore whispered in his ear. Lucian helping the blond jezebel with her wrap. Lucian staring at the camera as he held the door for the fucking tramp!

Scout growled and threw the paper on the belt at her register.

"You all right over there, tiger?"

She looked at Nick. He could read. Snatching up the tabloid,

she marched over to his register and waited as he handed his customer the change. Once the customer left he turned to her.
"What's up, Ev?"

"Can you read this?"

"Uh, yeah, but I'd rather not. I don't really care who found
Elvis and what the latest crop circle design is."

"No, just this article."

"Um, okay. Why?"

She glanced around anxiously and leaned over his bagging station and whispered, "I can't read very well." Interesting that her
curiosity outweighed her pride. More irrational behavior she
couldn't make sense of. What was happening to her?

He tipped his head back as though he was prepared to laugh
like she were joking, but her desperation must've showed in her
expression, telling him she was quite serious. "For real?"

"Yes. Please don't say anything. I can read small words, but
not a whole article."

"Okay," he said, calmly taking the magazine. "But why this
article? Why not read something with substance?"

She stabbed her finger at the picture. "I know him."

"*Lucian Patras?*"

"Yes."

He chuckled. "Well, aren't you full of surprises."

Scout glanced at their empty lines, knowing they didn't have
much time. "Will you please read it to me?"

He nodded and folded the paper open. "Okay." He cleared his
throat. "*New Woman in Billionaire Patras's Love Life. Lucian Patras
was spotted attending a swanky private event with a new bombshell
on his arm. Admirers are wondering what happened to the mysterious brunette he attended many affairs with this past winter, but
are also pleased to see he's paired up with Nicole Nottingham, young
heiress of Nottingham Cosmetics and budding actress. Although
Patras would not offer any comment as to what happened to the*

blue-eyed brunette he'd spent the winter beside, sources say the couple called it quits sometime last April, just before Patras was spotted doing business at his hotel in Paris, France.

"When Nottingham was asked if she and Patras were an item, she giggled and said, 'Depends how you define the word.' She then fled into a private benefit with the man in question. Followers are wondering if this one will be The One. *The Annual Rose Bowl Charity event takes place this coming Saturday, and enthusiasts are anxious to see if Nottingham will again be on the arm of Folsom's most eligible bachelor. The event is open to the public and tickets are five hundred dollars a plate. Tickets can be purchased at . . .*

"It just goes on to tell you where to buy the tickets," Nick commented.

Scout was going to be sick. That son of a bitch!

You asked for this!

Her mind took offense to the bitter swirl of jealousy souring her stomach and burning her heart. She'd pushed him away, made him leave, and he'd done exactly what any man would do. What made her so special to assume she deserved more?

Love.

She loved him and he was supposed to love her, but he was moving on. Outrage had her trembling. What if she'd truly pushed him away for good? The idea of a life without Lucian was too empty to contemplate. She realized that in the back of her mind she'd always assumed they'd get past this. But how?

She was going crazy. One minute she hated him. One minute she wanted him. The only constant emotion that wouldn't go away was the fact that she still loved him. She searched her mind for some stable thought, but her head was a mess.

"Hey, you okay? You don't look so good."

She shook her head, afraid that if she spoke she'd puke. Snatching the tabloid, she marched it back to the rack and stuck it with the other rags. Her stiff body slipped back into the space behind her register and she tapped her foot.

He'd betrayed her. She deserved time to cope with her emotions, figure a way to make sense of them. The urgency now suffocating her only complicated matters more. Would she ever think clearly again? Apparently the answer was no, because she was about to do something incredibly stupid.

"Uh, Ev? You gonna be okay?"

Her gaze snapped to Nick. "You're single, right?"

"Last I checked."

"What are you doing this Saturday?"

"Nothing. Why?"

"Will you go with me to that function?"

His eyes bulged. "It's five hundred a plate, Ev!"

"I'll pay for everything. I'll even rent you a tux if you don't have one."

"Where the hell are you gonna get that kind of money?"

She laughed dryly. "Mr. Lucian Patras himself will sponsor our date."

He hesitated, seeming reluctant to agree. "What's your relationship to that guy? Isn't he a lot older than you?"

"He's not that much older and I just . . . know him, okay? Will you go? There will be good food and probably an open bar."

"I guess, but I'm not sure if we'll fit in. People like us don't mix with people like Nicole Nottingham and Lucian Patras."

"Ugh. That woman is a skank!"

Nick held up his palms. "Okay. She's a skank."

"Sorry. I'm just . . ." What was she? What was she doing even thinking about going to that function? She didn't even know what a Rose Bowl was.

She sighed. This was probably a really bad idea, but after she last saw Lucian, she'd been softening. This was good. This showed her exactly why she couldn't trust him.

A war of indignation and jealousy battled inside of her. There was a point to be made, but she couldn't predict which point it would be—that she still wanted him or that he didn't deserve her. Hurt and anger were both unwelcome, but seemed all she had in that moment.

He could take his new phone and sweet words and give them to someone else. She was going to catch him right in the act with that blond trollop and then what excuses would he have?

Slut!

SCOUT sighed as she glanced in the mirror. Her stupid plan had cost her almost fifteen hundred dollars. Why had she ever agreed to do this?

She'd blown her hair out and left it wild, giving her that freshly fucked look. Her eyes were lined with kohl, making the crystal blue of her irises pop dramatically. She wasn't good at makeup, but refused to visit Patras to ask the girls at the salon for help. She wanted to catch Lucian completely off guard, and someone might've seen her if she went to the hotel.

Her dress was a find. It was nothing like the gowns Lucian had bought her. This was made of slinky black material that fit her hips like a second skin and only reached the middle of her thighs. The top of the dress was loose, hanging in a gathered halter that covered her breasts and drooped almost to her navel. A thin rhinestone chain linked the material at her cleavage. She wore nothing underneath, as even the tiniest G-string would show, and the back of the dress was completely bare to her hips.

Her shoes cost three times as much as the dress. They were strappy black satin with a rhinestone buckle at the ankle. She wished she had a full-length mirror to see if she looked as much like a horse's ass as she felt, but she didn't. She'd just have to wait and see Nick's reaction when he came to pick her up.

As if on cue, there was a knock at the door. Scout grabbed the little purse thingie the girl at the shoe store suggested she buy, and wedged her phone and keys inside. She'd already stuffed it with enough money for the evening and the tickets for the event.

"Coming!"

Shutting off the lights, she carefully took the stairs, very mindful of her shoes' ability to kill her. She hated high heels, but these babies were serving a purpose. Reaching the bottom, she unlocked the door and pulled it wide. "Ready?"

Nick looked quite debonair in his black tie. His hair was freshly cut and his tailored tux fit him to perfection. Her gaze traveled from his shiny patent leather shoes to his face. His mouth hung wide as he stared back at her.

She drew in a breath, incredibly self-conscious. "What? Is this too much? Should I try to find something else?" Not that she had anything else. "Maybe we shouldn't go."

"Ev, you look . . ." He swallowed. His voice was a mere rasp. "Wow. I mean, *wow*!"

"Yeah?"

He shifted and stood a little taller. Tugging the lapels of his tux, he held out his arm. "Your chariot awaits." She smiled and took his arm.

Nick drove a well-loved S10 truck of the ugly duckling sort. It was a loud and bumpy ride to the Marion, the hall hosting the Rose Bowl, but Scout didn't mind. She was just glad he'd agreed to go.

When they arrived, there was a parking attendant ushering a long line of luxury vehicles down the sectioned-off shoulder of the road as valets relieved drivers of their keys. Scout withdrew into herself a bit when she noticed most females were dressed in long, flowing gowns. She glanced at her exposed knees and became very aware of the sharp angle of her bare shoulders on display.

She swallowed. "Maybe we shouldn't do this."

Nick glanced at her, then back out the windshield as the line eased forward. "What are you talking about? We're all gussied up and you spent a ton on the tickets. Might as well have fun."

Her fingers fidgeted with the billowy material barely concealing her breasts. Never before had she dealt with jealousy. That's what this was: pure, stupid jealousy because Lucian was moving on just like she told him to do.

Disappointment in her actions made her feel even smaller. She didn't deserve to go to a function like this and that money should've gone toward more important things. None of this was part of her well-thought-out plan.

"Do I just give them the key? Do I need to tip or is that later? This is nicer than my prom was. Holy shit, is that Harvey Geswaldi?"

Scout glanced out the window at the tall man Nick was asking about. She had no idea who Harvey Geswaldi was, and Dugan always drove them so she didn't know what the parking protocol was. "I don't know."

"Hey."

She turned to Nick and found him studying her, a slight kink to his brow. Her lungs drew in a deep breath.

"You okay?" he asked.

"Yes. No. I don't know. I'm regretting my decision to come here."

His expression blanked. "Because of me?"

"No, God no. I just . . ." She sighed. "Can I tell you something?"

"Always."

"I wanted to come to make someone jealous."

His assessing gaze traveled from her knees, up her thighs, over her unsupported, barely covered breasts, to her face. "Is it Patras?"

"Yeah. Stupid, I know. I'm going to stick out like a sore thumb and he'll be so preoccupied with his stupid little actress he won't even see me."

His frown reappeared. "First of all, Ev, you can't go by the tabloids. Second, have you seen your reflection? You look crazy good, but not only tonight. You're really pretty every day. Everyone in there with working male anatomy and heterosexual thoughts will notice you. And third, you're fun. That Nicole chick can't compete."

Scout smiled at his attempt to cheer her, wishing his words could actually calm her nerves. "Lucian's in his thirties. She's more his age."

"You call him by his first name? Wow, you really did meet him, didn't you?"

Oh, she'd done more than meet him. "I know him well. We sort of had a disagreement."

It was Nick's turn to look nervous. "Did you two hook up or something? He's not gonna come after me for showing up here with you, right?"

"No. Lucian always handles himself with class." *Except with Parker, and surely that was an exception.* She hoped she was telling the truth and that the sophistication of the event would prevent any unwanted scenes. "Besides, he probably won't even notice I'm there."

Nick smiled. "Well, don't let age throw your confidence. It's just a number." He glanced over his shoulder. "You want to make him see what he gave up? Okay, we'll put on a nice little show. Come on, let's get you a drink and have some fun. We'll pretend we're rich folk for the night."

The attendants opened the doors and they were assisted out of the truck. Nick handed over his keys and was given a small white ticket, which he stashed in the breast pocket of his tux.

Someone held the door as they stepped over the threshold, and a throng of guests checking their bags and wraps immediately surrounded them.

"Do you want to check your bag?"

Scout looked at her petite clutch and shook her head. She was territorial when it came to her stuff, and she didn't want to hinder a fast escape.

Nick took her arm and guided them away from the congested area. She scanned the crowd, and her stomach bottomed out when her gaze settled on Lucian's tall form. He looked impeccable in his tuxedo.

His dark hair was slicked back naturally like a model lifting out of a swimming pool during a cover shoot. The romantic lighting showed his distinguished, if premature, salt-and-pepper temples, and he had just the right amount of shadow lining his jaw to give him that dangerous tycoon look. He grinned as someone spoke to him.

His tall body was easy to separate from the rest. Broad shoulders filled his jacket and, as her gaze traveled over him, the blond woman beside him distracted her. Nicole Nottingham wore a sequined red gown that displayed her lithe body with an air of class Scout couldn't muster.

A waiter walked by with a tray of champagne flutes and she snatched one, guzzling down the bubbly liquid fast. Her mouth was incredibly dry. She stashed the empty flute on a mantel to their left and stared as Lucian dismissed the person he was speaking with. He nonchalantly pressed his palm to Nottingham's bare back—which felt like a punch to Scout's stomach—and ushered her into the ballroom. Something about the casualness of his touch made it all the more painful to witness.

Scout sucked in a breath as they disappeared. "Do you have the tickets?" Nick asked.

She withdrew them from her bag, self-conscious of the way she'd folded them. Pressing them flat, she handed them over and he gave them to a woman at the desk. Another waiter passed and she grabbed another glass of champagne. This one went down just as fast, but seemed to settle her a bit.

"Ready?" Nick asked.

She took his arm and they followed the guests into the main

room. Soft music played as invitees mingled with acquaintances. The chairs were all trimmed in soft shades of rose, and topiaries spilled like waterfalls from the center of each round table.

There were so many flowers, the room smelled like a garden. Crystals hung and candles flickered. The volume of the soft chatter collided with the easy music, creating a low roar that made it difficult to hear.

"I think our table's this way," Nick said, guiding them to the back right of the ballroom.

Most of the women wore gowns. Some had short dresses on, but nothing like the dress she'd selected. A cool dew of sweat formed between her breasts, as she grew more uncomfortable about her choice of attire. What was she thinking, wearing a dress like this? She looked like trash.

Men uniformly looked the same. The only telltale differences were in their build and age. It was disorienting, being surrounded by so many men in black. Her steps depended on Nick's lead as her legs went into autopilot so her eyes could search for Lucian.

They reached their table and Scout took a seat so she was facing the crowd. She wanted to be able to observe from the corner. At their place settings, Nick found a menu and commented on the formality of the courses as she continued her fruitless game of I Spy.

"Champagne?"

Scout turned as a waitress held out a tray. "Thank you," she said, replacing her empty glass with a full one.

"You may want to slow down. We haven't eaten yet," Nick whispered. "I'm going to go up to the bar and see about getting a beer."

She nodded, ignoring his warning, and sipped from the flute. The room grew louder as more people arrived. Where was he? Her gaze snagged on a flicker of red and she spotted Nottingham. And there was Lucian, right beside her.

Her molars locked. He wasn't touching her, but the woman stood stoically by his side, clearly staking her claim to him.

Someone must have said something funny. Nottingham laughed and her tiny, scarlet-painted nails caressed the sleeve of his jacket.

Scout finished her champagne and guzzled the water at her place. She was incredibly thirsty for some reason. Magically, a white-gloved hand swept her empty glass away and replaced it with a new one.

Nick reappeared with a glass of dark amber beer. Its heady scent mingled awkwardly with the pure fragrance of roses. "So what happens now? Is it like a wedding? Do we dance after we eat? I've never been to anything like this."

"I'm not sure."

They each silently sipped their drinks and surveyed the room. "Hey, there's your guy. You gonna say hello?"

Scout's gaze didn't leave them. The more she watched Lucian and Nicole, the more she admitted how beautiful they were to-gether. She didn't know if she should be happy for him or cry. The champagne was going to her head. She hadn't eaten much that day and now her bladder was painfully full.

Her mind searched for courage she didn't have so that she could make it to the ladies' room. "I need to use the restroom," she whispered to Nick.

"Okay. Hey, check it out. They have an omelet station. Rich people are funny."

Nick was wonderful at going with the flow, she decided. She envied how comfortable he was with his station in comparison to the rest of the guests. There were likely others like themselves there, but Scout couldn't pick them out of the crowd.

Her eyes searched dimly lit doorways around the room and found a sign with fancy script. That could be the ladies' room. She stood and was relieved her legs were working. However, as she tucked in her chair and took her first step, she swayed with the effects of the four glasses of champagne she'd consumed in the past twenty minutes. She needed to slow down.

She shuffled through the crowd, mindful of some eyes—mostly male—watching her make her journey. She was so afraid Lucian might see her. She didn't chance looking at him. Head down, she made her way to the door she hoped was the restrooms.

Once she reached the perimeter of the ballroom, it was easier to slink by. She turned into the small hall and spotted a woman coming out of a door. Scout pressed the door wide and breathed a sigh of relief when she found a wall of sinks.

She took care of business and washed her hands. It was jarring, seeing herself in the full-length mirror of the ladies' room. In her high heels, her legs looked a mile long, especially because her dress was so short. Her butt was a tight little ridge covered in black, and her back was completely bare except for where her hair hung past her shoulders.

"I love your dress."

She turned and found a woman in a blue cocktail dress washing her hands. "Thank you."

"I wish I had the guts to wear something like that. Although, I don't know if my husband would want to leave the house then." She laughed. "He already gave me an earful about dragging him here again. But what are you going to do? If it was up to him we'd never go anywhere."

Scout laughed nervously. "Yeah."

"Well, nice talking to you." The woman left.

Scout glanced back at her reflection. *Shit.* She wished there were a service exit so she could sneak out. What was she doing there? Lucian was with a date, and she'd told him to move on. It wasn't right for her to come spying on him. She didn't belong there. It was a painful and expensive lesson, but she got it.

She pressed through the door and decided to tell Nick she changed her mind and wanted to leave. Her head was fuzzy and it took her a moment to locate her table. Had something changed in the room? It appeared different from this vantage point. Her footing slipped and she quickly grasped the arm of a man passing by. "Excuse me. Sorry."

She was drunk. Hopefully the first course would be served soon and she could get something in her stomach before they left. Or maybe they should just hit a diner. Scout looked up and spotted Lucian, smiling as an older woman pulled his lapel to whisper something in his ear. His eyes scanned the room, and when they landed on her it was as though a thousand silent words came crashing down.

His expression fell as their gazes locked. Whatever the woman whispering to him was saying, she was sure he wasn't listening. His lips parted and Scout could see the questions running through his head as his brow creased. He glanced to her left and right, perhaps looking for her escort.

Her heart raced as her breath came fast. This was a mistake. Maybe if she left before he caught up to her, he'd think it was a case of mistaken identity. He didn't need to know how immature she was and that she'd come here to spy on him.

He turned to the older woman and appeared to excuse himself. Nottingham straightened like a lap dog prepared to follow her master, but he gestured to her with a steadying movement of his hand to wait and handed her his drink. She looked crestfallen and frowned at the two glasses now awkwardly filling her dainty, manicured hands.

The second he stepped in Scout's direction, panic set in. She spotted their table and, with as much grace as she could manage, quickly worked her way back to Nick. Her hip bumped into a guest and she apologized quickly, glancing back to see Lucian hot on her tail.

She didn't bother to take her seat when she reached the table. "Come on. We have to go!"

Nick glanced up at her, startled. "Already? Why?"

"Because—"

"Ms. Keats."

Nick's gaze darted over her shoulder. "Holy shit," he muttered.

Scout swallowed, feeling the blood rush from her face, and turned. "Mr. Patras, nice to see you here."

He scowled. His gaze traveled over her barely there dress and over her shoulder, giving Nick an assessing glare. "I didn't expect you to be in attendance."

"It was a last-minute thing."

"A very expensive last-minute thing," he muttered. He extended his hand to Nick. "Lucian Patras."

Nick stood. "Nick Ramsey. Nice to meet you."

They shook and Lucian turned his gaze back to her, his displeasure at her presence slightly concealed, but very much obvious nonetheless. Her spine stiffened at the indignity of being caught and made to feel foolish. She was mad at herself but linked it all back to the intimidating man staring her down.

Her chin lifted. "You'll have to introduce me to *your* date," she said succinctly.

His lips tightened. "Might I have a word?"

She glanced back at Nick, who shrugged. "I think they'll be serving dinner soon—"

His fingers wrapped around her arm. It was a casual gesture, but there was steel behind his grip. "Just a moment of your time."

She barely had a chance to shoot Nick an apologetic glance before Lucian dragged her away from the table. "You're hurting my arm," she hissed as he deftly worked his way through the crowd. "Where are we going?"

He didn't answer. Her feet worked hard to keep up with his clipped pace as he shuffled her down a corridor and out a door. They were in a courtyard when he finally released her. She glared at him, rubbing her arm.

"What are you doing here?" he hissed.

It was her turn to scowl. "Celebrating the Rose Bowl."

"Do you even know what the Rose Bowl is, Evelyn?"

No. "Yes," she answered indignantly.

He gave her a look that called her a liar. "Who's the guy?"

"I believe introductions have been made."

He stepped closer and she stepped back. "Don't play games with me. Who is he?"

"A friend," she quickly relented.

"What *kind* of friend?"

"Lucian, are we really going to do this?"

"Oh, we're doing this," he growled, stepping closer again and causing her to take another retreating pace back. She glanced around the garden. It appeared they were alone.

"I think we should go back inside."

His eyes narrowed. "That's some dress you're wearing."

"I . . . I misunderstood the formality of the evening."

"A slight breeze and your nipples will show."

She uncomfortably crossed her arms over her chest. Damn him. His finger trailed over her bare shoulder, and she shivered.

"You've had too much to drink and they haven't served dinner yet."

"I'm fine."

He stepped closer again and she found it impossible to step back. "Why are you here?" he whispered, his fingers gently tugging her arms away.

Her hands tingled and she insisted it was a result of the champagne. The tip of his index finger trailed over the slight swell of her breast, sweeping beneath the billowy fabric and coming dangerously close to her bare nipple.

Unwanted company interrupted the moment. "Lucian?" He stilled and she sucked in a breath. Slowly he lowered his hand and turned.

Nicole Nottingham stood at the door they'd exited, her long

arms crossed over her perfect chest as though she had a chill. Scout stepped away. The woman's face was questioning. Lucian paced back and Scout nearly cried at what the act implied.

Lucian was with Nicole. She was his date and it was inappropriate for them to be out there in the garden alone.

He looked up and Nicole walked with the grace of a floating angel to his side. Scout hated her for being so perfect. She glanced at Lucian then to Scout questioningly. "Nicole Nottingham, this is Evelyn Keats."

The sting at having her name second in the introduction burned through her. She extended her hand and Nottingham did the same, turning her palm downward as though she expected her to kiss it. The shake was a mere gripping of fingers that carried much more class on the other woman's end.

"A pleasure," she said slowly then turned to Lucian. "Dinner is about to be served, darling. We should go inside."

Darling? Scout was going to be sick.

"I'll be in in a minute."

The woman's delicate smile twitched as though she didn't want to leave them alone out there, but she retreated anyway. Once she was gone, Lucian turned on her. "Stop drinking. You've had enough."

"You're not my father."

His jaw ticked. "No, I certainly am not. Come, I'll walk you inside."

Was that it then? Was he really okay with her presence? He took her arm, this time without the force he'd used to get her out there. Her world was spinning and she was again thirsty.

The volume of the room was stifling. Her steps slowed as her pace was unsteady. Lucian turned and frowned at her. "Are you all right? Do you need to sit down?"

She tugged her arm out of his grip. "I'm fine." She was on the verge of tears. Why had she come here?

He glowered. "I'm calling Dugan to take you home."

"Lucian!" she snapped. "I am not a child. I have as much right to be here as anyone."

Easing close he hissed, "You're drunk and your body's about to fall out of that scrap you're passing off as a dress. I'll be damned if you take another sip of alcohol and have that boy putting his paws all over you as he helps you out the door. Who the hell is he anyway?"

"It's none of your business. You have your own date to worry about."

His onyx eyes turned challenging. "What's the matter, Evelyn? Having second thoughts?"

Her palm twitched and she had the urge to slap him. "Not at all, *darling*. I'm just here to enjoy myself. What you do is your business. Now, if you'll excuse me. I must get back to *my* date."

She turned to walk away as his punishing grip closed on her arm again, cutting off her fast escape. He growled in her ear, his warm breath a hot caress over her neck. "Don't fucking play games with me, Evelyn. You won't like the result."

She laughed derisively to cover her discomfort. "Oh, you don't need to worry about me playing games, Lucian. That's your style, not mine."

He released her arm. "We'll see."

She took her escape the moment it was available. When she returned to their table, adrenaline was coursing through her veins so quickly her limbs were shaking.

"You okay?" Nick asked.

"Fine." She turned. "Where's the waitress?"

"Why?"

"I'm out of champagne," she grumbled, very much wanting another drink.

He gave her a measuring look and she tried for a reassuring smile, but failed. "I'll go get you one."

Nick stood and went to the bar. Scout's gaze traveled to Lucian's table and saw him making apologies as he took his seat next to the trollop in the red gown. A waiter passed and Scout managed to snag a glass of champagne and drink it down before Nick returned.

Lucian's gaze landed on her, heavy with warning. She lifted her glass and saluted him from afar. His eyes narrowed.

Nick returned and she looked away. She smiled as he placed a fresh glass in front of her. Servers brought out the first course, a light salad with mandarin oranges and some sort of raspberry dressing. Scout didn't have much of an appetite, but it was in her best interest to eat.

The first course was cleared away and replaced with a lovely pasta dish. Delicate little pillows of pressed pasta were stuffed with a salmon mousse and drizzled in a vodka sauce.

As her stomach adjusted, her equilibrium seemed to right itself enough for her to have another drink. The people at their table were nice. They breezed over casual topics and by the third course, Scout somehow managed to forget Lucian's presence, and by forget, she meant force herself to look in his direction only once a minute rather than steadily scrutinizing his every move.

After dinner her stomach was happy and her body felt light. Music changed to a more upbeat selection, and couples slowly made their way to the dance floor. Scout turned and realized there was a band as well as a prerecorded selection of music.

Her gaze returned to Lucian and found him watching her. Nottingham chatted with the woman to her right. Her mind went back to the first affair he'd ever taken her to. Scout recalled her fear of dancing that evening. She didn't fear such things now. They'd taken many private dance lessons, something she now realized she missed.

Her lips curled in a soft grin and she made a barely perceptible nod, calling a momentary truce. His eyes softened and she wondered if he was recalling the same memories.

Their connection was severed as Nicole stood. Scout's stomach knotted as she leaned down and whispered in Lucian's ear, her dainty hand brushing lightly over his shoulder. Nottingham left, and when Lucian looked back to Scout she lowered her gaze, no longer wanting to play at this game.

"Want to dance?" Nick asked.

She swallowed. "Sure." She'd dragged him here and he'd been a great sport so far. The least she could do was dance if that was what he wanted to do.

The music was an older song with a Motown swing to the beat. They slowly trotted around each other, and she forced a smile on her face. The alcohol in her system helped her to not overthink the fact that Lucian was watching them. When the song ended, she grinned at her date and caught her breath.

"May I cut in?"

Her steps faltered as she pivoted and found Lucian at her back. She glanced nervously at Nick, who swept his arm out invitingly and stepped aside. The song was not anything like the one that was just playing. A slow climb started on the piano as only one man sang slowly into the microphone.

Lucian stepped in front of her and took her hand. Her fingers curled over his and her palm settled on his shoulders, his scent a sweet form of torture to her senses. Peace swept over Scout as he pulled her close. He led them slowly in circles and his presence enveloped her. She closed her eyes and breathed in the welcoming, familiar scent of him.

"You look beautiful tonight."

His voice climbed into hidden places of her soul that shook with a longing almost impossible to contain. She was tired of fighting. "Thank you."

"I asked them to play this song for us."

Her lashes fluttered open. She glanced at him then to the band. Violins played softly from the shadows of the stage as the pianist sang. She focused on the words as Lucian glided with her.

"I've never heard it before," she said.

"It's by One Republic. It reminds me of you."

"Oh, Lucian . . ." She couldn't do this.

"Shhh, just let me have this moment of holding you without arguing about the past. I miss you, Evelyn."

She smiled sadly and blinked back tears. Her cheek rested over his strong chest, the beat of his heart echoing beneath the beautiful, lyrical vocals.

"Maybe I'm just dreaming out loud, but until then . . . Come home. Come home."

Her eyes closed as the words washed over her. Her heart wanted to simply wish away the past month and start back where they'd been before he broke her. As the song concluded and their steps slowed, she considered saying fuck it all and telling him just that. But as they stepped apart, her eyes caught on the stunning beauty in the red dress observing them.

Scout's peace faltered as she drew in a deep breath and stepped away. "Thank you."

"Evelyn . . ."

She shook her head. "You're here with her, Lucian. Go be with her."

He blinked. His eyes creased and she thought perhaps he might deny that they were together, but he simply nodded and stepped back. Scout watched him turn away first and then retreated to the ladies' room, fighting back the emotions threatening to break the fragile façade she held by a string.

Locking herself in a stall, she pressed her cheek to the wall and held her stomach as she cried silently and without tears. Would she ever stop loving him? Even after everything he'd done, she couldn't deny that she loved him more than anyone in this world and she'd never overlook the fact that he gave her away.

Once Scout had her emotions under control, she brushed her hands down her dress and tried for good posture. With trembling fingers, she unlatched the stall door and came to an abrupt stop.

"Enjoying yourself?"

Scout's lips parted as she eyed the beautiful Nicole Notting-ham in her glamorous gown and long blond hair. She was even more stunning up close, intimidatingly so.

Scout was too taken off guard to answer. Nicole took in her appearance, an assessing expression in her calculating eyes that told Scout she wasn't impressed with what she saw. It took every-thing she possessed not to cover herself. Instead, she stood straight and met the blond bombshell's challenging glare.

"I must say, I thought you'd make an appearance before now. When you didn't show up over the past few weeks, I assumed you might not. Your presence this evening took me by surprise. Lucian also seemed a bit put out by your attendance."

Scout narrowed her eyes. "I don't usually clear my schedule with him."

Nicole's painted red lips quirked. "Of course not. I've looked into you, Ms. Keats. Interesting that before you dated Lucian, you didn't exist. However did you two meet?"

She'd "*looked into*" her? What the hell did that mean? Scout didn't need some rich heiress traipsing around in her past. If her background was exposed it would embarrass Lucian, something he claimed not to care about, but Scout had worried over frequently.

Scout refused to show any sign of insecurity. "Kind of you to care so much. If you have questions, I suggest you ask Lucian. Or isn't he open with you?"

Her manicured eyebrow arched slowly. "You're a feisty little thing. I just want to make sure that we're perfectly clear. Lucian's here with me and he's leaving with me. I'd like to leave the bag-gage at the door if you know what I mean."

Scout jerked back. "Did you just call me baggage?"

"It was the kindest word I could think of," Nottingham said haughtily.

Scout's mouth gaped and she snorted. Wasn't this little viper interesting? "Really?" She tilted her head and smiled, amused. The champagne had apparently given her a solid pair, and Scout was grateful for the false courage.

"Well, let me enlighten your stunted vocabulary, Ms. Nottingham. The only baggage here is under your eyes. And as far as where I came from, or what I am to Lucian, it's none of your damn business. You can try to intimidate me all you want, but your first mistake was following me in here at all. It reeks of insecurity. You're nothing but a high-class act on the hunt for a better name, when I know the man behind the name.

"If you think coming in here and cornering me will impress him or intimidate me, you're wrong. I thank you for the display. It's enlightened me as to how hollow this charade the two of you are putting on actually is. You don't know him. And while you may have his company, I have his heart. So, if you'll excuse me, *darling*, I must be getting back."

Scout swept past the willowy creature and came up short when she called her name. "Scout."

She involuntarily turned and Nicole smiled wickedly. "Like I said, before Lucian, you didn't exist, but I did find some curious information on who you were, *Evelyn*. For instance, you also go by Scout and your mother's a junkie." She made a patronizing pout with her lips that smacked of pity, and Scout's stomach dropped. "I'd hate for that sort of personal information to fall into the wrong hands. Patras is a name that can afford some bad press, but wouldn't tolerate being sullied with the sort of filth that shows up at a sophisticated affair dressed as a hooker."

It was Scout's turn to gape. How had she found out about Pearl? She stepped into the woman's personal space and the she-bitch had the good sense to ease back. "I think you've made a mistake, Ms. Nottingham. You see, there's only one whore here, and she's wearing red. Come near me again and I'll show you exactly how low-class I can be."

Scout turned and marched out of the room. Her legs carried her right to the bar. "May I please have a shot of tequila?"

The bartender raised a brow and poured the crystal liquid from a stout bottle into a tiny glass. He placed a slender green lime on a napkin and slid it across the bar. With trembling hands, she tipped the shot back and savored the burn as it made its way down to her shaking insides.

"Hey, are you okay?"

She turned and found Nick. "Can we get out of here?"

He frowned and eyed her suspiciously. He jerked around and glared at Lucian. Scout followed his gaze. Nottingham was whispering to Lucian, who was scowling. He stood and turned away from his date, and scanned the room.

When his gaze fell on her, she narrowed her eyes. Lucian's brow lowered. He glanced back at Nottingham briefly, seeming to blow her off.

"Can I get you anything else, Miss?" the bartender asked.

"Do you want me to get the truck?" Nick asked.

She turned to the bartender. "I'll have a tequila sunrise." He nodded and went about concocting the drink. She turned to Nick. "Did you ever just want to say fuck it and do something crazy?"

"Sure."

She couldn't keep up with her emotions. Jealousy teetered between shame and indignation. It was all a mess. *She* was a mess. "Do you want to stay or go?" she asked, letting him make the decision.

He turned back and gave Lucian an assessing glance. "Did he say something that upset you?"

"No, but the slut he's here with basically called me white trash in the bathroom."

His nostrils flared and he mumbled something that sounded like "Fucking rich people." Sighing, he held out his arm. "Well, lovey, shall we show them how trashy people dance?"

She smiled and took a hefty sip of her cocktail, the sweet cherry a perfect complement to the tangy tequila. "I'd love to."

With the dinner hour over, the band kicked it up a notch. Scout didn't know music and she wasn't a great fast dancer, but she knew how to fuck and she decided dancing was like fucking, but with clothes on. Turned out, Nick was a great dance partner.

His large hands held her hips as she ground her behind into him. Her arms dangled high above her head as she let the rhythm seep into her limbs. A light dew of sweat coated her skin and by the third song, the liquor permeated her brain and she let go.

It didn't matter that they were making a display. Everyone had drawn their conclusions the moment she stepped foot into the room wearing a dress too showy for their elitist tastes.

Nick turned her and laughed as he dropped low on his haunches, bobbing with the beat. She did the same and when she tried to bounce up, she lost her balance and tipped back. Her hand reached for him and he quickly pulled her back up to her full height.

She lurched to the left when something yanked on her arm. Dizzy with exertion and too much champagne and tequila, she stumbled and came face to face with Lucian. He glowered at her and growled, *"Enough!"*

"Hey," Nick called, coming to her aid.

Lucian turned like a panther ready to attack. "Back off, kid. She's drunk and you're not helping."

Scout snatched her arm from his grip. "I am *not* drunk, Lucian." That was a lie.

He leaned close. "No? You almost fell on your ass. You're making a scene."

She drew back. "I'm not the one making a scene. You are! You and that waspy bitch you came here with. Now if you don't mind, I'm going back to what I was doing. Nick—"

Lucian spun her so quickly she nearly *did* fall on her ass. "I said enough."

She shot up on her toes and got in his face. "You don't call those shots anymore. I'm a grown woman and can take care of myself."

His chest expanded as he drew in a long breath. Through gritted teeth he said, "I'm giving you one minute to pack it up and leave. Either that, or I'll have you escorted out of here."

Mortification and hurt had her lips trembling. How dare he? She stood there indignantly, daring him to embarrass her like that. If he followed through on his threat, she'd never forgive him.

She glanced around. People crowded them, gyrating and dancing in a world of their own. Past the dance floor, she spotted Nottingham speaking animatedly with a woman holding a clipboard. She pointed at them and the woman spoke into a microphone at her ear.

They had every right to be there, but knowing Lucian, he likely paid a great deal to whatever the hell a Rose Bowl was and was a prominent sponsor. They'd lick his ass if he asked them to. He had the power to get them kicked out, which she didn't believe he'd truly do. But there was no way she'd give that red-lipped slut of his the satisfaction of seeing them escorted off the premises.

Her vision shimmered with unshed tears. She pressed her lips tight and glared at him. "I hate you," she whispered, and marched off the dance floor.

"Ev, wait up." Nick hustled after her.

When she passed the coat check, she halted and stomped her foot. "I forgot my bag."

"Hey, don't let that asshole make you cry. We were just having fun and he's pissed because he wants you."

"Oh, he doesn't want me, Nick. He just wants me to leave so he can have his little actress."

Nick sighed. "I'll go get your bag and meet you out front."

He quickly turned and went back into the ballroom. She turned and rushed through the door, her heel catching on the runner and causing her to go down with a thump that would've likely hurt had she not been so drunk. Strong arms lifted her off the ground and she shoved them away, brushing the hem of her dress down her thighs.

"Ms. Keats, are you all right?"

She looked up at the familiar voice and when she saw it was Dugan helping her up, his eyes creased in concern, she lost it. A wall of tears shimmered and collapsed over her lashes. "No," she sobbed. "I'm definitely not all right, Dugan."

His lips parted beneath his thick, handlebar mustache. "Here, let me help you."

He gathered her in his arms and escorted her away from the door. She sniffled and wiped her nose with the back of her hand. "I'm drunk," she admitted pathetically. "I'm really drunk and I embarrassed him."

His lips pursed as he opened the passenger door of the limo and helped her sit so her feet hung over the pavement. He squatted down and withdrew his handkerchief. She winced as he blotted the scrape on her knee.

"Pardon my French, Ms. Keats, but any man who lets you walk away is a fucking idiot and deserves to be embarrassed."

Her sob cut off and she looked at him, shocked. Was she that drunk or did he really just say that? She suddenly cracked up, giggles pouring from her lips as she draped her hand on his shoulder and held her stomach. "You're right, Big D. He *is* a fucking idiot."

"Am I interrupting?"

She and the chauffeur drew up short. Lucian towered over them, an unimpressed and quite put-out expression marring his beautiful face. His eyes traveled over them and stilled when he noticed her knee.

Dugan stood and Lucian took his place. He peeled back the handkerchief and made a sound of exasperation. "Goddamn it, Evelyn."

"I swear it was the shoes," she said. Dugan handed him a bottle of water from the limo and Lucian wet the handkerchief and dabbed it over her abraded skin. She winced and hissed at the sting.

"Stay still," he snapped.

Fucking idiot. She giggled and hiccupped. Crap, she was definitely plastered. As he doctored up her knee, Dugan producing a small bandage and some ointment, she watched how the streetlights turned Lucian's dark hair almost blue. Without thinking, she ran her fingers through it, and he stilled.

His gaze slowly traveled to her face and the air became charged. Dark eyes stared at her, not seeming to trust the energy between them. "Why did you come tonight?" he whispered in a voice so low, she could barely hear it.

"I needed—"

"Lucian!"

Jerked out of the quiet moment they each turned. Nottingham stood glaring at them, a gold wrap draped over her long arm. Lucian stood and Scout spotted Nick waiting with his keys and her clutch. The truck was idling behind the limo.

Dear God, when would this nightmare end?

She slowly climbed out of the limo and touched Dugan's arm. "Thank you, Big D, for coming to my rescue yet again."

Nottingham scoffed and rolled her eyes. She stepped close to Lucian and handed him her wrap, turning her back expectantly. She might as well have peed on his ankle.

Lucian held the gold wrap dumbly for a moment and then as though pulled on puppet strings, placed it on her narrow shoulders. His fingers never touched her. He nodded to Dugan, who gestured to the back door of the limo. Nottingham turned her picturesque face, and a slow, wicked smile curled her lips.

"It's nice to see that they know when to take the trash out around here," she muttered snootily.

Scout unsteadily stepped forward and Lucian held up a hand halting her. Nicole gracefully slid into the limo and Lucian stepped to the door. "Darling . . ." The shadow of her arm extended over the seat and Scout could imagine her self-satisfied grin.

"Dugan, take Ms. Nottingham home." He slammed the door.

"Gladly," Dugan said, rounding the front of the car.

Scout stood paralyzed. He'd sent her away. For some reason the triumph at seeing the car drive off was bittersweet. Nothing would erase the scene she caused tonight, but Scout knew she'd won in some fashion.

Lucian turned and faced her, his hands in his pockets. His anger seemed replaced with something else. She caught the slight way the side of his mouth kicked up as he stared down at her. She didn't know what to say.

He turned to Nick. "I'll be seeing Ms. Keats home this evening. Thank you for bringing her."

"Uh . . ." Nick looked at her for confirmation. "Ev?"

She glanced nervously at her coworker, betting he never imagined their evening playing out like this. "It's fine. Lucian can take me home. I'll see you on Monday."

Lucian frowned.

She ignored him. "Thank you for being my date."

Nick nodded slowly and handed over her purse. She took it and they watched as he climbed into his truck and drove away, the roar of the engine fading away in the distance. Lucian turned and glanced at her. He didn't say a word, just watched her.

She shifted on her ridiculous shoes. "Is Dugan coming back for us?"

"No."

"No?"

"No."

"How are we getting out of here?"

"I'll hail a cab." His hands remained in his pockets as if he were forcing himself to keep them there. "Why did you come here tonight, Evelyn?"

She looked down. "I don't know."

"Yes, you do. Tell me."

"I wanted to see . . ."

"Me?"

"Her," she admitted. "I wanted to see who she was."

"She's nothing."

She laughed without humor. "Don't tell *her* that."

"I'm sorry she spoke to you that way."

Scout met his gaze. "She wants you."

He smirked. "She can't have me."

"Did you sleep with her?"

"No."

"Kiss her?"

"No."

"Are you attracted to her?"

"I'm attracted to you."

"That doesn't answer my question."

He drew in a slow breath. "Nicole's an attractive woman, but she isn't my type."

"She looks nothing like me."

"Exactly," he said. A few beats passed. "How do you know Nick Ramsey? Who is he to you?"

"He works with me."

"Are you attracted to him?"

She smirked. "He's not my type."

Lucian smirked and stepped closer. His hand slipped from his pocket and he ran his fingers down the filmy sheath of her dress. "This dress is something else. Did you buy it for me?"

She shut her eyes and breathed him in. "No."

"Liar."

"Lucian—"

"Will you come home with me?"

Her eyes shot open. She was frustrated that her intoxicated brain was not as sharp as it should be. "I can't."

"You can. You just have to say yes. I'll take care of you. Get you something for your hangover in the morning."

His hand traveled up her neck to her ear, tugging on her lobe softly and sending shivers chasing over her shoulders and down her spine. Her lashes lowered as she tipped her head back. She could fall asleep. "We shouldn't."

"I won't touch you. It'll kill me, but I'll behave. I know you're drunk. Come home with me, Evelyn. I miss you in my bed."

She breathed through her nose, swaying just enough to remain upright. "Now who's lying?"

"Say yes," he rasped.

She barely made a sound. "Yes," she breathed.

That one word snapped him into motion. A cab was hailed and she was tugged inside. The broken-in leather was sunken and soft. She shut her eyes and moaned as the car lurched forward. Her stomach was not happy.

"You okay, baby? Want some water? I still have the bottle Dugan gave me."

She held out her hand blindly and heard him unscrew the top. Drawing the bottle to her lips, she drank greedily, causing the plastic to crackle in her grip. Lucian sat quietly in the dark. His fingers delicately traced up and down her thigh. The motions of the car made her insides swirl nauseatingly but his touch kept her grounded, a tight smile pulling on her lips.

Visions of the evening danced in her head, distorted and not lining up with what she recalled. Red dresses and sharp tongues, tuxedoes and sunrises. Bodies writhing and pounding music thrumming in her ears. Slowly, the visions faded away and all that was left was the gentle sway of the car and Lucian's touch caressing her knee.

"We're here," he whispered.

"Mmphh." She was too tired to form words, afraid if she opened her eyes the dizziness would intensify and make her ill. Her body was lifted and slid into warm fresh air and then familiar scents, rich with nostalgic meaning, greeted her nose. His shoes clicked on the refined tile underfoot as he carried her to wherever they were going. Something pinged and the scent changed to faded perfume and floor polish.

The world grew still and her mind slipped away. She gasped at the sound of another bell. "Shh. I have you."

She smiled and snuggled deeper into his hold. "Lucian . . ." If she was dreaming, she never wanted to wake up.

eight

TAKE TWO DOSES OF REALITY AND
CALL ME IN THE MORNING . . .

SCOUT'S mind eased into consciousness and she winced, her entire body protesting as she stretched. Her hands swept away a mass of knotted hair and she gripped her head. Who the hell was hammering an ice pick into her temples? She moaned.

As her leg extended, something didn't feel right. Her bed was way too soft and . . . big? She shot bolt upright and winced, moaning again, as the movement sent pain knifing up her spinal cord into her brain. Her hands swatted at the rat's nest that was her hair, and she opened her eyes. "Ohmygod."

Her head snapped around as she recognized Lucian's room, but she didn't see Lucian. Glancing down, she noticed she was stark naked. "Son of a bitch!"

She quickly crawled on the high bed made up like something from Arabian nights, and scrambled to the edge. Her feet tangled in the ridiculous amount of heavy down blankets, and she reached too soon for the table to catch her balance, missing completely and falling in a loud clatter to the floor. Her bones radiated with pain and something was squeezing the life out of her head.

Rolling to her knees, she hissed, reminded of her scraped knee.

Her arms batted at the offensive blankets and she cursed. She was a hot, tangled, mess.

"Evelyn?"

She stilled. Using her arm to lift the curtain of hair off her face, she slowly pushed into a seated position and peeked over the tall bed. Lucian stood by the door, and when he spotted her he cursed and charged in, likely to help her.

She threw out her hand. "Don't come any closer." He jerked to a stop. "I'm naked."

He laughed. "I know. I undressed you."

"What?"

"Evelyn . . . be reasonable." He stepped farther into the room and she quickly gathered the myriad of blankets around her, covering her woman parts. "Love, you were tanked last night. You barely moved once we got to the hotel. You were helpless."

"So you decided to take off my clothes?" she asked, outraged.

"I've seen it before."

"Well, I didn't invite you to see it again."

He sat on the edge of the bed and smiled down at her. His perfectly put-together appearance made her feel insufficient. "I have a peace offering."

She narrowed her eyes. "What is it?"

Reaching into his pocket he produced two small white pills. "Something for your head."

He handed her the tablets and retrieved a glass of water from the nightstand. She swallowed them down and guzzled the refreshing water until there was nothing left. Handing him back the glass, she eyed him suspiciously. "Did we . . ."

He chuckled. "No. You were comatose."

"What if I wasn't?"

"As tempting as that is, the answer would still be no. You were drunk and I gave you my word."

"Oh." She sat back on her heels and considered how this made her feel. He hadn't touched her. Good. Right?

"You're sober now, however," he said teasingly.

She shoved off the floor and stood. "Forget it. Where's my dress?"

"On the chair. I ordered breakfast."

She hobbled to the chair and found her dress. Frowning at the minimal swatch of black fabric, she hesitated. Her eyes glanced at the puffy down comforter wrapped around her. She looked like a Sumo wrestler in a toga. Turning back to him, she asked, "Do you mind?"

He sighed and shook his head, but didn't leave. Rather, he walked into the closet and she heard the opening and shutting of drawers. He returned a moment later with a pair of her jeans, a T-shirt, panties, and a bra. He handed them to her.

"These are mine."

"Who else's would they be?"

She blinked at the clothing. "But . . . I haven't lived here for over two months."

He drew in a slow breath and released it. "Evelyn, I did a lot of things wrong. I've apologized and will continue to apologize, but I need you to believe that I never anticipated you'd be gone for good. I still don't accept that as reality. You belong here. I'll wait as long as I have to."

"But you're dating."

He frowned and drew back his head. "No, I'm not. I attended a few events that required I bring a guest. That's all that was."

She scoffed. "That's not what the she-bitch on your arm last night said."

"What did she say?"

Scout thought for a moment. Her memories were sketchy at best. "Well, she cornered me in the bathroom and told me I looked like a hooker."

His brows shot up. "*She what?*"

"Yeah. Nice company you keep."

His eyes narrowed. "I'm sorry she spoke to you that way. You looked beautiful last night. You always do."

"Then she called me trash."

He rolled his eyes. "I was there when she said that and you saw my reaction. She has no room to talk. She'll blow anything with a zipper, and her behavior last night was the furthest thing from classy."

"I don't like her."

"Yeah, well, neither do I."

She smiled. "Really?"

"Really. There's no way I'll put up with someone talking to you like that or making you feel like you aren't good enough."

His words made her feel vindicated. A smile split her face, then faltered. "Shit."

"What?"

"She said something last night, but I can't remember what. Lucian, she knows about Pearl."

"How?"

"I don't know, but she also knows I go by Scout."

He shook his head. "She won't tell anyone."

"Wanna bet? She basically threatened to do exactly that."

"*She threatened you?*"

Scout flinched at the lash of his voice. "Yes."

"Motherfucker," he hissed. He turned away and paced. "Fucking people! I swear everyone is out for blood. Evelyn, I promise you'll never have to deal with that woman again. Son of a bitch." Clearly preoccupied with his own take on the previous evening, he ran his hand through his hair and walked out of the bedroom mumbling. He came back in and said, "Take a shower and get dressed. We'll talk more about this after I make a phone call."

He left her there, wrapped up like Stay Puft, holding her clothes. "Jeez, bossy much?"

After showering and dressing, Scout felt a world better. Her head still throbbed with a dull ache, but the painkillers were kicking in and the shower helped clear her mind.

It was strange being back in the penthouse. She knew where everything was and there were remnants of her there. Lucian still had her toothbrush sitting right next to his. Maybe he was being honest when he said he always expected her to come home.

Padding into the common area, Scout found him sitting on the couch watching some boring broker thing on CNN. He smiled and held his arm out to her. She went to him and froze. What was she doing?

He frowned. "Come sit with me."

Her fingers rubbed slowly over her thumbs. It was weird being there and not being there as his lover. She could so easily fall back into the old swing of things. "I better not."

"Evelyn—"

"Lucian, I can't. Please understand that. I just . . . can't."

He shut off the television and stood. At the table in the corner he plucked the metal lid off the plate and tossed it aside carelessly, letting it clatter against the other dishes on the table. "Eat your breakfast."

He was angry. Well, what did he expect? Last night she hadn't been thinking clearly. It didn't change anything.

She walked to the table and took a seat. He sat across from her, but didn't touch his food. The French toast at Patras was her favorite. Raphael, the chef, made homemade cream like nothing she'd ever tasted. Then there were the strawberries, floating in their own juicy sugar . . .

"I want to know what made you go there last night. You said you wanted to see Nicole. Why?"

She chewed slowly and put down her fork. "Are we really going to talk about this?"

"Why the hell wouldn't we? You tell me to move on. I can't, but I do my best to look like I am and you suddenly show up with some date and crash a party you'd never normally attend."

"Who says? I could be a huge Rose Bowl fan."

He raised an eyebrow. "What's a Rose Bowl, Evelyn?"

She grimaced. "A tournament in gardening?"

"No. It's a football game played at the beginning of the year. This year's players were honored last night for Folsom U."

"Oh. Well, I felt like being philanthropic."

"Can we please stop playing games and try for some honesty?"

She pursed her lips. She didn't want to do honesty. Honesty meant being honest with herself, and she was doing much better lying to herself lately. Her head still ached and she was tired despite just waking up, tired of everything.

"Talk to me, Evelyn."

Several long moments of silence passed and she finally whispered, "I never had anything, but I thought I had you, and losing you was just too much to bear."

The confession should have made him grateful. It was headway, but his expression crumbled. "I'm sorry," he said in a hoarse voice.

Time passed where neither of them seemed to know what to say next. Finally, Lucian asked. "If we could go back, would you?"

Impossible. "You can't take away the past."

"But I can give you all of my future. I wanted to, but you said no."

She recalled the night he proposed, how desperate he seemed. It all made sense now. She'd started the process of moving on. She had a plan. Lucian was a liability to her sanity. She never had someone get so deep inside of her that she couldn't think. He did. He touched places she never knew existed.

She stood. "The answer's still no."

His jaw locked. He'd shown restraint in the past few days that had boggled her mind. Lucian had never in his life been told no or that he couldn't have something, yet she'd told him nothing but no over the past two weeks.

"Friends. Can we be friends?"

She sighed. "I don't know if that's such a good idea either."

Lucian looked up at her, his hands folded over his lap, white-knuckled as if he were forcing himself not to reach for her. "How much longer do you expect me to go on like this, Evelyn? I'm not used to this sort of opposition."

Her anger surfaced. "I told you to move on."

He shot to his feet. "And I heard you, but I refuse to believe that's what you want. Not when you spent over a thousand dollars to run into me at a benefit you know nothing about."

"Last night was a mistake."

"No. It wasn't."

She stepped back. "Lucian, I . . . You're asking too much."

He crowded her and she eased back, but didn't take a step. His hand hovered at her jaw, yet he never laid a finger on her. "What will it take?" he whispered. "What do I have to do in order to touch you again? To have you back in my life and believe you're mine? I hate this void between us."

"You broke my trust," she choked. "I don't know if there's any coming back from that."

"It was a mistake. I realized it in a matter of hours. I broke my word and came for you, but I was already too late."

Her jaw locked. Everything she wanted was right in front of her for the taking, but there were valid reasons to deny herself. Yet, she couldn't help wondering if this torture of abstaining from him was some twisted form of self-inflicted penance.

Her eyes closed and she breathed. He was so close, but not touching her at all. In barely a whisper, she confessed, "He touched me, Lucian. I wanted to erase your mark and I let him kiss and hold me. I didn't know he saw me as a possession. He was my friend and I blame you for letting me go under such a misconception."

"I told you he was trouble. I told you he loved you."

"And I thought you were jealous."

"I *am* jealous! Think of how you felt when you thought Nicole and I were an item. How do you think your situation with Hughes made me feel? She's nothing to me, but he . . . he has pieces of you I never will. I know you, Evelyn, but he knows Scout. He knows what it was like to be there, on the streets, to go hungry. He knows what you were like as a young girl. He has all these puzzle pieces and I hate that he used that to his advantage."

"I want to hate you both. I can hate him, but I can't seem to hate *you*." She was weakening. That hard shell of ice she tried to encrust her heart in was thawing, and he was working his way through the fragile cracks. "I trusted you more than I've ever trusted anyone. You took care of my mom, Lucian. Do you know what that did to me? What it does? She's the only thing I've ever had in this life and I was going to lose her. You saved her."

Confessions spewed from her lips before she could draw them back. "That day that you found me, I thought, 'Oh my God, he's my hero.' And you were. But then I come to find out . . ."

Lucian gripped her shoulders. "It changes nothing. I still found you. Don't you see? I would have done anything to find you. Imagine what it did to me to have to agree to his terms, to let you go. I made sure there was a loophole, but you weren't ready for that. I'd do it all over again, Evelyn. It'd kill me, but I would. I'd save you again and again, no matter the cost, because that's how badly I need to know you're safe."

She opened her eyes and waited for the tears to clear. Blinking, she focused on him and recognized the staunch determination in his face. He was telling the truth.

His thumbs swept along her jaw as he gently clasped her neck, scrutinizing her. His pleading gaze was desperate. Her chest hurt. "Lucian . . ."

His head slowly lowered and he brushed his lips over hers. "I need you, Evelyn." He stepped closer, tilting her head back. "I need you more than the air I breathe." His mouth kissed the corner of hers. "Nothing is right when you're absent. I own the whole damn city, but when you aren't here, I can't find home."

A tear slipped past her lashes and he caught it on his lips, kissing it away. Her hands gripped his shirt. "You're my home," he breathed, turning her face to meet his kiss.

His lips slanted over hers and her lips parted. The press of his hand cupped the back of her head. "I love you," he rasped, lifting her into his arms.

Her legs wrapped around him as her face pressed into his throat. He carried her to the bedroom, the unmade bed beckoning with rumpled sheets and imprinted pillows.

They fell onto the mattress and his body pressed over her, igniting the longing that never stopped smoldering deep inside her. She arched as his mouth worked down her throat to the sensitive curve of her shoulder.

Cool fingers slipped under her shirt and over her belly. She lifted as he removed her shirt. Easing up on his knees, he crossed his arms over his belly and pulled off his own shirt, tossing it to the floor as well.

She stared up at him, truly seeing him. He was beautiful, so different from other men she'd seen. Lucian's olive skin was smooth. His muscles showed all over his trim body beneath a dusting of hair. He was entering the prime of his life, but he was no less gorgeous.

Her fingers traced up his torso and he cupped her hand, dragging it over his heart. They breathed heavily, the moment weighted in such intensity. Curling her fingers over his, she pulled his hand down to her chest and pressed it over her breast.

Her need outweighed her self-preservation, and the truth of what she wanted could no longer be denied. Strong fingers squeezed gently and she arched into his hold. Fingertips stuttered over the lace trim at the swell of her breasts, teasing her nipple into a tight point. He undid the clasp at her back as she lifted for him and the fabric pulled over her arms and fell away.

In the dim morning light, blocked by the curtains, Lucian's skin glistened in hard splendor. He slid off the bed and she watched as his fingers slowly undid the snap of her jeans. Once stripped away, along with her panties, he removed the remainder of his clothing.

Something was different about this time. Yes, the urgent need to have him inside her was there, but there was something so potent, it was tangible. This would change everything. Not back to the way it was before, but to something new and perhaps even more powerful than what either of them had ever known. This was a validation of their need, honed by willing abstinence.

The mattress dipped as he climbed over her. His motions were measured. His body braced above hers and he lowered his head. Lips tickled hers as his mouth opened, not giving her his full kiss. Head tipped back, she arched, seeking more, but he continued to tease.

His body was a welcome weight over hers, encasing her in his strength. Heat singed her where their flesh touched. The weight of his arousal hung heavily on her belly, and she parted her legs.

Toes pointed, she slowly draped her knees around his hips. They rubbed their skin together softly, teasing, tempting, bringing each other slowly back to life. "Kiss me, Lucian."

"If I kiss you, I'll never be able to stop," he whispered into her mouth as their bodies writhed.

"Then don't."

His lips crashed over hers as he took her mouth. His muscles bunched under the grip of her fingers. His hand traveled up her thigh, squeezing, massaging, and settled on her hip. His erection landed in the seam of her folds and grew slick with her arousal.

He ravished her mouth and she gave every drop of passion she had into that kiss. Tearing his lips from hers, he kissed and sucked her throat, biting softly at the tender spots and making her keen with need. She held his broad shoulders as he kissed a trail down to her breasts.

Easing back, he cupped her breasts and licked at the sensitive tips. It had been so long since she had been touched like this. Need burst inside of her. Her nails pressed into his muscled flesh as he pulled one turgid tip into his mouth and suckled hard.

His hands gripped her ribs, holding her in a way that made her feel delicate next to his strength, small and cherished. The fire inside of her built. Flames licked at her belly as his mouth traveled lower. Heat blazed in her loins.

He kissed a tender spot on the side of her stomach, and her back bowed. Lips traveled down to her hips, and fingers trailed through the soft patch of hair at the apex of her thighs.

"You're different," he whispered and heat burned her cheeks.

She'd lost weight and not been to the salon in well over a month. "I haven't needed to . . ."

He smiled. "I know. I like that no one else has been here. This is mine, Evelyn. Don't ever give it to someone else, or I may have to commit murder."

She smiled. Her body belonged to him whether she'd accepted the reality of that or not. When she'd kissed Parker, there was something fundamentally lacking.

His fingers trailed over her dewy folds and teased her sensitive bud. "What are you thinking about?"

"You. What you do to me. No one else has that effect on me, Lucian. Sometimes it's scary."

"You do the same to me. I can't choose to give you up. My body and heart forbid it. You're like a drug."

His head dipped and the soft glide of his tongue over her crease had her arching in his grip. She moaned at the gentle probing of his tongue.

"God, I've missed the taste of you." His mouth closed over her, and a thousand volts of electricity shocked her back to life. Sprays of light flashed behind her eyes as he sucked at her tender skin.

His hands slid beneath her bottom and lifted her to his mouth. His tongue delved between her slick folds and he gently began to fuck her with his tongue. He pressed deep and her body jerked at the profound penetration, remembering what it was to be filled in such a tender way.

He nibbled at her flesh, flicked his tongue over her sensitive clit, and proceeded to fuck her with his fingers. She came in a rush, crying out his name as waves burst from within, rippling her body. She jerked in his grip, but he never let her go. His mouth was relentless, driving the currents of pleasure further and further out, then pulling them back in.

He eased her down onto the mattress, dragging his fingers up the underside of her trembling thighs. Cupping beneath her knees, his hands pulled her legs farther apart, exposing her.

"You're all glossy and pink. Beautiful."

There was no shame in having Lucian see her this way. He adored her feminine parts and taught her to never hide from him. His arm extended and he pressed his middle finger into her sex slowly, reaching for that soft patch of nerves hidden deep within. Her heels pressed into the mattress and she lifted into him.

"Very good, baby. Show me you need it. Show me how much you missed my touch."

Oh God, she missed it. Another finger joined the first and then a third. Her body stretched around the intrusion. He tickled her G-spot, and soon his hand was fucking her hard, the wet slaps of his fingers sinking into her the only accompaniment to their heavy breathing.

She rode his hand, arching, her back coming fully off the bed as she came hard. Her second release surpassed her first, and she shook violently. He removed his fingers from her slick sex and rolled her on top of him.

Her hair formed a curtain around them. Her legs straddled his hips, her breasts clinging to his chest as she leaned over him and found his mouth. He tasted of her. He tasted of *them*. She kissed him hard, licking and biting at his lips, unable to get enough.

Her mouth traveled over the stubble of his sharp jaw, down his throat. Fingers combed through the hair traveling over his cut abs. She flicked his dark nipples with her tongue and he moaned.

Sliding lower, she gripped his cock in her fist. His flesh was burning. She squeezed him and his hips lifted. Meeting his gaze, she whispered, "I want you so much right now I can barely control myself."

His lips parted and she was suddenly gripped and thrown to her back. Lucian's mouth slammed down on hers and he kissed her almost violently, yet his touch was controlled. Fingers ran over the high arch of her cheekbones. His thumb smudged over her lips. Neither shut their eyes, staring intently at one another as he pressed his lips to her jaw and whispered. Each word dragged over her flesh like its own caress.

"I'll come. I haven't been with anyone since our last time at the estate. I want you so desperately right now, Evelyn, I'm afraid I won't last."

"Let me have you. I want you to come in my mouth."

He growled and rolled to his back, pulling her on top of him again. She crawled down his body and fisted him, pumping in two long solid strokes that had him groaning before she took him into her mouth.

He was already salty with precome. Her scalp pinched as he fisted her hair. Hissing, he pressed her down. Her lips stretched over his thickness as he pressed to the back of her throat. She worked her fingers at the root, her other hand cupping him, massaging gently as he pulled and pressed her over him.

Her nails softly teased at the underside of his sac, tickling the path of skin just below. He groaned. "Touch me, Evelyn." Her fingers explored his body. "Yes, that's it, baby. Make me come."

He growled through gritted teeth. She jerked him hard, scraping her teeth lightly up his shaft as she sunk down on him, engulfing him in the heat of her mouth.

He lurched and arched, nearly severing their connection. His hand fisted in her hair as he rapidly fucked her mouth. She pressed deep and his guttural moan filled the room. "Fuck! Enough. I need to be inside you."

Scout kissed up his trembling belly and he grabbed her. Her legs wrapped around his hips as he sat up, hugging her tightly, his face pressed into her throat. He nuzzled her through her wild hair. "I love you so much," he whispered fiercely.

He was still hard against her flesh. They sat upright, trembling, as his mouth kissed over her breasts. When his lips found hers, they stilled and stared at each other through hooded eyes. His potent need was clear in his smoldering gaze.

Scout lifted her hips, shifting her position, as he guided his cock to her sex. Their eyes never wavered as they each were locked in that moment in time. She was drenched with need. As his length filled her, Scout's moan paralleled his. The shock of pleasure broke their intense stare. Back arching, she fanned her fingers through his dark hair, fisting and pulling his head back as she came down on him and bit at his rough jaw.

Strong hands gripped below her breasts, spanning her waist as their bodies slowly began to move in tandem. Skin clung to skin. Breath mingled, and whispers of affection and pleasure filled the room. It was possibly the most intensely beautiful moment of her life.

Dark eyes stared into hers and there was not a secret between them in that moment. Everything was raw and honest and undeniably carnal. Their bodies glistened with sweat. Fingers dug into tender muscle as nails titillated and scraped. They would each wear marks of their possession.

She seated herself and his cock pressed into her G-spot. His mouth sealed over her throat and sucked as she rode him, rotating her hips and stealing her pleasure. Hot breath beat at her neck. "That's it, love. Take what you need. Let me feel you come all over my cock."

Bowing, her mouth opening in a silent plea of pleasure as desire exploded into something unnamable and delicious. Her body pulsed and twitched as he held her. Warmth erupted into her channel as he came, his own cries of pleasure mingling with hers.

Tipping back onto the bed, trembling, holding tight, she never wanted to let him go. Harsh gasps for air filled the quiet room as she stared into Lucian's expressive, dark eyes. Her thumb combed over his dark brow and he gently kissed her lips. "I love you, Evelyn."

It was time, time to face her reality. She caught her breath and met his stare. "I love you too, Lucian. Please don't hurt me ever again."

His eyes closed and his grip tightened. She knew how long he'd waited to hear those words. They were offered freely, without coercion, without guile. They were the only truth she had in this world. She loved him and that love terrified her, because it had the ability to tear her to shreds and leave nothing behind.

lucian

nine
·····

BREAKTHROUGH

The destruction of a seemingly strong defense,
often by means of sacrifice

LUCIAN sighed. Contentment was not an accurate enough word for the peace filling him. His fingers brushed the hair out of Evelyn's eyes and he watched as she slowly drifted to sleep. He almost couldn't believe she was there in his bed, in his arms. It was impossible to stop touching her after such a long period of not having the luxury.

Things had to change. They couldn't go back to where they once were. Too much had happened. She'd opened up parts of him he never shared with anyone. When he thought he'd lost her, he became crippled with regret. Losing her again was not an option.

His mind contemplated the ring in his drawer. His fingers idly played with hers. Her unconscious state allowed him to explore and study the many facets of her sleeping body. He wanted to slip that ring on her finger now, but knew that would upset her.

Was it him or something else? She'd admitted she loved him. There had never been more precious words. Did that mean she'd reconsider being his wife? He was never letting her go again. It simply wasn't an option, so why not marry him?

The sound of his phone vibrating from the floor distracted his thoughts. He ignored it and continued to observe her as she slept. She was so beautiful. Her dark lashes gathered like the feathers of a quill, making soft shadows over her cheeks. Her lily-white skin was softer than the petals of a rose. There was no one as beautiful as Evelyn.

He considered Nicole. She'd royally fucked up last night when she called Evelyn trash. He wanted to retaliate, but feared what the woman would do in return. The last thing he needed was some escalating game of tit for tat, especially if what Evelyn said was true and Nicole knew about Pearl and her past.

It didn't bother him, where Evelyn came from. Nor should she be held responsible for her mother's poor choices. But his baby was a prideful little thing, and that sort of exposure would crush her. She'd feel like she embarrassed him, which was bullshit, but it would be a challenge to convince her otherwise. If he could avoid a situation like that altogether, it was best for everyone.

He had a ton of shit to do. He'd been backed up with work since Evelyn had moved out. His mind just wasn't in it. There was one deal in particular that was weighing on him.

For over a year he and Shamus had been persuading Labex to move their green energy plant into the care of Patras Industries. The site was ready, blueprints drawn, and the nearer the deal came to closing, the more he wanted it done. There was a ton of money and man-hours at stake, and everyone was getting anxious the longer the preliminaries dragged out.

His phone buzzed again, and he carefully slipped from the bed and found it in the pocket of his pants. Climbing back into bed, he ignored his call log and texted Dugan.

Go to the apartment on Cypress. Take Manuel and Frank. I want all of her stuff packed up and brought back to the penthouse.

The phone vibrated a moment later.

What of the small apartment on the boulevard?

Lucian pursed his lips. That was *her* place. He couldn't touch her stuff without her permission. It irritated him that he not only had one apartment to consider, but two. In the past month, Evelyn had lived in four different places. The most he could do was take care of the apartment he'd rented for her. That was a mistake he'd be happy to never revisit again.

Just the one on Cypress for now.

He stayed in bed all morning, simply holding her. Around noon, she became restless and he sensed her waking up. His lips pressed into her temple. She sighed and stretched.

"Hi."

He smiled down at her. "Hi. Did you have a nice nap?"

"Very nice. I thought it was all a dream."

"Nope. It's real." He took her hand and brought it to his growing cock. "This is very real."

"You're gonna have to give me a minute. I'm out of practice and a little sore."

"Did I hurt you?"

"No. My body forgot what it feels like to be thoroughly loved."

He was silent for a moment, hesitation caused by his knowledge that he'd never let certain things go and that his question may totally destroy the peace of their morning.

"What is it?" she asked, snuggling closer.

"Will you tell me?"

Her brow crinkled. "Tell you what?"

"What happened when I was in Paris?"

Her expression shuttered, locking those secrets away tight. His need to know what happened with Hughes ate at him every day. Did he touch her? Fuck her? She said she hadn't been with anyone else that way, but what if she was lying?

"I don't want to talk about that," she said, rolling away.

He caught her hip and stilled her escape. "Fine. We'll put it away. For now."

"Forever, Lucian," she said sternly. "Bringing it up is only going to make us fight."

True, but his curiosity was tormenting him. He automatically imagined the worst. When he'd returned from Paris and gone to the apartment on Cypress and found nothing but empty pantries and her key on the counter, he feared he'd lost her forever.

The only thing worse than that fear was finding her in Hughes's bedroom half dressed, knowing he might be too late. He'd beaten the living shit out of that fucker and wanted to do it all over again every time his imagination played games with him.

He gritted his teeth. Now wasn't the time. Their reconciliation was still new and delicate and he didn't want to push her too hard. "How about a bath?"

She smiled. "A bath sounds lovely."

HIS knees pressed into the porcelain walls. Evelyn's back weighed lightly on his chest as he soaped her breasts with a sea sponge. "Where are you working, Evelyn?"

"I don't want to tell you."

He stilled. "Why?"

"Because it's always a fight, me working. I like my job and I intend to keep it."

"I don't have a problem with you working."

She snorted and turned, the water lapping at the walls of the tub. Her breasts swayed as she faced him, tiny droplets laced with suds traveling over her curves, gravity pulling them back to the water's surface. "Since when?"

"A lot has changed. Someday . . ." He drew in a breath, preparing for her opposition. "Someday, I'd like you not to work, to be at home, our home, taking care of our children."

Her smile melted away to a blank expression. "Lucian . . ."

He held up a hand. "I know. I'm not talking about tomorrow

or even next month. I'm talking about the future, our future. It *will* happen, Evelyn."

"And what if I don't want children?"

He frowned. "Of course you do."

"Why? Because other women my age do? I'm not like them, Lucian. Children need good parents. Otherwise it isn't fair to bring them into this world."

"Are you saying I wouldn't be a good father?"

Her lashes lowered. They were spiked from the humid air. "No. I was talking about me," she quietly admitted.

He grabbed her chin and tilted her face until she met his gaze. "Hey. You are not Pearl. You would make a wonderful mother."

"I'm very single-minded."

"That's because you've spent your entire life trying to survive. In time, you'll learn that you can trust me and I'll take up that burden and you'll never have to worry again."

"I do trust you, against my better judgment," she admitted. "But I'll never be able to surrender my independence. I've worked too hard for it."

He couldn't hide his grin and ignored the second part of her admission. "That's a start."

She sat on her bottom, this time facing him, her legs pulled up, her feet now tucked against his hips, a somehow possessive touch. "You wanted to know about Parker."

He stilled, not expecting her to readdress the topic so soon. Something had changed? But what? "Some. Only what I can handle without going on a rampage."

Evelyn wouldn't meet his gaze. Her finger slowly chased a cluster of tiny bubbles along the surface until they dissolved into bath oil, leaving nothing more than an iridescent film on the surface.

"He was different," she whispered so low he had to strain to hear her. "When he touched me, he always asked." Was she saying she preferred that? Lucian wasn't someone used to asking permission.

"One time, he kissed me and I *wanted* to like it. I needed to feel something other than the hollow ache you left behind."

His throat worked to swallow. He'd asked for this and he'd listen, but knowing he was getting his way did nothing to alleviate the pain or jealousy raging inside of him.

"At first it was nothing, and I realized there was a great deal to be said for chemistry. We had nothing like what you and I share, what you can do to me with just a look in a crowded room. But I wanted to like him. I hated you for abandoning me and I don't know if it was a self-preservation thing or because I wanted to punish you."

Her brow creased and she blinked as though she were recalling something and still trying to make sense of it. "The one time he kissed me, I forgot about you for the briefest moment." Her words sliced through him, but he remained silent, allowing her to carry on. "I don't know why. We'd been laughing and the ever-present awareness that gutted me again and again after you left, just somehow slipped away. But then . . ."

She paused and he quietly asked, "Then what?"

"Then he'd pause as if to ask if what he was doing was okay and I knew it wasn't. I didn't want to be loyal to you, but by letting him kiss me I was being disloyal to my heart. But it was more than that. When I'm with you, something happens to me. I slip away to a safe place where I don't have to worry or think. I couldn't find that place with him. He'd hesitate and reality would come crashing down and break any peace I felt."

"That's what surrender feels like, Evelyn. That's the peace I can give you when you give me your submission."

She met his gaze. "Is that normal, to feel that way?"

"Do you care?"

She lifted a narrow shoulder, the motion delicate, reminding him of her innocence. "I guess not. I've just wanted my entire life to be normal, like everyone else. I was afraid you broke me somehow . . . for all other men."

His eyes narrowed. "If I did, I'm glad. The thought of some other man seeing you the way I do, watching you fall apart when you come, seeing those exposed moments of vulnerability—they're mine, Evelyn. The idea of someone else seeing you like that is excruciating."

"I feel the same way about you." She looked back at the water. "When I thought you moved on, I felt like my insides were rotting. Something so dark and angry came over me. I just kept thinking about stupid things, like how you wake up just before dawn and sit at your desk to watch the sun rise. It killed me imagining her intruding on those moments."

He understood that level of jealousy, the covetous way she thought of his habits and behaviors. "And with everything you've just told me, what hurt the most to hear was that Hughes had your laughter. Those are my smiles. I'm a very possessive man, Evelyn. I don't ever want to share you. Not your body, not your mind, your smiles, certainly not your laughter. I covet all of you in a way I've never experienced greed before."

She smiled and it was just for him, secret and somewhat carnal, hidden at the corner of her plush mouth. He held out his hand. "Come here."

She pushed through the water, causing it to ripple in her wake. He pulled her to his lap and her legs went around his hips. His mouth kissed over her damp skin slowly, drugging her with tiny nips and licks until she softened completely.

His hand reached to fit himself to her sex. She leaned back and slid down on him, engulfing his cock in sensual heat. Her tight little pussy gripped him. It was *his* pussy. Never had it known another's touch. The notion did things to him.

Grasping her nipped waist, he guided her slowly, pumping his flesh in and out of her. He'd need a solid week to make up for lost time, and he wanted to spend every moment of it buried inside of her.

His spine tingled as she came. Her soft whimpered cries, tiny treasures to his ears. "Say it," he whispered, dragging his mouth over her damp shoulders. "Say you love me."

"I love you."

His muscles tightened and he filled her with his release. Briefly, he resented the tiny man-made device hidden deep inside her that prevented pregnancy, but his emotions were hot, her words compensating for the little things he could not yet have from her.

She loved him. She loved him and she'd admitted it. It made everything, in a way, seem worth it, just to have those three magic words.

THEY decided to go to dinner. It had been a long time since he'd taken Evelyn out and their last trip to a restaurant had been tainted with fear and guilt of what was to come. Lucian wanted a fresh start and planned to make one tonight.

"I don't have anything to wear."

"Your clothes are here." When she frowned, he explained. "There are still some in the closet, but Dugan retrieved your belongings from the apartment on Cypress. Everything's at the hotel, I just need to call down and have it brought up."

Her mouth twitched. "You had my stuff brought back?"

He wasn't going to apologize. "Yes. Is that a problem?"

She lunged at him, catching him completely off guard and tackling him to the bed. Her mouth opened over his and she kissed him with unleashed passion. "Thank you. I hated that place and I never wanted to go back."

He rolled her to her back and parted her robe. "I hated that place too."

His hand cupped her breast and squeezed. Her knees came up and gripped his hips. He arched a brow. "Again?"

She nodded. "Take me, like you used to."

Something dark unfurled inside of him. His fingers gripped her wrists and lifted them over her head, pressing them into the mattress with one hand. The position caused her tight nipples to lift. He pinched one pink tip and pulled, twisting slightly. She moaned.

Releasing her breast, his hand went to his cock. He pumped his flesh, eyeing her intently. "Tell me what you want."

"I want you inside me."

"Beg me."

She writhed, her hands remaining above her head like a good girl. "Please fuck me, Lucian. I miss your cock. I want it."

He growled and kissed her, his hands yanking the robe wide. His mouth went to her breasts and he pulled one tight nipple into his mouth, sucking hard enough to bruise the delicate flesh.

He forced her legs apart and slid a finger deep into her wet slit. Her arousal coated his fingers as he fucked her with his hand. His mouth moved to the other breast and left it dark and wet from his saliva. Withdrawing his fingers, he flipped her to her stomach. "Up on your knees. Good girl."

Her pert ass rose and he glided his palm over the soft flesh. He gripped her cheeks and spread her. Once his eyes spotted that tiny rosette, he couldn't resist. He leaned forward and kissed the tiny pucker. Evelyn purred and rocked into him.

"Stay still," he said, standing and swatting her ass. He went to the bathroom and found the oil. When he returned, she was exactly as he left her, his handprint leaving a delicate pink star on her cheek.

He climbed onto the bed and uncapped the oil. "Do you want me to fuck that tight ass of yours, Evelyn?"

She moaned her agreement. There was nothing more satisfying than knowing her desires matched his, equally dark and insatiable. He rubbed oil over his fingers and cupped her cheek, pulling it aside. Her little rosette clenched in anticipation and her folds glistened with arousal. He thumbed the little knot until she relaxed.

Once she was at ease he lined up his finger and sunk it deep into her back entrance.

Her spine stiffened and her shoulders shook as she tried to remain still. "That's it, baby. You love my finger in your ass almost as much as my cock, don't you?"

"Yes," she moaned, her damp hair fanning down her back and shoulders.

He withdrew and drove the oiled digit back in. She rocked slightly, but he saw the effort she was making to control her movements and remain still. He slapped the inside of her thighs and she spread her knees wider. The fingers of his other hand cupped her pussy and her body trembled.

He pushed two fingers into her sex and she lurched forward, catching herself on her elbows. "Where are you?" Her fingers formed the signal that told him she was okay and didn't want him to stop.

Twisting his finger in her ass, screwing her with each pump of his wrist while the fingers of his other hand pressed deep, searching for that soft spot deep inside her. He found her G-spot and applied pressure.

Her hips bucked. "Ohmygod, ohmygod, ohmygod!"

"I want you to come so hard my sheets are wet. I'm going to make you come that hard, do you understand?"

"Yes!"

He slid another slicked finger into her ass and began to fuck her harder with his hand. He pressed down on her G-spot. "Now, Evelyn. Come for me now. Scream my name."

"*Lucian!*" Her cry sunk into the mattress. Her body convulsed as her sex contracted in rapid pulses over his fingers and her snug little asshole tightened. She gushed over his fingertips and he withdrew both hands.

Flipping her on her back, he wrenched her trembling legs apart and licked up every drop of her release. Sweet ambrosia coated his tongue. Nothing had ever tasted so good, so right, as his Evelyn.

He loved making her come that way. He still remembered how sensitive she was the first time she realized a woman could come that way. She flinched and jerked under his gentle laving, her body overstimulated and vulnerable to the most delicate caress. Once he had licked her pussy clean, he sat up and extended the hand that had been in her sex.

"Open." Her lips parted and he pressed his fingers into her mouth, slowly fucking them over her tongue. "Suck them clean. See how good you taste."

She shut her eyes and moaned. His fingers withdrew with a pop. "Good girl. Now turn over. Cup your ass and spread yourself."

He held her arm as she slowly adjusted her position. Her face pressed into the bedding, her shoulders catching her weight. She spread her cheeks wide and he leaned forward. She gasped as he licked her from the tip of her sex to the tip of her spine.

"Are you ready for my cock, baby?"

"Always."

He uncapped the oil and coated his length. Dribbling a generous amount over her ass, he speared it inside her entrance with his finger. Easing up on his knees, he pulled close.

Withdrawing his fingers, the tip of his cock pressed into her tight muscle. She hissed and her back moved with the rapid way air filled her lungs. "Take me, Evelyn. Remember how I taught you."

She exhaled slowly and the tension in her body eased. He pressed in, stretching her, careful not to go too fast or hurt her. A long sigh escaped both of them as he seated himself to the hilt. Blanketing her, he leaned forward and kissed her nape. "Beautiful. You can relax your arms."

Her fingers released her cheeks, the soft weight folding around the base of his cock, cushioning him. Her arms curled under her head and he slowly pulled back, nearly exiting her completely. "Hard and fast or long and slow, Evelyn? I'll give you the choice."

"Whichever pleases you most," she panted, sounding on the brink of madness.

Jesus Christ, he nearly came. Could there have been a more perfect answer? He slammed back into her and her head shot up. He thrust into her without relenting. He'd had her mouth, he'd had her pussy, and now he was reclaiming her ass. By the end of the week there wouldn't be a single spot on her that didn't wear his mark.

Sweat burned his eyes as his hips snapped forward. She mumbled and moaned curses and prayers of pleasure.

He pounded into her and his climax built so powerfully he felt it in the soft undersides of his feet. He withdrew and yanked on his cock. Hot jets of come shot across her back and up her shoulder.

Collapsing beside her, he cupped the back of her head and dragged her mouth to his, kissing her with everything he had. "You are . . ." he said between kisses. "The sexiest . . . woman . . . I have ever seen in my entire life." She smiled through dazed eyes, her expression completely sated. "Don't ever change," he whispered.

"Only if you promise the same."

AFTER yet another shower, the boxes were delivered. Evelyn was in the bedroom, sorting through her old belongings, when Lucian noticed Dugan looked bothered. He walked him away from the bedroom door and toward the front of the condo.

"What is it?"

Dugan glanced back at the bedroom and lowered his voice. "Fucking paparazzi." Lucian relaxed. That was nothing new. "We've had the cops here twice already. I don't know what's gotten into them. They're like vultures today."

Lucian sighed. He hated the press. There was little to no peace away from his homes, which was why he'd become quite the hermit in his adult years. "Some things never change."

"Do you want me to pull the car around to the service entrance?"

Lucian considered it. "No. Let's see what they want. I'll throw them a comment about whatever they're after and that should satisfy them for a while."

Dugan nodded and took his leave.

When Lucian returned to the bedroom, Evelyn was pulling on the heel of a dainty sandal. Her hair was down and reached almost to her ass. She wore a slim little number, the color of jade, accentuating every fine curve she had. He came up behind her and smoothed his hands over her hips.

She chuckled. "You, settle down. I've already had two showers and a bath. I'm hungry and you need to feed me if you expect me to be up for anything else."

He grinned into her soft hair. "I'm just touching."

She swatted his hands away and turned. "Touching leads to fucking."

"Can you blame me? You look incredible."

She blushed. "Thank you. You look quite handsome yourself. Where are we going?"

"I made reservations at DeLuna."

She grabbed her purse and followed him to the door. He shut out the lights and they settled on the elevator. She turned and caught him looking at her. "Stop looking at me like that. I need food."

He grunted. "Feisty when you're hungry."

They rode in silence to the first floor and Lucian spent the entire time eyeing her legs. As they stepped off, he asked, "How's your knee?"

"Ugly, but I'll live."

"You need to be more careful with how much you drink."

"You need to not make me want to drink."

His arm wrapped around her and guided her through the lobby. He understood he was partly responsible for her actions last night, but that didn't excuse her carelessness. She'd been plastered and with a guy he knew nothing about. Sometimes her invincible attitude made him crazy.

He let his concerns go for the sake of their evening. He didn't want any unnecessary stress. They'd have dinner, talk, laugh, and enjoy themselves. The doorman held the door and she froze as a hundred flashes went off in their faces.

"Mr. Patras, can you tell us what happened with Nicole Nottingham?"

"Lucian, is it true you rescued Ms. Keats from a shelter?"

"Ms. Keats, did you threaten Nicole last night?"

"Where is your mother?"

"Ms. Keats, how old are you? Were you an adult when Mr. Patras seduced you?"

Jesus fucking Christ! He grabbed Evelyn's wrist and dragged her through the crowd of vultures. Dugan held the door to the limo wide as they fled inside.

The door slammed and the flashes of cameras beat against the glass. He was seeing spots. The car lurched, its wheels squealing as it pulled into traffic. He rubbed his eye sockets and faced Evelyn. Fuck. She was white as a sheet.

ten
. . . . .

CHEAPO
Swindling a win or drawing from another's position lost

LUCIAN pulled out his phone. "Dugan, drive to Isadora's. Call her and tell her to have food ready." His fingers flipped through his contacts and dialed when he found the number he was searching for. He reached his arm out to Evelyn. "Come here."

She looked lost and small. Her eyes weren't blinking and her mouth was flat, her lips vacant of color. She slid into the crook of his arm and he squeezed. "It'll be okay." The other line picked up. "DeLaCruz, please. Lucian Patras."

As he waited for his attorney to pick up, he kissed her temple. He needed to reassure her, but first he needed to start the long line of damage control.

"Lucian, what can I do for you?" The lawyer's voice, smooth and cultured, gave him some sense of ease. This would be taken care of, and soon.

"We have a situation. Nottingham found out some private information in Evelyn's background and exploited it to the press. I want her dealt with. I also want to make sure no harm comes to Evelyn's mother. She's vulnerable and doesn't need the goddamn media climbing her walls while she recovers."

"You sure it was Nottingham?"

"I'm almost certain. Question Hughes as well. Anyone who caused this is going to pay."

Sliding his thumb over the screen of his phone, he tossed it aside, turning Evelyn to face him. Her expression was so vacant it worried him. He kissed her and drew her close, hugging her. "Hey, this sort of thing happens. It's all right. I have people straightening it out now."

When she still didn't say anything, he tipped up her face. "Evelyn, you know none of this is your fault. I'm not angry. Not with you anyway."

Her lashes lowered. He was going to strangle Nicole next time he saw her. "Evelyn, talk to me. What's going through your head?"

Her face tightened and she drew in a deep breath. "I'm so sorry."

"Hey! I told you. There's nothing to be sorry for. This isn't your fault. I don't give a shit about what people think. I care about the stress the attention puts you under."

"This is all that bitch's fault!" she snapped with more venom than he was used to from her. "I should have knocked her on her ass when I had the chance." Her eyes shimmered with unshed tears.

"Hey, hey, she's not even worth your aggravation. That's exactly what she wants."

"That's not all she wants. She wants to expose me and humiliate you so you leave me and go to her."

"And do you know why that is? Because she's intimidated by you. You scare her. She can say you're just a girl from the tracks and expose your family's flaws, but that doesn't change the fact that you're still a better person. Sinking this low and playing dirty isn't wise when she, too, holds a position in the public eye. She's a fool for throwing the first stone."

Evelyn shook her head. "Calling her stupid doesn't take away what she did. This won't just get swept under the rug, Lucian. We have enough challenges on our own. All our crap is about to be thrown out on the lawn for everyone to see."

He considered her words. She was right. This wouldn't just get swept away. People would want to know. But he had nothing to hide. He merely wanted to shelter Evelyn. "What is it you are afraid of them finding out? Is it Pearl?"

She gaped at him. "It's *all* of it, Lucian. I'm an embarrassment to you! I was homeless for Christ's sake. I ate out of dumpsters and slept in the dirt. My mother fucked strangers for drugs. I was born addicted to heroin. I was illiterate until I was in my twenties and I can barely read now. You're Lucian fucking Patras. Do you have any idea what this will do to your reputation?"

Rage seethed inside of him. His jaw clicked. Her voice had grown shriller with each proclamation. He gently shook her. "Listen to me. You are *not* worthless. All of those things, they may be true, but look at you now. Who fucking cares about the past? You've overcome more obstacles than almost anyone I know. I refuse—*refuse*—to sit here and listen to you degrade yourself. Do you understand me, Evelyn? You do that, and all those assholes who told you you'd never be anything more, they win. Do you want them to win?"

"No." She was breaking, but he needed her to see herself the way she really was.

"You have pride in spades, Evelyn. Don't let them shake it. You're smart, determined, beautiful, and caring. Anyone who doesn't see that is a fucking asshole. And as far as all those other accusations, I'll come out with a statement and own up to every single one, just give me the word. I don't give a shit about what conclusions they draw. I love you. *You*, Evelyn, all of you."

His words seemed to sink in. She nodded. "Okay."

"Good." He hugged her. He didn't let her go until they reached his sister's. Climbing out of the limo, he reached for her hand.

"Will Isadora be upset we popped in?" Evelyn asked, adjusting her clothing.

"She's used to it." He led her to the door and Sophia, Isadora's maid, greeted them.

"Good evening, sir."

"Sophia." He nodded. "This is Ms. Keats."

"A pleasure," the maid replied. "Isadora's in the kitchen cursing you at this very moment."

"Wonderful," he commented, leading Evelyn to the kitchen. Escorting Evelyn through the grand entrance, he found his sister chopping peppers at her granite island, a scowl marring her otherwise pretty face. "Isa."

"Do I look like one of your employees, Lucian?"

He walked over and kissed her cheek. "Stop. We had a situation and needed to get out of the city. Evelyn was starving and we couldn't go to the restaurant where we had reservations."

Evelyn smacked his arm. "You're blaming me?"

His sister paused from chopping. "What situation?"

"Let's eat first and I'll explain over dinner." He plucked a slice of bell pepper from the butcher block and popped it in his mouth.

She scooped the peppers and dropped them over a salad, which she proceeded to toss. "Evelyn, will you tell me what's going on?"

She sighed. "Lucian got involved with a she-devil—"

"I told you to stay away from Nicole. That girl doesn't do casual dating. She can misinterpret a wave as a marriage proposal." She turned to Evelyn. "He never should have accepted her invitation to the Slavonia affair last week."

"Not helping, Isadora," he grumbled in a warning voice.

His sister arched a brow. "What? You're completely in love with Evelyn. You should have worked your crap out before involving that spoiled little Pomeranian." Turning to Evelyn once more, she added, "I never liked her."

Evelyn's dimple appeared as she allowed herself a conspirator's smile. Wonderful. "Well, I don't like her either. She 'looked into' me—whatever that means—and she got the paparazzi involved. We were nearly trampled leaving Patras."

Isa poured a glass of wine and offered them each one. They sat at the table and she sighed. "Dinner's in the oven. You're lucky I have casseroles on hand. So, what kind of dirt did she find? You're very lucky you come from an ordinary background. The press can be relentless once they sink their teeth in."

Evelyn nearly choked taking a sip of wine. She wiped her mouth and blushed, then looked at him with panic in her eyes. *Here goes.* Lucian took a deep breath. "Evelyn's past isn't exactly ordinary."

Isa stilled. "What do you mean?"

"She actually has quite an extraordinary story, but it's hers to share."

His sister looked at Evelyn. "Will you share it?"

"Don't pressure her, Isa."

"It's okay," Evelyn said quietly. "I'd rather her hear the truth from me than some distorted version of it from the tabloids." She cleared her throat. "I was born in the wintertime, I think twenty-three years ago."

His sister frowned. "You think?"

"I don't know. Until a month ago, I didn't exist."

"What do you mean?"

Evelyn sighed. "My father died before I was born, shot during a drug deal. My mother has been an addict all my life. She gave birth to me in an alley and I never had a home until now."

Isa's face slowly fell. She glanced at Lucian. "Is this a joke?"

"It's not a joke," Lucian said softly.

His sister looked at them both, gauging their sincerity. "How on earth did you two hook up?"

"Evelyn was a maid at Patras. I caught her rummaging through my stuff."

His arm was smacked again. "Lucian! Don't tell her that. I was *not* rummaging."

He laughed and kissed her temple. She pushed him away and rolled her eyes. "Your brother made a rather inappropriate proposition and rather than sue his ass off, I took him up on his offer. I figured it would help my mother in the long run. Which it did, but in no way close to what I imagined."

"You were . . . homeless?" His sister said it like it was a word foreign to her vocabulary.

Evelyn nodded. "Lucian helped me."

He needed to cut in. "She didn't need my help. Don't let her fool you. Evelyn has more determination than anyone I know, including myself. She would've gotten there with or without me, but I'm glad I was the one to help her."

Isadora sat back, her arms crossing, one hand catching her glass of wine. "Wow. Does anyone else know this?"

"Dugan. Shamus. Slade."

"Everyone will know now," Evelyn commented hopelessly.

"Does Toni know?" Isa asked.

"Not unless Jamie told her, but I don't think he would."

Isa nodded. "Me neither. They aren't there yet."

Evelyn sat up straighter. "Jamie's with your sister? Since when?"

He grumbled. "Apparently for some time now. I was the last to know."

"Oh, stop bellyaching," Isa snapped. "It's only been for a couple weeks, and who knows where it's going. Those two fight about the dumbest stuff. They don't get along long enough for anything to be consummated."

"Nobody's consummating anything," he snapped.

"Oh, I bet they're consummating like bunnies right this moment," his sister teased. She knew he couldn't accept that his best friend was sleeping with his little sister. She turned back to Evelyn. "So, how did that little twit find all this out?"

Evelyn shrugged. "I have no idea. I'm more worried about what this could do to Lucian and your family."

Isadora laughed. "Honey, the worst it could do is humble him. The paparazzi can't hurt him with this petty crap. It'll just add to the legend. Besides, that's your past. You've come a long way. I never would've guessed you were homeless when I first met you. You own that!"

He smiled, loving his sister for affirming everything he tried to say on the ride over.

"But it will embarrass him. And he'll lose business." Evelyn was still protesting.

He tried not to, but knew he scowled at her. "I told you to stop that. You are not an embarrassment. I'm proud to have you beside me. I don't give a furry rat's ass what your past is."

"And really, Evelyn," Isa cut in. "If people aren't doing business with the Patras name, who will they do business with? We're everywhere."

Lucian was surprised to hear his older sister make such a pretentious statement. It was true, but of all the Patras relatives, she was the most unimpressed with their wealth. Almost to the point of holding it in disdain because of what it did to their family.

Isadora turned back to him. "So what happens now?"

"Damage control. DeLaCruz will issue a statement when Evelyn's ready. I find some homemade porno or some dirt on Nottingham and nail her to the wall. Our biggest concern is making sure this doesn't affect Pearl."

"Pearl?"

"Evelyn's mother."

"Oh. Where's your mother, sweetie?"

"She's in a rehab. Did that woman really make a sex tape?"

Isa snorted. "Probably. She's a whore. And if she didn't, we can at least start a rumor that she did. That's always fun."

"Isa!" Evelyn gasped and laughed. "We all know it was an affair with her cousin. It's not nice to joke about."

His sister and Evelyn cracked up, carrying on with Nicole Nottingham's scandal, each time adding more fuel to the fire. He sat back and relaxed, glad to see the stress of the evening washing away. His sister was good for Evelyn in that manner. Good for him too.

The scandal would still be there when they returned to the hotel and likely in the papers tomorrow morning, but his greatest worry was protecting Evelyn. He'd grown up in the spotlight, but Evelyn's privacy was something she cherished. He needed to make sure all this mudslinging didn't hurt her.

eleven

MATCH

A competition between two individuals

EVELYN dozed in the crook of Lucian's elbow as the limo cruised into Folsom. Her shoulders tensed and he shifted. "What's wrong?" he asked.

"We're going toward Patras?"

"Yes?"

She sat up. Her hair was slightly mussed and looking particularly adorable. "Lucian, I have to go home."

They'd tiptoed around the reality of their situation all day. He'd been dreading the moment it came up. His jaw locked, but he forced his temper back. "My home is your home," he said with measured patience.

Her eyes closed as she drew in a breath. This should be good. "Lucian, I have an apartment now."

"Evelyn, we lived together before. You moving to yet another place is only a step backward."

His molars locked as she scooted back. He didn't like the stiff set of her shoulders. That's how she looked when preparing to argue. "We *did* go backward. You can't expect us to jump back where we were. Besides, I have work in the morning."

Fuck. He'd forgotten she was working again. He was a selfish man, and her working always seemed to rub him the wrong way. He was worth billions for God's sake. She shouldn't have to work.

"Dugan will swing by so you can get your things and drive you to work in the morning." Then he'd know where she was working.

Her mouth tightened. "No."

"No? Evelyn—"

"Lucian, I said no," she practically snapped.

He frowned, then growled. "Why? Why do you need to go there? What sense does that make?" He sounded like a petulant brat, but didn't care. He wanted her in his bed. She'd said she loved him. They made love several times in the past twenty-four hours. Why was everything suddenly slipping through his fingers once more?

"Because it's where I live now."

"And for how long, Evelyn? Are we supposed to simply date like two teenagers who can't afford more time or better circumstances? It's ridiculous."

"Maybe to you, but to me it's smart. I need to look out for me. I have a plan and nothing's going to get in my way this time, not your demanding needs or sex or even luxury. I need to be practical."

"Which is what? All I keep hearing about is this plan, but you won't tell me a single detail. Why the secrets?"

"Because if I tell you you'll take over and I need to do this for myself."

He couldn't for the life of him figure out what she wanted to buy with thirty-five thousand dollars. "Why can't you confide in me? I only want to help you. If this makes you happy, I'll help you get it."

"You don't understand. Telling you would be like cutting corners. It would shave away the pride I get from finally doing something on my own. I need to be practical."

He changed tactics. "How fucking practical is it to live in a less than pleasant section of the city when you could have everything you need at the hotel?"

"Well, it's a step up from the shelter," she hissed, and he saw he'd hurt her feelings. Her arms crossed over her chest and she turned away from him.

He sighed and pulled her to him so her back was to his chest. Rubbing gently over her stiff arms, he waited for her to unclench. "I know you want your own place. If it's about taking baby steps, fine, we'll go slowly. I'll get you your own room. But the idea of you sleeping all by yourself, miles away, isn't working for me."

She scoffed and tried to pull away, but he tightened his grip. "I'm sorry, Lucian, but it's going to have to work for you, because that's how it's going to be."

"This is ridiculous," he growled under his breath. Then, more to the point, he said, "You're being stubborn."

"Guess where I learned that from?"

They were each silent for a moment, reining in their tempers. Finally, like a whipped, lovesick kid—*pathetic*—he asked, "When will I see you again?" *Jesus, what is she doing to me?*

As much as he could try to play her game, tried to be flexible in a way he wasn't accustomed to, her answer infuriated him. "Tomorrow night I have something to do. I guess Tuesday."

"What do you have to do tomorrow night?" He couldn't think of anything she'd be obligated to do aside from working at her job and she said that was in the morning.

In a small voice she mumbled, "I don't want to say."

His grip over her shoulders tightened. "Why?"

"Because it doesn't have to do with you and I want to keep it that way."

She was shutting him out. A terrible thought suddenly occurred to him. "Is it Hughes?"

She sat up and scowled at him. "I'm not an idiot, Lucian. Give me a little credit." Huffing out an aggravated breath, she mumbled, "It's my plan."

This fucking plan. He didn't want to say it, but the words fell out anyway. "You're with me." He flinched at how small his voice sounded to his own ears. What was this woman doing to him?

"Yes, I am with you because I love you. He never has nor could he ever compare to what I feel for you. But I will say this. I am not about to throw myself into something after going through these past few weeks. I need time. *Need it*, Lucian. It's not something I'm going to negotiate. You either accept that I have these boundaries or we go back to the way things were a few days ago. You choose, but I will not be manipulated. I have a plan and I'm sticking to it. End of story."

"Why did you need the money, Evelyn? Level with me. I know it's not about Pearl. Tell me."

She shook her head. "No. I just . . . needed it."

"Do you owe someone money? Are you in trouble?"

"I told you it wasn't anything like that."

"Then why all the secrecy?"

Her narrow shoulders lifted as she sighed. "Because of all the reasons I already told you. You'll get involved and then it won't be my own."

"What won't be your own?"

"*Me*, Lucian. The plan is to make a better me. I need to be better than what I am and I need to accomplish that on my own, for my own peace of mind."

She was being so vague he felt like an idiot. "I don't understand." Why did she need money to do that?

"Do you remember the first time you ever really succeeded in business? Do you remember what it felt like to do something completely on your own and know that—no matter what—no one could ever take away that sense of pride because you earned it? I need to earn this. For me."

His mind played over possibilities. Curiosity ate at him. "Is it a business venture? Maybe there's someone I could hook you up with to help."

Her palms slapped against her thighs and she huffed. "You see? That's what I'm talking about! No. Just . . . let it go."

For the next several minutes they rode in silence. She seemed to relax, but his mind was running wild over what she could possibly be using the money for. His best guess was something with her stones and crafts, but she'd left most of that stuff behind and he hadn't seen any clues to her plans in her apartment. There weren't a whole lot of places she could hide things.

"If I promise not to bug you about the money, will you come home with me?"

She growled. "Oh. My. God. Will you stop?"

He relented for a split second until his protective nature kicked in. "Your apartment isn't safe."

She jerked out of his grip so fast he missed the chance to pull her back. "Did you see the men the cops arrested? I'm not some fragile flower, Lucian. They grabbed me and I fought them off. My apartment has locks and I have wasp spray in case there's an intruder. I also have my phone back if I need to call the cops. For Christ's sake, I used to sleep with a shoelace tied to all my belongings with one eye open. I'm a hell of a lot safer now than I was in the past. Drop it."

He'd drop it. For now. But the argument was far from over. He'd put a man at her door just to be safe. She may have gotten out of that alley mostly unscathed, but that was only because the couple in the insurance office heard her scream. The thought of what could have happened was too grim for him to consider.

Conceding his point, he grudgingly instructed Dugan to drive her to her apartment. Maybe he would stay the night with her. He inwardly groaned when he considered her tiny bed, wondering if she bought such a small mattress on purpose.

The limo pulled to the curb in front of her apartment and she waited as if expecting something. Dugan opened the door and she hesitated again. "I'm walking you in," he said, making it clear he would not relent.

She nodded and appeared relieved. At times he simply couldn't figure her out. She was . . . independently fragile.

As they climbed out Lucian turned to Dugan. "I'll be back in a bit. Wait."

He followed Evelyn through the alley, scowling at the poor lighting and vacant sidewalks. This wasn't necessarily a residential area, which made it more dangerous at night. She withdrew her keys and he took them from her hand. Undoing the lock, he flipped on her lights and escorted her up the stairs.

When she reached the top she tossed her bag on the bed and faced him with a *now what* expression.

This whole setup is ludicrous.

He sighed. "Come here." She stepped toward him, which in such a little space wasn't difficult, and he cupped her cheeks. "What am I going to do with you?"

"Kiss me?" She offered a cheeky smile, and he sensed she was on the verge of gloating that she'd gotten her way.

Rather than continue to argue, he did as she asked and kissed her. Her petite body curved into his as she went up on her toes. His fingers slid beneath her hair, pulling her close as his lips slanted over hers, deepening the kiss.

Within a minute they were each breathing hard. His fingers pulled at the straps of her dress as his mouth coasted over her jaw and down her slender neck. She made soft kitten sounds that went right to his dick. He tugged at her dress, trying to get her out of it, when she shifted away. He tightened his grip on her hip.

"Don't," he warned. He'd surrendered enough control for one evening.

She relaxed and he lifted her dress over her head, tossing it to the floor. His mouth traced the slope of her breast as he cupped her. His thumbs slipped behind the lace and tugged the cups out of the way, revealing two perfectly pink nipples. He bent and pulled one into his mouth, sucking forcefully.

Her spine bowed as her knees went weak. He caught her in his grip and released the wet nipple with a pop. Glancing over his shoulder, he growled in frustration. There was nowhere to go. "Your apartment is too small."

"My apartment is just fine," she argued in a breathy voice as she dropped to the floor and tugged him with her.

His knees landed on the firm discount carpeting as he followed her down. She stretched out beneath him, extending her arms over her head invitingly. *Little temptress.*

His mouth found hers as his knees fit between her thighs and nudged her legs apart. He felt like a goddamn kid trying to cop a feel before his girlfriend's dad came home. Yet, he was so desperate to feel her, so reluctant to let her go, he'd settle for this improbable situation that was his temporary reality.

A tingle of excitement raced up his spine as a sense of urgency settled over him. He had to go soon and he didn't want to. He needed to make this time with her count.

His fingers plucked at her panties while his mouth kissed down her belly. She'd lost weight and he didn't like that. He'd make a point to see that she was eating enough and not falling into old habits.

She writhed impatiently as he teased her sex through her panties. God, she was fucking beautiful. If he lost her again, he'd never survive it.

"Lucian . . ."

The corner of his mouth cocked up in a half grin. He loved when she said his name all needy like that. Fingers teased over her folds, keeping the silk of her panties as a barrier. She wanted to date like children. He'd show her what that was like. Moisture dampened the fabric as he baited her.

He hid his grin when her frustration became evident. She grabbed for his shirt, but he restrained her, pressing her hands into the carpet and weighing her down with his body. The denim ridge of his arousal rubbed over her sex and she moaned. He could tell she wanted more. So did he, in more ways than one.

His erection moved over her until he found the perfect rhythm and glide. Her moans hitched as he nudged her clit just right. She'd get off, but it wouldn't compare to coming with actual penetration.

His body flexed over hers and suddenly her cries increased and her head tipped back, spreading her hair over the gray carpet. His cock was ready to explode, but he fought back the urge to take her. Slowly, he found her mouth and kissed her.

When he eased back and carefully stood, she frowned up at him. "What are you doing?"

His lips twitched, but he kept them firm. "I have to get home. You could come." He smirked, letting her know the pun was intended.

She didn't seem to see the humor. "But . . . we didn't . . ."

He nodded and pursed his lips. "I know. And now we have to wait until Tuesday to see each other again."

She scowled. "Is that what this is about?"

"Of course not. This is merely one of the disadvantages to our living situation."

"You don't have to go," she said pointedly.

"Do you want me to spend the night? I'd hate to impose on your newfound independence."

Her silver eyes narrowed and she sat up. She snatched her dress off the ground and covered her breasts. "You're right. You better go." Her words would've been alarming had he not detected the competitive challenge in her tone and the quiver of a smirk at her kiss-swollen lips.

He blew her a kiss and stepped away. "Sweet dreams, Evelyn. I'll call you in the morning." He edged his way toward the stairs. She was glaring at him. "And Evelyn."

"What?" *Oh, she was salty . . .*

"No coming. Rules are rules." Their circumstances might

have changed, but his rules remained the same. Her orgasms were his to give. And he would know if she broke a rule. She was terrible at hiding such things from him. He only wished she was just as terrible at keeping the other secrets, like where the hell she worked and what she needed all that money for.

She threw her shoe at him. "Good night, Lucian!"

He chuckled as he bounded down the steps. He locked the door behind him and his cheerful whistle echoed through the alley as he headed for the limo.

SITTING so still it was a wonder his lungs remembered to breathe, Lucian stared out the large window behind his desk, the sleeping city a quiet storm without wind. Lavender shades of silver and blue painted the world a still life that always entranced him with its peaceful qualities. He'd been sitting there since sometime after three, silently letting his mind wonder over the mundane and lulling his body in a way the quiet of his room never could.

While his gaze watched the silhouetted landscape reflect the colors of dawn, his mind dwelled on other forms of beauty. His mind should have been focused on business, but long, tapered legs and a cinched little waist filled his mind until his imagination lent her weight to his empty palms. She was back in his life. His Evelyn was finally back.

There was something incredibly tenuous about their reunion, something Lucian feared could shatter at any moment. Always so strident and sure in his endeavors, he was man enough to admit, for the first time in his life, he'd found something he coveted so much it terrified him. She was so much more than a possession. It was what she *gave* him. A soft security that never took tangible form, yet he felt it everywhere in her presence. What they had he cherished beyond measure, and it was changing him in ways he didn't understand.

Never one to backpedal or hesitate, she somehow gave him second thoughts. Thoughts of not rushing in, not jarring this delicate slice of peace she presented, thoughts of . . . compromising his desires for someone else's. He didn't understand how she made him feel so different, but she did and he was determined not to do anything hasty that could damage their love.

She loved him. That in itself was a gift beyond measure. He never—

His thoughts cut off at the soft vibration rattling over a sheaf of papers on his desk. He checked the antique pocket watch resting on his ledger and frowned. It was just past four a.m.

His hand scooped up his phone and a smile curved his mouth when he read the screen. His thumb slid across the screen and he brought the cell to his ear. "Did I conjure you with my thoughts?"

"Did I wake you?"

He settled back into his leather high-backed chair and turned to face the dawn once more, awaiting the brilliant show of light that never failed to rejuvenate him each day. "You know me better than that."

"Are you at your desk?" Her voice was sleep-roughened silk tantalizing his ears.

"Yes. Just thinking. Couldn't you sleep?"

She drew in a breath and let it out slowly. The soft sound of sheets rustling had him imagining her warm and cozy in her little bed. He loved that she'd call him at odd hours of the night. It was the next best thing to having her there. "I had a bad dream."

He glanced down at his legs as his brow drew tight. "You okay? You don't usually have nightmares. Want to talk about it?"

"We don't have to. I just . . . wanted to hear your voice."

"Want me to come over?"

She chuckled, her voice a raspy invitation he'd be more than happy to follow. "No. It's still dark out and I have work in a few hours."

He growled. "You and your work."

"Don't start."

"What was your dream about?"

The playfulness siphoned out of the space between. "Pearl. Me. It was more of a flashback but everything was different. I was older, but still young."

"What happened?"

Pearl was a burden he feared Evelyn would always feel responsible for. He couldn't blame her. Pearl was her mother. If having his mother back meant having her in the form of Pearl, he didn't know if he'd be able to turn down that sort of devil's deal. In that respect, he understood Evelyn's loyalty and need to save her any way she could.

"It was cold. It was so cold I woke up shivering. When I was little, my mom used to send me with money to buy her hits while she worked off the pay with some man that used to come around. I got lost."

"Did this really happen?"

"Yeah. I was only about eight, but in my dream I was older. I was so cold and scared. It was dark before I found my way back. There was a cop patrolling in a squad car and I almost asked him for help. Something made me hesitate though, made me think twice about talking to him. In that moment I knew he would help me, but if I asked for his assistance I also knew I would likely never see Pearl again. He'd take me and put me in a home she'd never follow me to."

Lucian grew uncomfortable in his own skin trying to imagine an eight-year-old Evelyn attempting to rationalize her way through a situation like that. This was partially where her fear of law officers stemmed from. He could remind her she was now an adult, but didn't see the point. Certain ingrained tendencies would be impossible to rewrite.

This was who she was. He'd take care of her so long as she let him.

"It was a stupid dream," she muttered.

"Everyone has fears, Evelyn. Some are rational and some aren't, but that doesn't make them any less frightening."

"This from the man who fears nothing."

"I have fears."

The echo of her gentle breathing filled the air. She whispered, "What are you afraid of, Lucian?"

Losing you. Ruining what we have again. Not being strong enough for you. "I'm afraid of what I can't control."

"Ah, but I thought you controlled the world."

"Smartass." He smirked in the dark. "I'm afraid of not being able to protect you. I want to always be there when you need me, when you're lost. I always want to help you find your way home."

He sensed her satisfaction with his answer and imagined her blushing in the dark as she attempted to deny her lips a grin. "Surely that will never happen with Dugan forever on my tail."

"Exactly." A few beats passed. "But that's not what I mean."

"What *do* you mean?" Her question was asked in a husky voice reserved for mornings and talks with cheeks pressed upon soft pillows.

"I mean I never want you to think you can't come to me, with anything, no matter what. I'd stop the world for you."

His mind filled with strobes of red and blue lights, flares lined along the shoulder of the road leading to his estate, and Monique's covered body on a gurney. But in his nightmares it wasn't Monique. It was Evelyn. Those were his bad dreams.

His request slipped past his lips, a hushed plea. "Come over."

"I can't."

"Why? I want to hold you and make you feel safe."

"You do. Just knowing that I can hear your voice is reassuring."

He sighed. "I feel like I just got you back and I can't reach you. It's making me crazy. Will you spend the night with me tonight?"

"I . . . I can't."

He frowned. "Why?"

"I have plans."

"Tell me your plans."

"Lucian," she said in warning.

"What are your plans?"

"I have a . . . meeting."

His brow kinked. "With?"

She sighed. "Don't do this. I told you there are things I need to take care of on my own."

"I'm not doing anything but asking you a question. You're the one being secretive for no reason. Be open with me. I don't understand—"

"Things are different now. I can't go back to the way things were. Not after . . ."

Right. Not after he royally fucked up. This was the shit that was making him crazy. He'd somehow placed himself in a certain kind of purgatory. How long would it take to get her to be open with him again?

He hated tiptoeing around, worrying he'd push too hard and somehow push her away. He needed to reel his temper in and trust her to open up when she was ready.

"When you're ready, will you tell me?"

"Lucian."

"Give me something, Evelyn. I'm trying to be patient here. At least give me credit for not insisting on full disclosure. I know it has to do with the money. I don't care. I want you to have it to do with as you please. I won't talk you out of whatever you're buying. Just . . . eventually . . . tell me."

There was a long moment of silence. "When I'm ready."

"Good enough."

twelve
.....

POSTMORTEM
An analysis of a game after it's over

"THIS is fucking bullshit." Lucian gripped his cell as he climbed into the elevator, maneuvering around the others filling the cramped space. A woman in a fitted suit smiled up at him. He ignored her and focused on what Shamus was saying.

"I can't figure it out either. This deal was in the bag. I don't understand what's causing them to procrastinate."

"Have you sent over the paperwork from Quincy?" The elevator paused as several riders exited. Lucian waited as the doors closed and it continued on its journey to the top.

"They got it yesterday. My understanding was that they were only waiting for the final draft. The board was all in agreement this was the best move. It doesn't make sense for them to pull back now. What's changed?" Shamus was clearly as frustrated as he was.

Lucian stepped off the elevator and walked at a clipped pace past Seth's desk. "Get me Quincy on the phone, and I want a copy of your notes from yesterday's conference call."

"Yes, sir," his assistant said, snapping into action.

Lucian shut the door and went to his desk, removing his jacket and tossing it over the chair. Today was going to be a pain in the ass. He could already sense it. His mind refocused on what Jamie was saying.

". . . The statistics are all in their favor. There are no other bids on the table now that Chrysler's withdrawn their offer. Could there be someone we overlooked?"

Lucian dropped into his chair. "Who? Bishop's not going to be interested. He's already on my shit list and knows going into this will only end in his company's bloodshed."

"No, I don't think it's Slade. Something isn't adding up though. For Labex to suddenly hesitate when they have everything they asked for on a silver platter . . . there has to be an offer on the table we aren't seeing."

"Are you saying there's a mole?" Lucian frowned and did a quick inventory of his staff. This deal was huge. Over eighteen months poured into schmoozing and negotiating in order to get Labex, a green energy provider, to put their accounts in the care of Patras. They'd be handling everything from the site modifications to warehousing their equipment to managing their accounts. "Who else could compete with our offer?"

"Aside from Slade? I don't know."

Flicking on his computer, he grimaced.

"Mr. Patras, I have Mr. Quincy on line one," Seth piped in over the intercom.

"Shamus, I do *not* want to lose this deal. It's a good partnership, and the mere idea of someone fucking with us is irritating. I want to find out who it is and I want them dealt with. Have Margarite do a search on all vacant warehouses in Folsom. I'll get Seth to arrange a dinner tonight, someplace nice. We'll do some ass-kissing and dig around. Whoever's playing with us is about to get a severe lesson in business acumen."

"You got it. Let me know how you make out with Quincy."

"Will do." He ended his call and snatched up his desk phone. "Quincy."

The long series of phone calls that followed did nothing but frustrate everyone involved. Lucian had a staff of over one hundred involved in this deal, and they were all running around like headless chickens trying to find where their plan had fallen short.

By two, he was ready to flip his desk and demand a meeting with Jacobi, the CEO of Labex Green, but knew that would only show his cards and not bode well for anyone. Dinner was arranged for that evening, and he and Jamie would do everything in their power to control the damage.

Finally, the call he'd been waiting for came. He snatched up his cell. "Dugan?"

"Got it," his chauffeur said.

Lucian smiled with great satisfaction. She had to know it was only a matter of time. "I'll be down in five."

He grabbed his jacket and left his office. "I'll be back in an hour. Text me with any news regarding Labex. Everything else can wait."

Seth nodded and continued to frantically compile the schematics Lucian requested for that evening. As he strode into the elevator, he slipped his master key into the grid, in no mood to deal with other passengers. The ride to the ground was made in luxurious silence. When the dial showed he'd reached the lobby without interruption, he withdrew his key and stepped onto the marble tiles.

Pressing through the revolving glass doors, he found Dugan waiting. His chauffeur opened the back door of the limo and Lucian glided onto the smooth leather seat. "Where are we heading?"

Dugan smiled. "Clemons Market, sir."

The door shut with a soft snick and they were soon on their way. He hadn't heard from Evelyn since early that morning. He wondered how committed she was to her "plans" that evening. It would benefit him if she accompanied him to their dinner meeting, making it seem more casual than manipulative, a sort of preemptive celebration of the partnership to come. Much of his success in business was the result of assuming victory from the first handshake.

He groaned as he considered that Shamus, if he intended to bring a date, would likely ask his sister Toni. Lucian could not wait for that ridiculous coupling to run its course and be over.

Toni was the furthest thing from reserved. She spoke too much and most of the time came off spoiled and unworldly. It wasn't her fault. She was young. He couldn't fault her for her lack of experience. It was her need to fill every bit of silence with mindless chatter that could hinder his plans for the evening. Evelyn was much better at knowing when words were necessary and when less was more in terms of finessing professionals.

He drew out his phone and texted Jamie.

Are you going stag tonight?

It only took a moment for his friend to reply.

Your sister would cut off my nuts if I took someone else. So, yes. It's better she thinks this is strictly business and no one's feelings will be hurt.

Lucian drew in a breath of relief. The one thing he couldn't deny was that his friend truly knew his sister . . . and her faults.

I may bring Evelyn. She already has plans, but I'd like her to go.

The time to reply exceeded the norm and Lucian knew his friend was laughing at his expense.

So she's speaking to you again? And plans? Without you? I didn't know that was allowed.

Lucian carefully typed each letter of his reply.

Fuck. You.

Shamus's reply was quick.

Lol. Would if I could. I'm very good. Ask your sister.

He wasn't touching that one. Wedging his phone in his breast pocket, he shifted as Dugan pulled into the market's parking lot.

The market was small, sort of a commercialized mom-and-pop feel to it.

When the limo eased into the fire lane, Lucian let himself out. Dugan met him on the curb. "I'll be out in a bit. You can park."

"Yes, sir."

The automatic doors opened to the scent of paper products and the hum of canned elevator music. He could not recall the last time he stepped foot in a grocery store. Perhaps he never had. A metal snake of shopping carts was parked along the front of the store. His feet carried him where his mind wasn't aware he should go.

Crossing the threshold of another set of automatic doors, he entered the main store. Shoppers glided by, perusing their lists and selecting goods, as mothers herded children in the desired direction. A stack of baskets sat just beside a display of cut flowers. He collected a basket and selected a bouquet of lavender tulips, dropping them into the green wire bin.

Sales marked the first aisle, and he wasn't quite sure where Evelyn would be. He drifted down the aisles, taking in the unique feeling of normalcy that came with being in such an ordinary place. Lucian stilled in the cookie aisle when his gaze recognized a type of pinwheel biscuit and his mind drifted to a memory he had all but forgotten.

His fingers curled around the simple white box with blue lettering as he returned to his childhood kitchen. He suddenly conjured his mother's perfume and felt the warmth of her presence as she handed him a pinwheel. Her smile was delicate and loving.

Strange that a cookie could present such a nostalgic recollection he didn't realize he had. The box of cookies landed in the basket, cozied neatly beside the tulips so as not to crush the blooms.

As he wandered on he looked for signs of Evelyn, but didn't find her. At the line of registers he saw the young man who had taken her to the benefit that weekend. No longer in a tuxedo, he appeared less of a threat and more of a boy. Odd that Lucian would see him as so young when he saw Evelyn as *his* perfect match.

He frowned as he considered the difference in their age. The media had been focusing on the question of her maturity like predators over a downed squirrel. Had he taken advantage of an innocent? True, she was a virgin when he met her, but she was also an adult.

The media would, of course, have no knowledge of such things, but it certainly didn't escape their notice that Evelyn was in her early twenties while he was in his midthirties. Should he feel some level of guilt for wanting her in such carnal ways?

"Lucian?"

All thoughts cut off as he heard her voice. He turned and found her stepping from a nondescript back door by the bakery section. "There you are." He smiled and approached her.

Lips parted in surprise, she stared at him. "What are you doing here?"

"I wanted to see you."

"I'm working." She scowled. "How did you find out where I worked?"

He rolled his eyes. "Come on, Evelyn . . ."

She made a sound of disgust. "And you wonder why I want my privacy on other issues."

He frowned. The sense that he was unwelcome irritated him, another barrier that hadn't existed before. "Well, I needed to pick up a few things."

The disbelieving look she gave him made him smirk. She never bought into his bullshit, but at least she didn't challenge him. She peeked into his basket. "Cookies and flowers?"

He stepped closer and whispered, "Shh, you aren't supposed to see the flowers." He had the strongest desire to kiss her, but knew she wouldn't want such attention in her place of work.

Rather, he slowly traced a finger down the delicate curve of her jaw.

A door opened, the one she had just exited, and she suddenly stiffened and stepped away.

"Evelyn, you will also need to—" The man who emerged cut off his request when he spotted Lucian standing there.

He was young, but appeared older in the way he carried himself. His face was groomed with a dated mustache and his eyes were hidden behind thick lenses, making his age difficult to discern. Lucian's gaze snapped to his badge and noted that he was the manager.

"I didn't realize you were assisting a customer. Please return to my office when you're finished."

There was nothing inappropriate in such a request from a manager to an employee, yet the set of Evelyn's shoulders and the blank expression on her face told him something was off. The manager disappeared through the doors again and Evelyn drew in a shaky breath.

Before he could ask what the guy's deal was, she turned and hissed, "You have to go."

He frowned. "Do you not like your manager?"

"He's my boss. I don't have an opinion about him, but he'll certainly have an opinion about me holding social calls at work."

No, there was something definitely off with her, and it definitely had to do with the manager. "If you think I'm leaving because some little twerp with his picture in a dollar-store frame wants it so, you're mistaken."

She huffed and shifted on her feet. "Lucian, I have work to do—"

"Is that his office?"

She turned and glanced at the door. "What? Yes."

"Why were you in his office?"

"He had to go over some things with me."

"Like?"

"My receipts. Lucian, I really need to get back to work."

That was his little worker bee, always so concerned about keeping her job. She really was an admirable employee. However, she was also vulnerable because of her age and the drive to maintain her job.

"Does he ever request the other employees join him in his office?"

Her fingers pinched the bridge of her nose. They were manicured, but no longer polished the way they had been when she'd stayed at the hotel and had the use of the salon. He'd make her an appointment.

"I don't know. I need to go see what he wants *now*. I'll call you when I'm done working." She turned and disappeared through the back door without giving him a chance to reply. Dismissed indeed. He had a moment of *what the hell is happening to me* as he stared at the nondescript door, dumbfounded.

He decided he'd wait. *Let's see how long Mr. Manager decides to monopolize his employee.*

Lucian drifted to a display of rotisserie chickens that smelled surprisingly good. He waited for several moments. And when the door finally opened, Evelyn marched out and made a beeline to the registers on the opposite end of the store. There was no mistaking the irritation that set her shoulders. His eyes narrowed as he placed his basket beside a tank of lobsters and adjusted his cuffs.

Walking over to the door he pressed through and found a cramped little storage room with a ratty filing cabinet and the manager behind a beaten-down desk. The man's mouth dropped open beneath his mustache.

"May I help you?" Clearly shoppers were not permitted in this area.

Lucian took his time taking in the small space. The guy had pictures of himself on the wall proclaiming he'd been employee of the month more times than any other. Instinct told him something was off and his gut said it was more than simple territorial paranoia for Evelyn.

He brushed his thumb over the edge of a dusty crate. "Mr. Gerhard?" It was easy to get his name off one of the many plaques on the wall.

"Yes?" The manager's confusion about his presence showed signs of unease. It was a simple enough task. Lucian was older, better dressed, taller, and unarguably more powerful. The manager was outmatched and knew it, even if he didn't know the game.

"I'm Lucian Patras." There, that did it. Game on.

His brows shot over the dated frames of his glasses and he stood, instinctively offering the well-known name the respect it deserved. He held out his hand. "Mr. Patras, well, what a surprise. I hadn't recognized you. Is there something I can do for you?"

Lucian kept his expression blank, but narrowed his eyes in a manner he knew could intimidate even the most powerful man. Gerhard got the unspoken message and withdrew his proffered hand.

"I imagine you've worked quite hard to obtain your position here at Clemons, Mr. Gerhard. Did I mention I know the Clemons family? They and the Patras family go back a long way. I'd hate to have to contact them beyond the courteous Christmas card."

"I'm not sure I understand," the manager said, his posture protective.

Lucian eyed the watermark on the ceiling with disinterest. "Evelyn Keats is someone very special to me. I understand that she's new here and may require direction as she becomes oriented with her new duties, but do *not* make the mistake of taking advantage of her work ethic." He met the other man's gaze, which was magnified by his thick glasses. "I look out for her and will continue to do so. I want to make sure she's being treated the same as the other employees. She may appear to be just another clerk here, but I assure you, she has an arsenal of attorneys at her disposal if, say, an employer were to overstep the bounds of proper management. Are we clear?"

The man swallowed noticeably. "Perfectly."

"Very well. I'll continue with my errand." He turned and exited the office, sweeping up his basket and making his way to the registers.

LUCIAN approached the hostess's station and was recognized immediately. "Mr. Patras, lovely to see you again. Your party is waiting right this way."

He followed the young blonde to his usual table and recognized Jamie. Confusion knit his brows when he noted his friend's scowl. The hostess left them as he settled across from Shamus. "What's wrong?"

"You'll see," Jamie grumped and Lucian turned just as his sister slid into the seat beside Jamie.

His gaze widened for a split second. "Antoinette, I wasn't expecting you."

His sister made a great show of hauteur as she adjusted her napkin and raised her chin. "Lucian, always a pleasure. No Evelyn this evening?"

"She had plans."

"Ah, so she was *invited* and simply couldn't make it. How interesting." She shot Jamie a derisive glance and his friend rolled his eyes. This was not what they needed this evening.

Lucian tilted his head to Shamus, his eyes asking *What the fuck?* Jamie simply shook his head and said, "George and Preston should be here any minute. Let's order some drinks and get on with this. They're both gin-and-tonic men."

They waved over the waitress and ordered a round of the house's best gin, and drinks for the rest of them. Toni ordered a daiquiri or some other juvenile display that was inappropriate. This entire parade was making his jaw tense. What the hell was Shamus thinking, entertaining a relationship with his little sister? This was exactly why the idea was ludicrous. Not only were Shamus's tastes too dark for Lucian to contemplate when involving his sister, their lifestyle required a certain level of class that came not with money, but with time and experience the likes of which Toni had yet to learn.

Lucian sighed and sipped his brandy. They discussed the strategy for schmoozing their associates, and Toni remained quiet. However, her disinterested expression, the one that said they were boring her and she'd rather be shopping, grated on Lucian.

Toni fidgeted like a child in church. He wanted to slap his friend for not taking control of the situation and demanding she stay home. This wasn't fucking *Romper Room*. It was a multimillion-dollar merger that they were rumored to lose.

Shamus hissed a warning to Toni, who replied with an indignant glare when their guests arrived. Luckily, by the time George and Preston were escorted to their table, his sister's expression had morphed into serene acquiescence.

The five of them shook hands and Antoinette was introduced. Ice was broken and orders were placed with no regard to price, and every bit of emphasis placed on the unspoken acknowledgement that the Labex men were their honored guests. No comment was made to hint there was any chance the deal could go to another bidder. Confidence and the assumption of success were all part of the game of persuasion.

Throughout the meal, Shamus and Lucian made a good play to lull their associates into a state of comfort that seduced them into believing this was right, this was where they wanted to be and it was in their best interests to stay.

Toni remained silent through most of the meal and Lucian was relieved. She preened prettily and batted her eyes at the other men. Ironically, this play of flattery outwardly annoyed Jamie, although he quickly hid it.

When the meal was concluded, Lucian felt confident they'd done a good job of firming up their ties. However, he was smart enough to know their work was far from done. Like sex, there would have to be some morning-after cuddling and follow-up throughout the day to prove to their counterparts they were valued and memorable even after the interaction.

Seth would send a well-thought-out thank-you that would trickle down to their subordinates. Quincy would readdress the plans, putting them in a new, shiny light that left the impression of Patras covering every base and ensuring every T was crossed and ass kissed. It was all routine bullshit that came with the game.

Preston even commented on Antoinette's bracelet, saying his wife would like something similar. Lucian would have Seth send him the gift in the morning.

He took care of the bill and they exited the restaurant together. Once the valet retrieved George's Mercedes, they shook hands and said good-bye.

Toni let out a breath of air as if the entire evening had been unbearable. "Next time I get mad you don't include me in business dinners, remind me how boring they are. Jeez, I should have stayed home and watched the Kardashians."

Dugan arrived with the limo, and the three of them slid onto the seats. As the car jostled, making fast progress to Shamus's condo, Toni said, "Where's Evelyn?"

That same question had been in the forefront of his mind all evening. It was tiring, this new position he was taking with her. He didn't enjoy constantly reining in his temper and his need for control, but he was trying to redevelop the trust he'd lost, and that meant trusting her.

"She had an appointment." There was no need to make excuses to his little sister about things that were clearly none of her business.

"An appointment where?"

Jamie cut in before he needed to. "Antoinette, mind your own business."

Toni crossed her arms and huffed. "Whatever."

Ignoring the irritating lovebirds, Lucian gazed out the window until they reached Jamie's. When Dugan opened the door he was surprised to see Toni exit the car as well. Nothing like having the visual of his sister being debauched driven home. He gritted his teeth and pretended everything was as it should be, wanting nothing more than to end this evening and find Evelyn.

He wanted to text her, but texting was an issue for them. He couldn't call until he was alone.

"I'll see you in the a.m.," Shamus said, leaning into the open door.

Lucian nodded and Dugan shut the door, closing him in welcome, dim silence. When his chauffeur returned to the wheel, Lucian instructed, "Knights Boulevard."

The limo stealthily merged into traffic and headed in that direction as he pulled out his phone and dialed Evelyn. Her cell rang three times before dumping into her generic voice mail. He frowned and dialed again, only to end at the same result.

Shifting on the soft leather seat, he loosened his tie. This secretiveness was not palatable. As a matter of fact, it was infuriating him more and more with each passing minute. He removed his pocket watch and flipped the antique cover open. Her plans *must* have concluded by now.

As the limo approached her apartment he immediately caught the illuminated, unadorned window. She needed curtains. Lucian let himself out and faced Dugan on the crippled patch of sidewalk.

"Should I wait, sir?"

As he prepared to answer, something caught his attention. A man, roughly in his late twenties and carrying a leather messenger bag, exited the alley. Both he and Dugan stared as the man stepped from the mouth of the alley, the alley that led only to Evelyn's door.

A fire snapped to life in his gut as all sorts of insinuating scenarios ran rampant through his mind in a blink of an eye.

"Oh, excuse me," the man suddenly said, stepping around them, clearly not expecting others to be on the walkway at this late hour. Their presence was likely as surprising as, say, a man exiting Evelyn's home at such an hour.

They trained their gazes on his progress to the little Toyota parked across the street and, as if reading his mind, Dugan said, "Follow him?"

Lucian's teeth were clenched so tight it was a wonder his tongue found the space to form words. "Yes."

His man nodded and returned to the idling limo, making no secret of trailing the Toyota. As he stood on the pavement alone, Lucian collected his wits. A thousand assumptions played devil's advocate in his mind. When his temper was somewhat under control and he'd waited long enough to discount any perceived coincidental meetings, he entered the alley and knocked on Evelyn's door. Seeing the newly installed security lights brought him comfort, but he made a mental note to have the landlord agree to security cameras. He'd handle the cost and installation as well as the monitoring feed.

The peephole darkened, followed by the opening of the door. Evelyn appeared surprised to see him. "Lucian."

"Evelyn. May I come in?" She was wearing a sweatshirt and jeans and her silver eyes appeared weary. What the hell was going on?

She nodded and led the way up the narrow stairs. He was reminded again just how miniscule her chateau was as he ducked under the low-slung ceiling at the top of the steps.

"I wasn't expecting you." A small table had been added to her meager collection of furniture. Two chairs. She made quick work of collecting a stack of papers from the surface of the table and stashing them in a cabinet. The paperwork confused him and he regretted not having the gall to demand she let him see what it was. The bed was neatly made.

"How was your evening?" he asked.

"Fine."

They faced off in silence, Evelyn's gaze landing everywhere but on his own. This was bullshit. He had the urge to demand she 'fess up to whatever secrets she was keeping. What had the loan been for? Who was that man?

His senses prickled as a subtle trace of the man's cologne drifted to him. His molars locked in place. The pregnant silence weighed heavily, so much so he wondered if her dollhouse of an apartment could withstand the laden presence. She fidgeted with the string attached to the worn hood of her sweatshirt.

His chest expanded with hot breath until he fought the urge to scream.

"Did your dinner go well?"

Small talk? Really? "Fine."

She glanced at him and quickly averted her eyes. These were the signs of submission that went right to his cock. So strong and capable yet so delicate when handled rightly thus. He stepped closer and her fingers fluttered to her side. "You've been pushing me away."

Shock registered in her stare. Her lips parted. They were so soft and pink without the need for gloss. "I . . . I was with you last night."

"That's not what I mean and you know it. Today, at the market, your clandestine plans, which you refuse to enlighten me on—how many walls are we going to erect before we are two completely separate beings?"

"It's only because . . ."

He stepped closer, interrupting her excuse. She made a sound of confusion low in her throat and looked at his shoes. Her feet were bare. Did that other man see her toes?

Her breath was shaky and the slight space between them became charged with his need to possess what he saw as his. He sensed her need building as well, the ever-present chemistry between them that was impossible to deny. His fingers reached for her chin and tipped up her face until she met his gaze.

There was no apology in those stern eyes that played between crystal blue and tinsel gray. She was stubborn as a foothill, and he needed to see her bend in some manner to satisfy his wilted confidence. No other woman had ever made him second-guess his actions the way she did.

He reached between them and gripped the sagging front of her cotton shirt, bunching it within his fist and yanking her across the last gap that separated them. No space.

"I spent nearly a month without you. I won't do it again, Evelyn. Not in word or action will I tolerate such distance between us. I want you, in my life, in my days, in my bed, and I don't intend to acquiesce all that much. You want your independence? That's fine . . . for now. But there's only so much a man can take."

The soft pink curve of her lower lip trembled as she processed his words. His thumb dragged over the fleshy pillow just before his mouth lowered and took what he needed. Breath audibly drew in as she permitted his kiss. So much had changed, somehow tilting the axis of everything he was accustomed to and tipping the balls until they all came crashing down into her court. Enough.

She could hold on to her individuality and massage her pride, because he recognized that was something she needed, but he wouldn't give in to her every whim like some docile, dickless yesman. The need to assert some force of authority raked at him until he was nearly clawing at his flesh.

Ripping his mouth from hers, he breathed heavily as he stared

into those eyes, darker now, dilated with lust. "I want you naked."
She hesitated and before she could answer, he mumbled, "And tomorrow we're getting you curtains. Anyone could see in here if
they took the time to look."

The side of her mouth kicked up. "Not feeling your inner ex-
hibitionist?"

"There's a difference between fucking you on my terms at the
risk of being witnessed and displaying your beauty where I'm not
welcome to stay and keeping onlookers at bay. You're by yourself
here. You need curtains."

All humor faded from her teasing expression, as she understood the danger of accidentally tempting a stranger with a window
show. She went to her bed and removed the coverlet. After a
minute the window was blocked with the makeshift drape.

Turning, she said, "The value of submission is in the will to
surrender, Lucian." She removed her sweatshirt, a glint of challenge in her eye. No bra. Goddamn it. There had been another
man here.

Drawing in a calming breath, he said, "And your pants."

Her fingers toyed with the snap and zipper. "I think we both
understand you own my body and my heart." Denim met the
floor and she wedged the jeans and panties off her feet with her
heels. "You can take what I freely offer and accept that this is the
most I can give at this time, or you can go."

His cock pulsed at the image of her so beautifully naked before him. He wasn't going anywhere. His smart little woman had
discovered the power of surrender. He wasn't surprised. "I'm not
leaving."

"It's a two-way street. I refuse to give what you won't. Compromise. Accept that this is who I am and respect my need for
independence, and I will tolerate your need for control in other
things."

Well, wasn't she just full of conditions tonight? So stubborn.

So headstrong. So much like him. She made him proud and her stick-to-itiveness made her surrender all the more sweet. "You're pushing me."

She smiled. "And you're pushing me. I'd say we're well matched. If we can agree on the rules, we can play."

She knew him so well, understood the logic he approached life with every day, and could bend him the way no one else could. She was treading on a fine line, playing with his need for control and demanding her own.

She bowed her head, her body a display of everything he wanted to possess, yet he also wanted her secrets. He wanted her mind. She made it . . . interesting. "Show me."

When she gazed up at him, there was acceptance dappled in anticipation showing beneath her full lashes. "What do you want, Lucian?" Her soft whisper glided over his flesh like a caress. In the face of such driven self-reliance, her submission disarmed him. His need was so potent, beyond wanting, beyond simple lust. His desire to possess her was tattooed upon his bones.

She'd stripped his dominant side raw with those simple words. She laid him out, taking all distractions off the table and surrendering herself purely for him. In this manner, they always complemented each other.

So many women believed submissiveness was a weakness, mindless subservience enacted to inflate a male's ego. They were wrong. It was strength. Her strength was the trigger. The strength to let go, the strength to trust in another's ability to know how much they might take, the strength to believe they're utterly beautiful without façades and conceit. Raw.

It was a woman bared in naked truth, secure enough to give over to her man, surrender every bit of struggle to be a queen at the top of the king's mountain. There was such a high esteem in his mind for the strength it took to surrender here, yet remain empowered in the outside world. He felt nothing but utter admiration for any woman capable of collapsing such self-preservation after just one command.

"You're beautiful," he whispered as she folded her hands behind her back. If he asked her to undo his pants and suck him off she would, but he wanted to pleasure her. This was the one area she truly let go and trusted him. He lamented that he could so freely have her body's submission and somehow she still held back part of her heart. He'd work on it.

Lucian walked slowly to the bed and removed his suit jacket. After loosening his tie the rest of the way, he slid it out from under his collar and draped them over the corner of the low mattress. Easing down until his back rested on her pillows propped against the wall, he said, "Come here."

She obligingly stepped in front of him. When he arrived, he wanted to claw off her clothes and mark her like an animal. Now, however, something in her calmness had tempered his need. He wanted only to be with her, please her, make her cry out in a way no other man could.

He sat up and drew her to his lap. Her knees straddled his thighs and settled onto him. His fingers curled over her hips, thumbs teasing at the undersides of her breasts. He loved her.

Quiet moments like this seemed to scream the truth. He loved her and would do anything to protect her, to witness those limited moments of unburdened happiness that showed so seldom in her knowing eyes. She had had such an arduous life before him. He hated that his poor choices had somehow added to her strife.

Apologies rang in his head. He'd been such a careless bastard. How could he have allowed things to get so out of hand with Parker? Never again, he vowed. Never would he let her slip through his hands again.

With intrepid gentleness, he sifted his fingers through her hair and drew her into his kiss. Petite hands squeezed at his shoulders as her knees tightened at his sides. He kissed her slowly, but intensely, laving at her neck, lips, and shoulders until he slowly eased her to her back and pressed his weight into her.

The world fell away, hidden beneath the sensual fog that swallowed them. The tiny bed squeaked beneath their weight as he removed his clothing and pressed into her hot core. Her legs held him and her hands glided over his skin as he slowly filled her, his only intention to love her.

Fingers pressed into flesh. Mouths pulled upon tender parts, and their bodies tangled with unanimity. Gone were his worries of business and poachers. She was his and she owned him equally, mind, body, and soul.

After bringing her to climax several times, he allowed himself to let go and bathed her womb in his release. Her sigh of contentment matched his own. So rarely had he enjoyed plain old missionary vanilla sex, yet with Evelyn, there was no line of ordinary. It was all potent and all-encompassing.

His body collapsed beside hers as they caught their breath. Her dainty fingers found his and entwined themselves there.

"I'm staying the night," he announced and she let out a resigned sigh, clearly sensing there would be no getting rid of him.

After several moments of simply basking in the aftermath of their lovemaking, she rose and went to use the bathroom. His eyes returned to that cabinet hiding her paperwork. What would a woman who can't read beyond a primary student's ability need with so much paperwork? He worried she could be signing something under misconceptions, and his need to protect her rode him hard.

He ignored his urge to investigate, feeling a bite of some unnamable esteem for his exercise in restraint. Trust. For some reason he knew it would mean so much more if she came to him with her secrets than if he demanded she share them. It was a difficult exercise in control and trust, but one he could savor the burn of—like a marathon he didn't want to run, but found the value in walking.

Reaching in his pocket, he found his cell phone for distraction. His thumb swiped over the screen and found Dugan's text.

2424 Glacier Place.

Residential area near Susquehanna Ave.

Appears to live alone.

Lucian quickly replied and tucked his phone away.

Run a check on the address and find out who he is. I'll see you in the morning.

On cue, the reflection of the limo's headlights danced over the blanket covering the window as Dugan pulled away.

THERE had never been a time Lucian was grateful for Evelyn's literary shortcomings until now. As he glared down at the rag sprawled upon his desk, he felt like hurling his coffee across his office. In bold ink, his and Evelyn's names sat like graffiti on every page. Never before had he resented the paparazzi so much.

Their assumptions of her background were preposterous and at the same time a little too close to the truth. What frightened him most were the references to Pearl. There was definitely a Judas among them, and when he discovered who it was, they would be handled accordingly. He wondered if the person tampering with his personal life and leading the media to his door through crumbs of truth was the same person trying to swindle him out of his deal with Labex Green.

He'd run through all possibilities and unwittingly kept returning to the same suspect. There was only one person who knew of Evelyn's past in such detail and only one person brazen enough to face off with Lucian in business. He'd hoped it wouldn't come to this, wishing the fallout of their partnership and threats to disembowel the other man's company would be enough to keep him in check, but it was time to admit he'd been wrong.

Tossing the paper in the trash, he punched his finger into the intercom. "Seth, get Slade Bishop on the line."

"Yes, sir." A moment later the intercom buzzed. "Mr. Patras, I have Mr. Bishop on line one."

He picked up the receiver and Slade was the first to speak. "Lucian, this is unexpected."

"Is this really how you want to handle this?" Lucian asked, cutting right to the heart of matters.

"I don't understand."

"Cut the crap, Slade. I know you're feeding the press. I have to say, I'm impressed with the size of your balls, but it will only make it easier when I cut them off."

The other man cleared his throat. "Lucian, I read most of the articles, but I'm afraid you're off on this one. I haven't spoken to the media about you *or* her."

Lucian calculated for a minute. He sounded sincere, but after the stunt his ex-partner pulled with Parker Hughes, Lucian would never trust Slade again. "And what of Labex? You have nothing to do with that either?"

"I heard about your deal with Green. I assumed it would be wrapped up by now. Am I wrong?"

Lucian frowned. If not Slade, then who? His brain compiled a list of variables. Who would want to see Evelyn dragged out in front of the masses? Nicole was suspect, but surely she'd know this would do nothing to win her favor. She also would have no interest in a company like Labex, which meant if she were the one slandering Evelyn, it was completely unrelated to the business deal hanging by a thread.

Who had the manpower and resources to poach Labex? One name came to mind, but that was so farfetched he dismissed it immediately. No way had Hughes climbed that fast. Impossible. Didn't matter who his father was. Such rapid success was unheard of.

He realized Slade was talking. ". . . Really like to sit down with you."

As Lucian pieced together what he'd missed in the conversation, he almost laughed. "While I'm glad to hear you decided against interfering further in my personal life, I have to say I'm not flattered to the point of social calls. We passed that the minute you assisted someone I consider my enemy, lending yourself the same title."

There was a pause. "Luche, I'm not your enemy. I never was."

"We continue to disagree. I'll let you get back to your work."

As he leaned in to hang up the phone, Slade's voice rung out and gave him pause. "I saw what you did to Hughes."

Lucian drew the phone back to his ear.

Slade rushed on, assuming he regained his attention. "I saw what you did and I assume you got her back."

"I merely collected what's mine."

"I want you to know, for what it's worth, my role in the situation was . . . regrettable. I apologize."

As much as Slade's apology should count for something, it didn't. His actions spoke louder than words, driving home the point that the man could not be trusted. "We're through here." He ended the call, thereby ending his association with Slade Bishop. One Judas down. How many more to find?

THE email came through at three fifteen.

Jason Dodd
Mother: Rebecca Esperanto-Dodd
Father: John Dodd
D.O.B. September 2, 1981
Current Address: 2424 Glacier Place, West Folsom, PA
Previous Address: 192 Lenox Ave, Cincinnati, OH

Prior places of occupancy: Room 206, Parks Dormitory, Triton University

No criminal record.

No unpaid tickets.

Moved to Folsom last June. Currently employed with the 34th school district as a behavioral specialist. Vehicle registered in his mother's name. Home leased through a man by the name of Gregory Lutz. Aside from residing within a couple miles of Ms. Keats, I cannot find any cause for association. How much deeper do you want me to dig?

-D.

Lucian replied via text.

Follow him this evening and see where he goes.

Dugan's reply was immediate.

Already done. He left work at two forty. I've been behind the Toyota since.

Lucian frowned. If Dugan was texting, he was parked.

Where are you now?

The reply took longer than usual and before he read the message, his sour stomach already guessed the answer.

Knights Boulevard. She just got home from work.

"Son of a bitch!" Lucian cursed and stood. His hand shook as he texted Dugan back.

Stay there.

He went to his call log and dialed Evelyn's number. The call went to voice mail. Shoving his arms into his jacket, he dialed again. Voice mail. "Evelyn, it's Lucian. Call me as soon as you get this."

He marched past Seth's desk and jabbed his thumb into the elevator call button. "I'm going out."

As he rode the elevator to the ground floor, he seethed with each call to her voice mail. Why wasn't she answering? Why was that guy back at her place?

He exited the elevator in the cool shade of the underground garage. His keys filled his fingers as his thumb tightened on the fob. The chant of his Mercedes unlocking in the distance was followed by the purr of the automatic start. Folding his body, he slid into the buttery bucket seat and threw the car into gear.

Cutting his turns tight, he belted onto the main road and dug in the console for his shades. It was in the low seventies, so he pressed the control on the dash and the soft top lowered, tucking itself neatly into the compartment above the trunk.

The car sped out of the congested traffic and took back roads toward West Folsom. Sure enough, when he spotted the limo on the corner of Knights Boulevard, the Toyota was only a few spots ahead, parked.

He peeled into the spot, shoving forward the gearshift just before his bumper went into the Toyota's ass. Jumping out of the car, he pocketed his keys and ignored Dugan's raised, bushy brow. Enough was enough.

Yes, she was allowed to have friends. Yes, she was allowed to have a life aside from him, no matter how much it made him crazy. Yes, she was entitled to her privacy. But this guy was in her fucking home, her home that consisted of a small cramped space dominated by a kiddie table and a *bed*. A line had been crossed. She wanted equality . . . He knew she'd never accept the situation if the shoe was on the other foot.

evelyn

thirteen

. . . . .

THE STRESSES OF ENTERTAINING

EVELYN was nervous, which was a major distraction. "Can I get you something to drink? I have milk, water, iced tea, or apple juice." She sounded like a moron. Certain words didn't fit in her vocabulary, too awkward in comparison to the life she had and the way she attempted to live now.

Jason settled into the chair at the table and sifted through his bag. "Iced tea would be nice."

With shaky hands she twisted the ice trays and plopped two cubes in a glass. Jason knew a little about her background, but she didn't want to volunteer too much. The last thing she wanted was to appear illiterate *and* uncultured. He'd already discovered how little she could read, so she gave him her favorite glass in hopes that it compensated for some level of sophistication. Smart people usually had nicer things.

Settling into the chair next to him, she slid him the beverage. He sipped it and thanked her. "How did you make out yesterday?"

Her hands slid the paperwork in front of him and she waited anxiously. Most of the stuff she had to go through at work whenever there was a lull in shoppers. Luckily, Nick was there to answer any questions and Mr. Gerhard was surprisingly quiet today, not getting on her back over every little thing like he usually did.

"Um, it was okay. I think I understood most of it. I didn't get very far. Oh, before I forget . . ." She reached into her pocket and removed the envelope of cash.

Jason took it and smiled. "Thanks. It's a lot easier for me to deal in cash with things like this. I appreciate it."

"Thank *you*. I'm glad I found you. That's only two thousand. When you need more let me know."

His eyes bulged. "Uh, Evelyn, most people pay me by the hour."

She knew that, but she was so afraid he'd get frustrated and quit on her that she wanted to pay him in advance. "Well, consider your first twenty hours handled. We already used four of them anyway."

He shook his head. "Then let's get to work."

There was a sharp knock on the door and she frowned. "I'm sorry, let me see who that is. The people in the office downstairs said my electric bill would be in soon. That's probably them dropping it off."

"Not a problem. I'll look over this stuff."

She stood and quickly rushed down the steps and unlatched the door. She came up short when she peeped through the hole and found Lucian glaring on the other side. Her hand fumbled to unlock the door. "Lucian? Wh-what are you doing here?"

"Is this a bad time?" His dark eyes narrowed on her, full of suspicion. Chances were, if she peeked around the corner she'd find Dugan—who was really starting to piss her off. Didn't these people have work? "As a matter of fact—"

"Invite me in."

She stiffened. Okay, clearly he knew she had company. Not wanting to make a scene, she eased the door closed and stepped into the alley. "Why are you doing this?" she hissed.

"Who is he?"

Once again, he'd bulldozed into her personal business with no regard to her privacy. "Damn it, Lucian, you can't keep doing this! Not every part of my life is open to you, and you need to accept that."

"Bullshit. This is your private home. I get that you need this right now, but how would you feel if some woman was visiting me at the penthouse? Call it whatever you like, Evelyn, but fair is fair. You can't hold a double standard."

She gripped her temples, very aware of her pricey minutes with Jason ticking by. "Can we talk about this later?"

"I'm not leaving until you give me some answers."

Just once, she wanted something to be her own. Bristling with frustration, she snapped, "Do I ask you for every detail of your private dealings? No. Why can't you draw a line? I draw plenty for you!"

He stepped close enough that she could see the fine silk threading of each button on his jacket. "Let's not beat around the bush, Evelyn. You want me to admit I'm jealous? Fine, I will. There's a man I don't know in your apartment right now, only a few feet away from your bed. Don't pretend this is all right. Not when you crashed a benefit just this week because the thought of another woman accompanying me was enough to get you to interfere."

He was right. Jealousy was a new emotion that wasn't sitting too well with her. No matter how much she wanted to throw his accusation in his face, declaring she'd never stoop so low, she couldn't. The idea of him dancing with someone else, dating someone else, was simply disgusting to her. She had no idea she owned such possessive tendencies, but when it came to Lucian Patras, he was hers.

Part of her liked that he was equally possessive, but at times like this it was a huge inconvenience. Before she could come up with another excuse, his fingers brushed against her cheek and he whispered, "There's nothing you could confide in me that would make me stop loving you, Evelyn. I trust you. It isn't that I think you're having an affair, it's that there's a man in your apartment and you won't tell me why. I don't know *him*. How am I supposed to trust a stranger in such a setting with the woman I love when I know nothing of his purpose? Confide in me. Let me in. I promise not to interfere, just . . . let me know what's going on."

All of her life she'd studied people from afar, assuming she could predict the most logical reaction to an event, but there was something completely illogical about knowing someone up close and personal the way she knew Lucian. It frightened her, how often he'd surprised her. There was nothing predictable about him.

Their relationship had taken a severe detour over the last month, but this was not the man she left behind. This was someone sensible and understanding, someone who needed her reassurance as much as she needed his. He didn't compute with the arrogant man she'd met last year. And while she liked it, she didn't know if she could trust this open side of him.

Shades of truth played in his eyes, begging her to trust in him. That look telling her all he wanted was to know she was safe. It was as if he needed the assurance as much as breath.

Last night he arrived in a mood she was sure would lead to a fight. Something in the tone of his voice had transformed the energy into something sexual. But he'd blown her away with his gentle possession of her body. He was still Lucian, but there was something more there, something that fascinated her and made her want to lean into that illusion of security. *Was* it an illusion?

Taking a huge chance, she let out a long breath and pushed open the door. "Come on."

Opening the door, she led him inside. Slowly marching up the stairs, he followed. He wasn't the creeping giant she once feared. He was her friend. She'd been so afraid of exposing her flaws to his perfection, but with every step she acknowledged just how ungrounded her worries had been. When she reached the top step, Jason turned.

The man's face showed surprise that they were not alone. "Hello," he greeted politely. Jason was easy to talk to and she liked that about him. That was why she hired him.

Lucian stood, a tower of authority to her left. "Good afternoon."

"Lucian Patras, this is Jason Dodd. He's helping me get my GED."

The expression on Lucian's face was one of utter surprise. Whatever he'd expected her to say, it wasn't that. Jason stood and extended his hand.

"Wow, I've heard of you. How do you do?"

It was uncharacteristic, how taken off guard Lucian was. His shock registered in every motion, from the slow progress of his handshake to the way he glanced back at her and blinked. Strangely, there was a hint of regret in the now-soft set of his eyes. Perhaps the reminder of how uneducated she truly was had become too much for him to bear.

"Now you know," she muttered.

Her eyes went to the primary worksheets and handwriting lessons scattered about. Lucian slowly approached the table and picked up a sheet. It was a simple vocabulary page that had taken her several minutes to work through.

Lucian cleared his throat. "Jason, would you mind giving us a minute?"

Her tutor glanced at her then back to Lucian. "Uh, yeah, you know, I think I left a book in my car." He found his way down the stairs, and the door quietly shut behind him.

Lucian's thumb and forefinger rubbed over the thick paper with a childlike illustration on the top beneath the directions. "You're getting your diploma?"

Her lips pursed. "Eventually. I heard it takes fifteen hours a week. I'm a little behind, but I know basic math and once I get a handle on reading, I think I can do it."

"I have no doubt," he agreed in a voice laden with emotion. Was it shame? Pride? She couldn't guess what was going through his head.

"You probably get why I didn't want anyone to know."

His gaze snapped to hers and his eyes narrowed. "Let's get one thing straight, Evelyn. The only thing I feel in regards to your initiative to educate yourself is esteem. There's no question in my mind you'll achieve your goal."

She hadn't realized how afraid of his reaction she was until the tension rushed from her shoulders as a near sob of relief shook her frame. "Thank you."

His fingers traced her jaw and tipped her face up. "Hey, you're one of the strongest women I know. Not everything is measured in reading, writing, and arithmetic. You *will* do this. I have no doubt."

His confidence left her breathless. Yes, he was her friend.

"Can I ask something of you?"

She blinked, not understanding the sheen of tears suddenly blurring her vision. "Yes."

"I know your first instinct will be to say no, but think about it. Don't give me your answer for a few days, until you've truly considered my request."

Emotion was pushed aside for practicality. Who knew what he was about to ask? "Okay."

"The money, the thirty-five thousand, it's for your education. Let me pay for it, Evelyn. Let me give you that one thing, not because you asked, but because I want to be the one person who gave you something you truly wanted and truly deserve."

She took a deep breath. "I'll think about it."

He nodded, apparently content with her consideration. "Good enough." Placing a kiss on her cheek he asked, "What time is your lesson over?"

"Ten."

"Will you stay with me tonight?"

At that moment she was so attracted to him—not because he offered her a free and clear education, but because he accepted her as she was and still desired her all the same—there was no way she could turn down such an offer. "Yes."

"I'll have Dugan pick you up at ten fifteen."

"Okay."

He smiled. "You know, sometimes I don't always do the right thing. I'm sorry my curiosity got the better of me. A part of me wishes I would've waited until you were ready to confide in me, but then a selfish part of me is glad that I know what's going on and that I don't need to beat up this Jason fellow."

She chuckled, knowing he was kidding. "Are you really okay with this? I know it's weird. I'm just trying to be a normal person—"

"Hey, I am beyond okay. I'm so damn proud of you it's . . . I don't know what. I never felt like this before. Sure, it would've been nice if your tutor was a woman so I didn't have to worry about him peeking down your shirt, but I'm beyond happy that this is what you're investing in. You. It's about time somebody did."

Something soft and gushy and entirely girlie bloomed inside of her. Without thinking, she propelled herself at him, wrapping her arms around his broad shoulders and squeezing with all her might. They were always so controlled around each other until that jolting moment when the sexual tension became too much. This was different. This was unprecedented. This was the first time in her life she felt no shame for being exactly who she was, because in his eyes, no matter what, she was beautiful.

EVELYN awoke after a long bout of lovemaking and crept through the dark condo to find Lucian exactly where she knew he would be. His expression softened the minute he noticed her, his arm lifting invitingly.

She climbed onto his lap and rested her head on his bare

shoulder as those strong arms closed around her. Breathing in his familiar scent, she realized, like the scent of burning leaves or the scent of the cots at the shelter, his rich musk now held a very special nostalgic place in her heart.

He always smelled so fresh and good. Her mother, when she was clean, had a stronger scent that wasn't unpleasant, just . . . different. Pearl often smelled of cold weather, briny and sort of metallic, like winter. Parker smelled like most boys. Evelyn wondered what she smelled like.

Pressing her nose into Lucian's throat, she inhaled deeply. *Lovely.*

His hand coasted over her tangled hair. "I miss you being here all the time."

She missed him too. It was a difficult predicament. Part of her demanded this physical space between them, but another part longed for the convenience of always having him near. Her independence was something she longed for. She'd always had it, but this time it was different. It was on her terms, not based on uncontrollable circumstance. She wanted to hold on to that hard-earned freedom with both hands.

She wasn't sure when she'd be satisfied, but expected one day she'd be comfortable enough to let it all go and surrender to the currents of life. The tides had changed. She no longer had the sense of drowning.

Her exhaustion was welcome. It was one that followed a hard day's work and too much thinking over written words and elementary math equations. It was a good sort of tired, nothing like the unending hunger that came with her previous nomadic existence. Yet it was all so new, and that was why she had trouble trusting its perpetuity.

"I know. I miss it too."

"Will you ever come back to me?"

She loved these moments tucked away in the shadows of the

night. It was their confessional, where eyes needn't meet and secrets could be told. "Yes. When I'm ready."

Warm lips pressed into her temple. "How often will you see Jason?"

"As often as he can manage. I have years and years of missing out to make up for. I want to learn as fast as my brain can manage."

"Don't burn yourself out."

"I don't understand that concept."

"I know you don't. You're like the little engine that could. Quitting's a foreign term to you."

"It's grueling," she admitted.

"What is? Never letting yourself give up?"

"Yes. There were times I thought about not moving. About just giving over to the frigid lock on my bones and the hollow feeling in my belly. There were days it was simply impossible to move my fingers, all my energy going into shivering uncontrollably, where my hunger became an emotion I couldn't contain. But I always forced myself to find food and something to keep that fire burning."

"I can't fathom that sort of existence. It's so far from the privilege I've known. It's a wonder we found each other."

Yes. It was. "Do you know . . . out of all those freezing winters and hungry nights, the emptiness I felt when we were apart put those aches to shame."

He stilled, even the breath in his chest coming to a halt. "I'll never regret anything as much as those days apart. I was a fool and I'm so sorry I did that to both of us."

Her lashes lowered and she found comfort again in his scent. It was the affirmation that she needed, telling her he was truly there. So many nights she'd tried to conjure his scent, searching for it in items he'd left behind, but it didn't exist. "I don't think I'd go if you asked me to leave again."

"There are lots of things I wish to ask you again. Leaving's not one of them."

He was referring to marriage. No matter how much their time apart taught her how she needed him in her life, marriage was still something she wasn't ready for. Oddly, they fit each other. While some might assume debutantes of high society would be better suited for a man of Lucian's stature, they were wrong. Something inside of her—some very stingy part—knew he was made for her and she was made for him. But the time to confirm such feelings was not now.

She wondered if she'd ever reach a point that she could agree to such commitment without a thread of uncertainty. When she'd met Lucian, she'd assumed intimate relationships were as black and white as anything else. She couldn't have been more wrong.

Love was like piloting a jet through a mountain range, blind. It was freeing and exhilarating, but at the same time, at any second the person risking their life piloting that plane could crash and burn, shattering into nothing but dust—all for one glorious ride.

When the sun came up they ordered breakfast. Her body was tired from many hours of lovemaking and not enough hours of sleep. She savored every bite of her delicious scrambled eggs. Raphael, the chef at the hotel, must have known it was for her. He slipped in a small triangle of French toast generously dusted with powdered sugar beneath a dollop of homemade cream. A strawberry, carved into a starburst, perched at its side.

She ate until her belly could hold no more, and then it was time to leave. "Will I see you tonight?" Lucian asked as he made a production of kissing her good-bye.

"Jason's coming at three, but tomorrow I have off."

He growled and nibbled her lip, his fingers slipping beneath the waist of her wool pants. "I feel myself coming down with something. Perhaps I better tell Seth to reschedule my appointments."

"You do feel warm. Hot even."

His mouth trailed down her throat as he cupped her ass. The flesh of her nipples tightened and she moaned softly, wishing she could stay. His lips found hers. It was a kiss filled with dark promises. She groaned as her sex twitched, asking for more. "I can't be late. I don't feel like getting called into the office for a lecture."

He drew back. "Did you have to go to the office yesterday?"

"No, but I wasn't late."

"Don't let that manager of yours take advantage. I want to know if he treats you any differently than the other employees."

She rolled her eyes. Even little old Clemons was not out of the Patras jurisdiction, apparently. He smacked her ass.

"Don't give me that look. I'm serious."

"Okay," she said with little conviction.

His phone rang and he glanced at the screen before answering. "She's on her way down now." He hung up and kissed her one last time. "Your chariot awaits."

EVELYN pushed aside her worksheet when customers began loading groceries on her belt. "Hi, how are you today?"

The older woman strategically grouped her refrigerated items and boxed nonperishables and mumbled some form of reply. The rhythmic beep, beep, beep of the scanner filled the silence as items tallied on her register. She efficiently bagged the objects and when the order was complete, Evelyn instructed the woman to slide her card. Not everyone was having a bright and cheery day here at Clemons Market.

The next few customers were a little more pleasant. In between orders, Evelyn returned to her studies. Today she was working on combination vowels like in the words *boat, coat,* and *oat.* It wasn't rocket science, but she was immensely proud of herself.

Jason was a patient teacher. Being the only qualified instructor she ever sat down with, she noticed an impressive difference in how her mind was beginning to process the squiggly lines, putting sounds to letters, and grouping sounds to form words. He encouraged her when quitting was tempting and he never let her get overly frustrated.

Much of the process of learning to read was frustrating. Directions were difficult. Luckily, Nick knew her secret and he was always a register away if she had any questions.

Mr. Gerhart had been MIA for the last few days. That made sneaking in her studies between customers a bit easier. Anyone who saw what she was working on would clearly know she wasn't as educated as she should be. She'd gotten in the habit of putting her dictionary over the juvenile illustrations of tugboats, puppies, and sand pails. By next week she'd be on the second grade workbook and she hoped the pictures would be a bit less infantile. Getting rid of the baby format was just another motivator in her long journey.

A young woman stepped into her aisle and began unloading items. Evelyn pushed her paper aside and scanned the tub of coffee. "Hi, how are you today?"

The girl had auburn hair and an easy smile. She looked about twenty-five. "I'm good. How are you?"

"Good, thanks. Do you have any coupons?"

"No."

Evelyn continued to scan and bag the order while the woman waited. The customer glanced at the register area as she played with her cell phone. "Do you have a child?" she asked, motioning to the phonics sheet.

Heat tickled the back of Evelyn's neck. Hiding her discomfort, she turned and bagged three boxes of cereal. "Um . . ." Should she lie? It was only a customer. "Yes."

"How old?"

How old was a first grader? "Six."

"Boy or girl?"

What was this woman, writing a book? "Girl."

"That's nice. What's her name?"

Sometimes Evelyn preferred the grumpy, quiet customers. "Pearl." She said the first name that popped in her head.

The girl's manicured brow rose as if Pearl was an inappropriate name for a little girl. Evelyn lifted the filled bags onto the metal apron of the checkout. The girl pushed her cart forward and loaded the sacks of food. She returned to the card device and continued to play on her phone as she processed the rest of the order.

There was a quiet snick and crunch sound that caught Evelyn's attention. She didn't recognize the sound. When she heard it again she turned and blinked at the tiny white flash of light. *Snick-crunch, snick-crunch, snick-crunch.*

The girl appeared to be dialing something, maybe playing a game or texting—Evelyn stilled. "Are you taking my picture?" Indignation tightened her brow.

The customer had the good grace to blush and lower her phone. She quickly slid her card. "It says wait for the cashier."

Evelyn's jaw dropped as she stared at the girl and her phone. She repeated herself. "Did you take my picture?"

The customer's mouth opened to form a reply, but said nothing. Her lips curved in something of a satisfied smile and she suddenly said, "You know, I don't need any of this stuff after all."

Dodging the cart full of groceries she tucked her phone away and turned to flee the store. *What the hell?*

"Hey!" Evelyn called. She abandoned her register and caught up to the girl at the automatic doors just before the chain of shopping carts. Her fingers curled around the girl's sleeve. "Why did you take my picture? What about your groceries?"

She smirked and Evelyn's blood ran cold. "Thanks for the interview." She tugged away and bolted into the parking lot.

Fucking paparazzi!

Evelyn's knees tightened as she thought to chase after her.

"Evelyn." She stilled at the sharp tone in Mr. Gerhard's voice. Gritting her teeth, she turned to her waxy-faced boss. "What's going on?" he asked.

Speechless, she fumbled for an explanation. That woman had stolen pictures of her and—oh God, what had she told her?

"My office. Now." Her manager turned and stalked to the back of the store.

Anger boiled up inside her chest. She marched back to her register and flicked off her light.

"What the hell was that?" Nick asked as he sent a customer on their way.

Hands trembling with outrage, she snapped, "That woman took pictures of me and left all her crap here!"

"Pictures? For what?"

She grabbed the stack of tabloids she'd collected over the week. Inky words mocked her and surrounded pictures of Lucian and his limo. Slamming them on the belt of Nick's register, she gritted her teeth. "She was a reporter."

He glanced down at the newspapers and cursed.

"Evelyn, please come to the back." The intercom interrupted the cheery music filling the store and her stomach seemed to bottom out. Now she needed to deal with *this*.

She pressed the Process button on her register. The woman had slid a card, and Evelyn wanted a name. Steering the cart out of the way, she trudged back to Mr. Gerhard's office like she was visiting the gallows.

Her heart clattered in her chest as her knuckles grazed the door.

"Come in."

Her steps grew heavy as she pressed into the office. The floor, where she forced her gaze, was dusty. A crumpled receipt sat in the shadows beneath his wooden desk. She waited for him to speak. The words *you're fired* rang like a taunt in her head.

"Mind telling me what just happened?"

She shrugged.

"First I see you leave your register. Then I see you accost a customer. This is unacceptable." When she said nothing, he said, "Shut the door and have a seat."

Keeping her breathing steady, she pressed the door the remainder of the way closed and slowly paced to the chair across from his desk. Dropping into the seat, she kept her gaze down.

"You're going to have to explain your actions."

Her eyes closed and she sighed. "That customer was taking my picture, and then she said she didn't need her groceries and left."

"And you thought the right thing to do was chase after her and grab her? We could have a lawsuit."

She glared at him. "She was taking photos of me!"

"That's no excuse for your actions." He sighed and leaned back in his chair, his fingers tapping his manicured mustache. He appraised her for some time then announced, "I'm changing your shift. I think you'd be better suited for evenings."

Her breath froze like tiny vines of ice in her lungs. If she worked nights, she wouldn't be able to continue her lessons. "I can't do nights."

"You're still in the preliminary stage of employment. You need to be flexible if you intend to become a permanent employee."

She didn't want the evening shift. That meant walking home after dark. Less time with Lucian. No more working with Nick. And worst of all, no time to get tutored. All forms of pride took a backseat as she blinked back tears. "Please, Mr. Gerhard. My schedule works for me the way it is. I don't want it to change."

"I think you'd be better under Monica's supervision."

"Monica?"

"The evening store manager."

Her mind ticked over solutions rapidly as she tried to figure out a reasonable argument. Maybe she should go back to her housekeeping job at Patras. Maybe she could talk to someone above Mr. Gerhard. She hadn't even earned her first paycheck yet, and she had the sinking suspicion there wouldn't be another.

She stood. "I'm sorry you feel that way. My schedule doesn't allow for me to work a night shift. I'm afraid if you insist on changing it I'll have to put in my resignation."

His brows shot up from behind his coke-bottle glasses. "Now, I didn't say you had to leave."

Maybe this was for the best. Lucian offered to pay for her tutoring and the more she considered his offer the more grateful she became. Over the past week things had changed. She was seeing more and more reasons to trust that he wasn't going to abandon her. A very romantic part of her believed, wholeheartedly, he'd always be there. She could figure something out. She was a survivor.

As she thought of possible solutions, she realized her manager was still talking. ". . . Now, I'm sure we could come to some agreement. What do you say we discuss this more over lunch? It is completely *your* choice however."

As she caught his suggestion, a frown pinched her face. That slimy feeling returned, the one she usually got in Mr. Gerhard's office. Why was she back here more than anyone else? His smile was patronizing beneath the mop of his mustache, and his eyes were hooded and magnified behind those thick lenses.

Deep down, she knew he was crossing a line, and she knew if Lucian found out he'd kill her manager. More complications she didn't want to deal with.

The scent of peppermint and coffee was suddenly suffocating. Her gaze slipped over the washed-out grease stain on the breast pocket of his pink Clemons shirt just beneath the narcissistic name tag proclaiming he was something better than the rest of them.

"I'm trying to be your friend here, Evelyn."

Her gaze flashed to his and something inside of her snapped. "No, you're not. You're trying to manipulate me. You've asked me to lunch over and over again and I've continually made it clear that I'm not interested. Have you ever asked Nick or Gary or Todd to lunch? No. And I imagine it has a lot more to do with their lack of breasts than their job performance."

She was really doing this. Her fingers went to her name tag and snatched it off her shirt. "That woman violated my privacy. Rather than sympathize with your employee, you used the opportunity to further your creepy advances. I'm. Not. Interested. I quit."

She tossed the name tag on his desk and exited the office. When she reached her register, she was trembling. Her fingers clumsily collected her papers and books and shoved them into her bag.

"Hey, you all right?"

"Do me a favor," she said as she slung her bag over her shoulder. "Make sure they get my address to mail me my check. I quit."

"What? Why?"

"Because that waxy motherfucker asks me out nearly every day, and he just tried to change my shift. He's always leering at me and brushing up against me and I can't take it anymore."

"You need to tell someone if he's harassing you."

"I'll be sure to *write* a letter to management," she snarled, needing to take a jab at herself in that moment for some unknown reason. "I am so sick and tired of being treated like a piece of flesh. Goddamn it! What does a girl have to do, not to be some sort of object in this world? People are writing about my personal business! Taking pictures of me at work! I just want to blend in! That's all I've ever wanted! To blend the fuck in."

Nick was suddenly at her side, ushering her away from the registers and into a quiet corner behind a juice display. "Hey, hey. Calm down."

Her breath quaked and to her horror, drops of tears fell from her cheeks, blooming into dark, rosy puddles on her pink shirt. She only wanted a normal job with a normal boss and a normal life. Why could nothing ever be normal?

She'd gone from the gutters to an ivory tower to what she finally hoped was average, and now, because of her stubborn temper, she had nothing.

The heel of her palm scrubbed away her stupid tears and she shrugged off Nick's touch. It was only meant to comfort, but at the moment she didn't want the weight on her skin.

"Gerhard's a jerk. I see the way he watches you. Seriously, Ev, you can complain to management."

More attention she didn't want.

Pulling herself together, she shifted and sniffled in a deep breath. "No. This isn't where I want to be anyway. No offense. I just . . . I'll figure it out."

"But I like you working here," he admitted. "We have fun."

They did have fun. It was nothing tangible, but Nick made her laugh and helped speed along the hours. Something inside her told her this might be the end of their . . . friendship. The word settled in her head like a battleship trying to parallel park in a shoebox. He was her friend.

He didn't want anything from her. Theirs was a mutual respect for silly jokes and meaningless chatter. She never had that before. With Parker, there had always been an underlying sense of struggle, a weight that siphoned away all those free opportunities to simply *be*.

Her relationship with Pearl was work. When had it become so much work to have a mother? Perhaps it had always been that way. No, there was a time when Evelyn was merely a child expected to sit and have her hair braided by her mother's fingers and go to bed in her mother's arms. Those days seemed lost, worlds away.

Then there was Lucian. He made her laugh. He made her

smile. He made her do a lot of other things that were fun. Every other face from her existence paled in comparison to his. Her emotions calmed at the mere thought of him.

She grinned at Nick. "I really liked working with you too, Nick. Maybe in a few weeks we can get together and hang out. Grab lunch or something."

Her friend smiled sadly. "That would be cool. I can introduce you to my new girlfriend and maybe you can bring your bazillionaire."

She laughed. "Maybe." Would her life ever be ordinary with a man like Lucian in it?

They hugged and said good-bye. She felt marginally guilty for leaving the cart of food for the others to put away, but she was done. Another job, another chapter in the life of Evelyn Scout Keats.

fourteen
.....

"Hearts can never be practical until they can be made unbreakable."

~THE WIZARD OF OZ

THERE is something so contrived about winter. It's long, and bits of warmth are stolen from fabrications of man. Evelyn always favored the warmer months, and on days like this she savored every replenishing kiss of sunlight as it heated through her clothes and hugged her in a way her skin desperately needed.

For once, her feet simply trotted over ground with no direction as to where she should go next. Sharp, white blades of sky blurred the tops of buildings as she wandered aimlessly through the streets of Folsom. It was barely noon and she had hours to spare before her lesson, before Lucian finished work, before . . . anything.

Her body sunk into a bench, its metal planks forcing her posture into a pose she had no energy to hold. This dogged existence of climbing from one ladder to the next was wearing out her limits. She ached to crawl out of her skin and be someone else for a day.

People steadily passed in cars and on foot. She watched in a clouded form of wonderment. Where were they going? What did they do? Was there a purpose to their day? It all appeared convoluted and arbitrary at the same time.

Feeling like she'd run a marathon a lifetime long, she welcomed this jumbled form of inertia. Maybe Lucian was right. Maybe she was burning herself out, trying to cram too much in. Outlasting all else was her desire to be on par with others. She was twenty-three years behind in the game, and her struggle to catch up was beating her down like an iron fist.

It wasn't fair. None of it was. Her life was a peephole, a tiny snippet of skewed reality that flipped upside down in the blink of an eye. Lowering her lashes, she eased her head back, drawing warmth from the rays that warmed her cheeks and the bridge of her nose. Her mind traipsed over sporadic clips of her past, visiting some longer than others for no reason in particular, clinging to certain specific memories.

"Wait. He's a big coward!" Evelyn recalled her outrage at having borne the entire length of L. Frank Baum's The Wonderful Wizard of Oz. *"It's all fake." She shifted from her seat on the carpet of the library. Her back ached from lounging against the jagged bookcase display.*

Parker folded the paperback over his thumb and frowned. "Well, it's fiction, Scout."

"Then why didn't they make him real?"

"Because that's not the way the story's written."

Her disappointment was a cramp in her heart. "He's just a man."

"It's symbolic."

Her lips twisted derisively. "Symbolic of what? How disappointing all their hard work to reach Oz is?"

"No. It's a metaphor. All the pomp and fanfare, it's all just glitz to disguise normal men. He's just an ordinary man."

"Exactly."

Parker crossed his legs, tucking the book beneath his knee. The fabric was torn there much like she imagined the legs of the wilted scarecrow. Cynically, she said, "None of them even knew. The little dog figured it out."

"*Maybe they didn't want to know. Maybe they wanted to hope there was something more out there, a man so powerful he had the ability to change their fate,*" Parker argued.

"*Maybe this book doesn't make any sense.*"

"*It's a fairy tale. It doesn't have to make sense.*"

But she wanted it to, desperately. She wanted to join the band traveling along the yellow brick road and be taken away to a better place. "*Fairy tales are supposed to be happy.*"

"*Maybe that's what makes this such a popular story, that it isn't wrapped up in unattainable perfection. It's flawed because there is no real magic, but the magic of an ordinary man willing to tell the people they're more than ordinary travelers. Do you want me to keep reading?*"

"*Why bother? They went all that way for some measly trinkets. I don't get why they're so happy.*"

"*Because they were seeking validation,*" Parker said as if she were missing the whole point. Maybe she was. "*Their struggles are representative of the journey every person makes. There's confusion and mishaps and villains along the way, but in the end it's up to each individual to get where they want to be. We don't need wizards or magic. That's the point of it all. We just have to try and we'll eventually get there in some form or another.*"

Evelyn blinked through the blinding sun that bleached the darkness from the shade of her eyelids. She felt like Dorothy: lost, alone, meeting strange people along the way. When Parker finally finished the book, it had all been just a dream. Maybe that's all they all were—dreams in the mind of some superior being.

Could you dream up something a little easier?

Sighing, she pushed herself off the bench and looked at the time on her phone. 12:47. She counted the cash in her pocket and decided to make use of her time until Jason came at three. Hailing a cab, she made up her mind to visit Pearl.

• • •

THE halls to the rehab always smelled the same. Deodorized air shone over motes of dust that hovered in shards of light cutting through the white blinds at the reception desk where she signed in. The staff smiled at her, but otherwise ignored her presence as she made her way to her mother's room.

She tapped her knuckles on the door, which eased open silently. Pearl was watching television and turned at Evelyn's presence.

"Scout, what you doing here?"

She hadn't realized how much balanced on the gamble of her mother's recognition, but when her mother distinguished her as more than just a stranger, something broke inside of her and she started to cry.

"Oh, baby, what happened?" Her mom stood from the ugly mauve recliner and stepped close. When Pearl's frail arms drew her in—*physical contact*—every bit of preservation fled and she sobbed into her mother's meek form. She hadn't felt her mother's touch in years and she needed it so badly.

Tears erupted from Evelyn's eyes as she drew in stuttering breaths. "I'm so lost, Momma."

"Here. Sit." She was drawn over to the bed and collapsed, her shoulders hunching forward in defeat. "What happen?"

The anomaly of her mother's nurturing touch and sympathetic tone was her undoing. She wept like a child. She wept for all those times there simply wasn't room for tears. She wept, because sometimes, no matter how old a person was, they simply needed a mother and today she had one.

Pearl waited quietly for her to explain herself. It was a novel form of patience displayed by her mother, and Evelyn wondered if this was the break she had asked for.

She was tired of pretending; pretending she could read and

write, pretending the children's books in her bag belonged to someone else. The unending marathon of her life had exhausted her and the finish line felt just as distant as ever.

And now she was back with Lucian, but not back to the way things had been. There had to be a happy medium, but she didn't know if he could truly bend the way she needed and she feared losing him again.

All she ever wanted in life was to be normal. Was it even possible to be normal and in love with a billionaire? He was larger than life, and she valued the small things that most took for granted. She didn't know where she belonged, and her heart was leading her down a very impractical path she'd never traveled before.

Once her emotions were back under control, she blotted her eyes and looked at her mom. She looked well. In soft cotton pants and an ordinary cotton T-shirt, she looked nothing like the woman who raised her or stood by teaching her to raise herself.

Gaunt fingers, no longer stained with grime, brushed a strand of hair from her face. Muddy brown eyes, once so velvety tan, like chocolate, searched her face. "You okay now, baby?"

What could she say? Pearl's standard of living was a version of poverty littered with squalor and accepted sacrifice that was never good enough for Evelyn. Pearl merely existed until it was time to clock out.

Evelyn had always been different. She'd wanted to run from the time she could walk. Her hunger had always been for something more than what was immediately available. Maybe she simply wanted too much.

"I'm so confused, Momma."

"Confused 'bout what, baby?"

"Life."

There would be no logical advice from her mother's lips, but her presence of mind in that moment was worth more than any nostalgic diatribe of life's dos and don'ts. She shut her eyes and breathed.

"Life's hard, Scout," Pearl slowly said. She blinked at her mother's unexpected comprehension. "I 'member back when I's met your daddy. We had some good days. Once we even had a place to stay. It was real nice. Had a bed and toilet. We's had that place till just before you came along."

Her expression shuttered. That was the place her father was murdered. She didn't know much about the man who created her, only bits of what she'd heard over the years. Pearl had been right next to him when he was shot point-blank to the head.

"He should'a been your *real* daddy. Not those men that came by. No. Not them." Pearl's head shook in slow denial and Evelyn frowned. "Them's men was evil. They's come and take everything we had. Took your daddy. Took our stuff. Even took me and left me near for dead."

Evelyn's lips parted as she tried to voice her question in the most delicate way possible. "Momma, did those men hurt you?"

Her mother's stare became vacant, drifting off to blind moments of a past Evelyn hadn't been present for. "Yes."

Images flickered through Evelyn's mind of her mother before life demolished her softness, before a life of drugs and prostitution eradicated all optimism for something better. She struggled to voice her question. There was violence and then there was defilement. "Did they hit you?"

"No. They's come in shouting and shot your daddy. I was so shocked I cried and screamed. They just held me down and did what men do as I cried. Then they's left me there to die. But I didn't die. And then I's had you."

How had they gotten on this topic?

Her mother made a sound as if the memories caused her pain. "It was so hot that spring and as I lay there all I could smell was the blood. Smelled like copper pennies."

Evelyn swallowed as something cold and unwelcome slithered through her insides. These details had always been coveted because they were mostly unknown, but now she wanted to erase them from her mind.

All Evelyn knew about her birth was that it happened in winter. How long were women pregnant for? Her father couldn't have died in springtime. "Momma, what color eyes did Daddy have?"

"Brown like mine."

Evelyn glanced at the mirror over the sink in the corner of the room and stared at her light blue eyes. *Oh God.* She'd never met her father, only held him as a memory of some piece of her she'd never know. But if what Pearl meant was that he had never truly been her father in any sense of the word—*oh God*—she felt robbed of everything and nothing at all.

"I have to go," she wheezed.

Pearl turned, coming out of whatever trance she'd fallen into. "I'll come with you."

Evelyn stood and smiled sadly. "No, Momma. You have to stay here."

All softness morphed into cold, hard angles as her mother glared. "No. I'm gonna come with you. We gonna go home. 'Nough of this place and pretendin' to be people we ain't."

Evelyn shut her eyes and waited as Pearl, the mother who just held her the way she so desperately needed to be held, transformed into the selfish woman Evelyn knew too well. Her mom was sick. There were tests they could perform and specialists they could visit, but for what purpose? Beyond her physical ailments was an endless heap of mental issues. Labeling them solved nothing.

She slowly collected her bag as her mother argued. Her voice grew shrill with accusations, too cruel for Evelyn to listen to. As she backed out of the room, shutting away the raving woman on the other side, her mind shut off.

She walked the halls with no recollection of scenery or others passing by. It was all a blur until the moment she pressed the green button on her phone and heard Lucian's voice on the other end.

"Evelyn?"

"Can you come pick me up?"

He was quiet for a moment. "Are you at work? Is everything all right?"

Thankfully she was out of tears. "I'm at Pearl's."

He didn't ask how she'd gotten there or what had transpired in order for her to leave work early. He only said what she needed to hear. "I'll be right there."

Sliding the phone back into her bag, she realized she was outside once more. She walked to the curb and sat on the low lip of yellow-painted pavement and waited. The rehab was closer to Lucian's estate than her apartment or the hotel. It would take him some time to drive there. As the minutes ticked by she thought of nothing beyond the ache in her back and the invisible weight on her shoulders.

Time passed in increments of devastated hope. The little bit she had in the world had just been cut down by half. The loss of those childhood imaginings, of a heroic father she lost before he ever got to hold her, were stripped down to nothing more than the remnants of a criminal act. She was the leftovers of the monsters who decimated the only home her mother had been able to lay claim to.

The insignificant pieces that amounted to her existence became the flesh and bones that held her together. And for the life of her, she couldn't find the nerve to go on.

The slight pelting of drops barely registered as the sky gave way to spring showers. Her heated clothing grew damp and clung to her body, another weight to bear.

A delivery truck of some sort pulled into the lane separating her from the courtyard beyond the parked cars, as puddles pulled at her feet and darkened the hem of her gray pants. She wished she could simply wash herself away, float on to an easier place and forget these aches that added up to the sum of her.

The prattling engine of the truck came to life after the slide of a door. It grumbled as the driver pulled away from the curb and, as if the clouds parted to give way to the only spot of hope in her life, there stood Lucian before the sleek length of the black limo.

Separated by wet puddles upon pavement, the thread that tied him to her heart tugged as she met his gaze. There was no pity in those onyx eyes. Only clouded understanding that drew her in faster than gravity takes hold of a falling soul. Her knees flexed as she pressed her weight off the ground.

His expression was blank, an intrepid mask that lured her in. One foot moved in front of the other as she crossed the lot. His arms opened and she fell into his strength, drawing breath from his warmth and solitude from his unshakable stature.

She asked him to come for her and he came. No questions asked. He simply was there because she needed him.

"I love you." The words fell out of her mouth and nothing inside of her wanted to draw them back. It was the simple truth, she loved him and she would always love him, because beyond his flaws and after his stubbornness, before his need to serve himself, he would always put her first. That was something no one in her life had ever done.

Her breath hung suspended like fragile icicles in her lungs as she waited for his reply. Perhaps it was her new knowledge of how she came to exist that insisted she hear his reassurance. Always less and now a bit lesser, her tattered dignity required the words. She needed his vow of love. It was the only bond that could possibly forgive and accept the shame of her conception.

"I love you too." His arms sheltered her from the rain as he escorted her to the car. A thousand weighted worries eased with his easily given reply. She shivered in the cool interior as he settled in beside her.

It all made sense now. He would move hell and high water to protect her. It was an unfathomable awareness that nothing she could ever do would change that. There was no distance he would not cross to reach her if she called to him. Even when it came to what he'd done in the past, he merely let her go only to bring her home, surrendering everything he desired just to ensure she was safe.

The limo eased away from the rehab facility and she breathed a sigh of relief as he pulled her close. "Tell me why you came here in the middle of the day?" Lucian asked in a soft voice as he peeled a strand of damp hair back from her temple.

"I quit my job at Clemons."

His shoulder tensed under the weight of her cheek. "How come?"

"A woman in my line started taking pictures of me. I think she was from the press. I chased after her and apparently we aren't supposed to accost the customers. My boss was pissed and I over-reacted because he wanted to change my shifts so I walked out and basically told him where he could stick the job."

"Do you want your job back?"

She smirked. If she said yes, she had no doubt he'd somehow manage to resolve the situation for her. "No. I wouldn't have stayed there forever. Maybe this is for the best."

"So you left work and came to visit Pearl?"

"Yeah."

"I assume it didn't go well." His large palm coasted over her damp clothing, pressing heat into her chilled skin.

"She recognized me for a change. It actually started out as an okay visit. I mean, I was upset, but . . . she . . . listened and made me feel better."

"But that's not how she was when you left?" He knew enough

about Pearl and the way she treated her to know nurturing was not her mother's strong suit.

"No." She had the urge to let it all out, bare all, and hope he could catch all the broken pieces and mend her back together. "I don't know who my dad is. I never did, but the amalgam of a man I concocted in my head, the image I carried around like a kind of a talisman since I was a little girl, that's not him."

She wasn't making much sense. He waited for more of an explanation so she went on. Shame laced her confession. She never imagined her station in life could grow farther from Lucian's, but it had. All within the span of a few moments with Pearl. She needed to tell him.

"The people who killed the man I believed to be my dad . . . they raped my mom. I think that's where I came from."

His grip on her tightened as soft lips pressed into the top of her head. The sigh he expelled spoke volumes of his regret. Something told her it was regret for her shame, however, not his. Inexplicably, she believed, after all he'd already accepted of her past, he wouldn't be ashamed of her now.

"I'm sorry, baby."

"It's stupid to be upset about something so irrelevant. It changes nothing. It's just another shift in the pieces I've stood on all my life, another unstable chip in who I am."

"You're right. It doesn't change anything. You're still you, and you're more a compilation of your strength of will and personal experiences than anyone who played a part in the making of cells."

"So why does it hurt so much?"

His chest expanded and he exhaled slowly. "Because those made-up memories were yours, and someone took them away. When you don't have a lot, I imagine every bit counts, whether we acknowledge those parts of who we are or not. But this doesn't change anything, Evelyn. You're still the same person you were this morning."

"Who is that?"

"Pardon?"

"Who am I?"

"You're a young woman trying to find her way. You're smart, courageous, loving, and honest."

Her lips curled into a sad smile and she chuckled. "I'm Dorothy, the Tin Woodman, Scarecrow, and Cowardly Lion all rolled into one."

He laughed. "What?"

"Nothing. I was thinking about that story earlier and how much it frustrated me."

"*The Wizard of Oz?*"

"Yeah. I was so mad when I found out the great and powerful wizard was just a man behind a curtain."

Lucian turned and softly said, "That's all we all are. We're just ordinary people trying to do great things."

"Yeah," she agreed, for the first time feeling at ease with that mediocre explanation of people and life. "I guess we are."

THE soft press of lips to the corner of her mouth had her lashes fluttering open. They were still in the limo. She'd fallen asleep.

"I want you to call Jason and cancel your lesson for tonight."

She blinked as words crammed to the forefront of her mind, preparing to spill out in argument.

Lucian cut her off. "Either you call him or I will. You're exhausted. I'm taking you up to the penthouse where you will take a long bath while I order dinner, and then I'm putting you to bed."

"Lucian, there are some things I need more than sleep."

He wasn't angry, but his expression also told her he wasn't budging. He held out his hand. "The phone, Evelyn."

Her head was fuzzy and her nose was stuffy from crying. Rubbing the heel of her hand into her eye, she sat up. Maybe she should call it a day. The more her brain awoke the more she recalled why she wanted to sleep.

Shoving thoughts of Pearl and her morning away, she lifted her hips and dug out her cell. Lucian reached and she pulled her hand back. "It's my responsibility. I'll handle it." He relented and she dialed Jason's number.

After leaving a quick voice mail saying she wouldn't be able to make their appointment that evening, she suffered an uncomfortable sort of guilt. She didn't like making excuses.

"It's for your own good," Lucian said, rubbing his arm over her shoulder and easing her to the door of the limo.

She didn't like that he knew what was best for her before she did sometimes, but he was probably right. She was muzzy headed and tired, emotionally drained. Still, she couldn't give him too much credit or he'd slowly start deciding everything for her, and she wasn't ready for that. "I wouldn't have made the call if I didn't think it was the right choice."

His eyes narrowed, studying her, but there was a slight quirk to his lips. A smile. "So tough. Come on."

The walk out of the limo was made in haste as it continued to rain, an otherwise beautiful day turned into a dreary smudge of inconvenience. Shoes squeaked over the pristine lobby floor, and all sound was buffered as the elevator doors closed around them.

When they arrived at the penthouse, Lucian walked her straight into the master bath and proceeded to prepare the tub. Soft citrus fragrances wafted to her nose as bubbles frothed against the porcelain walls. He helped her off with her shirt, expertly sliding each little button through its hole.

These were the moments she valued surrender. When they were alone and he took control, she was able to let go and simply be. She valued that time, loved his gentle authority. Somehow her needs in privacy were quite contrary to the control she needed of her own life outside these walls.

Her legs were stripped down to nothing, and he helped her step over the high lip of the tub. She settled into the warm water and groaned at the delectable way the heat seeped into her bones.

Lucian disappeared and returned with a plush, folded bath towel and sat on the chair at the vanity. She sensed his need to say something, so she faced him and turned off the faucet.

"I want to talk to you about our arrangement. We can talk at dinner or after you rest. I'll leave it up to you."

She frowned. The term "arrangement" didn't sit right with her, not after she'd come to an understanding with her heart. "What is it you want to discuss?"

He shook his head. "Not now. Relax for a while. It'll keep."

"You can't do that. You can't say something like that then expect me to relax. And why are you suddenly calling it 'our arrangement'?"

His thick lashes blinked at her in confusion. "I meant our living arrangement. And it isn't anything bad, we just need to get a few things clear." He stood and her body refused to go after him, too comfortable in the heat of the silky water.

"I'll order dinner in a half hour so you have time to unwind and clear your head."

Yeah, like that was going to happen now.

He kissed her hair and left the room. Evelyn soaked for what she assumed was fifteen minutes, then climbed out of the tub and did a quick rinse and scrub in the shower.

On Lucian's bed she found a white dress shirt laid out for her and slipped it over her shoulders, buttoning it down to her thighs. The scent of dinner wafted through the hall, and her hunger announced itself as she settled into the chair across from him.

He smiled. "Feel better?"

"Yes." She lifted the cover off her dish and found a succulent slice of beef cradled in a nest of fresh greens. Lucian nodded at her, quietly prompting her to eat.

After several bites, he said, "There's a party at Antoinette's condo this weekend. It's for Jamie. It's his birthday. I'd like you to go with me."

"Sure." She nibbled on a sprig of asparagus. "I guess he and Toni are really an item now, if she's throwing him parties at her home."

He grumbled something under his breath, telling her he still didn't approve of the match. "Shamus doesn't know about it. It's a surprise."

"Oh. Will he mind?"

He cocked his head and lifted a shoulder. "We'll have to wait and see."

"Are you going to get him a gift?"

"I ordered his gift this morning."

No time like the present, she thought. "What did you get him?"

"A Spider."

"You got him a bug?"

He laughed. "No. I bought him a McLaren Spider. It's a high-performance sports car he was drooling over at a trade show we caught last time we were in California on business."

Wine went down the wrong pipe and she choked. "You bought him a *car*?"

His lips twisted. "To call this a car is an insult. It's a quarter-of-a-million-dollar machine that can travel up to two hundred and four miles per hour. It's built for racing so the safety features are extraordinary, yet it's luxurious as well."

Her jaw unhinged as she stared at him. She'd never be able to conceive that type of money. The fact that Lucian had it freaked her out. Sure, he lived in the lap of luxury and invited her to many fancy places, but good grief! *She* couldn't justify buying nongeneric cheese.

When she continued to gawk, he placed his fork on the gold filigree rim of his dish and asked, "What?"

"You bought him a quarter-of-a-million-dollar car! What do you mean, *what*?"

He shrugged. "Shamus is a good friend."

She scoffed. "I can't even comprehend why such a thing costs so much. And who in their right mind wants to go that fast? Where do you even *go* to drive that fast?"

"The Autobahn."

"What's that?"

"A federal expressway in Germany with no speed limit."

"Are you trying to kill him so he stops dating your sister?"

He frowned and she winced, regretting her words. He wouldn't find that joke funny, not after losing his ex-lover in a motorcycle accident. "No. I thought he'd like it, but now you have me second-guessing my gift."

She shook her head. Who spent that kind of money on gifts? "What did you buy your sisters for their last birthdays?"

He tilted his head as he thought about his answer. "Well, I gave Toni her condo, and Isadora—she's a little more difficult to please—I gave a chateau in Italy. She visits there each August."

Her skin felt heavy on her face. There was no precedent set to react to such an outlay of money. "Don't *ever* spend that kind of money on me."

He pursed his lips and said, "Are you finished eating?"

Yes, she couldn't stomach another bite. "Yes."

"Come sit with me. We need to talk."

Her stomach twisted. Each step toward the sofa was heavy with trepidation. Her body settled beside him and she waited. Whatever he needed to say was going to be big. She could sense it.

He loosened his tie, the shadowy skin of his throat as tanned as the back of his hands. Once he settled comfortably into the cushions, he announced, "This isn't working for me."

The blood drained from her face in a whoosh that left her dizzy. "What?" she croaked.

"Our situation, it isn't enough for me. I want more."

Shockingly, no tears filled her eyes. His words trod over her like little daggers, each one burying itself deep in her heart. It was too much, too much agony, too much reality, too much shock.

Warmth surrounded her fingers. "Hey, you're shaking. Evelyn, take a breath. Do you want some water?"

She must have nodded, because he stood and returned a moment later with a glass of cold water. She guzzled the entire thing and still was thirsty.

Where would she go? Back to her apartment, she supposed. But then what? She couldn't go back to that place where she and Lucian didn't exist.

She'd become so dependent upon him being in her life. Shock was an agony she could cauterize. She'd thought, after the last twenty-four hours, they'd reached a place of security and agreement.

He came for her, said he loved her, and she loved him. Love was all she could offer, but her ever-present fear of not being enough cut her down quick, and she choked on a sob as everything she held so dearly threatened to rip away.

"Maybe you should lie down. I should have waited to talk to you about this until after you rested."

She had the instinct to run, but her body was so numb she feared she'd barely be able to stand. Her throat was dry. It was work to swallow. When she managed to produce a normal amount of saliva in her mouth, she asked, "Why?"

"Well, for one, I want you living under my roof. This nonsense of living apart is a step in the wrong direction for us and—"

"Wait, what? I thought you were breaking up with me."

His eyes widened as he drew back in apparent shock. "Why the hell would you think that?" He actually sounded angry.

"Because you said it wasn't working out, that you wanted more."

"Yes. More of *you*!"

Oh. As her mouth hollowed around the silent word, she blew out a shaky breath.

"Evelyn, I've told you, you're not getting rid of me. Ever."

A tumultuous smile stretched her lips as pure satisfaction purred from somewhere within her chest.

"Can we talk now?" he asked, face tight, reflecting a cross between amusement and suspicion.

Her confidence slowly reestablished itself. "Yes. Let's talk."

Watchfully, he nodded. "Like I was saying, I want more. I know things have . . . escalated between us. I doubt either of us predicted falling in love, but I do love you and you love me. I'm not going to press for marriage until you let me know you're ready, but I see no need for this distance. There are certain things I need in life and you're one of them. I want you here, by my side, always there when I wake up in the morning."

Images of her apartment broke away like figments of clay. Moments ago, the idea of having only her apartment to return to seemed like the most desolate end. It was only an inanimate structure. When she mistakenly thought she was losing Lucian, she realized how lifeless and empty her place truly was without him. But she wanted them both. She wanted her independence and him. That apartment symbolized more than four walls to her.

"I can stay over, but I won't give up my home, Lucian. It's important I have a place outside of what you give me."

"Why?" This obviously wasn't what he wanted to hear, but he seemed to be open to discussion.

"Because I've never had such a thing, and I won't give it up before the novelty wears off."

"But you expect the luxury of having your own place to wear off?"

She shrugged. "I don't know what to expect. All I know is what I want. I want you and I want my own home. If you want me, you'll have to compromise and accept that this is something I need right now."

If she were being honest, she missed living with him as well. But this was an important stepping-stone for her. She was proving she could stand on her own two feet. Lucian should understand that, being that he held such high regard for control. He'd shown her firsthand how empowering control should be, and she was finally taking charge of herself.

"Assuming we agree that you keep the apartment—"

"*Accepting*, Lucian. Because I *am* keeping it."

Narrowing his eyes, he continued. "I still want you to treat my homes as yours. I'll hire a decorator and you can remodel the penthouse as you see fit. We can do the same at the estate and when we visit my other homes, if you want to change them, you can do as you please."

"Other homes?"

He smirked. "I have eight homes, Evelyn. My estate outside of Folsom; one in Aspen; one in the Hamptons; another off the coast of Florida; a condo in Vegas; a small cottage in Carlingford, Ireland; a mansion in England; and a brownstone in Manhattan. Huh, I guess that's nine, actually, if you count my home here at the hotel."

She pushed every word away, not equipped to process such wealth and possession. Her mind focused on the salvaged table and chairs she'd bought the other day. She didn't know the first thing about decorating. Stupidly, she said, "Maybe we can start with new placemats or something small." He was insane giving her that sort of authority.

"Whatever you want. I want my homes to be equally yours."

But they aren't.

"I want to take care of you, Evelyn. Every time you ask me for something, whether it's to come to your rescue or simply kiss you good night, it gives me a rush, a feeling of purpose I've never experienced before. I want you to be independent and focused on bettering yourself so that you're happy, but I like that you need me. I want it to be my responsibility to keep you safe. How do you feel about that?"

Warmth bloomed in her chest as she remembered how it felt to see him come to her rescue that afternoon. "Well, that's sort of your role whether you ask me or not. I do see you that way. I know I can come to you with anything and you'll help me. But I can't go back to the way we were. You'd go off to work and I'd wander the condo. I need my life to be more than that."

He hesitated a moment, then asked, "Once you get your education, which you will, what do you want to do? I can help you get there."

"That's the thing. I don't know myself well enough to know what I'm passionate about. This is the first chance I've had to take time to do for me, and I *need* it. I need my own stability. I'll stay here from time to time, but I need a home to go to."

"You have several."

She smirked. He was insistent. "So long as you respect that one is solely mine."

He sighed. "I can accept that. For now."

"Good," she said, not seeing the point in putting a time limit on what she didn't yet know.

"Good. On that same line of trust, I want to readdress the issue of a safe word."

Her body had a gut reaction as she recalled the only time she'd ever needed to utilize her safe word. He'd pushed her too hard, not physically, never that, but emotionally. She didn't like the presence of that memory in her mind and tried to force it back into some dark cavity of her brain.

"I just want to be clear," he continued, "that, no matter what, your safe word will always be respected. No matter what. This time, however, it won't mean our time's concluded. It'll mean we stop whatever we're doing, regroup, and discuss matters once everyone's calmed down. Agreed?"

She liked having that sort of safety net. "Yes."

"Do you still want your word to be 'checkmate'?"

She nodded. There was nothing more fitting than a word that meant the king was pegged. This was all very familiar to the terms they started their association with. She didn't understand why he felt the need to readdress such matters. Then he dropped the bomb on her.

"I want the dynamic of our relationship to grow in trust, and I think the only way we can do that is to jump right in. I want you to try something with me. Over the next month, I want you to surrender to me, not just sexually, but completely. I want you to trust me to make the proper decisions regarding your well-being and safety. When I say you should do something, I want you to do your best to get it done. When I say no, that's the end of it. No arguing. You trust me to have your best interests at heart."

She held up her hand. "Checkmate." His brow arched and she explained, "You're going too fast. Submission in the bedroom is an entirely different practice than submitting my independence."

"You will always have your independence. I can't change who you are, nor do I want to."

Objections sprinted to the tip of her tongue. There was sexual surrender and then there was free will, something she always held tightly to. "Lucian—"

"One month, Evelyn. If you don't like it, we go back to the way things are. It doesn't mean we're over. I believe this is right for us. All of your life you've had to decide what was best. I want to give you this gift, unburden you from all that stress. I swear I'll never treat you as anything other than my equal. Surrender takes more strength than authority demands. I'll take full responsibility for your health, happiness, and general well-being, and you'll let me. I see it as a win-win. I'll be there to take care of you no matter what, but in return I want your complete honesty and trust."

They'd traveled this road before. When they first met they'd had similar discussions, and her answer was always the same. Trust could not be forced and free will could not be surrendered. "It won't work."

"How do you know if you don't try?"

"Because I know me. I'm stubborn and when I want something, I won't back down."

"If there's something you want, and there's no harm in having it, I'll provide it for you. All you have to do is ask. What you're missing is the fact that I'm relieving you of the struggle. I want the gratification of granting you life's simple pleasures."

"Why is what we have not enough for you?"

He took her hands. "It is enough. *You* are enough for me, but I believe we can have more. There are certain things I want. I like authority and order. I've watched you come such a long way from where we started, and there have been moments I've suffered through silently, watching you struggle—knowing I could fix a situation for you—but I held back because I didn't want to bruise your pride.

"You're a remarkable woman and that's a compliment I've never paid another female and, in my business, I've met my share of impressive women. All of these secrets and unnecessary shame, they're taking something incredible away from us, and I don't think you even realize it. There's nothing you could tell me that will diminish my love for you.

"Imagine what it would be like, Evelyn, no longer having to worry about money, to have everything you need at the tip of your fingers. I want to see you accomplish your goals as much as you do. I too draw pride from your success. All I'm asking for is thirty days. Try for me. Surrender. You can continue to see Jason and I'll arrange for anything else that helps you get where you want to be. I can give you anything if you'd just let me."

Well, there wasn't much to complain about there. Thirty days, not a lifetime. What was the harm? She'd wasted more time trying things the hard way, and here was this incredible man offering her the world on a silver platter.

"Would I still get to see Pearl?" There were certain things she simply couldn't give up.

"Of course, but I don't want you to work, at least not now. I believe you'd be much better off focusing on your studies. Most students don't work. Embrace this stage and the next will come in time. Tackle one dream before you try to conquer the world." He laughed affectionately and dragged a finger over her ear, tucking her hair behind it. The affectionate gesture made her feel safe and warm.

Work wasn't really an issue for her after today, and the idea of finding another job, yet again, was daunting. "What if I want something, really want something, and you tell me no."

"Then you have to trust that I'm making the right choice for everyone. I'm not perfect. You're always entitled to a different opinion, but there will be times we won't agree and I expect us to discuss the matter respectfully and honestly. Truth is a major part of this sort of relationship. You can never lie to me, Evelyn. Never."

"What if I know you're making the wrong decision?"

"You'll just have to trust me. I'm sure to make mistakes, which I'll take full responsibility for, but they're my mistakes to make. Thirty days, that's all I'm asking. Then the choice to continue or go back to the way things were is yours. You have all the power here. You're simply entrusting it to me for a short period."

Her head rolled from side to side on her shoulders as she weighed her options. Was what he suggested really that different from how they lived now? Thirty days would tell.

"All right."

His brows lifted. Clearly he hadn't expected her to agree so easily. A slow smile curled his lips and she caught a glimpse of his perfect white teeth. He leaned close and traced his lips over hers. "You make me a very happy man, Evelyn. Thank you."

Breathing deep, her blood and bones melted into warm liquid heat as the touch of his mouth seeped all the way to her sex. Her body tightened expectantly. She wanted him.

Moaning softly, she leaned into his kiss and he pulled back. A satisfied smirk played on his lips, creasing his eyes. "You need to sleep."

The lightness of her expression crumbled into a pout. "I'm not tired anymore."

He raised one dark brow. "You've been going a hundred miles a minute. You had a rough day, and there are dark circles under your eyes. I don't want you coming down with something because you've exhausted yourself. I want you to go to bed."

If she went to bed, she'd stare at the ceiling. She truly wasn't tired anymore. She wanted to make love. "I—"

"Surrender, Evelyn."

Her lips pursed as her chin dropped. *Well, this wasn't fun.*

Whatever her expression was, it made him laugh. His palm touched her knee and patted her bare skin. "Come on. I'll tuck you in."

She stood and her body ached. "I'm not a child."

"Of course not. If you were, the things I'm planning to do to you when you wake would land me in jail."

Grumbling under her breath, she climbed onto the thickly made-up bed. The cool satin covering the down comforter sunk beneath her weight, and she turned to collapse in the cloudlike pillows. Sweet heaven, this bed was so much more comfortable than the one she'd bought.

Her hips lifted as he drew back the coverlet and tucked her

legs under the pressed linens. This was a bed made for sleeping—among other things. Her eyes drooped heavily as he switched off the bedside lamp.

Leaning over, his dark eyes creased. "Not tired, my ass," he said as he kissed her good night.

"Are you going to be working?" She sounded groggy, but she still wanted to make love.

"For a bit. I have to finish up some things I left behind. Seth's coming by to drop off some papers on this deal we're hoping to close soon, and then I'll be in."

"Wake me up when you come in." Her eyes closed and she sighed.

The weight of his fingertip traced her brow, dragging down the arc of her nose and to the curve of her lip. "I decide. You sleep. I love you."

Bossy. "Love you too," she mumbled as her mind clouded with dreamlike images that made no sense and she let go.

fifteen
.....

THE BEAUTY OF ABANDON

IT was a feather tickling her cheek, enough to rouse her from a deep slumber. Evelyn's mind pixilated until under the dark cloak of night, a vision formed in her head, paralleled by the caress teasing her awake. Heavy limbs folded over her and she sighed, arching into a diminutive stretch, purring like a cat begging to be stroked.

That was what he did to her, made her a feline of sorts, proper and proud, but deep down a slut for his touch. She didn't care. Every trace of his finger and touch of his tongue was like being anointed with something sacred she'd never known before him.

Her life was compiled in seasons. There were warm months and cold, but nothing took relevant shape until she'd met him. He made everything matter. *He* made *her* matter.

The heat of his mouth pressed into her sleepy smile. "Mmm, I want you." His gravelly confession warmed her limbs as heat seeped down through her belly and coiled in the depths of her where everything feminine waited, just for him.

The blanket pulled away and she stretched beneath him, extending her arms to the pillows as he worked each little button of her shirt. Cool air bit into her flesh like a minnow's kiss, tightening. His chest rasped over her soft breasts, beading her nipples another degree.

Breath moistened her skin above her shoulder in the curve of her neck, and the press of his nose to her throat was a vow of unspoken need. The hard, silken weight of his arousal rested upon her hip, leaving damp little kisses over her soft skin. Hands contoured her ribs, cupped her breasts and traveled lower still to brace her curves.

As his bulk slid lower, her need ratcheted. Stretching and undulating slowly like a cast spell coming to life, she twisted with desire. Fingers tightened over the protrusion of her hips, and breath ruffled the dusting of hair at her apex. Shades of purple filtered through her lashes, but she kept her eyes closed.

His knees locked over her legs, pressing her thighs tight like a mermaid's tail, forbidding access to where she wanted him most. Then, like a slow lick of fire, he found her most sensitive spot and flicked his tongue slowly over her bud. She moaned and her body pressed into his kiss, but his strength set her deep in the bedding.

Slow traces of his tongue eased her clit out of hiding, and soon his lips closed over her. Her thighs brushed with little movements as he restrained her legs and tortured her slowly. It was enough to make her come, but the release was precise. A throbbing linked to her heartbeat pulsed low in her belly, a slight quivering beneath his lips.

She trembled as he kissed her swollen bud, prolonging the gentle, rhythmic burst of pleasure. Sighing, she tried to turn out of his grip, wanting to repay the favor of being woken so splendidly.

"Stay."

Her motions halted as her chest rose and fell with breathless desire. "I want you," she whispered into the dark.

"Shh. I'll give you everything you want."

His fingers curved around her inner thigh, slowly drawing her legs apart. Warm, openmouthed kisses anointed the soft flesh from her pelvis to the underside of her knee. The other leg was treated much the same; again and again, slow torturous kisses drew her senses out to play.

Her lips parted as her sex was bathed in her own arousal. Finally, his heated breath cooled her damp folds. Licks traced every crevice, but his tongue never entered her sex. She felt hollow without him there. He was her missing piece. His mouth sucked at her flesh and pressed her thighs wide.

"You're so beautiful here. So pink and perfect."

His tongue rimmed her opening, and he growled. The weight of his finger was a welcome intrusion. He did not plunder her, but rather traced her walls, slowly delving deeper and deeper with that solitary finger.

When she arched, his other hand pressed like a starfish into her belly, anchoring her back down. "Stay still."

His touch was sexual indeed, but there was a feeling of being examined as well that left her on the precipice of something dark. Emotions surged and urges to cover herself weaved with the intricate reaction of her desire to let him continue.

Surrender. Be his. Trust.

The tension that had her squirming fell away as her legs opened the remaining distance until they settled softly into the bedding. "That's a good girl."

She was rewarded with a deep press of his finger that settled right over her G-spot. Her back bowed reflexively as he tickled there. Hot lips nibbled and sucked her clit, and she was coming once more, this time her release forceful. Waves of pleasure consumed her, and she cried out with the ecstasy of it.

His fingers fucked into her sex as he extended her pleasure. When her body was a puddle of bones and flesh holding her heartbeat inside, he withdrew his touch and kissed up to her breasts.

Evelyn had no idea what time it was, if it was close to morning or just after dark. Time didn't matter when they were together. Nothing did. The world simply fell away.

Her body was turned as his lips kissed and nibbled over her shoulder. "Come here."

She opened her eyes, and even under the dim twilight shadows, she blinked at the vividness. He sat on the bed, his back facing the headboard, but not leaning in. Guiding her body, he scooted her to his lap so her back was to his chest. "Put me inside of you," he whispered, taking a nip from her shoulder.

She lifted and her fingers curled around the solid length of his velvet cock. Bracing her weight on her knees, she fit him to her slit and sunk down. He filled her completely and they each moaned at the pleasure of such a union.

Strong hands curled around her ankles before she had a chance to move. "Slide your legs back and lean forward so you're resting with your belly on the bed."

She worried she'd hurt him in that position, but he was large enough to keep them connected as she eased forward. His palm pressed softly into her back, slowly guiding her all the way down until the cool satin sheets pressed into her breasts. Her arms wound around his calf muscles and when her legs extended, knees pressing into the bedding and thighs bracketing his hips, he grabbed onto her hips and gave a little tug.

The position seated him deep in her sex, pressing firmly into her front where all those delicious nerve endings lay. Fingers massaged her cheeks as he eased forward. "Now fuck me, Evelyn."

It took her a moment to find her bearings. She wiggled and every little motion seemed to anchor him deeper in her sex. She decided she liked this position very much. Once she understood the mechanics of it, she realized she could use her upper body strength against his calves as leverage. Pulling at his ankles, the wiry hair covering his legs tickled her fingers as she rocked.

Dear God he was deep. He grunted and began to rock back into her, every counterstroke to her rhythm a delectable brush to her core. Her limbs grew slick with exertion as she soon mastered the pose. Just as she was about to come again, he slapped her ass hard and she sucked in a breath and stilled.

"My pleasure, Evelyn. I saw to yours. Now see to mine."

Indeed. Her greedy body wanted more, but her mouth pulled tight in a smirk. The orgasm vanished, leaving nothing but a tell-tale quiver. Frustrated with being deprived of such selfish pleasure, she put her efforts into milking the best climax he'd ever had. Her force of each stroke doubled. She clenched her sex at precisely the right moments, and when his fingers dug into the firm flesh of her ass, almost punishingly, she knew he figured out she was playing with him.

Her body became an instrument of pleasure. Delirium set in as she worked at her task. Body slicked over body as fingers tightened to leave purple kisses like the subtle, bruised painting of rose petals. The muscles of her arms and legs cried out for mercy, but her determination to shatter him to pieces overruled their protests. The bed rocked like a lullaby of sin, and he cursed.

His grip bit into her flesh as the warmth of his seed spilled into her womb. His cock, buried so deep inside her, hammered, each jet of his release a pulse into her sensitive sex, and she cried out as her orgasm collided with his. He nearly dislodged himself with the force of his release, hips bucking, leg muscles constricting. Opening her eyes, Evelyn had the satisfaction of literally seeing his toes curl.

The urge never announced itself; she merely transcended into an animal claiming her mate, and her teeth bit down on the muscle of his calf. He twitched and pinched her ass, jarring her enough to loosen her jaw. She giggled and rested her dewy cheek on his leg. Spent.

The room echoed with their labored breaths, and somehow

Lucian managed to untangle their limbs. When he withdrew from her sex, as always, the unwelcome emptiness that followed provoked a little whimper. Strong arms pulled her to his chest and slid the covers up to their shoulders as he eased their heads onto the pillows.

"You're amazing," he whispered. His lips pressed into hers, hard. The kiss was packed with direct admiration.

She softened and he followed suit. Her fingers threaded through his silky black hair, and she tugged. "So are you."

They settled in, hips nestled within hips, ass to groin. His arm coiled around her, and his hand found a home possessively over her breast. A kiss to her shoulder, and then they rested, replete, well loved, and blissfully content.

EVELYN stretched her sore muscles, basking in the gentle afterburn of great sex, as the hot, pounding water soothed her body. Slippery suds traveled over her skin, detouring in the gully of her breasts, gliding over her hips and down to her toes, swirling away at the drain on the marble floor.

Her fingers shampooed her long hair. She never grew tired of the ritual, too familiar with the notion of having to go without. Turning her face toward the spray, she closed her lips and let the suds rinse away. How glorious it was to be clean.

Lost in a whirlwind of visions from the night before and cozy in a feeling of contentment, she jumped when Lucian's body stepped into the shower behind her. His arms snaked around her belly and the long length of his arousal settled in the crease of her ass as he bent to kiss her shoulder. She smiled and leaned into him.

"I thought you had work to do," she said, suggestively wiggling her ass.

"I do, but I kept picturing your mouth, and then my cock got hard, and then I heard the water and knew you were naked and you can guess where my mind went next." He caressed her hip, running his knuckles through the damp curls at her apex. "We need to get you waxed again."

"You say that so easily, but no one's pouring hot wax over your manly bits and ripping it off."

He chuckled and bit her shoulder. "Thank God for that. Wax can be fun though. Maybe that's something we should look into."

"No, I think I'm set. Those torture artists you employ at the salon downstairs kick my ass enough."

His thumb and forefinger pinched her nipple. "Are you telling me no?"

The ache at the tip of her breast spread into heady need. Breath catching, she remembered their agreement. "No. I suppose it's your decision."

He flexed his hips and growled. "Correct. Do you know what I want right now?"

His fingers continued to toy with her nipples. Her head rolled back on his chest. "What?"

"I want to see your pretty mouth stretched over my cock."

Her pussy clenched and she turned into him. Her mouth licked at the drops of water, and the flat of her tongue dragged over his dark nipple. Fingers tightened at the back of her head in the tangled, wet mop of her hair, the grip of his hold urging her down.

She lowered to her knees, the unforgiving tile slick beneath her weight. His fist released her hair and she looked up at him, awaiting his command, hands folded delicately over her thighs.

"God, you're beautiful," he rasped, dragging a finger around her ear and down her jaw.

She wasn't beautiful. She was too thin. Her eyes were too gray. And her skin was too pale. But he made her feel like a work of priceless art. Blinking slowly under the soft spray of water misting over his broad shoulders, she preened at the compliment. "Thank you."

"I love seeing you like this, on your knees for my pleasure."

Oddly, she loved being that way for him. His thumb rubbed over her mouth, pressing softly into the plump swell of her lower lip. He widened his stance and stepped closer, bracing his weight in a way that made the thickly corded muscles of his legs flex.

She opened and he breached her lips, sliding his thick cock to the back of her throat. Her satisfied moan mimicked his. Brushing the damp hair out of her eyes, he stared down at her. His erection pressed and withdrew, slowly at first, but building momentum with each thrust.

She rose up on her knees, lifting her weight off her heels, and gripped the root of his cock. He stilled. "Hands behind your back."

Blinking up at him, she did as he said. His fingers wound her hair like long lengths of ribbon, fisting it tight at the back of her head. He was in control, and she melted at the sensation. Although he kept a strong hold on her, he wasn't rough. He never went too deep or too fast. He merely directed their rhythm in a way that allowed her to let go, not think, and simply feel.

The press of his fingers to her throat warned her that he was ready to come. Going up on his toes, he groaned and dragged her head back, withdrawing his flesh from her lips.

Shoulders tight with her fingers laced behind her spine, she watched as he tugged at his length in quick jerks. Ribbons of hot, white come splashed onto her breasts and chest, marking her.

His shoulders expanded with each breath. His hand reached out and she unlaced her fingers, placing her palm in his as he carefully hoisted her off the floor. He took several minutes kissing and bathing her. When he toweled her off, her skin was buffed to a glowing pink.

His lips found hers and lingered there for several minutes. When he pulled away, he said, "I need to go to the office in a bit. I'll be back soon. I've left Jason a message asking him to meet you here."

Her brow tightened. "You called Jason?"

"Yes."

She understood she was supposed to hand over some authority to him over the next thirty days, but this was not what they discussed. "But he's *my* instructor."

"I've arranged for you to use a boardroom on the ninth floor for your lessons. There's a Smart Board and other items that may help. Welcome to school, Evelyn. Today you'll be visiting your first classroom."

She stilled, processing what he'd said. A classroom. Not her rinky-dink table that barely had a large enough surface for two books. Perhaps this was what he'd meant by making things easier for her. He hadn't done anything but provide a space for them to work more efficiently, a space that likely would have been vacant on a day like today.

While most people might dread the idea of passing endless hours in a classroom, it was a novel experience for her, and she looked forward to it. Many times over the past week she and Jason had struggled to make room at her tiny table. Between the books, worksheets, and other notes there was a lot to manage. A larger table and classroom would be ideal.

"Thank you. That'll probably make things a lot easier."

He smiled and kissed her nose. "The room is yours as long as you need it. I've ordered the concierge to mark it as occupied until otherwise instructed. Feel free to hang things on the walls and leave your books there so you don't have to lug more than you need back and forth. Your clothes are laid out on the bed."

She flinched at the sudden change of subject. Glancing to the unmade bed, she saw denim and cotton folded neatly beneath a wisp of black lace. "You're picking out my clothes now?"

"You never wear shorts. I wanted to see you in them."

She thought for a moment, supposing she never wore shorts because they were impractical. Skin was the body's best defense against outside objects. Long jeans were a precautionary form of armor. More than once she'd cut her knee slipping under a chain link fence.

He didn't wait for her acquiescence. When he disappeared into the walk-in closet, she stepped over to the bed. The shorts were khaki and the shirt was a soft pink button-down with capped sleeves. There was also a white tank top to go underneath, no doubt to cover up the black demi bra he'd selected. Matching panties rested in a tiny drape of fabric.

Slipping out of her towel, she made quick work of dressing. Peeking out beneath the dust ruffle were two small sandals. She scooped them up and examined them. Flip-flops. Another type of clothing she never attempted for sensible reasons.

"Here, it may be chilly later and the boardrooms maintain a lower temperature because of the electrical equipment." He stepped out of the closet, holding a white cardigan, and stilled. "You look lovely dressed like that."

His gaze traveled down her legs and her cheeks warmed. "Where are all these clothes coming from?"

"The girls at the stores we visited in the fall have a record of your sizes. I told them you were in need of a summer wardrobe."

It seemed her Lucian had truly returned, making snap decisions at the speed of light. "When did you contact them?"

"Last week when I noticed your sneakers were getting a bit worn. There are several new pairs in the closet."

His fingers deftly flipped the navy silk of his tie and knotted the loop, cinching it tight at the collar. He slipped into his jacket and kissed her again. "I'll make an appointment for your torture session downstairs and have them call up with the time. They'll fit you in before Jason gets here."

"Lucian, I have to go home."

He turned and frowned. "Why?"

"Because I don't live here."

He stepped close and smiled. "What would you do at home until your lesson?"

She frowned. Nothing. She had everything she needed here: clothes, her books, her phone. She didn't even leave a dish in her sink. There was no reason for her to leave.

She had intended to go to the salon eventually, knowing he preferred her waxed with only a trimmed patch at the top. Looked like he'd thought of everything. She supposed she could indulge him for his thirty days. What was the harm? So long as he wasn't interrupting her plans with Jason, she saw no trouble in humoring his request. "I guess I could stay here."

"Good." He kissed her lips, a satisfied grin on his face.

She took a few experimental steps in her flip-flops. The smack of the shoe against her heel made her frown. God, she was like an alien, always trying to get used to new things. *Get over it, Keats. They're shoes.*

Lucian hustled in and out of the room, sorting through his money on the bureau, returning to the bathroom to tidy his hair, and finally to kiss her good-bye. When he left, the condo was filled with impenetrable silence. She wandered around for several moments, pondering what she should do for the next few hours.

The sharp ring of the house phone startled her. "Hello?"

"Ms. Keats?"

"Yes?"

"This is Camille from the salon. Mr. Patras asked me to call and inform you your appointment is at eleven."

She glanced at the clock. It was quarter to. "Oh, okay. I'll be right down."

"He wanted me to remind you to bring a book so you have something to do during your paraffin treatment and pedicure."

So he *had* decided what she would be doing with the remaining hours of the day. She smiled. If she shoved away the initial offense at being coddled, she could actually get used to feeling so cared for. "Okay. Thank you."

She hung up the phone and went to her bag. Evelyn wasn't going to bust out her elementary workbook at the salon, so she grabbed her dictionary. She'd practice reading words. Jason had been working on combination sounds and consonant blends with her. She'd play around in the *ph* section for a while, because that still threw her off.

sixteen
· · · · ·

SPEAK EASY

OVER the following days, Evelyn discovered a side to herself she only knew from distant musings. Lucian decided everything for her, from the type of panties she wore to what vegetables she ate with her dinner. She couldn't imagine how such an arrangement was benefiting him. She, on the other hand, was making out like a bandit.

She saw no fault in temporarily indulging his request to take better care of her, so long as he didn't override her decision to continue with her education. Her lessons with Jason took an incredible amount of time. The work she did on her own often left her tired, but Lucian was encouraging her every step of the way. His determination to control the little details was actually helping her focus on her top priorities.

The freedom of not having to make one decision after another cleared her head into a state of purity she never experienced before. Her tasks were simple: focus on her schooling, rest, tend to Lucian—which was never a chore—and simply be.

It was a vacation from herself in a fundamental but intangible way she was quickly learning to live with. And she *liked* his choices, from the style of underwear to the menu. He knew her so well, knew what she liked, and appeared to understand exactly what she needed.

On Friday morning, Lucian arranged for Dugan to take her to visit Pearl. Evelyn complained, still feeling beaten down from her last visit with her mother, but he felt it was for the best that she replace her recent memories with better ones. In the end, she was glad he pushed her.

Pearl was quiet, somewhat withdrawn, but the presence of sullen doubt and jaded opinions helped to put Evelyn's world back on its proper axis. As always, her mother complained about her stay at the rehab as though she were an imprisoned criminal, voicing falsehoods of how good she used to have it on the streets.

Evelyn took stock of the increased thickness of her mother's wrists, the fullness of her hair, and the lack of sallowness in her skin. These were the evidence of better living. Lucian had done this as well. Her mother, who had been malnourished and withered since Evelyn could remember, was finally beginning to look like a somewhat healthy person. Her jaded, cynical opinions of the world said otherwise, as did her nonsensical ramblings that indicated mental illness, but Evelyn had grown used to such tendencies.

Nevertheless, Lucian had suggested setting Pearl up with a specialist capable of performing evaluations of her mental health and possibly getting her on additional medication. Evelyn agreed it wouldn't hurt to utilize the professionals at her mother's disposal, but it was still a lot to take in. Her mother was not normal and would always be a little bit broken. Seeing physical improvement at least made up for something.

Once her visit with Pearl was over, Evelyn saw that Lucian was again right. Seeing her mother had healed some of the hurt from her prior visit. Once back at the penthouse, she'd called Lucian and thanked him, telling him she'd like to see her again soon. Lucian seemed touched by her gratitude and wished her a good rest of the day. Next it was off to her lesson with Jason.

AS she sat, distracted by the clock, impatient for Lucian to return home, Jason read a page from the light chapter book they were working on. It was about a seal named Sam. Or was he a starfish? She wasn't paying much attention.

"Evelyn, it's your turn."

She looked away from the clock on the wall. "Oh. Sorry."

He laughed. "Just like the rest of my students. Here," he said, pointing to the paragraph they were on.

She fumbled over the words slowly, mispronouncing several. Jason never gave her the answers like she sometimes wished he would. Rather, he prompted her to take a second look and notice certain letter combinations. Evelyn easily became frustrated with her inability to simply read, but Jason had patience in spades.

"Very good," he said when she finished the paragraph.

He read the next one, and she admired the way his voice easily flowed over the words. She hoped one day she too could read so smoothly. It was as if he somehow predicted the tone in which the characters intended to speak. Her words always came out jagged and segmented in a way that made it difficult to comprehend the purpose of each sentence.

They worked for several hours and she was getting hungry. His phone vibrated quietly on the table. He glanced at it and she paused in her reading. "Keep going," he said, typing into his phone and putting it aside.

When she finished he shut the book. "We're done?" she asked.

"Looks that way. Lucian asked that I wrap things up."

"Oh." She should've never given him Jason's number.

"I'll be back tomorrow at ten, so no homework tonight."

"You're coming tomorrow?"

"Yes, but not again until Monday afternoon. I'd like to see you do the pages I circled in your workbook by then. And I have another assignment for you, a sort of project."

"Okay," she agreed.

"I want you to start texting. No abbreviations, real words only. You have a smartphone, so there's auto correct. Seeing the full spelling pop up will help with your recognition and increase your fluency. You'll start picking up on sight words from the first syllables. I want you to try to send a text every hour you're awake. Do you know how?"

She shook her head and he reached for her phone. He explained how to open the little speech bubble icon and plugged Lucian's name in from her contacts. "Once the message is opened, all you have to do is click on the line and type your text. Try writing 'On my way.'"

He slid her the phone and she searched the keys. "They aren't in order." Where the hell was the O?

"You'll get used to that after a while. Just take it one word at a time."

After several minutes of hunting for the right letters, she typed "On my wa," and then auto correct plugged in the *y* she didn't know went with "way."

"Good. Now hit Send."

She did, and her phone made a little *vip* sound that sent a little thrill through her. "I did it!"

"Yup." Jason stood and collected his things. Her phone whistled and she frowned at the screen. "Did he reply?"

She slid her thumb over the screen and there was a text from Lucian. "It says . . ." The words were big. "I can't read it."

Jason looked at the phone and frowned. "We'll have to tell him to start with smaller words. That first word is *anxiously*. You try reading the rest. Remember to break them down."

She sounded out the next word. "A-wait-ing you."

Jason smiled and she grinned as well, feeling her cheeks warm slightly. "Better get going."

They parted at the elevators and she traveled up to the penthouse suites. The private elevator announced her arrival with a soft chime and her phone whistled. Reaching in the pocket of her shorts, she withdrew the cell just as she slid her key into the door. It was another text from Lucian.

Stop

She stilled, knowing the word stop. The door shut behind her and her phone whistled again. Her feet remained planted in the entrance of the suite just by the coat closet.

Clothes off

Her lip curled in a half smile as her neck stretched, trying to spot him. His tie coiled in a circle on the small accent table to her right. He was home.

She removed her shirt and shorts and toed off her flip-flops. Her thumbs glided under the band of her panties, and her arms slid out of her bra. Lastly, she undid her ponytail.

Her fingers snatched up her phone from the table and texted back. It took forever to find the keys. She tried to type *done*, but the word didn't look right. So she went with a word she knew.

Off

She heard the soft buzz of his phone receiving the text and assumed he was at his desk. A moment later, her phone whistled.

Let me see

She smirked and left the phone on the table as she slowly walked into the sitting area. Lucian sat behind his mahogany desk, fingers steepled beneath his chin, collar undone. He looked handsome as hell.

"Hi."

His gaze traveled over her form. "You learned to text," he said, smiling.

"I did."

"I like it." He slid his chair back. Warm sunlight filtered through the enormous glass wall behind him, catching highlights in his ebony hair. "Come here."

Her bare feet pressed into the carpet as she stepped around his desk. Papers were piled haphazardly over the surface. Her body stood in the space just outside of the V of his knees. His gaze roamed up her legs and settled on her breasts. He didn't move, just watched her.

"Do you remember the first time we met?"

How could she forget? He terrified her. She thought he was a guest at the hotel and, because she had inadvertently knocked over some things on his desk, was going to get her fired. "Yes."

"I've left something for you in the guest room. Go put it on and come back here."

She turned and followed the hall to the spare room. When she entered, there was an object sitting on the bed in a pile of folded satin that looked like an animal. Approaching the bed, she saw it was a feather duster. She laughed.

Her fingers pushed it aside and lifted the satin, discovering a maid's uniform. It was nothing like the uniform she'd worn while employed at Patras. No, this was sinfully provocative.

The bodice was a whaleboned black corset. The skirt was more of a ballerina tutu made up of crinoline with a short lace apron tied up with ruched bows. Beneath the costume sat a matching lace bonnet and wide-net thigh highs topped with bows. Looking down, she spotted a very dangerous pair of platform pumps.

Is he kidding with the shoes?

She picked them up and her eyes widened. Clearly a man invented them. The heels reached from the tip of her middle finger to her wrist, easily over six inches. The soles were devil red. It simply wasn't natural for a foot to arch that far.

She sat on the bed and shimmied into the costume. Cool air

brushed her bare cheeks peeking out of the ruffled skirt as she pulled on each thigh high. Taking a deep breath, she slid her feet into the shoes. Someone could get a nosebleed at this altitude.

She grabbed her bonnet and wobbled over to the mirror. After fitting the band to her head and finding her balance she—*carefully*—walked back to the common area, grabbing her feather duster along the way.

She entered the room, and in her best French accent, she said, "*Bonjour*, Monsieur Patras. You called for housekeeping?" She didn't know where the French words came from. She supposed, after so many months at the hotel, she'd picked it up from some of the staff.

Great satisfaction filled her as his lips parted and he breathed, "Jesus."

She smiled. "Shall I dust for you?"

He cleared his throat and shifted his weight in his seat. "Yes. I'd like you to dust my desk."

Trying hard not to snap her neck or break an ankle, she did her best impression of a sexy walk. When she was within arm's length of him and his desk, she pouted. "Oh, but I have strict instructions not to touch Monsieur Patras's desk."

"You'll have to be careful not to make a mess."

She smiled over her shoulder and bent enough to give him a peek at her bare behind as she proceeded to dust around his many papers. A ghostlike touch traced up the inside of her leg, and she paused. Her body arched over the right side of the desk and she continued to dust. A sheaf of papers on the far left corner tumbled to the ground, and she stilled.

"You knocked over my papers," he said. She knew full well he deliberately pushed them over on purpose. "Better pick them up."

She lowered herself to the ground and crawled to the papers. After stacking them in some sort of order, she slid them onto the desk. "I'm so sorry, Monsieur. Perhaps I can make it up to you?"

He grinned. "How?"

"I'll do whatever you ask."

Raising an eyebrow, he said, "Take out my cock."

Her belly tightened as she crawled between his knees and undid his zipper. He was hard when she pulled him out. She looked to him for instruction.

"Put me in your mouth."

Leaning forward, she engulfed him with her mouth and proceeded to suck him off. He didn't touch her as she worked his flesh. When his length twitched over her tongue like he was about to come, he said, "Stop."

His cock slid from her lips as she settled back on her heels. Something hot and liquid tightened in the pit of her belly.

"Do you like sucking my cock, Ms. Keats?"

"Yes, sir."

He growled. "I'd like a scotch on the rocks."

She rose from the floor. Her shoes elevated her, and the netting of the stockings sensitized her legs. The short skirt rustled, and cool air touched her sex as she carefully sauntered to the bar. Fishing out three cubes of ice, she poured the amber liquid and carefully carried the glass back to the desk. She handed it to him, but he didn't take it.

"Straddle me."

Glancing at the desk, she looked back at him askance.

"Put it on the coaster." She did as instructed.

Balancing on one wobbly foot, she lifted her leg over his knees and lowered her body. He caught her hips and drew her close. His cock stood between them as he reached for her bodice and split the fabric wide with a quick tug. The satin material shredded to her bellybutton. She gasped and his hands cupped her breasts, fingers brushed over her nipples until they drew into sharp little points.

He growled and released her, reaching around for the glass

and taking a sip. Her eyes watched the curve of his throat, his Adam's apple slowly rising as he took a long swallow of scotch. He placed the glass back on the desk and leaned forward to capture her nipple in his mouth.

She hissed at the cool touch of his tongue and realized he'd stolen an ice cube from the glass. The brush of frozen water to her heated flesh sent chills up her spine and down her chest. She shivered and he chuckled as he moved to her other breast.

He played with her nipples until she felt like she might come. His fingers tugged and pulled at the nubs while his frosty mouth teased. She rocked over him, grinding against his cock, and he gripped her hips. "Are you stealing from me?"

She frowned. "What?"

"Were you just trying to steal an orgasm without my permission?"

"I'm sorry, sir."

His hips lifted and he tucked his cock away. "Stand up."

She trembled with anticipation. As she stood, the top of her uniform hung in tatters, leaving her breasts peeking out through the shreds of fabric.

"You are so beautiful, Evelyn. I don't even think you realize how stunning you are, which only adds to your beauty."

Her face heated. "Thank you. I think you're beautiful too."

He tugged her close and she lost her balance. The heat of his palm burned over her cheeks as he rubbed her ass. "You have an amazing ass." The smack took her by surprise. She gasped as heat spread over her. He rubbed the tender flesh and smacked again. Her sex clenched and she moaned. The third swat landed between her spread legs, his fingers grazing her wet lips. Fingers dragged over her skin and suddenly filled her.

He fucked her with his digits, using fast thrusts. She came in a matter of seconds, feeling her cream coat his fingers and crying out. His mouth slammed into hers. The kiss was greedy. His tongue took her mouth. Teeth pulled at lips. They became possessed by dark need.

The chair rolled over and papers fell. And then she was being lifted and pressed into the glass window. Her legs wrapped around his hips. Her weight leaned into the glass. His pants were again undone and dropped to his thighs. He filled her in one hard thrust.

There were various levels of their sex. Sometimes it was slow like summer rain. Sometimes it was intense like a winter storm that built gradually and ended in something beautiful. And then there was good old chaotic fucking. That's what he did to her. Like a tornado crashing into a hurricane, he swept in and changed everything.

His body beat at hers in smooth licks like a rushing brook over the bellies of rocks. Thunder built in his chest and they came in an eruption of cries. He broke her open, split her every nerve wide, and left her without a shred of cover: bare, exposed, sheltered in nothing more than him.

He breathed into her shoulder harshly, pinning her to the window. Her six-inch heels dangled at his back. Her lips pouted as she caught her breath.

"I've never had better service," he rasped and she laughed, tugging at his hair.

WITH a final sigh of satisfaction, Lucian collapsed beside her in the bed. It was now early morning. She was truly enjoying waking up beside him each morning.

Evelyn breathed deeply through a smile. She'd never slept with anyone else, but she doubted anyone was as good as Lucian.

He sighed. "Tonight should be interesting."

It was Jamie's surprise party at Lucian's sister's. "Are you not looking forward to it?"

"Hmm, looking forward to it? Not necessarily, but I'm sure we'll enjoy ourselves. I've made arrangements for you to get your hair and makeup done at the salon."

That was good. She wasn't very confident in her grooming abilities and would rather have a professional tell her what looked right. "Thank you."

He leaned in and kissed the arch of her cheek. "I'll be crossing paths with you at some point. I need a haircut."

Her fingers ran through his dark hair flopped over his forehead. Strands of silver shined in the thick black mass, giving him a salt-and-pepper look at his temples. "Your hair *is* rather long at the moment."

"I'm getting too old for longer hair. Makes me look like I'm clinging to my faded youth."

She laughed and shoved him. "Shut up. You are *not* old."

"Older than you." His lips tickled the soft skin behind her ear and her toes curled.

"I like that you're older."

"You do?"

"Yes. I don't see you as old, though. You're . . . distinguished. I see your age as credibility. You deal with many people in business who are older than you. I think if you were my age you wouldn't be taken as seriously. People my age don't have the success you've accumulated."

"Ah, but I was worth millions in my early twenties."

"It's not the same. That was your family's legacy. This"—she waved her hand outward—"the hotel and everything you've created, that was fueled by what's in here." Her hand rested over his bare chest. "Not what was given to you."

His lips curled in a soft smile, and his thick lashes lowered slightly. His voice became husky. "What you just said, the way you put that, it makes me feel good. It's nice to hear someone give credit to the man behind the name for a change."

She curled into him and nestled her nose against the stubble covering his throat. "You deserve it. You work very hard."

"I'll accept some of the credit, but not all. My family has contributed generations of visionaries to my success. Their success gave me the means to make my own."

Her fingers brushed over his hair and tucked it behind his ear. "Just don't forget to give credit to yourself from time to time."

"Do you see how it works?" he whispered, dragging his fingers over her hip. "They gave me the means and I had the ambition to do great things with those means. You're ambitious too, Evelyn. I like giving you the means to become something great. I believe you will someday be my wisest investment."

Her breath caught. He hadn't said it, but for the first time her mind slipped away from her, as though his thoughts snuck into her head and hijacked her own. She saw a startling vision of herself standing on the lush green grass at the estate, just in front of his mother's lilacs. Riots of purple danced behind her in the perfumed breeze as she called for Lucian.

But Lucian wasn't who came to her in that vision. No, it was a small boy with startling dark hair and crystal blue eyes, much like her own. The little boy ran to her and threw his arms around her waist, pressing his face to her abdomen, which was heavy and swollen under her clothes.

"Evelyn? You all right?"

"What?" The image vanished.

"Your cheeks got all flushed and you smiled in a way I never saw before."

"I . . . I was just thinking."

He smirked and pressed his lips to hers. Keeping them there, he whispered, "I like seeing you smile. You do it much more than you used to."

They wound up rolling around in bed, sharing soft whispers and gentle, teasing caresses that eventually led to more, until it was time for her to rush out the door to see Jason. She hadn't had time to shower, and through her entire lesson she found the scent of Lucian clinging to her skin incredibly distracting.

When she returned to the penthouse, Lucian was gone. She took a long shower, and as she was drying off there was a text from him on her phone.

Salon at 1:00. See you there. Love you.

She smiled once she carefully read the text. She sounded out the word *bossy* until auto correct got it.

Yes, bossy pants. Love you too.

When she arrived at the salon, she was immediately greeted with smiles and ushered to the back. The staff was wonderful. They always made her feel like royalty, which was so far beyond her wildest fantasies, she wondered if such treatment would ever stop feeling surreal.

Her hair was twirled into hundreds of tightly coiled curls and plastered around her face, which had been made up in a way that transformed her. The makeup artist had somehow made her lips into sharp peaks of red and her eyes seemed wider, accented with long lashes beneath narrow, groomed brows. She looked nothing like she normally did when done up, but didn't question their expertise.

Lucian appeared in the reflection of the gilded mirror. Her belly pinched with excitement at the sight of him. His hair was damp and parted to perfection, long locks gone. She smiled. "Aren't you handsome."

The hairstylist greeted him and stepped aside as Lucian kissed her cheek. "You look stunning. Here."

A small red velvet box, the size of a book, was placed in her lap. "What's this?"

"For tonight. Open it."

Her fingers flipped up the ornate bronze clasp, and the box opened with a creak. White netting and ivory-sequined detail filled the faded velvet. It had a scent of time, a little musty with the trace of oiled perfume. The scent reminded her of an empty church. The fabric pulled like a delicate web as she lifted it with her fingers. "What is it?"

"It's for tonight."

The hairstylist, Fernando, admired the gift. "Very nice. Authentic?"

"Yes," Lucian said. "From an antiques dealer outside of the city."

"May I?" Fernando asked.

Evelyn still wasn't sure what it was. It looked like a decorated sack of sorts. She handed it to the hairdresser, who examined it admiringly and then placed it on her head. It was a hat or a band. The peculiar way he had done her hair suddenly came together. The reflection blinking back at her was a photograph from back in time.

Lucian smiled. "It's a speakeasy party."

"Speakeasy?" She knew that word. "Like from the days of Prohibition?"

"Yes. Everyone will be dressed in costumes from the 1920s era."

"A costume party?" *How fun!* She'd never been to anything like that.

"Yes. I have your dress upstairs. I'll wait while Fernando finishes up."

Lucian disappeared into the front of the salon, and Fernando pinned the delicate cap over her hair. She looked like she'd fallen back in time. It was amazing how he'd transformed her with a few curls and some fancy makeup.

Lucian escorted her back to the penthouse. When they entered the master bedroom, a gorgeous ivory gown was hanging from the sconce. She gasped. It was . . . majestic.

"Do you like it?"

"I love it. It's so luxurious." The soft material was like layered wisps of clouds running through her fingers, weighted with tiny beads. Detailed bits of lace showed here and there, and the vintage accents told of tired fingers and handmade thoughtfulness. She decided she liked this era.

"It was worn by a famous singer in the twenties. There are photographs of her performing on stage during that time."

"Oh, Lucian . . ."

"Let me help you put it on."

The material was so light, but layered in such a way the dress was weighted. She slipped out of her clothing, careful not to muss her hair, and he helped her with the dress. It slid over her bare skin like a silken sheath.

"Do I need a bra?"

"No. Nothing underneath."

The gathered fabric hung heavily over her shoulders. Cool beads weighed on her skin. He buttoned up the back and turned her to the full-length mirror, his knuckles dragging seductively from her shoulder to her elbow.

It was spectacular. Sheer layers of ivory draped over her unfettered breasts, resembling the attire of a Greek goddess. The scoop over her chest was wide. Modesty was protected with an intricate shield of lace, beaded in swirls of roses and white peacock feathers.

Beneath the swoop of the neckline, the dress fit to her hips, mimicking the same intricate lace covering the span of her breasts. Midthigh, a seam traced to her legs, and billowy layers of the softest sheer silk gathered and poured to the ground like the clouded mist of a waterfall.

"You put the original wearer's beauty to shame," he said.

This was, perhaps, the first time she ever—truly—agreed with him in terms of her beauty. She looked . . . picturesque. A shock of vanity had her blushing. She cleared her throat. "What are you wearing?"

"A tux. Here, I have shoes and gloves for you."

He bent to his knees and slid a pair of ivory closed toed shoes onto her feet. He carefully tightened the buckle and stood. "I'll be dressed in a few minutes, and then we can be on our way."

He disappeared into the closet, and she allowed herself a few vain moments to admire her reflection. Lucian emerged and she turned, drawing in a long breath. He had taken all of two minutes to trump her beauty.

Broad shoulders were encased in black. The cut of his jacket was different than his usual tuxedo. This one had tails. A starched white collar peeked over his white bow tie and a pristine, snowy vest with diamond-encrusted buttons covered his chest. "Shall we?"

"You look fantastic."

Paying the compliment no mind, he filled his pockets with the usual items and mumbled a quick thank-you. As they walked through the lobby, guests stopped to stare. It was quite an experience. Rather than fidget and worry what onlookers were thinking, she held her chin up with newfound confidence she couldn't recall discovering.

As they stepped onto the red runner with gold tassels, she looked for Dugan. He wasn't there, nor was the limo. A Patras attendant beamed and opened the door to a sleek Mercedes that had to be close to a hundred years old.

"You rented an old car?"

"No. I own it."

It was the color of the darkest chocolate. Long fenders bent like shapely legs. In her mind the car was definitely female. The wheels had polished white walls. Rounded headlights protruded from the chrome grille. It was all body with only a little cockpit left for passengers. If there was a roof, it was hidden. Caramel leather seats beckoned behind the slight metal-framed windshield.

"This may be the prettiest car I've ever seen."

He squeezed her hand through her satin glove. "Get your license and it's yours."

She gaped at him. The doorman opened the passenger door—from the front, rather than the back, the way car doors usually opened. She slid in and her dress shushed against the soft seat. He tucked her gown into the car and gently shut the door. Lucian slid in beside her. The car was already purring.

"Ready?"

She smiled and nodded and they were soon on their way. The summer heat cooled as it filtered around the windshield to tickle her hair and tease her shoulders. Driving a car without a top was loud in a hypnotic way. Lucian handled the car like he did everything else, with expertise and refined control.

She grinned as pedestrians stopped to admire them. A few people took pictures with their phones as they waited at traffic lights and for the first time in a long time, Evelyn thought about the paparazzi.

Lucian had been very careful to keep the papers out of sight. Trepidation curbed her curiosity as far as their cutting words went, so she didn't mind his keeping the news clippings out of her sight. She knew the horrid things they were saying linked back to real shame, and she'd rather not witness how badly her personal business was being exploited when there wasn't really a solution to stop their attacks. Lucian said he'd handle it, and she trusted him to do just that but knew the media hype wouldn't vanish overnight.

They were still making headlines, and the media was making all sorts of assumptions about her and her past. Lucian had given a statement to his PR team, admitting only that he was in love and the media would have to wait for further details. He'd told her it was up to her, if she wanted to offer explanations for her presence in his life, but he remained very protective, constantly reminding her that no explanation was required.

Beyond the distraction of their own personal relationship seemed to be rumors regarding Lucian's business relationship with the green company he'd been trying to work with. She didn't know much about his professional doings, but she hoped both issues were resolved sooner rather than later. It surprised her that someone would have the guts to face off with Patras Industries. However, the opposition wasn't all that brave if they continued to keep their identity secret. The moment Lucian discovered who was leaking information about his deal, Evelyn had no doubt all opposition would crumble.

When they arrived at Toni's building, her excitement took a tumultuous turn, swirling in her belly at the unexpected. A valet complimented Lucian on his car and took the keys as a doorman greeted them. They took the elevator to the top floor, and soft music could be heard from behind Toni's door. Lucian knocked, and she was surprised to see Dugan answer.

"Mr. Patras. Ms. Keats."

"Dugan."

He didn't let them in. He was also dressed in a tux. A white scarf was draped over his shoulders, and she spotted the hints of a holster beneath the breast of his coat. "The password . . ." he said, holding the door in place.

Lucian said, *"Lá breithe shona duit."*

Dugan nodded as he opened the door, and Evelyn's jaw unhinged. She'd never been inside Toni's condo, but she was sure this was not the way it usually looked.

The walls were draped in heavy damask fabrics drawn back with thick cords of gold. Crystal chandeliers hung from the high ceilings, and a jazz quartet played in the corner. Boxes of booze and hay were stacked with well-planned detail to look haphazardly smuggled. A sleek bar filled the corner of the grand living room. The bartender was dressed in vintage attire, his dress shirt complete with vintage bands around his shirtsleeves.

Palms of ostrich feathers topped the well-dressed tables. Polished silver accented each place. There were crowded counters set with dealers and games. Lucian squeezed her hand. She'd been standing there staring.

"Toni does love to entertain," he mumbled. She turned to him and simply shook her head, speechless. "Shall we find my sister and say hello?"

"What did you say to Dugan to get in?"

"It's a speakeasy. I had to give the password of course. I said, *Lá breithe shona duit.* It's Gaelic for 'Happy Birthday.'"

"Because Jamie's Irish?"

"Yes."

As they made their way into the room, Evelyn was in awe. The place was like a portal back in time. Every guest had taken time to dress the part. Not a single detail was overlooked.

As Lucian said hello to acquaintances and made introductions, she took the time to envy Toni's ability to do something so grand for Jamie. Evelyn hoped to someday do something along these lines for Lucian. She'd ask Toni for help of course, because she could never be this creative.

When they found Lucian's sister, she squealed. "You guys look incredible!" Toni's gold dress was so beaded, every move she made jostled the long strands. She looked lovely. Her dark hair was down in smooth waves. A feathered gold band wrapped around her forehead and her lips were as red as Evelyn's.

She pulled her in for an affectionate hug. "What do you think? Do you think Shamus will like it?"

"As always, you've outdone yourself, Antoinette. I'm sure he'll be surprised."

She beamed and bounced giddily, her short dress dancing about her curves. "Come on, Ev, let's get a drink."

Lucian's hand tightened over her gloved fingers. She glanced back at him. Drawing her close, he pressed a kiss to her cheek and whispered, "I have plans for tonight. Three drinks and that's it. Pace yourself."

Evelyn narrowed her eyes, but didn't argue. He was in charge and she was a lightweight. Besides, she'd much rather see what he had in store for her than get plastered. Last time she had too much to drink she'd made a fool of herself.

As they went to the bar, Evelyn forgot she was in Toni's home. Everything was so grandiose. The splendid guests laughed and the quartet played. Even the bartender seemed to be a bit in character. Toni tittered on about how anxious she was for Jamie to arrive. Soon a guest Evelyn didn't know pulled Lucian's sister away.

Servers began to butler hors d'oeuvres, and she scanned the now-full condo for Lucian. When she didn't see him right away, she stepped closer to the wall, trying to blend with a feathery palm. There had to be over a hundred guests there.

She took note of every man connected to a tuxedo, looking for his handsome face. When she spotted dark hair, she smiled then stilled as the man turned slowly from the woman he was speaking with. It wasn't Lucian, but he also was no stranger.

Slade.

Her smile faltered as those piercing blue eyes connected with hers. He tipped his head ever so slightly in acknowledgement of her presence and she tightened her lips. Not only had that man never liked her, he'd betrayed Lucian. She was half tempted to march over to him and tell him just how unwanted his acknowledgement of her presence was. Screw him.

As always, he seemed to pay her no mind. He turned and she watched his head move as though he were looking for someone. She had a feeling they were searching for the same person.

"He's on his way up! Everyone, quiet!" Toni yelled.

The guests and quartet hushed as everyone collectively turned to the door where Dugan waited. Just then, she spotted Lucian stepping in from a balcony door she hadn't noticed. A man whis-

pered in his ear and Lucian nodded, his eyes scanning the area. He
was looking for her most likely. She turned back to Slade and saw
that he had indeed been searching for Lucian. His gaze welded to
Evelyn's lover in a way that had her bristling protectively.

She abandoned her feathered shelter and found her way to
Lucian's side. He smiled and took her hand. "Alistair, this is
Evelyn."

"Pleased to meet you, Evelyn. I've heard lovely things about you."

The man clasped her gloved fingers lightly and she replied in
kind, though she'd never heard of him before.

There was a knock, and rather than ask for a password, Dugan
opened the door wide. The room bellowed a heartfelt "Surprise!"
and Jamie's jade eyes went wide, his fair skin flaming a bright
shade of red. Toni clapped and laughed, then threw her arms
around him. He smiled tightly and gently pushed her away.

"Well," he said, with a grin that seemed slightly forced. "This
is certainly unexpected."

The guests laughed and Toni wound her arm through his and
escorted him through the crowd. The chatter continued to es-
calate at a gentle roar. Evelyn caught sight of Isadora and whispered to Lucian that she'd be right back.

She made her way through the crowd, and Isadora smiled when
she saw her. Lucian's sisters were so very different. While Toni was
a bottle of energy and youth, Isadora was a tower of elegance.

She wore an emerald gown trimmed in gold. Her dark hair
was slicked back into a simple bun that only a woman with such
elegant bone structure could pull off. She didn't have the acces-
sories some of the other women opted to wear. Yet, in Evelyn's
mind she was the most stunning woman in the room. It struck her
as odd that Isadora was always alone.

"Isadora," she greeted.

Lucian's sister smiled and kissed her cheek. "Evelyn, you look
stunning. Are you enjoying yourself?"

"Yes. This is incredible."

"Toni loves to put on a party. I think Shamus would like to strangle her, but he'll get over it. She means well."

They laughed and chatted about the guests and touched on her plans to visit Europe in the upcoming months. There was something mysterious about Lucian's older sister, but not in a suspicious way. She radiated kindness and always seemed to put Evelyn at ease, whereas Lucian's younger sister seemed to fill her with a sense of urgency.

The Patras siblings were like seasons. Lucian was beautiful, but could freeze someone with his icy stares and intense moods. He was the winter while Toni was summer, vibrant and bursting with light. She couldn't decide if Isadora was spring or autumn. While she was nurturing and maternal, there seemed something innately sad about her. That unnamable sadness was what reminded Evelyn of fall.

Evelyn finished her drink and traded it for some hors d'oeuvres. Isadora had nothing but kind things to say about everyone she appraised. Toni was ushering Jamie through the melee. Her laughter could be heard from time to time over the quartet. Deciding to find Lucian, Evelyn excused herself.

Strangers smiled at her, and many men chivalrously stepped aside for her to pass. Cool vents rippled the dressed walls and when she peeked out on the balcony, the sultry air seemed stifling. Guests partook in cigars and voices bloomed with liquor-scented rowdiness. Lucian was nowhere to be found.

She made her way back through the living room and searched the bar. He wasn't there, but while she waited, the bartender made her another drink. It was some sort of signature drink made with crushed fruit and gin. She didn't really care for it, but drank it anyway. She noticed a door she hadn't seen before and decided to look there for Lucian.

Making her way back through the crowd, she paused at the

entrance. The last thing she wanted to do was inadvertently go trespassing in Toni's private space. She decided she'd use the excuse of looking for the restroom if anyone questioned her.

Her gloved fingers touched the knob and the door glided open with little effort. It hadn't been closed tightly. She stilled when she heard a deep voice whispering.

"I will apologize again and again. I see now what you saw in her. I was wrong. All I can say is that my intentions were at one point honorable and somehow got twisted into something selfish along the way."

She frowned and remained hidden behind the door. Her feet casually stepped closer to the heavy curtain suspended about a foot from the wall so not to appear as if she were eavesdropping, although she was.

"I'm not losing any sleep at night, Slade. I suggest you cut your losses and move on. What's done is done. I'll continue to tolerate your presence out of respect for my sisters and Shamus, but other than the lingering business ties we have, our association is over."

Her ear cocked to attention at Lucian's statement.

"Lucian, please. We were friends. I made a mistake."

Lucian's curt voice rang of exasperation. "I told you I loved her then and I love her now. You betrayed me and nearly cost me the only person who has ever made me feel this way. You don't know what it is to fear losing someone you love with an intensity that eats up every hour of your day. What either of us felt for Monique doesn't compare to what I feel for Evelyn. I can overlook what you've done, but I'll never forgive it completely. Until you love someone the way I love her, I don't expect you to understand that. Now, if you'll excuse me."

The sound of footsteps had her jumping back behind the curtain. Lucian passed in a blur of black and she heard Slade sigh and mumble something. Enough. Striding out from the shadows, she stepped through the narrowly cracked door and shut it quietly.

Slade's head jerked up at the sound of company. She expected to see those stormy blue eyes and experience the jolt of shame his disdainful scowls usually provoked in her, but she didn't. The whites surrounding those blue irises shimmered and appeared slightly pink in hue. He cleared his throat and quickly blinked and looked away.

"Evelyn. Lucian just left." His voice was grave, but curt. She was clearly being dismissed.

"I know. I heard you talking."

He turned back to her, all signs of being humane gone, replaced with the hard mask he usually looked down at her with. She waited for him to say something, but he didn't. He just glared at her, intimidating her, but she didn't let it show.

The room was some sort of den. A desk sat in the corner with a laptop closed on the surface. Club chairs perched around a modernized gas fireplace. This was Toni's usual style, she assumed. Evelyn entered the space with a show of courage. Slade's days of making her feel unwelcome were over.

"You know," she said in a soft but steady voice as she ran her hand over the back of a plush red chair. "While I appreciate you helping Parker, I hope someday he betrays you the same way you betrayed your partner. I hope you feel what it truly is to be the victim of someone else's ill-intentioned motives."

He sighed and looked to the ceiling as though he'd allow her this moment to say what she needed to say, as if it were her due.

She swallowed and refused to take her eyes off of him. "You decided not to like me from the first time you met me. It didn't matter who I was or where I was from. You never gave me a chance and never denied it. Well, I have news for you. Your opinions are worth less than dog shit, not just to me, but now to Lucian as well. You meddled in our lives and cost yourself a valuable friendship. That's your loss. But you also managed to cost *me* a friendship too, and I hope Lucian never forgives you, because I can be selfish too. I think you're nothing more than dressed-up scum. And those people you pretend to help at the shelter, but turn your snide nose up at, they have more right to the graces of this world than you'll ever deserve. I don't know what you want from Lucian, but leave him alone. He doesn't need friends better suited as enemies in his life."

She turned and he said, "Scout."

She stilled but wouldn't face him. She'd said what she needed to say, and now adrenaline was causing sweat to gather under the silk of her gloves.

"You don't understand," he whispered. "I never meant to hurt you."

The audacity. She pivoted, the motion charged with outrage. "You must think I'm stupid. Your sole intention was *to hurt me*. You humiliated me, exposed me, and manipulated me, every chance you got—"

"Only because you had what I wanted."

"What? His time? His ear? I never tried to take advantage of him or what he could offer, but you dove at the chance to make it seem that way, thinking I would trade him in for some other man with money if the benefits were in my favor. Unlike everyone else in this world, I'd take him with nothing at all. I love *him*. The rest is just fluff."

He nodded, and she didn't understand the tired expression on his face. "I'm glad you feel that way." His tone and expression didn't ring true with his words. "Too many people see the money and prestige before the man."

"And you don't?" she asked indignantly. Slade's professional life was no doubt suffering since Lucian had cut him off.

"No," he rasped. "I never did." The quiet confession sounded raw on his lips, as if it had to travel from somewhere deep in his soul.

Her face slackened as her lips parted. Suddenly she saw something she doubted anyone else saw in this man, not even Lucian, not even Jamie. She'd met a myriad of people in her life, and where she was from, most hid their vulnerabilities as carefully as they hid food, money, or drugs. But she always had a gift for seeing what others missed. That's why they called her Scout.

"Oh my God," she breathed. It was all suddenly so clear. "This has nothing to do with your grief over Monique or your hatred for me. It's *him*."

He cleared his throat and looked away. He didn't deny the accusation.

Her lips parted as her heart beat against her ribs like a caged bird. "You're in love with him."

Sharp blue eyes sliced into her, and she knew her statement to be true as a slight flush showed under his collar.

"She was just a convenient cover for you, and when you lost her you lost him." Lucian never showed any signs of being interested in men. But Slade must have hoped.

"I cared for Monique very much," he argued unconvincingly.

"But not as much as you cared for him."

As he swallowed, his Adam's apple made a slow journey up and down, traversing the long line of his throat. "He doesn't know," he rasped.

Yes, she believed he didn't. Tilting her head, she quietly said, "You could have told him. He loved you like a brother. You could've told him and saved your friendship."

He nodded sadly. "But I didn't, and that will be my regret to live with for the rest of my life."

How did two men entertain a relationship with one woman for years and not know one of them was bisexual? "Is it just Lucian or have there been other men?" She shook her head. "Sorry, I shouldn't have asked that. It's none of my business."

His shoulders lifted and he let out an audible breath. "None of it matters now."

How had she gone from hating this man to suddenly pitying

him in the span of a minute? Perhaps it was because she knew what it was to love Lucian Patras and not have him.

"You played a part in taking him from me," she said fiercely. "I know what it is to love him and not have him. I actually can empathize with you. Maybe that makes me an idiot. But I'm not some prattling little girl you and so many people think I am. So let me make this clear. I'm sorry you will never have the person you love, but he's *mine*. I won't share him and I won't take kindly to anyone who tries to take him from me, ever again."

He nodded. "For the record, if I thought you were just some ditsy piece I never would've felt threatened by you, Scout. You're strong. You have scruples. And you tell it like it is. I saw it in you the first time I met you, and that's why I panicked. You're everything he needs, deserves, and wants."

She didn't like getting compliments from people she didn't trust. They were usually backhanded and she tensed at the niceness, awaiting the sting. When it didn't come, she simply said, "Thank you."

The door opened and they both turned. Lucian stepped in and scowled. "What the hell is this?"

"Nothing. We were just talking," Slade said, his voice again cold and emotionless. She couldn't imagine living such an act.

Lucian came to her side and placed his arm protectively around her. He gazed at her as though appraising her emotions.

"Everything's fine. I was looking for the restroom and got lost," she covered.

He glared at Slade then whispered to her, "It's the fourth door down the hall. I'll meet you there in a few minutes."

She nodded and left, but paused at the door. Slade didn't get a chance to explain. Lucian's voice was a low growl. "Stay the hell away from her."

"Lucian—"

"I don't give a fuck about your explanations. I don't want you talking to her. End of story." At the sound of his retreating steps, she lifted her gown and quickly found her way to the restroom.

The rest of the evening passed in a surreal succession of events. Lucian never left her side and there were no more signs of Slade. There was dancing, cake, and plenty of drinking, but she never had her third. Lucian was overly attentive and seemed curious about what she and Slade said to each other. She wasn't sure if she should tell him.

Part of her felt sorry for the friendship lost, but the part of her that sometimes missed Parker and knew they would never be friends like they once were resented Slade Bishop for playing a part in that and hoped he'd rot in misery.

Then there was a very insecure part of her she didn't want to face. A part that worried if Lucian knew, he might leave her. Perhaps he harbored similar feelings. She dismissed that worry quickly, but insecurities lingered. The part of her that was never sure she was good enough wasn't entirely convinced.

At the end of the evening she was tired. The ride home was peaceful. Her head rested on the soft leather seat as the world buzzed by in a breezy wash of black sky. It wasn't until they reached the highway that she realized they weren't heading back to the hotel. "Where are we going?"

"The estate."

She frowned at his clipped tone. Trying to make light conversation, she asked, "Did you give Jamie his gift?" They hadn't opened presents, but there were stacks and stacks of beautifully wrapped packages sitting around by the time the party was over.

"I left the keys in a gift box with the other presents."

"Didn't you want to see him open it?"

"No. I know he'll like it."

She would've liked to have seen the car. No matter how he explained it, she couldn't imagine it. "Oh."

He didn't seem to be in the mood for conversation. She scooted closer and he gently rested his hand on her knee in between shifting gears. When they arrived at the estate, she was ready to pass out. Her hair smelled like summer wind and her cheeks were slightly chilled.

Lucian opened her door and escorted her to the front of the house. Lucy didn't greet them, which was odd, but she assumed that was because it was nearly two in the morning.

Once inside, she slipped off her shoes. They dangled from her fingers as they made a silent stroll up the grand staircase. In the master bedroom, they quietly slid out of their clothes. Lucian helped her from her gown and she shivered as he hung it in the closet.

He emerged from the walk-in and tossed a satin bag on the bed. He was already in his silk sleeping pants. His expression was unreadable. She wished he'd say something.

When he spoke, his words did nothing to relieve the awkwardness that accompanied them since leaving the party. "On your belly."

She blinked and eyed the satin bag.

"Do I need to repeat myself?"

There was a bite to his words and she frowned. "No," she whispered and climbed on the bed.

The thick down comforter was cool beneath her weight. Her nipples tightened as she lowered herself. Her arms lifted to rest above her head in the plush pillows. The soft whisper of Lucian stripping away his pants came just before the bed dipped under his weight.

Gentle lips pressed into her spine and kissed a trail down to the backs of her thighs. Her body reacted, but her mind detached. Why wasn't he speaking to her? The little satin satchel disappeared, and there was a snap followed by cool liquid being drizzled over her creases.

His finger massaged the oil over her back entrance and something inside of her panicked. Not because he intended to take her this way, but because he'd done little to acknowledge it was she he was taking. As he hoisted her hips off the bed and his thighs pressed into hers, her mind began to play tricks on her.

Was this because he saw Slade and this was what seeing him made Lucian crave? Was he being silent because he was imagining someone else? His fingers fondled her sex. Outwardly she breathed and reacted the way her body normally responded to his touch, but inwardly she tensed.

When his cock pressed at her tight entrance she gasped suddenly. "No!"

He stilled. "What's wrong?" He sounded genuinely worried.

She quickly crawled away and faced him, only after she'd snatched a pillow to cover herself. She was on the verge of tears. "I don't want to do that!"

His head tilted in confusion. "You usually enjoy *that*."

Her head shook and she swallowed. "I don't want to do that now."

"Why?" He sounded frustrated.

"I just . . . don't."

"That's not an answer. You're supposed to be honest with me at all times, Evelyn."

Because I'm afraid you're thinking of him. "I don't know why."

"Yes, you do."

"Can we just do something else?"

He frowned then his expression softened with concern. "Did I hurt you the last time?"

"No. I just . . ." The frown was back. "Please."

He appraised her for a long moment. "You aren't telling me something. You've been acting strange ever since I found you in the den with Slade. What did he say to you?"

"Nothing."

"Too fast, Evelyn. Now I know you're lying."

"I told him to leave you alone and that he didn't deserve your friendship."

His lip twitched as his brows shot up. "You were defending me?"

"Well, yeah. Someone has to."

He chuckled and looked down. His finger traced over her knee and slowly snagged the fringe of the pillow covering her. He pulled it away and tossed it to the floor. "I appreciate the sentiment, but would rather you leave that sort of thing to me. I don't trust Slade and prefer you to keep your distance. Now, tell me what else is going on."

She hunched into the pillows and looked away. His strong fingers clasped her chin and turned her so she was again facing him. He gave her a stern look.

Quietly, she admitted, "You weren't talking to me. It felt distant. I didn't like it."

He exhaled and seemed to sag a little. "I'm sorry. I was irritated because I couldn't find you and when I did, you were with the last person I wanted to see you talking to. I'll let it go."

She nodded and whispered, "Okay."

He climbed over her and pressed his lips to hers. "I still want your ass." She stiffened and he drew back. "What the hell is going on, Evelyn? The truth now."

Her breasts lifted with each deep breath. "Why do you want to have sex with me that way?"

Half his face tightened. "Why the hell not? Because I like it and so do you. *Why* are you questioning me when you should be submitting to me?"

"I'm not a puppet."

He threw up his hands. "Goddamn it, Evelyn. Don't pull this shit. You know that isn't what I want."

This is why she knew she couldn't be submissive all the time, because there would be days like this where submitting to him would feel demeaning, and her insecurities would run rampant in her brain and make her second-guess everything she knew about him. "Not tonight."

His eyes narrowed. "Are you calling checkmate?"

"If I have to."

Lips thin, he finally said, "Fine." He stood and pulled on his pants.

"Where are you going?"

"When you're ready to be honest with me about what's going on, I'll be down in the library."

"Lucian, don't leave. I don't want to fight."

"I asked for your honesty and surrender, Evelyn. That includes your secrets. I don't keep secrets from you. I don't appreciate you being secretive with me."

He turned and as he was about to walk out the door and leave her there, she blurted, "He's in love with you."

He stilled and slowly turned. "Excuse me?"

Her throat was dry as she swallowed. "Slade. He's in love with you."

"I think you misunderstood—"

She shook her head quickly. "No. He admitted it the moment I said it. He's in love with you. It was never Monique. His grief was partly for her, but mostly because she was the only link to being intimate with you."

His face contorted. "Slade and I were never intimate. We shared her. It wasn't like that."

"I know, but he hoped that would change."

"That's insane. I've known Slade almost my entire life. He's been with countless women—"

"If you don't believe me, Lucian, ask him. But you asked for the truth and that's what I'm giving you."

His expression fell as his eyes drifted as though he were seeing events of the past. "I'm not gay." The words were whispered as if he were clarifying things for himself, excusing the entire confession based on his own preferences. Relief filled her at the uttered assurance, but she knew that all along, didn't she?

"I know."

He looked at her, eyes sad. "And he's never said anything . . ."

She swallowed again. "If he did . . . would it have changed anything?"

Shaking his head emphatically, he looked utterly shocked. "No, but it would've explained a lot."

"I don't think he ever really wished to hurt you, Lucian."

His face hardened as his dark gaze locked with hers. "The road to hell is paved with good intentions, Evelyn. I couldn't give two shits about what he did to me. The moment he hurt you, our friendship was over."

She didn't know what to say to that. "Does knowing his feelings change anything for you?"

"Hell no. He's a grown man who needs to deal with his shit on his own time. I—" He was suddenly silent. "Is this why you said no?"

She met his gaze. He was furious. "I didn't know if you knew and were maybe . . ." She shrugged, and he turned and cursed.

"Evelyn," he sighed and came to sit on the bed. "First of all, when I make love to you it's always you I see. Second, I never have, nor ever will I, want a man. I'm simply not that way. Since I met you it's only been you. I will never make love to you and think of anyone else, man or woman. And third, the reason I enjoy fucking you that way is because I enjoy the psychological release it gives us. You seemed tense. I wanted to get you out of your head."

"But, Lucian . . . this was different." She shook her head trying to pin down what was actually bothering her. "The intimacy wasn't there."

His face softened. "I'm sorry, love. I didn't mean to come off cold. I was intent on getting you to relax. The last thing I wanted was for you to feel anxious."

His dominance didn't usually bother her like it had tonight. Perhaps he was stressed, but no matter what he was going through, if he wanted the responsibility of her submission, something she wasn't altogether sure she was prepared to surrender, he needed to communicate with her.

She liked losing herself to him in moments of passion. She didn't know if she'd ever allow herself to completely let go, however. He swore she was submissive, but she was too mesmerized with the idea of her independence. This trial period she was humoring him with wouldn't make it another day if he didn't explain himself along the way, especially when she was feeling vulnerable.

"You can't expect me to surrender if you don't explain your intentions."

His eyes flashed to hers. "I suppose I could be a bit more clear. You usually love when I touch you like that."

"There are always exceptions, Lucian. Some days I like soft, some days I like hard, but *every day* I like to feel I'm entitled to know what's going on between us."

"Understood," he said, running his hand over her foot. "Do you understand *why* anal sex has a different effect on you, Evelyn?"

She frowned. "I don't know what you mean."

He took her hand. "Deny it all you want, but you *are* submissive at heart. You get bogged down with the outside worries of your world and need to let go, but don't know how. When I take you—*truly take you*—you surrender those burdens. Anal sex just happens to be a very cut-and-dried way for a man to dominate a woman. If you pay attention to the times you crave it, it's usually when you're highly stressed."

He was right. "Oh." She stared as his fingers wrapped around her ankle. They tightened until his touch was all she could feel.

"Perhaps I'm just feeling a bit . . . delicate . . . emotionally. I don't like feeling the weight of other issues between us."

His head tilted as he studied her for a long minute. His fingers traced down her neck. "I don't like that feeling either. I think we were both feeling the presence of other issues tonight and we should have talked it through before we went to bed. I'm sorry I didn't handle the situation more delicately. I'll try to be more aware. I know you're giving a lot of yourself, and I need to look deeper than I do sometimes."

Her heart raced. There was something so sexy about an understanding Lucian. If he could truly be that intuitive it made the temptation of surrender so much greater. This trial period was good. They were both learning from the experience.

He pulled her close and continued to stroke her bare skin. "You see, it doesn't have to be that way, but I know you take pleasure from it as do I. It's the adrenaline rush we get from the act, me exerting my strength over you, and you being placed in a vulnerable position where your only choice is surrender, but the point is, you choose it. That choice is never taken from you, Evelyn."

Perhaps she just needed to hear that.

Easing up, he gripped her other ankle and tugged her down the bed so she was lying flat on her back as he towered over her, a mischievous glint in his eyes. "Push me away," he whispered.

She moved to press her palm against his chest, but he caught it before she made contact. Her arm was forced into the pillows and he kissed her. She gasped and her heart pounded, the mood shifting that quickly.

"Do you feel how badly I want you, Evelyn?" He dragged the weight of his cock pressing through his pants against her sex.

She sucked in a breath and he said, "Push me away again."

She used her other hand. This time, when she made contact with his shoulder, his hand clamped down on her sex, cupping her tightly. She gasped and her fingers curled around his bicep.

He chuckled, his eyes gone smoky. "You see? You're supposed to be telling me no, but your body's crying yes. Go ahead. Exert yourself. Deny me. I'll make you beg for my cock and I'll take all the blame so you don't have to think. Push me away."

He was right. Her blood tingled and she felt herself shrinking away to some hidden place inside her filled with lightness that only he could lead her to. He released her wrist and balanced his weight on his thickly muscled arms, causing the mattress to dip around her. She shoved at his chest, and he ground his erection into her sex almost punishingly.

When he leaned in to kiss her, she turned away. He bit at her neck and growled, sucking and pulling at her tender flesh. She moaned despite her physical protests. It was indeed a psychological game he was playing. King of the mountain. He tried for her mouth again and she slithered out of his reach.

Sitting back, he grabbed her calves so she couldn't turn to her belly, and wrenched her legs wide. "Your pussy's wet. I can see it glistening from here. Do you want to be fucked, Evelyn?"

"No," she rasped, her breath coming fast as she told the lie, hiding her smile.

Leaning forward, he pinched her nipple hard and she cried out. "Little liar," he laughed.

She pressed her foot into his stomach, not hard, but enough to force space between them. His strong fingers caught her ankle again and tugged roughly. She gasped and watched him as he slowly sucked a long finger into his mouth and proceeded to slide it into her pussy.

Her body contracted around the digit, but he made no further move to pleasure her. "You're happy simply feeling me in you, knowing I hold the control to make you come. Admit it."

"No."

He tipped his head back and groaned. "Oh, that word. You know what it does to me." He twisted his wrist and pressed his finger into her G-spot, causing her to arch off the bed. His other palm flattened over her stomach and anchored her back down. He tickled her deep in her sex, and she whimpered with denied need.

"Ask me. Ask me to fuck you."

"No." Her lips twitched. She wanted to smile, but wasn't sure why. They were playing. This was *playing.*

He removed his fingers in one quick withdrawal that made her gasp. Her wrists were caught and pinned as heat engulfed her breast and there was a tug of teeth. Her knees locked on his hips. If he pressed his cock against her sex, she'd break.

Lips released her tight nipple, damp from his sucking, and took the other. It was a painful yet pleasurable pull that connected directly to her womb. Her thighs softened and her hips unlocked, allowing him to fall into the cradle of her hips. His restraining hold on her arms was transferred to her hands, but her fingers intertwined with his in mutual consent.

His body blanketed her, riding over her in powerful waves. Every touch of flesh, every drag of his tongue brought her plea closer to her lips. He was making her crazy. She arched into him and he continued to tease and torment her, stimulating her further, but never really fulfilling her with what she wanted most.

Words whispered over her damp skin. "Tell me . . . ask for it . . . beg me . . ."

When he tried to kiss her, again she turned away. This time he caught her hair and took what he wanted. She bit at his mouth, giving him the fiercest kiss she'd ever given, and he took everything she had to offer. His fist tightened in her hair. "Ask me nicely."

"No," she panted, forcing her smirk back.

He made a sound of disapproval. His hand pulled out of hers and reached between their bodies. He slapped her clit and she made a sound between a hiccup and a gasp. Heavy, dark eyes stared into hers. "You're only denying yourself, Evelyn. All the power, all the pleasure, rests in your surrender."

He slapped her there again and she moaned. Strange, once the shock of the action faded, familiar pleasure bloomed. A few more slaps and she would—*slap*—yes, she could definitely come this way.

She pressed her wet sex into his palm, a silent plea. The satisfied smile pulling at his lips told that he knew she was weakening.

"You won't ask because you love it when I make the choice. Admit it."

She wasn't admitting to anything!

"Stubborn," he whispered as he leaned back on his heels, taking his touch with him. His hands tugged at the waist of his silk pants, and his cock sprang out. "You're going to suck my cock now. And only when I'm about to come will I fuck you."

Had she even moved? Her body reacted so quickly. She was on her hands and knees, taking him deep into her mouth.

His fingers caught in her hair and he thrust to the back of her throat, forcing her to take quite a bit of him. She was lost in a white haze of passion, determined to bring him more pleasure than any other woman—or man—ever could.

"You see, Evelyn," she vaguely heard him whisper over her head as she worked his flesh. "I set the conditions, and you fight me almost every time because you're so used to fighting for every scrap of pleasure you have in this world. You have more self-discipline than any woman I know, and when I take you to that place of surrender and you give over, you do so beautifully. Never mistake yielding for weakness. Your resilience, your choice in the matter, is what makes your surrender so priceless. I may strip away your boundaries, but true courage comes when you bare all in the face of our love."

She stilled and released him. Slowly, she sat up, his words playing again and again in her mind. All else faded away until the *need* to surrender was all that remained. She had the choice. She finally understood.

She met his gaze and whispered, "Please, Lucian, take me."

He toppled her to the bed and they kissed madly, laughing and moaning as he filled her. His physical potency blanketed her as the emotional sense of strength he stimulated inside of her exploded. He erased every questioning doubt she'd entertained over the past two hours as his desire for her and her alone stifled every insecurity and satisfied every need she had.

His mouth dragged over her flesh as he praised her for being exactly who she was and vowed to always be what she needed. "I love you, Evelyn. Only you. Forever."

"I love you too."

It was in that moment, as he took her without apology, that she embraced a certain kind of oneness he often provoked in her and she realized, while not everyone worked under this sort of sexual dynamic, *they did*.

He made sense of her and she did the same for him. They were two parts of the same twisted whole. She knew in that moment he was her future, and she recalled the vision she'd had of a young boy running to her, resembling both her and Lucian. She was going to marry him someday, and perhaps he loved her just enough to wait until she was ready to face those fears of letting go as well.

seventeen
.....

FALLING IN

BY mid-June the city was sweltering. If leaving the hotel could be avoided, it was. Yet, Evelyn made a point to return to her own apartment at least once a week. She didn't know why she did this, perhaps it was a needed reminder to both her and Lucian that she still stood apart from *them* and held a very fundamental part of *her*.

He grumbled when she made excuses to go home, and she usually returned by way of Dugan once Lucian's patience ran out. But he never forbade her this private space and time, and she loved him all the more for granting her that significant escape. However, as time went on, she realized her apartment was not as magnificent as she'd once thought. It was shelter, and with that shelter came pride, but after a few hours wandering around the small vacant space, she'd soon begin to miss him.

During those quiet moments she did find time to contemplate her career. She wasn't lying when she told Lucian she didn't know what she wanted to do. Time would tell. As Jason taught her language arts he also broached other subjects. Her passions were still budding and eventually she'd choose a specific future to chase.

Until then, she decided Lucian was right. She was better off focusing on her studies rather than working part time trying to make ends meet when he'd already met all her needs.

At the condo, even when he wasn't there, he was. His scent was on the furniture. His personal items scattered throughout wore his mark. She realized she was beginning to wear the same mark. Lucian was simply so overwhelming he left fingerprints everywhere he touched. His fingerprints, she suspected, were taking shape on her soul.

Evelyn found it interesting that this was the first summer she'd actually held on to all of her belongings. Usually she was forced to stash a great deal of her things because lugging them around in the heat became unbearable, but this year all of her stuff was safely put away in closets and drawers.

When her bank statements showed up at the condo, she was grateful she'd never gone through the trouble of changing her information.

"You have mail," Lucian said as she walked into the living room one hot afternoon.

"I do?"

"Yep." He held out the envelope.

Her hands slowly took the paper and stared dumbly at it. She'd never had mail before. Her finger slid under the lip of the envelope and she unfolded the paper. There were the details of her account with a bunch of other stuff written on the statement. She smiled.

"I should really give this back to you if I'm not using it for my education."

Lucian was busy doing something on his laptop. His glasses perched at the end of his nose, reflections from the computer screen showing on the lenses. He didn't look at her. "Knock it off."

She stuck out her tongue. "You're grumpy today."

"I'm losing a deal."

She stilled. "The green deal? The big one?" She knew the deal was being threatened, but she never suspected he might actually lose it. It was Lucian. He didn't lose.

"It's always a big deal when you put over a year into something that never comes to fruition."

"I'm sorry. Is there anything you can do to fix it?"

"I've tried. I don't know who I'm up against, and it's pissing me off to no end. Somewhere in the past few months another company fell into the mix and they've taken arbitrage to a certain form of espionage. I'll get over the loss, but I want to find out who's screwing with my interests."

"What's the name of the company again?"

"We're procuring the rights to a company called Labex. They build windmills all over the country and deal in cleaner energy."

He was not in any sort of joking mood, and she wasn't sure anything she could say would be welcome or helpful. Giving him his privacy, she grabbed a muffin off a tray and disappeared into the other room.

She turned on the television and nibbled her snack. There was something very unsatisfying about not being able to solve problems for Lucian. As she ate her muffin she watched *Gilligan's Island* and tried to think of ways to put him in a better mood. Her mind ran over various images and she stilled when she thought about what he'd said, actually considered his words.

Cleaner energy. She wasn't exactly sure what that was, but she knew what windmills were. There weren't any in Folsom and being that she'd never left Folsom except to visit the estate, she wasn't sure how she knew what they were.

She frowned as her mind kept returning to the same images of a man in a hard hat standing next to an enormous white tower surrounded by nothing but blue sky. There was another image floating around in her head of an enormous turbine in a warehouse.

Where had she seen that? On television? In a book? She sat up straight and her eyes suddenly went wide. "Parker."

Tossing her muffin in the trash, she went to the bathroom and made quick work of getting ready. As she stared in the mirror, fixing her hair, she remembered images of the multiple books stacked throughout Parker's apartment. The majority were worn-out paperbacks and novels, but there were some that caught her attention because they were nothing like what he usually read.

Several had pictures promoting eco-friendly trends, showing vibrant pictures of a greener earth. There were ones about solar energy and definitely some about windmills. She'd only flipped through them once, barely able to comprehend what she had seen, but that was where she'd seen the pictures.

Anger had her breathing heavily as she threw on shorts and a T-shirt. She needed to get past Lucian. Hopefully he was still distracted enough that she could make up some lame excuse and get away for an hour. So help her, if it was Parker—

"Are you going somewhere?"

She jumped and turned to find Lucian standing in the closet door. "I, uh, left a book at the apartment. I figured since you were working I'd go get it and do some studying." Guilt burned through her as the lie passed her lips.

"Oh, okay. Isadora called. She wanted to know if we felt like coming by for dinner. She's leaving for Italy soon and I'd like us to spend some time with her."

"Sure."

He stretched and pulled his glasses off his face. "I'm going to shower and get back to work. I'm getting a headache. You going to study?"

"Yes." Well, research was more like it, but same difference.

He kissed her and disappeared into the bathroom. As soon as she heard the water turn on, she grabbed her sneakers and left.

On her way past Lucian's desk she stilled. His cell sat on top of his closed laptop. She glanced back at the door and, on impulse, grabbed the phone and set it to silent. She was on the elevator rushing to the ground three seconds later, her heart racing.

As the doors to the lobby parted, she finished tying her shoes. There were ways to be sneaky that reeked of guilt and knowingly doing something wrong, and then there were ways that were so in-your-face people missed the fact they were being outmaneuvered. There was little chance of her getting away with this blame free, but she decided to own it and go down fighting.

"Good morning, Mademoiselle Keats."

"Good morning, Claude. Is Dugan around?"

The doorman pointed to the long line of cabs and cars. She spotted the limo at the end of the block. Taking quick, determined steps, she walked in that direction. Dugan must have spotted her. He stepped from the limo and gave her a curious look, then checked his phone.

"Ms. Keats?"

"Hey, Big D. I need a ride."

He met her at the door and opened it. "Mr. Patras didn't send me a text."

"He's in the shower." The limo driver's eyes narrowed beneath his bushy brows. "Look, I'm with you. I'm being honest. Text him if it makes you feel better, but I need to leave now and I'm either walking or getting a ride from you."

He shut the door and withdrew his cell again. Moments later he was behind the wheel. "Where to?" he asked, easing the car from the curb and into traffic.

"Parker Hughes's apartment building." His head jerked and she met his challenging stare in the rearview. "Should I walk?"

Rather than answer her, he brought his phone to his ear and dialed. Lucian was likely just getting out of the shower, but he wouldn't hear his phone ring. Deceit sat like heavy oil in the pit of her stomach, but it was better she deal with Parker than leave it to Lucian.

The entire ride there, Dugan's phone never left his ear except to press Call again. He never made a peep, which meant he never got through to Lucian. He did, however, manage to take the longest possible route from A to B.

The limo pulled to the curb of Parker's building and she got out. Dugan placed himself between her and the entrance. "I'm not sure what's going on, Ms. Keats, but I know this isn't okay with Mr. Patras."

She shifted her weight and tried to reason with him. "Look, Dugan, I need to go in there. I told you to call Lucian if you want to and I had no doubt you would. I'm not hiding anything. This is only a detour. Just . . . please let me go."

She brushed past him and he caught her arm. "Evelyn." It was the first time he'd ever called her by just her name. She looked at him and his eyes were softened by age and worry. "You didn't see him before. Don't do that to him again. He loves you."

She placed her hand on his. "I know. I love him too. That's why I have to do this. Ten minutes, that's all I need."

Before he could stop her again, she rushed inside and took the elevator to Parker's floor. The route to his door was familiar. Had she really lived here only a couple of months ago? It felt like a lifetime ago.

When she reached his door, she took a deep breath, made a fist, and knocked hard. She heard movement inside and knew he was home. The door opened and he stared at her, confusion and a mix of concern tightening his brow.

"Scout? What are you doing here? Are you okay?"

He looked different from the last time she saw him. His face was no longer battered and he'd gained more weight. He was still fit, but gone was the gaunt look of years of starvation. He was no longer a lost cause. He was a man.

"I know what you're doing."

"I beg your pardon?"

"With the company Lucian was dealing with. I know it's you messing with him."

His expression immediately shuttered. "What? Is he sending you to do his dirty work? Shows how much he—"

"Oh, cut the crap, Parker. You're messing with his livelihood."

He laughed, but it came out more as a snarl. "His livelihood? Are you kidding? He's Lucian fucking Patras. He'll get over it."

"Will *you*? What you're doing is wrong and you know it."

"What I'm doing is business."

"Business like the way your dad conducted his."

His lips tightened. "I'm nothing like him."

"You may want to check your reflection again, Park. You aren't playing the game on even ground. That's how it all starts, isn't it?"

It was the first time Parker ever directed his anger at her. He stepped close and hissed, "What do you want me to do? Give it back? That isn't how the real world works, Scout. I worked my ass off for this deal and if I get it, it's because I'm the better man."

"Will that help you sleep at night?"

"You have no idea what gets me through the night."

"Why? Because I'm not there? This is all some pathetic game of revenge because I didn't want you! I *did* want you, Parker. I wanted you to be my friend. But all that crap about just wanting me the way I am was just that. Crap. Having me as a friend was never going to be enough for you, and you ruined everything."

Her voice cracked, but all the words she'd never had the strength to say suddenly came pouring out. "Why was that not enough? You say you loved me? When did you once prove it? You were my friend and you betrayed me and took our friendship away without asking."

His face wavered from indignant to apologetic. He stiffened.

"I can't undo what's been done." The elevator bell sounded and she knew she only had a few seconds left.

"I know. That would be too much like the gentleman you claim to be and too far from the self-serving prick you truly are. That's why I'll always pick him first. He'd surrender anything if I asked it of him."

"You think that—"

"I *know* that," she snapped with absolute assuredness.

"Evelyn."

She didn't need to turn to see that Lucian found her. She looked up at Parker and said, "Our friendship is over. You hurt me and friendship can forgive some things, but I will *never* forgive you for going after him."

When she turned, Lucian's expression was assessing, but blanked. He'd clearly caught the last of her words and was piecing everything together. She didn't need to justify coming to his defense.

She walked up to Lucian and said, "I know you're pissed. I'm sorry. I can't help that I want to protect you as much as you want to protect me."

He brushed his finger over her chin and there was something inherently sad in his eyes she didn't like. "Lucian?"

"Sweetheart, Pearl ran away."

Ice shifted through her veins, and she forgot all about her mission. "Wh-what?"

"Pearl. She left the rehab this morning and no one can find her."

"That's impossible. Where would she go? She has no money."

"One of the nurses turned in a report that her purse was stolen. She didn't have much in there, but she had enough for cab fare."

Evelyn's world began to spin. She grasped her temples. "No, no, no, no, no."

"We'll find her. I have people driving around now and I put a call in to the local cab companies with her description. I can't turn in a missing person's report for a few more hours still."

Arms wrapped around her as her knees went weak. "We'll never find her."

"We will. I promise," Lucian said fiercely.

"What's going on?" Parker's voice rang like a distant reminder of his presence. Why did she come here? She wanted to be anywhere but here.

"It's not your concern," Lucian snapped, pulling her toward the elevator.

They'd have to go to the tracks. They'd have to go everywhere. Her mother was missing, and all she could think of was the sweltering stench of bodily waste and garbage that was going to greet them in every place they'd be forced to search.

"Goddamn her!" she suddenly hissed. "Why can't she just be normal? Why does everything she does have to tear me apart? I'll *never* forgive her for this! She was clean!"

She'd fallen into hysterics, which delayed their quick escape. Lucian cradled her face and spoke softly of things that should reassure her, but there was no getting Pearl back there once her mother realized she was free to leave.

The elevator made a sound and Parker held the door. "What do you think you're doing?" Lucian growled.

"What do you think? I'm going to help find her mother. I know the places she goes."

"Last time you offered your help it came with conditions. We'll manage without you."

"Whatever. I really don't give a fuck what you want. I'm helping Scout."

Lucian looked at her as she wiped her nose and eyes. He must have come to some decision, because the next thing she knew they were exiting the building as a group and climbing in the limo. Lucian's Escalade was parked at the curb, forgotten.

Once inside, Lucian directed Dugan to the tracks. The ride was made in awkward silence. She couldn't look at Parker. Her mind continued to arrange a slideshow of the worst-case scenarios.

When they reached the tracks, she went to open the door and Lucian held her back. "No."

"I'll go look," Parker said, letting himself out. The door quickly closed behind him. This was where Parker had found his own mother's body years ago. Would he find Pearl's as well?

They waited for what felt like days. Parker had disappeared under the torn chain link fence and vanished into the old abandoned mill. Her tears had dried and her skin was cold.

"How long ago did she leave?" she croaked.

"The nurse said they think she left around seven a.m."

"What time is it now?"

"Almost one."

It was about a thirty-minute ride from the rehab to the city. Would Pearl even know an address to give the cab driver? She could have told him Folsom and directed him once he got closer to roads she recognized.

The door suddenly opened and Parker slid in. "She's not there. No one's seen her in months. Do you have hand sanitizer?"

Lucian reached in a compartment and tossed him a small bottle. "Where else can we look?"

"She'd most likely come back here," Parker said as he cleaned his hands.

Lucian looked at her and she shrugged. "This was her home."

"Is there anywhere else she went? Where did she get her drugs?"

"I got them for her. It was either that or watch her sell herself until there was nothing left."

As he drew in a deep breath, she heard the way it shook. "Where did you buy them?"

She met his gaze. Showing him this side of her past was so much more painful than telling him about it. There was no diluting the truth when it was right before his eyes. "There's an old school about eight blocks from here. There's a house . . ."

The limo drove as Parker directed Dugan in the right direction. The few houses that marked the way were mostly abandoned or in ill repair.

She rubbed her head, weary from worry. The thought of what this day could still bring utterly exhausted her, but she'd get through it, because that was what she'd always done. Humpty Dumpty fell down, and she put her back together again and again and again.

The school came into sight. It was vacant beyond the fact that summer was here. Scout recognized the old familiar landmarks and pointed to a run-down house across the way. It was likely an apartment at some point, but had the bones of an old Victorian.

The siding was a faded shade of maroon. Trim was painted everything from green to blue. The crumbling cement steps were barely climbable. Graffiti was scribbled everywhere, even over the wood that filled the windows like patches over empty eye sockets.

The Victorian was the crack house where everyone went to get stoned. Next to it, the small, run-down white house with blue trim was where the dealer lived.

Lucian looked to Parker and he shook his head. "He'll only talk to Scout."

"I'll need some money."

Lucian scowled at her as if she were crazy. "You're out of your mind if you think you're going in there alone."

"Lucian, if you go, he'll shoot you. He'll think you're a cop or worse, someone poaching from his territory. Just give me a few dollars and I'll be right out. He's probably already loading his gun from the window wondering what the hell a limo's doing in his front yard. I just want to find Pearl."

"I'm going with you."

"No."

"Evelyn—"

Parker suddenly interrupted them. "I'll go with her. He at least knows who I am. He doesn't like me, but he'll recognize me."

Lucian's jaw tensed. "I swear, if anything happens to her on your watch I'm holding you responsible. You have three minutes and I'm coming in."

They climbed out of the car and approached the tiny white house. A sheet fluttered over the unbarred part of the window. They were being watched. She knocked, just as she always had, two quick, short raps.

The knob turned and the door eased open as if by a phantom touch. They pressed through and she was immediately bombarded by the tainted scent of meth and rotting waste.

Piled-up trash crunched under her shoes, and she was incredibly grateful she wore her sneakers that day. A half-naked woman slept on a bare, stained mattress in the corner.

"Well, well, well, if it isn't Scout. I'm getting one surprise after another today. You're looking . . . well." The dealer turned and scowled at Parker.

"Damien, we're looking for Pearl. Have you seen her?"

He shrugged. "I see lots of people. I'm a very sought-after gentleman. Hard to keep track of who I do and don't see." He sat slouched on a broken couch. She made out the shape of a gun under the worn cotton of his pants.

"Please." She held out the hundred-dollar bill Lucian gave her. "I only want to find Pearl."

She never let Damien know Pearl was her mother. While they may have resembled each other at some point, those days were long over. Giving a man like Damien that sort of information only gave him more power.

He took the money and eased back in his seat. Feigning disinterest, he flipped back the sheet over the boarded window.

Through the small cut-away space she saw the limo. They'd been gone about a minute.

"You're rollin' with a new kinda crowd now, eh, Scout? I'm thinking you could do a little better than this if you really wanted my attention. Why don't you run on out there and ask your sugar daddy for some more money and I'll help you find Pearl.

"Here, you piece of shit," Parker said, tossing another two hundred on Damien's lap. "Now tell us if you saw her."

Damien picked up the money and tsked slowly. The girl in the corner moaned. The smell was getting to Evelyn and she felt like she was going to pass out if she didn't get into some fresh air quick.

"I don't recall inviting you in, boy. Why don't you step outside so me and Scout here can have us a chat?"

"Not on your life."

Damien's lip lifted as if it were attached to a fishing hook. He laughed. "Ah, or maybe on yours."

"Parker, go wait in the car."

"Are you insane?" Parker hissed.

"Better do as she says . . . *Parker.*"

"I'm not leaving you here. You have about one minute before I'm the least of your problems so I suggest you talk."

Damien sat up, his hand going to his waist. "What's going on, Scout? Who's in the limo?"

"No one. No one who wants any trouble. Look, Damien, please just tell me if you've seen Pearl and we'll leave. If I'm not out of here within a minute, you'll have company I know you don't want. Just tell me what I paid you for and we'll go."

His bloodshot eyes narrowed. He seemed to be weighing his options. Unwanted company led to gunshots, which led to the police, which led to trouble for everyone. "A'ight. She was here first thing this morning. Bought her usual shit and left, just like you and boy wonder are gonna do right now."

She nodded, a thousand knives tearing at her heart. There went her mother's sobriety.

They left the house just as Lucian was getting out of the limo. She drew in a breath of fresh air that was hardly fresh. Everything around that place smelled of decay.

She quickly walked to the limo.

"Did you find out anything?"

"She bought heroin this morning. That means she's not far. If I know my mom, she went to the first dark corner she could find to get high."

The three of them turned and looked at the three-story Victorian. She was most likely in there.

Evelyn suddenly couldn't move. All of her life she'd had this despicable vision of finding her mother dead. Each time she knew Pearl had gotten high she feared it would be that moment come to life.

Chances were they'd find her all doped up, she wouldn't recognize any of them, and they'd be carrying her like a screaming banshee out of there. But the little girl in her, the one who many times tried and failed to wake her doped-up mom, feared that wasn't the worst they could find.

Dugan appeared and handed Lucian a gun. Fuck, things were getting out of hand. "I'll go look for her and come get you if I find her," she said.

Lucian nodded at Dugan in some sort of code. She looked up as Dugan's large shadow blocked the sun. The chauffeur stepped close. "I'm sorry, Evelyn."

She squinted at him. "What?" He grabbed her and she jerked, unsure why he was suddenly restraining her, but his grip was too strong.

Lucian turned to her. "Parker and I will go in while you wait here."

"What? No! I'm going in. It's my mother." He was already walking away. "Dugan, let go of me!"

"It's for your own safety, Ms. Keats." He dragged her to the limo and she struggled as he shoved and shut her inside. Her fingers jammed against the handle as the safety locks engaged. She smacked her palms against the glass and screamed. *"Let me out!"*

There were dangerous, rotted places in the house that wouldn't hold the weight of two grown men. Parker wouldn't know where those spots were hidden because he never went in there.

She abandoned the door, scurried across the carpeted floor, and climbed over the front seat. Her fingers shook as she found the main controls and unlocked the door, wrenching it open. Dugan cursed and grabbed her. His fingers bit into her arms and tears rushed to her eyes.

"You don't understand! I have to go with them!"

"I'm sorry," was all he said as he refused to let her go.

She struggled, urgent concern choking her. "Please, Dugan. He could get hurt. They could both get hurt."

"I'm sure they'll be back in a few minutes. Why don't you get back in the car?"

She nodded in defeat and turned to face the building. The cracked foundation and hollow windows were weathered beyond repair. Drawing in a deep breath, she winced, fully admitting to herself she was crazy, turned, and slammed her knee in Dugan's groin.

He buckled like she predicted and released her arm. "I'm sorry," she called over her shoulder.

As she raced into the building, the chauffeur wheezed her name. Her feet kept moving. The stench just inside the door was rancid. Her eyes adjusted to the sooty darkness. Floors that hadn't seen the light of day in years were covered with a slippery layer of dust marked with footprints.

Trash littered the perimeter, and floorboards whined under her weight. Moving quickly, knowing just where to put her feet from force of long habit, she listened for where Lucian might be.

A thick banister lined the broken steps. Peeking in the large rooms on the first floor, she saw junkies lazing here and there, mostly stoned out of their minds and uncaring of her presence. She didn't see Lucian or Parker, which meant they'd likely already searched those rooms for Pearl.

Taking the stairs, she carefully placed her steps. At the top, she knew to avoid a soft patch of floor. Remnants from a demolition that had started long ago and never completed were piled in the middle of the largest room on the second floor. As welcome as a beam of light would be, whenever the sun pressed through a crack, it only drew her attention to how putrid this place really was.

Something shattered beneath the weight of her rubber-soled shoe, small and narrow like a crack pipe. Steady footsteps sounded behind her, echoing with heavy breath. She rushed around the pile of nails, wood, and wire, in search of Pearl or Lucian.

The low baritone of male voices drew her attention. Lucian's broad shoulders filled the doorway of what was likely once a bedroom.

"Jesus, don't let that be her . . ." he whispered.

"I'll go check," Parker said and Lucian stilled him before he entered the room to inspect whatever they were staring at.

"She's looking at us."

Evelyn stilled. There was something so wrong with that statement. Her blood ran cold and her limbs trembled. Her sense of speech disappeared as she watched Lucian's expression. Her mother was dead. She had to be dead. Why did he look like that?

Halting footsteps echoed behind her, then someone grabbed her arm and she screamed. Dugan held her with unbreakable strength.

Lucian pivoted and his face contorted with outrage. *"Get her out of here!"*

Words she couldn't decipher were said and voices rose. Parker stepped out of sight and that's when everything stopped moving in slow motion and picked up double time.

There was a horrible creak and Lucian turned. He shouted and Dugan ran, albeit with a hunching gait, after Lucian. Evelyn chased after Dugan, who blocked her way. She wedged her body into the room just as Parker's body lost balance. The house moaned like a burg slamming into the earth from a thousand miles away. Lucian threw out his arms and Parker skidded across the floor. The noise became deafening and suddenly the floor collapsed, a cloud of dust and rotted wood particles rising in its place.

As the gaping hole came into view, every nerve ending tensed and she screamed at the top of her lungs. He was gone.

"Lucian!"

Dugan restrained her as she kicked and screamed, fully prepared to fall into hell after him. As the dust settled, her frantic eyes landed on her mother's face. She wasn't blinking. With all this dust, she wasn't moving, and a trickle of dried blood trailing from her discolored mouth matted with the dirt falling through the air.

It was too much. With superhuman strength, she threw Dugan off of her and rushed down the stairs, twisting her ankle on the broken step along the way.

She's dead. She's dead. She's dead. She's dead. She's dead. She's dead. She's dead.

Limping, she gripped the doorjamb. There was an enormous pile of scrap. *"Lucian! Answer me!"*

The dust was still settling. The leather sole of his shoe peeked out beneath a board hammered with rusty nails. "Jesus Christ!"

Like claws, her hands reached into the debris, careless of scrapes and cuts, her flesh tearing as she sifted the larger pieces out of the way. "Baby, say something. Please." Where was his face?

Hurling a large piece of wood out of the way, she finally found him. His eyes were closed and his skin was covered with fallen clay and dirt. She carefully climbed over the debris and touched his face, leaning close to hear him breathing. "Lucian, Lucian, baby, open your eyes. Please open your eyes."

Her face burned as tears smudged past her lashes. The grit was blinding. "He's not waking up! Somebody help me!"

There was movement above her, but she couldn't take her gaze off of Lucian. It wasn't right for him to lay there so unconscious and vulnerable. She pressed her lips to his and whispered, begging for him to please open his eyes. He groaned and she jerked back.

"Shh, it's okay. You're okay. Just relax. We'll get you out of here."

A crude curse rasped softly over her whimpered cries.

She started as Dugan was suddenly behind her. He lifted away the boards she couldn't move and did a quick check of his body. He cursed. "I'm going to have to call an ambulance. I don't know if anything's broken and I don't want to shift him and make it worse."

Dugan made the call and she continued to comfort Lucian any way she could. Within minutes the whine of sirens in the distance could be heard. Her body wouldn't stop shaking.

She's dead. She's dead. She's dead. She's dead. She's dead. She's dead. She's dead.

Her hands gripped her hair and pulled hard.

He's gonna be okay. He's gonna be okay. He's gonna be okay.

When the EMTs arrived, she slid into the corner, feeling more at home in the shadows of a crack house than in their presence. Silently, she rocked as a brace was clamped around Lucian's neck and a plank was slid beneath his body. Her mind was going a mile a minute.

Straps wrapped around him as he was lifted up, and then he was on a gurney. As they wheeled him away, the gaping void was too far to cross, too real, too painful, too terrifying. He was leaving her.

Pearl's empty eyes, Lucian's body being taken away, a mad carousel whirled through her head, mocking her.

What about Momma? Where do I go?

"*Scout!*" She jerked at the sound of Parker's voice.

"You need to go with him," he said and she vibrated with fear. "Do you hear me? He needs you. Get up and go with him before they leave."

She couldn't make any words come. Her legs refused to work. Her thoughts fragmented, snapping into a million pieces, each one too heavy to bear. The carousel went round again, her mother's lifeless, bloodshot eyes staring through that dust, and Lucian lying still as a corpse.

"Scout! Go!"

"*I can't!*"

"Yes. You. Can."

Her head shook senselessly. "She's dead. I can't lose him too."

"You're *not* going to lose him, now come on!"

Her body was yanked off the ground, dragged out of the horrid-smelling building and into the street. Her vision protested as the sun pierced her eyes. The ambulance conquered the limo in height. Parker hauled her along, and Lucian's feet came into view as he was loaded into the back of the ambulance. There were lights and people in uniforms and machines, and it was all very scary.

"She's going with him," Parker demanded.

"Who is she?" a man in a uniform asked.

"She's his fiancée," Dugan announced, barring any arguments.

She turned to Dugan. "My mom . . ."

"I'll handle everything, Evelyn. You go with Lucian now."

She blinked, suddenly wanting to hug him for being there, but all she could manage was a jagged nod.

She was lifted into the car and tried her best to sink into the stiff bench and hide. The doors closed and hands probed at Lucian's limbs. She knew they were helping him but she wanted to throw herself over him protectively and scream that they stop touching him.

A cuff wrapped around his arm and his eyelids were lifted so a man could shine a light in his eyes. His face was powdered with debris and a bruise tinted his temple. There was blood crusted on his lip. She looked away when he didn't respond to the light glaring in his eyes. The ambulance lurched and rushed over the roads, adding to her dizziness.

"Ma'am, hold on to that strap." It took her a minute to realize the man in the uniform was speaking to her. Robotically, she did as he instructed.

There was so much noise between the ambulance moving, the machines, the walkie-talkies, and all the equipment rattling on the walls. Every breath seemed deliberate and forced. Her hand reached out and touched the cool feathered strands of Lucian's hair. It was the only place she was certain she wouldn't hurt him.

Movement caught her eye as the EMT took a pair of scissors and began cutting Lucian's shirt away. "What are you doing?" she demanded.

"We need to check his ribs."

"You're ruining his clothes."

"That's the least of his problems," the guy mumbled, and she gasped, pressing her knuckles to her mouth and sucking back a sob.

"Sorry, I just meant after a fall like that he probably has a broken rib or two. His vitals are good, so there's no need to get too upset."

She ignored him. Why wouldn't he wake up? *Open your eyes and look at me! You said you'd never leave me!*

When they reached the hospital, things went from scary to terrifying. She hated these places for a reason. Lucian was hauled through a set of electronic doors, faster than she could keep up with.

"Miss? Excuse me, Miss! You're going to have to wait here until the doctor sees him."

"But . . . I'm . . . I'm his fiancée."

"Sorry. That's not the same as wife. I'll let the doctor know you're waiting."

She turned and the world continued to spin. Her mom was dead and she couldn't go wherever they were taking Lucian. Faces stared at her as she stood there, unsure of where to go. A police officer approached her and she took a step back.

Like an animal cornered, she shrilled, "I'm waiting for my fiancé!"

The officer held up his hands. "Okay, but you need to take a seat. You're blocking the patient entrance."

She nodded and jerkily walked to the closest chair and forced herself to sit. The officer looked like he was going to say something else, but then an alarm started to beep and a nurse called out a code. The doors she had been waiting by opened and her heart stopped.

Lucian stood, face haggard, sweat dotting his brow, shirt cut open, his weight braced on the wall. Nurses rushed toward him and he slowly lifted a shaky arm and pointed directly to Evelyn.

"She comes with me." He sounded nothing like himself.

Evelyn sobbed in relief and ran to him. "You're awake," she cried as her arms carefully hugged him and he winced.

"Sir, this is a hospital—"

"I'm aware. I paid for several wings. Now go back to your desk and get out of my way." His voice was stern and left no room for argument.

As they turned, he draped a goodly amount of weight on her shoulders, nearly collapsing her to the floor. An obviously irritated doctor scowled at him.

"Get me out of this curtained tent and put me in a real goddamn room before I find some other hospital to support. And someone contact Dr. Sheffield and get her here. Now!"

A nurse produced a wheelchair, but looked none too happy at

assisting Lucian. Evelyn gripped the hand that didn't seem to be bothering him as they raced down the long hall and entered an elevator. They rode in silence, Lucian appearing to have depleted his strength, but he never let go of her hand.

They traveled down one long corridor after another until they finally entered a room. It was nothing like she expected. The walls were creamy butter yellow and paneled in dark cherrywood. The bed was made in soft linens and the windows were draped with thick valances. A couch sat along one wall and a large sink adorned the other. Aside from the railing on the bed, it looked more like a hotel room than a hospital room.

The nurse grumbled a few words about the doctor and helped Lucian get settled. Evelyn once again felt pushed away, so she went to the couch and waited for the doctors to tell her he would be okay. She needed someone to confirm that he would be okay. By the time the nurse shut the door, his eyes were closed.

She backed up to the couch and lowered her weight.

Pearl's dead.

"Hey." He sounded like he swallowed a handful of gravel. His eyes were mere slits.

She needed to be strong. "Hey."

"I'm so sorry about your mother."

Her vision blurred and she nodded. "I always knew I'd find her that way."

"I'm still sorry. I wanted to help her. I wanted to save her for you and I couldn't."

For some reason it was easier to talk about Pearl than the fact that he was lying in a hospital bed. "No one could. She was her own worst enemy."

Silent moments passed. He drifted off as she wept. Her fingers were filthy and bloody.

"Why are you all the way over there?"

Startled by his voice, she sniffled. "What?"

"Come over here."

"You're hurt," she protested.

"I'm fine. Come here."

Slowly Evelyn stood and moved beside the bed. He sighed and grabbed her wrist. "*Here*. Come *here*. Lay with me."

"I can't. I'll hurt you—"

"Will you knock it off?" He tugged her and she climbed onto the bed, curling into his side, careful not to put any weight on him. He hugged her close. "It'll be okay, Evelyn. I'll be out of here soon and we'll work everything out."

She nodded and pressed her face into his shoulder. "I was so scared when you didn't wake up. If anything bad happened to you I don't think I'd ever be able to forgive her. All the things she's ever done to me, put me through . . . watching you fall through that floor trying to get to her—" Her words cut off with a sob. "It's her fault you got hurt."

"Shh. I'll be fine." He rubbed her arm, soothing swirls of fingers leaving goose bumps in their wake, and after several minutes he asked. "Did Parker get out okay?"

"What? Parker's fine."

"I didn't know if I got there in time. I saw him going down and I just reacted. I couldn't watch you lose your mother and friend all in one day."

The entire event rolled through her head, unfolding moments she'd been too upset to see before. "You saved him."

"I couldn't let him fall."

"Oh, God, Lucian." She was grateful he didn't let Parker get hurt, but angry he did so at the cost of his own safety. She needed to tell him. "Parker's the one who's stealing that company from you."

"I know. I put it together when I got Dugan's messages saying you made him drive you there. I heard what you told him. When will you stop trying to protect me and let me do the protecting?"

She swallowed. "I was so angry with him, but then, today,

after . . . after they took you . . . he forced me to get up. Made me keep moving. He told me you needed me. I was so scared, but he wouldn't let me quit on you."

His lips pressed to her temple. "Well, I'm glad you're here. Are you hurt?"

There was a knock on the door and Dr. Sheffield came in. Her slight figure showing under a white lab coat, hair and makeup perfect, posture impeccable in those tall heels. She held a clipboard and shook her head. "This looks about right. I get a call saying there's some problematic patient demanding all sorts of special treatment and my presence yesterday. I should have known it was you. What happened?"

Evelyn tried to sit up, but Lucian tightened his grip.

"Stay there, Evelyn. The scared ones need their security blankets," the doctor said as she moved to the foot of the bed. "It's nice to see you again, by the way."

"Very funny, Vivian. I fell through a floor."

"Well, that wasn't smart. Says here you got knocked out for a bit. What hurts?"

"My arm and my head."

She placed her clipboard down and reached in a drawer. Producing scissors, she made quick work of cutting away the remainder of his sleeve. Dr. Sheffield examined the arm and he winced. "Hmm. It hurts because it's broken. See this? That's not supposed to be there. You're going to need a cast, and if you argue with me about it, I'll plaster your mouth shut. How's your breathing? Your chart says your ribs may be broken."

"It hurts."

"I'm going to run some x-rays and an MRI. While you're gone doing that—and behaving like the quintessential good patient—I'm going to chat with Evelyn." She left for a moment and returned with a nurse and a wheelchair. "Bonny, this is Lucian Patras. He's very grateful you offered to take him down to radiology."

Evelyn sat up and helped Lucian out of the bed and into the chair. Reluctance to watch him leave again had her gripping his good hand. Just as Bonny was wheeling him out of the room, Dr. Sheffield called, "Oh, and Lucian, you're going to need a tetanus shot."

He cursed and then he was gone. The doctor faced her and smiled. "He's such a baby. How are you doing?"

"I'm . . . okay."

The doctor made a sympathetic smile. "You're limping. I heard about your mother. I'm so sorry, Evelyn. There are fantastic grief counselors here at the hospital if you want to speak to anyone. Lucian's name carries a lot of weight. They're at your disposal if you need them."

"Thanks, but I'd rather work it out on my own. Do you know how long he'll have to stay here?"

She sighed. "I was hoping you'd be the one to convince him to stay if it was for the best."

"Sorry. I hate hospitals."

"A match made in heaven. If his x-rays and MRI check out and it's just the arm and ribs, we can have him wrapped up in no time and home before dinner. If I spot any signs of internal bleeding or other issues, I'm going to insist he stays. I don't give a hoot what his name is."

Evelyn stared at the doctor for a long minute and then finally found the courage to ask what she'd wanted to ask since their first meeting. "How do you know Lucian? I mean, aside from being his personal physician? How did you meet?"

She smiled. "I'm shocked you waited this long to ask. I'm Shamus's sister."

Evelyn's mouth drooped open like a trout. "But your last name's Sheffield."

"Yes, and I'm happily divorced, but I was married when I got my MD. I've known Lucian since he was a baby and spent most of my adult years torturing him for all the ways he used to torture me when I was a girl."

"I see it now . . . in the set of your eyes and your smile."

"Well, I look more like my mother. Shamus gets his curls and freckles from my father."

"How come you weren't at his party the other week?"

"I was here. That reminds me, I may break Lucian's other arm for buying Shamus that death trap. Now, let me look at your ankle."

Evelyn lifted her leg and winced under the weight of her sneaker. The doctor's cool hands gently probed. "That's quite a sprain you have there. How about I wrap it for you?"

Evelyn nodded and the doctor left for a moment. The silence was too much. Her mother's face, unblinking eyes, haunted her every thought.

"Okay, this should do," Dr. Sheffield said as she returned to the room. "I'll show you how to wrap it and if you keep it elevated for—oh, Evelyn . . ." She tossed the bandage aside and Evelyn was suddenly wrapped up in the doctor's arms as sobs racked her body.

"I did everything I could and it still wasn't enough," she cried. "Everything! I was never enough, never a reason for her to stop killing herself. Why wasn't I good enough? *Why?*"

"Shh. Oh, honey, your mother's death has nothing to do with anything you did or didn't do. She was an addict. But that long, painful journey she always took alone is over, and now she's finally found some peace."

Evelyn cried beyond countable minutes. It hurt to love her mother from the time she was young. There were no selfless whispers of hope breathed to her in sleep. No encouraging expectations or coddling during the moments she was too weak. It was always the wrong way, her doing for her mother who loved her heroin—*always*—a little bit more than she loved her daughter.

The doctor's hair smelled of berries. Her embrace was a warm pillow wrapped around Evelyn's fragile heart. Once she got her sobs under control, Dr. Sheffield produced a damp cloth and washed the grime from her face as if she were a small child. Deft fingers with cherry-painted nails wrapped her ankle.

Just as the doctor clasped the small metal clip to hold the brace in place, Lucian returned.

"What happened to your leg?" he snapped, attempting to get up and slumping back into the wheelchair.

"Easy there," the nurse, pressing a hand into Lucian's shoulder, said.

He glared at her and Dr. Sheffield stood. "It's just a sprain, Lucian. She'll be fine. How did the x-rays go?"

The nurse and the doctor went over the x-rays. Lucian's arm needed to be set. Everything was done in an uninterrupted blur of one event after another. Scout held Lucian's good hand and never took her eyes off their intertwined fingers. It was long past dark when Dugan showed up and they were permitted to leave.

Lucian had three badly bruised ribs, a broken radius, a dislocated shoulder, and several lacerations on the shoulder that took the brunt of the impact when he fell. His temple was bruised, but he was not concussed. His lip was split, but the bleeding had stopped and there was no need for stitches. They wheeled him out because there was some rule about being wheeled out if you were wheeled in. She'd hobbled behind him until Lucian insisted she ride on his lap.

When they got to the limo, he shut her inside for a moment to talk to Dugan. Typically, she would have objected to being left out, but she was simply too tired to complain. By the time they reached the hotel, they were both dead on their feet. They made quite a spectacle, walking through the lobby, her limping along, him holding his ribs, as his casted wrist lay cradled in a sling over the only remaining shred of his dress shirt.

They walked into the bedroom without turning on a single light. Neither of them seemed interested in catching their reflection by chance. Silently, they assisted each other with their clothing until they were both naked.

She pulled back the covers and helped him in. Gingerly, she padded around the bed to her side. When she climbed in, he drew her close with his uninjured arm, and she pulled the covers over their tired bodies. And then they slept for what felt like days.

eighteen
.....

BREAKING OUT

THE curtains remained drawn, so there was no telling what time it was. Evelyn had woken at some point and stumbled into the shower. Beads of moisture spattered over the tile told her Lucian had done the same. She'd slept so deeply she hadn't heard him wake. Once the filth—what could be washed away—from the day before was cleansed from her skin, she climbed back into bed and slept.

Her dreams were a cruel kaleidoscope of her past. Distilled images of Pearl in places she'd never been. Every dream ended the same. Her mother's face turning to her, mouth gaping, eyes unblinking, and Evelyn woke up choking on dust that wasn't there.

They were her dreams. Her nightmares were worse. In her nightmares Lucian didn't wake up. His eyes were dull and flat. She couldn't get to him. She ran, but her legs were anchored with muscles made of wet sand. In one dream she caught up to him, but it was too late, he was tying off his arm and she observed helplessly, screaming, as the fluid flushed through the needle into his veins.

Each time she thought she could save him, and each time she

was either too weak or too late. It was such a dream that woke her up. She curled into herself, sobbing softly into the pillows.

"Hey." Lucian's voice was a whisper in the dark. It curled around her like a caress and chased away the confusing cobwebs of sleep. He eased her to her back and kissed her softly. "It's okay."

He drew her close and soothed her, brushing his palm over her back and calming her tears. Would he be mortified to know she wasn't crying over Pearl, but over her irrational fears of losing him? She was a bad daughter.

His mouth teased over hers and he looked at her with those beautiful dark eyes. "Better?"

She nodded.

"Some deliveries came for you while you slept. Dugan brought them up."

Had he been up and about? She assumed he only showered. "Deliveries of what?"

"How about you use the bathroom and then come see. I have bagels and some French toast. It's probably cold by now. I didn't want to disturb you."

She gripped his arm and he frowned. She needed to make sure he understood. "Lucian?"

"Yes?"

"I *love* you."

"I love you too, Evelyn."

He didn't get it. Seeing him fall made her realize just how much she needed him. This was different than before. This was irrevocable. This was to the depths of her soul, with a thread tying her to him that sewed her so tight she nearly puckered inside out. This was forever.

She'd show him. She'd show him and eventually he'd understand, everything had changed.

When she emerged from the bathroom, she hobbled to the common area. Her ankle was a constant reminder of everything that happened the day before. The scent of flowers had her breathing deeply. She turned the corner and gasped. Arrangements of stunning blooms and sprays covered every surface. "What is all this?"

"Your friends are sending their condolences."

"I . . . I don't have any friends."

He gave her a strange look, lips pulled to the side and his brows bending in a sort of question mark. "Sure you do. Don't be silly. Eat something and I'll help you read the cards. A lot of them are in cursive."

"Because they don't know I can't read, because they don't know me. Lucian, who sent all this and why?"

His head tilted like he didn't understand her confusion. "They're from people who care about you, Evelyn. These cards were written with one thought. They all hope you're doing okay. There wasn't room for thoughts about script or anything else. Trust me, they were all sent out of love."

Lucian was the only person to ever give her flowers. Now she was being bombarded with them. The sentiment was unfamiliar and slightly embarrassing. She didn't want people to worry about her.

He brushed a hand over her knee peeking through the slit in her robe. Her fingers picked at the French toast as he plucked a card from a spray of yellow roses. There were still flecks of dirt under her nails and she lost her appetite.

"This one is from Antoinette and Shamus. *Evelyn, it is with great sympathy for your loss that our heavy hearts are quiet today. May the love of those closest to you hold you tight and get you through.*"

He plucked up another card from a vase of tulips. "This is from Dugan. *Ms. Evelyn, It is only because you are so brave that I know you will get through this difficult time. Have the courage to cry and know that you are loved by many. If there's anything I may do to help, I'm always near. D.*"

Her lips trembled. They were from friends. Friends she never realized she had. Lucian read one card after another. There were flowers from Seth, Lucian's assistant; Patrice and the girls at the salon; Raphael and the others who worked in the kitchen of the hotel; Tamara, her old general manager; Nick, from Clemons; Parker; Isadora; Dr. Sheffield; Jason, her tutor; several people Lucian introduced her to at events; and even one bouquet from Slade Bishop. She never felt so much affection and care.

"Oh my God," she breathed. "This is . . . incredible. How did they all know?"

"You've been sleeping for nearly two days. I had to let people know where I was and that I'd be unavailable for some time."

"Why?"

"Evelyn, you just lost your mother. There's no way I'd leave you at a time like this."

"Lucian, where *is* Pearl? Dugan said—"

"Don't worry about the details. A private service is scheduled for tomorrow. The arrangements are handled. I don't want you to stress about any of that."

"What kind of service? Like a funeral?" Her people didn't have funerals. If they were lucky, someone identified them at the county morgue.

"Of course."

More flowers came throughout the day. Evelyn remained quiet. She felt like an outsider looking in. The dragon had finally swallowed Pearl whole and Evelyn, selfishly, existed without purpose.

A nagging urge for motion teased at her nerves all day. She should be moving, thinking, going, but all she could manage was breathing. They watched a movie and when Lucian's wrist started bothering him, she forced him to take the prescribed pain medicine Dr. Sheffield had provided. He was a terrible patient.

Her head rested upon his shoulder as he softly twirled the ends of her hair. Her foot was elevated on a delicate little pillow, and suddenly it was all funny. A jagged giggle escaped her throat and turned into a hiccup, which evolved to a full-on belly laugh.

Lucian twisted as much as his bruised ribs would allow and gave her a questioning look. "You okay?"

Covering her face with her palms, her skin heated. Why was she laughing? "I'm sorry. I know it isn't funny. I don't know what's wrong with me."

His expression slowly lifted with cautious concern. She was losing it. Her sides ached as giggles prattled from her mouth like champagne bubbles rising to the top. Sighing, she tried to get hold of herself, but the sigh burst into more inappropriate laughter.

"I'm sorry. I'm sorry. I shouldn't be laughing. Look at us. We're a mess and my mom's funeral is tomorrow. I think . . . I'm nervous."

"Don't apologize. Sometimes we just need to laugh. What are you nervous about?"

"I don't know. Nothing. Everything. I don't know what to do now."

His brow knit. Soft purple flesh darkened and she sobered. He was hurt. Her laughter fell away like autumn leaves lost in the wind. She was hysterical.

"No one expects you to *do* anything, Evelyn. We all just want to see you get through this."

"And then what?" she scoffed. "Then what, Lucian? I've never allowed myself to truly think outside of protecting Pearl. I've never left the city other than to visit the estate with you. I've never thought more than a day or two ahead. I don't know how to let go of the weight that's been on my shoulders since I was born."

His dark eyes blinked as though he were contemplating her outburst. Soft, sooty lashes, too pretty for a man, guarded those dark eyes that saw so much in her when the rest of the world merely looked through her. "Do you remember when I told you about the time I went to the circus?"

"Yes."

"Tell me a memory from your childhood, a time that you were happy."

She stilled. Images of hardship and empty, faded memories skated through her mind. "I don't have any."

"There has to be something," he said quietly, waiting for her to offer up some vivid recollection of happier times.

She wanted to give him that. Needed to ease his mind before that sympathetic look in his eyes turned to pity. Should she make something up? He'd know if she were lying.

The truth was, the only happiness she ever felt was linked to him. The first time she slept on a real bed, the first time she ever properly bathed, her first fulfilling meal, all things most people took for granted she had never known until meeting him.

Then she thought of something. "When I was little . . ." she said quietly. "I must have been very young. I could walk and I was talking, so I guess I was around four or five. We were standing in a field, or it looked like a field to me at the time. I don't really remember what buildings were around. I just remember the sky."

His head cocked. "Why the sky?"

"It was a faded blue I'd never seen before, dull and cold. I'd never seen it like that before. The air had a strange metallic scent to it, not like the tang of rain or the heaviness before a storm. This was different, lighter. Pearl was there, but she must have been preoccupied because I only recall her presence, nothing about what she was doing.

"There was this unfamiliar current, like a soft whisper that gets your attention faster than any scream. I looked up and the sky was swabbed with white cotton. The clouds were soft but impenetrable, and there was an eddy of gray just above us. I thought if I found a branch long enough I could pop those bloated gray billows. And then something amazing happened."

"What?"

"Soft, drifting flakes began to fall from the sky. It was like God was sprinkling the world with sifted sugar. What I saw as ominous suddenly became enchanted. I watched them fall, each one taking a slow journey down to earth, but I couldn't figure out what it was. It wasn't rain. It wasn't ash. It smelled pure and looked so pretty. I should've been scared, but I wasn't. When one landed on my arm I gasped. Ice in the shape of a star. I called my mom, but it melted before she saw.

"I was too young to conceive how something so small and delicate could amount to something so . . . consuming. I realized, over time, that snow was like a blanket of white death for people without shelter, but in that moment it was just magic being sprinkled from the sky."

They were silent for a long moment. "You've never left the city." It was a statement. He knew she hadn't other than their short trips to his country home. "I want to show you things, Evelyn. I want to see that look in your eyes like when you saw your first snowfall. I want to be there for all your firsts."

"You have been," she whispered.

He nodded. "I want to be there for all of them. There are so many more."

"I haven't done much. I could never stray far because Pearl always pulled me back. She was the anchor I carried. It's scary letting her go. Sad, like a balloon cut from its string. I'm afraid I'll just float away."

His fingers twined with hers. "I won't let you."

She snuggled into his side. The movie was over and neither of them seemed to care. He had a nick on his knuckle from the fall. She lifted his strong hand and kissed it. "I love you."

"I love you too."

She thought about the snow. It was the first peaceful memory she'd had in days. After several quiet minutes, Lucian asked, "If you could go anywhere, see anything, what would you want to see?"

Her world had always been so small, the mote in the eye of a giant. Lucian's world was limitless. *He* was the giant.

She wanted to experience everything, but never dared to hope for more than she was due. Perhaps she was owed something great. "I'd like to see the ocean."

He smiled. "Then that's where we'll start. I think we need to get away for a while. Your lessons will be here when you return."

For the first time she agreed with him. Her lessons would be there. She could take a break and return to her education. "What about your job?"

"That's the glory of being the boss. I can leave whenever I want. Tomorrow, after the funeral, we'll run away, just the two of us. And we won't stop until the ocean's at our toes."

Something warm unfurled inside of her. Maybe it was love. Maybe it was hope. But it was comforting and exciting and big. It was the tingle she felt in her heart whenever she was around Lucian.

It seemed appropriate that it rained the day Evelyn said good-bye to her mother. Tears from heaven clung to the tinted glass of the limo as they drove out of the city. Evelyn hadn't asked where they were going. She hadn't said much of anything since waking up that morning.

Funerals were something she'd only seen from afar, cars snaking through crowded city streets, people dressed in colors of mourning. She wasn't sure why people celebrated death, or perhaps they were celebrating life. Pearl hadn't lived a life of greatness and she hoped it would all be over soon.

Lucian seemed to think this was something she needed. Maybe he was right. Her world was small, filled with only a handful of people. Pearl had been there from the beginning, and losing her was like saying good-bye to a part of herself.

When they arrived at the estate, Evelyn was confused. Lucian didn't offer explanations. He simply held her hand and gave her a comforting squeeze from time to time.

Dugan parked the car and greeted them with a somber nod. Other cars lined the long drive, and she hesitated when she realized they wouldn't be alone. Lucian's strength enveloped her as he guided her into the house.

Lucy, dressed in her maid's uniform, but with a black armband, opened the door and softly whispered her condolences. Evelyn's shoes clicked over the marble tile and the silence struck her as odd. She knew they weren't alone.

Beneath her sleeveless black wrap dress, her skin prickled. She didn't want to see Pearl again. Her mother's lifeless eyes had haunted her for days, and Evelyn just wanted to forget. They approached a set of French pocket doors that led to another den, and Lucian turned to her.

"Are you ready?"

She hadn't known what to expect so there was no way to prepare. She nodded and he slid the doors open; the soft whisper of aged wood and gears wasn't loud enough to bring her back to earth.

She turned and sucked in a breath. In front of the large paned window was a polished coffin. The wood was dark and glossy. Brushed pewter rails ran along the trim. Her eyes devoured the detail of the casket so as not to see the body lying inside. There was no one else in the room.

He took her hand and helped her cross the threshold. With each step, her world closed in. The walls fell away and her vision shimmered. Where was Pearl?

They stopped walking and she realized it was because she was crying. Lucian gave her a few moments and then, drawn, like a butterfly to a bloom, she stepped closer to see the woman before her. No, it was not Pearl. It was her mother.

Gone were the lines of time and marks of tension in her face. Her skin appeared slightly flushed, vibrant in a way that Evelyn didn't recognize. Her hair was done and her lips held a serene pose. Her fingers were clean, and wrapped in her palm was a beaded crucifix more valuable than anything her mother had ever held.

Evelyn's lips parted as she took in this image of the woman who raised her. She was dressed in a divine pink suit. An ivory blanket covered her feet. She looked like a sleeping angel. She looked . . . peaceful.

Her fingers trembled as she slowly reached to touch her. A gasp echoed in her ears as the coldness beneath her fingers penetrated her foggy mind. She looked so young. This was how she should have appeared in life, Evelyn decided. It was astounding, how happy seeing her mother this way made her. Never before had she seen Pearl at rest, she realized.

For as difficult as Evelyn's life had been, Pearl's was as well. She'd fought every day against a monster no one else could see. The monster had won, but perhaps this was Pearl's victory. Rest. Eternal, uninterrupted rest.

"There is an ancient Chinese belief," Lucian said quietly. "That when dragons collide, pearls fall from the sky."

A dragon had destroyed her mother, and now she looked like a fallen angel. "Thank you for doing this for me," she whispered through tears.

He squeezed her hand. "If you're ready, the others will join us."

Again, she wasn't sure what to expect. She nodded silently.

Lucian left her with her mother and opened the pocket doors. Isadora was the first to enter. She stepped into the room with ethereal grace and came to Evelyn's side. Her kiss was soft upon her cheek and her hands warm.

"I'm so sorry for your loss, Evelyn."

Evelyn nodded. Isadora's perfect long fingers grazed Pearl's hands, and she watched in awe as Lucian's sister shut her eyes as though praying for a woman she never met. It was strange, seeing someone mourn for Pearl, but that is what they all did.

One by one, guests entered the den and paid their condolences. Toni, Jamie, Parker, Nick, the girls from the salon . . . it was surreal to see these people in Lucian's private home. There were no rivalries or politics in those moments, only grace.

After everyone came through to offer his or her sympathy, Isadora returned. She whispered to Lucian and then came up to Evelyn and smiled sadly. "When you're ready, I'll be waiting in the hall."

Ready for what? Evelyn looked to Lucian as Isadora turned away and quietly shut the doors. "It's time to say good-bye," he said softly.

Something protested inside her. It was a little girl waiting for her mom, the one who never gave up hoping she'd someday come around. Blinking back tears, she soothed the child who lived in her heart and finally admitted this was how it had to be.

Leaning over the casket, her lips pressed into her mother's cool cheek. "I love you, Momma. I always will."

Lucian walked her to the doors and Isadora waited quietly. "I'll be with you soon. Go with my sister," he said.

She didn't want to part from him, but allowed Isadora to take her hand and lead her away. They walked through the house and came to the back door, facing the gardens and pool.

"Here, put these on," Isadora said, handing her a pair of dainty black flats.

Evelyn did as she was told and followed Lucian's sister out into the balmy air. The rain had stopped and the sun gave breath to the ground as it steamed. The earth was soggy beneath her feet as they stepped off the cobblestone path.

In the distance, over a knoll of emerald blades of grass, she spotted the silhouettes of people waiting. There was a willow tree luffing in the stiff breeze, and the heavy scent of lilacs filled the air. Isadora held her hand as they climbed the hill.

When they reached the top, she realized where they were. Beneath the tree stood a stone carved with angels. She couldn't read the engraved writing, but knew the grave belonged to Lucian's mother. This was where Pearl would forever rest.

The somber faces of those who'd come into the den smiled softly, but not everyone was there. The men were all absent except for one she didn't recognize. From somewhere in the distance pipes began to play, and her heart raced with unsure expectancy.

Cresting the hill, several figures came into view, suited black silhouettes of strength. She breathed a sigh of relief when she spotted Lucian. Behind him were Shamus, Parker, Nick, and Slade. They were carrying her mother's casket.

When they reached the top, the casket was placed within a nest of flowers, and Lucian relieved Isadora of her duties. His hand curled around hers as he stepped close. The man she hadn't recognized began to speak.

"God our Father, Your power brings us birth, Your providence guides our lives, and by Your command, we return to dust . . ."

Evelyn listened but did not hear what was being said. The sense of losing someone she never had was peculiar and difficult to comprehend. Relief that this was where she would always be, only a short walk away from where she sometimes slept, struck her like an unfamiliar comfort that eased the unending search her life had been conditioned to perform. She'd be safe, blanketed in the belly of the earth, a garden for flowers to grow. There'd be no time, only peace. And for the first time ever, Evelyn let her worries for her mother go.

A rose was placed in her hand. Lucian led her to the casket. She could read the word engraved in the plaque. It simply said *Pearl*. There was a solitary white mollusk embedded in the pewter above her name. It was breathtaking.

They placed their flowers on the casket and walked away in silence. The scent of lilacs imprinted on her mind. They were Lucian's mother's favorite, and every year her mother would now share in their beauty, as they'd come to bloom. Strange that Pearl had been gifted the same standard of rest as a woman like Mrs. Patras.

The guests didn't return to the house with them. Evelyn had no concept of time. A meal was set for only the two of them on the terrace in the gardens. Her fingers picked at her food, but no taste touched her tongue. Lucian watched her but said very little.

He was right. She needed this closure and embraced the sad peace that came in its wake. Losing Pearl was like breaking away from who she had always been. She was a tired balloon cut from its string, floating on to places untold. But Lucian would be there with her, always, making sure she never floated alone.

THE limo pulled onto the airstrip, and Evelyn's face went numb. The jet was the size of a two-story house. "This is yours?"

He smirked as he gazed at his oversized toy. "All mine."

Her stomach flipped and continued to teeter. He wasn't kidding when he said he would be showing her many firsts. In a few minutes she would be leaving earth and rocketing through the sky at God knew how many miles an hour.

As they stepped onto the tarmac, the pavement was hot beneath her sandals. Dugan loaded their luggage on a cart, and Lucian clasped her hand. "Ready?"

Evelyn hesitated. Birds flew. People walked. These were the facts of life. "Um . . ."

Taking her other hand, he drew her close and kissed her softly. "It will be fine, Evelyn. My pilot has over thirty years' experience under his belt, and I not only trust him with my life, I trust him with yours."

Perhaps it wouldn't be so intimidating if it weren't so large of a jet. How did a thousand tons of metal just float through the air? She licked her lips nervously. She could do this. This was her first big step—well, more of a leap—in her plan to experience new things. The world was her oyster. Whatever that meant.

They climbed the steep set of stairs jutting out of the belly of the plane, and she gaped at the luxury awaiting them on the inside. Butter-colored leather and polished wood dominated the cylindrical space. Windows were adorned with dainty navy blue curtains. Seats were arranged aesthetically for conversation or dining.

Cool air pumped into the cabin. She'd seen the inside of an airplane on television. This was not a plane. This was a flying mansion.

"Our room's back here," Lucian said, carrying their smaller bags through the door.

She followed him. Yup, it was an actual bedroom. Against a wall, the king-size bed was made up with soft accent pillows. Two swivel chairs sat adjacent on the other wall, with a small glass table in between.

"Watch this," he said, smirking like a young boy. He really did love his toys. He typed in a code on a small hidden panel, and the wall began to move. She jumped back and stared in awe as blue sky came into view.

The wall literally extended and lowered, forming a balcony on the side of the plane. *Great. A plane with collapsible walls.* It didn't make her feel safer.

"Come see," he said, taking her hand.

Reluctantly she followed. It was disorienting, being so high. The limo seemed to have shrunk. She stepped back in the plane and he chuckled.

"Can you close it back up now?"

He sighed at having his fun spoiled. After pressing a few buttons, gears shifted and the wall rose, locking back into place.

"Is it locked?" she asked nervously.

"Yes, Evelyn. Relax. Let's have a drink."

They returned to the main area of the plane, and a flight attendant waited behind the bar. "Good afternoon, Mr. Patras. Can I get you a drink before takeoff?"

As Lucian ordered their beverages, Evelyn settled into a large upholstered chair. There was a long couch, but the chair seemed safer. Her fingers located the seat belt and buckled it, pulling the strap as tight as it would go.

Lucian tsked as he handed her a cool glass of something pink and fruity. "Are you planning on staying buckled the entire flight?"

"No," she sassed. "Only for the parts when we're in the air."

He shook his head, but a smile pulled at the corner of his mouth. "Drink your cocktail. It will calm your nerves."

The alcohol went right to her head, and soon they were speeding down the runway. Her heart dropped into her ass as they left the ground, and she may have whimpered a few times. She also may have punctured the leather armrest with her fingernails. The sense of hurtling upward eventually evened out and she breathed again. Captain Hertkorn's voice announced they were traveling at speeds Evelyn didn't want to contemplate, and Lucian unbuckled his belt.

"Would you like another drink?"

She glanced at her glass, about to decline, and was shocked to see it was empty. "Okay."

He pressed a button and the flight attendant returned. Where had she gone? Their drinks were replenished, and as Evelyn sipped her second fruity cocktail, she embraced its settling effects.

Lucian's fingers traced over the back of her hand. "Come in the back with me."

Her eyes widened. That would require unbuckling her seat belt. "I'd rather stay here."

"I wasn't asking."

"Lucian, I'm a turbulent sneeze away from wetting myself. I suggest you let me stay in my seat."

He reached over and clicked the button on her buckle. Her

breath caught. Leaning in, he swept her hair off of her shoulder and slowly kissed her neck. "Nothing will go wrong. The captain will let us know if things are going to get bumpy. Now, come with me. I have great plans for the next hour, great, distracting plans."

She rose on shaky legs and he led her to the bedroom. Her eyes immediately darted to the fall-away wall. Safety hazard! She jumped when his palm settled on her shoulders, tickling her skin beneath the straps of her tank top. His casted arm banded around her waist and tugged her close. He was already hard.

Warm kisses poured over her shoulders. He cupped her breasts through her shirt and slowly reached lower to undo the buttons of her jean skirt. "Your legs look amazing in this skirt. I'm going to start at your feet and kiss all the way to your sweet, pink pussy."

Before her skirt fell to the ground, he clasped his palm over the denim and gripped the V of her sex. Her heart raced. She leaned her backside into his arousal and he growled in her ear. It didn't take long for her to be thoroughly distracted.

Evelyn rolled to her back and sucked in a deep breath. Her body tingled from coming so many times. Lucian, who had indeed kissed every square inch of her legs and then some, toyed with her bare breasts. It was the first time they'd slept together since the accident, and they both seemed to have some pent-up energy to get out. The edge, at least, was off.

He reached to the floor and found his pocket watch. She laughed. "Are you timing yourself?"

He pinched her nipple. "No, smartass. I want to show you something."

"Please don't let it be another collapsible wall."

He rolled to his side. When he grunted, likely from putting too much pressure on his ribs, she quickly sat up.

"I'm fine." He eased off the bed and she had the urge to check his injuries, but he stayed her with an arrogant look that claimed he was invincible. "Here, put this on."

He handed her a robe and she drew back, her face scrunching up in revulsion. "Why do you have two robes?"

He frowned and glanced at the robe, then back at her. Making a sound in the back of his throat, he said, "Because I ordered this one for you. Don't be ridiculous, Evelyn. I have people who handle my planning to the last detail. This trip's for you, for us. Nothing I give you will ever be secondhand."

She relaxed, chastising herself for letting jealousy get the best of her for a moment. Her arms slipped into the wide kimono silk sleeves, and she tied the band under her breasts, then helped Lucian tie his since the cast kept getting in his way. He was impatient with his injuries. It was going to be a long few weeks.

He led her to the cabin and pointed to a small window. "Look."

She hesitated, trying very hard to forget she was in a glorified tin can careening through the clouds. He gave her a stern look, telling her to just do it, and she eased toward the little window.

Between wisps of cotton candy clouds she saw a floor of cerulean blue and gasped. "Is that—"

"The ocean."

"It's so . . . blue."

"The closer to the Caribbean, the more blue it gets. Next time you see it, your toes will be in it."

Her face split with a genuine smile. She turned and kissed him, hugging him hard enough to make him grunt. "Sorry. I keep forgetting about your ribs."

The landing was a little rough, but Lucian argued it was smooth. Bottom line, she was a terrible air traveler and hoped they wouldn't be flying too much on their trip.

A limo awaited them, and she suffered a bit of homesickness for Dugan. The chauffeur, a tall man with skin the color of molasses, took their carry-on bags and introduced himself as Clarence.

The air was thick with humidity. Evelyn's hair curled against her neck in tight little sweaty coils. Luckily, the limo was cooled and there were bottles of water chilled and waiting for them inside.

"Where are we going?" she asked once they were in the limo.

"You'll see. Here, I want you to put this on." He reached into his pocket and pulled out the black sash from her robe. Fun things always followed whenever Lucian blindfolded her, so she scooted close as he tied the sash over her hair.

"Can you see?"

"Nope."

"Good."

The drive took only a few minutes. They were soon exiting the vehicle, and she was again breathing the liquid air of Florida. Lucian carefully guided her steps. Their path changed from pavement to planks.

"I'm going to let go of you for a second. Stay still."

She heard the tinkling of bells and people talking in the distance. Then there was a strange licking sound. They were by water. She breathed deep, tasting the salt air on her lips. "When can I open my eyes?"

"Not yet. Take my hand and step carefully."

She had the sense of falling for a split second, but then her feet found purchase. Lucian led her up a somewhat steep and shaky slope, and her body teetered.

Another man greeted them, and Lucian made introductions. She couldn't see whomever they were talking to, but she imagined him with tanned, sun-kissed skin. Moisture gathered in a slick tear that pooled between her breasts, and the sun heated her shoulders. She could sense each bit of cool shade they walked through.

The man eventually excused himself, and Lucian's arms wrapped around her. "I can smell it," she whispered, as the weight of his chin rested on her shoulder.

His voice was gravelly, relaxed, and she imagined him smiling. "What does it smell like?"

Breathing deep, she said, "Nothing I've ever smelled before. It's wide-open, massive. The air tastes crisp, briny."

His lips pressed to the sensitive curve of her neck. "So does your skin. Tell me what it sounds like."

Her ears tuned out the distant chatter and soft rocking of boats. They were definitely on a boat, she decided, which was also a new experience. "It sounds . . . like secrets, deep, dark, and whispered."

His fingers toyed with the hem of her shirt, tracing soft swirls over the skin of her belly. He was arousing her with the slightest caress. His breath alone, as it echoed over the shell of her ear, was erotic. The balmy heat was moist, misting salt water over her sun-heated cheeks. She sighed and tilted her head back.

Strong fingers guided her hands to a railing and held them in place. She jumped at the roar of an engine. She amended her image of a boat to a big boat. "Do you own this boat?"

"I must insist you use the proper nautical terms so as not to offend my manhood. We're on a yacht and yes, it's mine."

"Another toy," she commented.

He nudged her backside with his hips. "I love my toys."

The yacht moved and she swayed, her fingers tightening over the rail. "How much farther?"

"Only a few minutes longer. Hold on tight."

Her body lurched into his broad form, but she didn't panic as badly as she did on the jet. So long as she was in his arms she was fine. Her hair whipped back as the yacht picked up speed. Moisture tickled her lips, and the temperate breeze went from stagnant to refreshing. Excitement, bottled up inside of her, came rushing out in bubbles of laughter. She was speeding over the ocean.

It was too overwhelming to speak. When the yacht slowed, there was more rocking, jostling, and eventually the motor was cut. A thrill of anticipation spiked up in her belly, tickling her smile with uncontainable joy.

"We're here," he whispered, lifting her arms from the rail.

Various voices called to Lucian, but he didn't stop to talk to anyone for more than a second or two as she was blindly ushered away. His hand repetitively squeezed her fingers and she could tell he was excited too. They walked down a slope and onto another planked surface. It was quieter there than where they'd departed from.

Soft ripples made delicate splashing sounds. Waves sloshed at a soothing pace. She wanted to borrow their rhythm. It was hypnotic. Her and Lucian's footsteps clanked along the planked path.

Lucian stopped and she halted. "Give me your foot." He removed her sandal. "And the other one. Now step."

She gasped as her feet sunk into soft sand. It was hot. Why hadn't she expected that? Chills raced up her spine, puckering her skin in strange places. Her entire body responded to the unique sensation beneath her feet. Her toes wiggled and she laughed.

"It's so soft."

"Come on. There's more."

Treading through sand was different than walking over a smooth surface. Her leg muscles tingled with each step. He tugged her arm, cutting off the slack of his lead, and she abruptly stopped.

"Ready?"

She grinned. She could hear how close they were, feel the open breeze. "Ready."

He took both her hands in his. Her fingers squeezed and brushed over the coarse plaster of his casted wrist. He pulled her forward and she sucked in a deep breath.

Cool water lapped at her toes, engulfing her bare feet, then licked at her ankles. He removed her blindfold, and light seeped through her lashes, causing a white glow. "Open your eyes, Evelyn."

Her lashes flickered. It was . . . incredible. There was no world on the other side of the horizon, only impressive sea and endless sky. The sun hung like a burning piece of fruit in the clouds. She'd never seen anything so impressive.

"Oh, Lucian . . ." She shook her head. "It's magnificent."

"Not nearly as magnificent as your expression right now."

They stood staring at the ocean for a long while. Eventually, they stripped off their clothes and waded into the surf. Lucian assured her their privacy was secure, as the crew had already departed the island on a smaller craft.

White, salty kisses marked her skin. Tiny urchins raced under the glass surface. Lucian could only wade out so far because of his cast, but he laughed as she dove under the waves. Euphoria surrounded her as much as the weightless water. She was a mermaid, falling through the silky waves and piercing the surface, her body buoyant and free.

Once she was sufficiently waterlogged, they lounged in the sand, the sun drying their skin. Imprints of broken shells and grit beveled her thighs. She leaned into Lucian and kissed him long and slow.

"What was that for?" he asked.

"Of all the things you've ever given me, I think this is my favorite."

He smiled, wrapping his arm around her shoulders and drawing her close. As he looked out to the horizon, his eyes crinkled and she knew he was happy. So was she.

The house was amazing. White cotton-covered windows waved gossamer sails rather than screens, and doors were never closed. They spent their days walking the private beach, making love wherever they pleased, and napping in hammocks under the shade of the tall palm trees. Lucian carved a coconut and she sipped the milk right from the fuzzy shell. It was a magical escape, better than the pages of any book read to her before. This fantasy was reality.

On the morning it rained, they remained tucked away in the

bungalow, wrapped in their own slice of heaven. She recollected tales of Robinson Crusoe and whispered remembered adventures to Lucian as the soft rain pelted the open sills. His fingers never left her.

Languid days folded into unforgettable nights. The world was far away, and the untouchable sanctuary they'd found was catalogued in her mind as the sweetest fairy tale she'd ever known.

One evening, after making love in the surf as the sun bowed brilliantly behind the horizon, they rested on the cool sand, wrapped only in a blanket of stars. Uncountable white stars winked through the inky canopy of night, and she considered never returning to the city again.

"We could live here." she whispered in his ear, her fingers slowly combing through his sea-scented hair.

"We could," he agreed on a contented sigh.

"Would you miss the city?"

"So long as I was with you, there isn't much I could miss."

She smiled softly. "Sweet talker."

They curled closer as the breeze chilled their skin. Soft ripples of the never-ending waves whispered over the sand beneath the hushed motion of the palms.

"Lucian?"

"Yes."

"What's going to happen with your deal? With Parker?"

He sighed and she waited as his eyes took in the fathomless sky. "When life announces its fleeting presence, things are sometimes thrown into perspective." His hand coasted over her shoulder, its weight a comforting presence. "I spoke to Parker the day after we found Pearl. He said, when you lost it after I fell, he realized the way you loved me would never equal anything he could make you feel for him. It was never about force with us, Evelyn. It was always about surrender.

"There's an old saying, that if you love something, you must let it go. He said he could never let you go completely, but he cares for you enough to let you be happy."

"You make me happy," she whispered.

His lips pressed into her temple. "I'm glad, because, for as much as I love you, I don't believe I could ever let you go. My only choice is to keep you happy for the rest of your life so you never want to leave."

She remembered that horrible afternoon when she'd thought she lost it all. "He made me go with you. He said you needed me and I was so afraid, but he made me go."

"As brave as I pretend to be, Evelyn, I'm glad he did. Seeing you in that house before all hell broke loose, knowing your mother was gone, I was terrified. All I've ever known is how to lead. I've always protected those I loved, because my father never did. But when I fell, I was helpless. My last thought was you. Being helpless to protect you is my greatest fear. I can only protect you when you're safely by my side. Not having you there is the worst torture I've ever known.

"In my mind, when he insisted you go to me, he surrendered. Men are made of pride. That wasn't easy for him, but it was the right thing to do and in doing so, he earned my respect. That's something Parker Hughes never had before."

"But what about what he's doing with the company you want?"

He chuckled. "I have a hundred companies, Evelyn. There's only one of you. He can have them all if that's what it takes."

She sat up, her hair pooling over his chest as she looked into his eyes. "But you put a year into that deal."

"And it will be a great boon to your friend. He'll get the security he's been searching for, the confidence he never had, and I'll get the rest of my life with you. Sometimes victory is won by surrendering something great. And in surrender, we unburden ourselves so clarity can come through. We're all just men hiding behind curtains and impressive toys, Evelyn. He can have whatever trinket validates his struggles, but he'll never have your heart. That's mine. I'll surrender everything, except for you."

She kissed him. Her heart overflowed with emotions there were no words for. As the chill of night subsided and their skin heated, he carried her to the bungalow and they made slow, sweet love. His proclamation that he'd sacrifice all in order to hold on to her heart was the most selfless vow she'd ever been given.

Every doubt she'd ever harbored, every condition she'd ever entertained, it all fell away as he showed her how much she truly meant to him. She had no riches to give, no companies to sacrifice or grand gestures to measure how much he meant to her. All she ever had, the one coveted part of her soul she protected above all else, was her heart. But it no longer felt like hers. She'd given it to him long ago and she knew, beyond the shadow of a doubt, that he would protect it above all else. Always.

They stayed on the island for seven days and seven nights. By the time they left they were both a warm shade of brown, toasted and freckled in a way she'd never been before. Her body and mind was so relaxed, the anxiety she suffered on the flight there was absent as she boarded the plane.

"I'm sad to leave," she said, staring out at the runway just before takeoff.

"We can come back whenever you'd like."

"Tomorrow?"

He laughed. "Tomorrow I suspect you'll be in love with our next destination."

Her mouth pulled into a smile. "Where are we going?"

"It's a surprise."

Their second flight was much longer than the first. When they exited the plane, she had no idea where they were. It was chilly and the air smelled of fresh rain and wood; gone was the briny trace of ocean. When their new chauffeur greeted them, Evelyn couldn't understand him. He spoke to her several times before she realized he was speaking a very heavily accented English, interspersed with expressions she'd never heard before.

"I can barely understand him," she whispered to Lucian.

"You'll get used to it. All Irishmen have thick accents, but your ears will adjust."

"We're in *Ireland?*"

"What better place to show you the breadth and scope of the mountains? Welcome to Carlingford."

Ireland was stunning. There were so many novel shades of green. The locals were lovely. They made new friends every night, laughing over pints at various local pubs. She laughed harder than she ever remembered laughing in her life. Lucian was at ease and she adored this freer side of him.

There was never time to be hungover, because before she knew it she was drinking again. Beer did funny things to her. It made her fearless.

One evening they were at a small pub, and the locals took turns singing. None were particularly good, but it was all in fun, until Lucian insisted she give it a shot, that is.

"I am *not* going up there."

"Have you ever sung in public?" he asked, brow arched in challenge.

"I've never sung, period."

"Well, this entire trip is about trying new things. What are you waiting for?"

"I don't know any songs."

"That's not true," he argued.

She honestly didn't know any songs well enough to sing. "Uh, yeah, it is."

He shook his head and stood, a devilish gleam in his eye. He approached the three-man band and whispered something to them. The men discussed and nodded in unison.

Lucian went to the microphone and said, "I'm here with a beautiful woman tonight, but she's being a little shy. You see, I promised her I'd help her experience everything she never tried before. It just so happens she's never sung. She knows a song, but may need some help. Who's up to helping her?"

The rowdy patrons cheered and lifted their mugs in the air. There was no hiding from their enthusiastic calls. Slowly she rose, shooting him a glare that promised retribution, and went to the stage. When Lucian tried to step down, she dug her fingernails into his arm. "Oh, no. You're not leaving me."

The man on the guitar began to play. She panicked when she didn't recognize the song. She knew she wouldn't!

Suddenly a man with a strange drum joined, and twinges of familiar rhythms flickered in her brain. She recognized it . . . sort of.

"Shall we start you off, lass?" the guitar player shouted. She nodded and he grinned. When he sang, it only took a moment for her to place the song. *"Just sit right back and you'll hear a tale, a tale of a fateful trip."*

Her mind prickled with recognition as her shoulders began to bob slowly to the cheery beat. It was her favorite television show! She jumped in, belting out the line about the mighty sailing mate and the brave skipper from that three-hour tour.

The audience echoed back the chorus. *"A three-hour tour!"*

The music picked up and so did her energy. It was a rush, singing like that. The next verse was sung with much more verve. By the time they were calling out the characters, everyone was shouting along.

She grabbed the microphone and tugged on Lucian. *"The millionaire . . ."*

He tugged her back, his eyes gleaming mischievously as he stared into her. *"And his wife . . ."*

Heat pooled in her belly, full of excitement, at that look of promise in his gaze. A smile tugged at her lips, and her voice fell away as she stood suspended in his arms, paralyzed by his potent stare. The patrons finished the drunken rendition on their own. Slowly, he leaned down to press his warm lips to hers, and everyone else fell away.

As the last verse was sung, she was dipped back and kissed properly, in front of the entire crowd. *"Here on Gilligan's Isle!"* They burst into applause and she blushed furiously.

After that night, Lucian never made mention of wives or marriage or anything else pertaining to wedding rings and the like. She was surprisingly disappointed, but still having the time of her life.

On their last night in Ireland, she watched the sun set over the mountains of Carlingford. Blushing clouds settled over the peaks as the sky faded from vibrant shades of burnt sienna to deep violet. She'd miss the simplicity of Ireland, but was anxious to see where Lucian would take her next.

As she suspected, life and work called on Lucian even as oceans separated him from the city of Folsom. He'd started using their quiet mornings to tend to business that couldn't wait for their return. She didn't mind, because he also set her up with an iPad that had an interesting program that let her videoconference with Jason.

Their online lessons were not as long, but just enough to keep her mind sharp. Jason would go over some examples, holding a notepad in front of the screen, and then she would complete her assignment in the workbook she packed. Lucian looked over her work and was impressed with how quickly she was learning.

Evelyn was surprised that they didn't return to the jet when they left Ireland. They took a boat called a ferry, and then a train. She'd seen trains before, but never ridden on one. Their next stop was England, and it was the most magical of all.

There were castles and villages hundreds of years old. It was as humbling as the ocean. Where the sea made her feel small in the presence of such unstoppable motion, England made her feel ordinary, lost in some span of countless time. Such emotions might not appeal to others, but they certainly appealed to her.

Her entire life, she only wanted to be ordinary. Lost among so much history made her feel exactly that. Ordinary. It also made her realize how fleeting their time on this earth was. Urgency rushed at her, tucked like a secret in those many still moments they found in England, and she wanted to embrace life and all of its greatness.

They'd taken a tour to Stonehenge, and it was there that she found something she never knew she wanted.

Her gaze locked on the impressive structures, wonder filling her as she tried to imagine the strong hands that had once placed them there, hands that belonged to hearts that loved and minds that held memories of their own.

"Do you think this is magic?" she asked, taking in the open space untouched by passing time.

"The stones?" Lucian asked.

"No. All of it." Her hand swept out over the encompassing distance. Waves of green rolled over the hillsides. There was so much immeasurable beauty and nature. It was so different than the structures she'd grown up under in the city. The impressive skyscrapers of Folsom, crafted by visionaries and demigods, paled in comparison to this impressive creation.

This openness was God's work, and no man could ever encompass such magnificence. Perhaps that was why these stones were so notable. They didn't try to overcompensate or compete with what already existed. They simply rested humbly in the presence of the greatness that already was.

"No, not magic, traces of history left untouched."

"Do you believe in God, Lucian?"

He took a long while to answer. "I believe there's something that created all this. But I'm not sure if I believe in a being that watches over us."

Her gaze went to the clouds rolling in the distance. "I actually spent a lot of time in churches. Sometimes, going to church was the only way to keep warm. People think every religion's different, but if you really listen, they're all teaching the same thing."

"What are they teaching?"

"Be kind. Be good. Be humble."

His arm draped over her shoulder. He pulled her close and kissed her temple. "*You* humble me, Evelyn." He squeezed her shoulder.

They'd been traveling for three weeks. The mansion in England was breathtaking. She found Lucian reviewing travel plans the evening before they departed, and she knocked softly on the study door. "Lucian?"

He grinned, plucking his reading glasses from his nose. "I thought you were in bed."

"I was." She slipped into the room and he pulled her onto his lap. "I couldn't sleep."

"Something on your mind?"

"Are we returning to the States tomorrow?"

"Yes, but not to Folsom." She wrung her fingers and he stilled her hands. "Did you want to see something else before we left?"

She took a deep breath. He'd showed her so much while in Europe, but there was one place he never mentioned and one person she'd like to meet. "I thought it would be nice to visit Paris."

He stiffened. "Just Paris?"

She turned in his lap and gripped his face with gentle hands, her eyes pleading. "He's your father, Lucian. You said he was ill the last time you visited. We're in Europe. Why not just make the trip?"

His expression was unreadable. When he didn't answer, she said, "I'd like to meet him."

"You'll be disappointed."

"I might surprise you. My expectation of parents is astoundingly low."

He laughed without humor. "My father isn't a nice man."

"Maybe he's changed."

"He hasn't."

She sighed. "Lucian, there is so much I wish I could have shown Pearl. Those moments to wish are over now. Don't let them slip away from you too. It isn't him you'll be punishing. You'll be the one outliving him and it will be your regret to bear, not his. Let me meet your father."

His chest rose as he drew in a slow breath. "Fine, but I don't want to stay more than a day."

She smiled. "Okay."

As his lips banished her grin, his hands slithered under her robe. She giggled and pressed her thighs together. "Open for me," he commanded against her lips.

Her thighs slowly parted and his fingers slipped inside her heat. She arched, hands tightening over his shoulders. His mouth trailed down the narrow column of her throat and found her breasts. Soon they were naked on the floor, equally satisfied and breathing heavily, all thoughts of the days to come vanishing in the presence of their priceless now.

Lucian was acting strange as the limo rode through the streets of France. She'd never seen him behave that way before. It took her longer than it should have to realize he was nervous. She wanted to put him at ease.

"You have a hotel here, right?" she asked, hoping to distract him.

"Yes."

"Does it look the same as the one in Folsom?"

"It's bigger."

Her eyes widened. "Do you have a penthouse you keep there?"

"No. I rarely come to France anymore."

She was silent. Her mind worked to think of a neutral topic. "Have you spoken to your sisters?"

"No. I should probably call."

"Do you think Jamie and Toni will get married?" she blurted.

He squinted at her. "Are you trying to stress me out?"

"No, just asking."

His legs shifted in his seat and he fidgeted with his tie. It was the first time since they left the States that he'd dressed up. It was a show of power.

"I don't know," he said after a long contemplative moment.

She frowned. "Don't know what?"

"About Shamus and Antoinette. I don't see it, but then again, my sister always seems to get what she wants, and she's always wanted Shamus."

He picked up her hand and his finger brushed over the knuckle of her ring finger. She wondered if he'd ever propose again. "We haven't played chess in a while," she said, remembering how he'd asked her.

"The last time I played, I lost."

"Perhaps you should try again."

"Perhaps."

The limo turned onto a rounded stone driveway, and an old mansion came into view. He sucked in a deep breath and sat more stiffly. "Brace yourself. Claudette will likely squeeze the life out of us."

"Who's Claudette?"

"My father's maid."

The car slowed to a stop and the chauffeur opened the door. Evelyn climbed out and stretched. Lucian paid the driver and took their bags. They climbed the stone steps and he rang the bell.

A female voice sang a French greeting and the door opened. If this was Claudette, Evelyn loved her on the spot. She was short, round, soft, and gray haired. Her face drooped, eyes wide, as her mouth fell open. *"Lucian!"*

"Hello, Claudette."

"What . . . what are you doing here?" Her accent was thick.

"This is Evelyn Keats. We were in England and decided to visit."

Claudette stared at Evelyn and back at Lucian. She rapidly shot off words in French that sounded as if she were praying. "My goodness, you have a woman!"

Lucian smiled. The maid trilled and lunged, her arms gobbling him up in a hug. Her small form somehow engulfed his towering body, and Evelyn grinned. He laughed and the maid released him. "What is this?" she demanded, pointing to his cast.

"That's nothing, a small accident. It will be coming off in another week or two."

She tsked and suddenly Evelyn's face was being pinched between chubby fingers that smelled of pastry. "And let me look at you, mademoiselle. Oh, you are quite lovely. You must be charming too, to capture *garçon*'s heart."

As the maid threw her arms around her, Evelyn whimpered. They were relieved of their bags and bustled into the house. "Your father is resting. Shall I wake him or would you like to settle in first?"

"We'll settle in upstairs first."

"*Oui*," she said. "You can use the room you stayed in last time. Will that do, *garçon*?"

"That will be fine," said Lucian, his voice level.

The maid's speech volleyed between French and English, sometimes using both languages in one sentence. It was overwhelming. When Lucian switched to French, something inside of Evelyn quivered.

As they carried their bags up the stairs, she admired the banister. The house was old, like Lucian's home in Carlingford, and Evelyn was strangely homesick for Ireland. Who would've thought she'd ever have a right to such emotions when she never had a home?

She followed Lucian down a wide hall and he opened the door to a bedroom. The furniture was made of thick, dark wood. The smaller pieces perched on ball-and-claw feet. The bed was adorned in dark velvet drapes pulled back at the four posts, and a chair and ottoman sat in front of the empty fireplace.

He placed their things on the bed. There wasn't much. Lucian had the majority of their clothes delivered to the jet. "You know," she said, shutting the door. "It's very sexy when you speak French."

He quirked an eyebrow and looked at her over his shoulder. "*N'est-ce pas?*"

She smiled. "I have no idea what you just said."

"*Alors peut-être que vous pourriez enlever vos vêtements.*"

Her body reacted, coiling and heating low in her belly. She laughed. "What did you say?"

He removed his jacket and draped it over the back of the chair. "I said, 'is that so?' Then I said, 'Perhaps it would help if you took off your clothes.'" His fingers plucked at the light cardigan she wore over her dress.

Her lips pulled to the side, hiding her smile. "Maybe you're right."

"I usually am," he whispered, pulling off the cardigan and dropping it to the floor.

EVELYN'S fingers went numb as they walked to the den. Lucian knocked briskly and opened the doors. Evelyn took a deep breath and followed him in.

Lucian's father, a tall and remarkably handsome older man, stood. "I could barely believe my ears when Claudette told me you were here. And with a woman no less."

"Hello, Christos. This is Evelyn Keats."

Christos Patras nodded with little evidence of affection toward his son. His hair was white as silver fox fur. He turned to

Evelyn, and she watched his unapologetic, dark eyes move over her appraisingly. "Keats. That isn't a name I'm familiar with."

"It's nice to finally meet you, Mr. Patras. And no, my name doesn't mean much."

"Who are your parents?"

"Dad." Lucian's tone was sharp and warning.

His father waved him off. "Calm down, Lucian. I'm only curious. This is a long way from Folsom. I imagine you'd only bring a woman here if she meant something to you." He turned back to Evelyn. "Are you in love with my son or his money?"

She bristled. His question was rude and took her by surprise. "I beg your pardon?"

"We may be a continent away, but we still get the news from home. I've seen your picture. I've read the stories. I've never been one for beating around the bush, so I figured I'd give you the courtesy of answering for yourself."

"That's just it, Mr. Patras, the only person I answer for, and to, *is* myself. If you want to know my intentions, I suggest you take the time to get to know me and make a decision on your own. That's the kind of man you are anyway. Am I correct? Words only hold a small value next to your instinct."

Lucian sniggered.

"She's feisty," Mr. Patras said to his son. "You'll have your hands full."

Lucian said something in French. His father's brows lifted and he replied quickly, also using French.

Lucian looked his father in the eye and simply said, "*Oui.*"

She cleared her throat and mumbled to Lucian. "Not sexy anymore. What did you just say about me?"

He didn't answer, and now his father was really studying her. "I see," Mr. Patras said. "Well then, the pleasure is all mine, Ms. Keats."

He shook her hand and she hated that he might feel her fingers trembling. "You can call me Evelyn."

"And you may call me Christos. Shall we have coffee?"

They settled into soft upholstered chairs that were too dainty and feminine for both men. Claudette brought in a tray of biscuits, and coffee in a polished silver kettle. She smiled sweetly at Evelyn and quickly bustled out of the room.

"So tell me, Evelyn, are the stories true? Did my son take advantage of you?"

She stilled, her biscuit suspended between her mouth and her tiny plate. "What?"

"You've read the rags, haven't you? Your age is a mystery. And then there was one rumor that you had a child in grade school. Are you a mother?"

"Christos, stop with the inquisition."

"I don't read the tabloids," she said, hiding her discomfort.

"Good girl," Christos commented, sounding so much like Lucian. "And the child? Are you a mother?"

"No. I have no family."

"How very . . . simplistic for you."

Lucian ran a hand over her knee. "Only you would see it that way," he said with dry acceptance.

"Indeed. So what brings you to Europe?"

"Lucian wanted to show me the mountains."

"Evelyn's never been outside of Folsom."

Christos cocked his head. "Really?"

The questions were growing tedious. She decided to put an end to them so that she could actually get to know Lucian's father and perhaps show Lucian something new. They only had a short time in France.

Placing her plate on the table, she faced the older man. "Christos, I also don't beat around the bush, so here's the truth of the matter. I have nothing. I've never had anything besides a name.

Your family's financial situation overwhelms me. I'm not capable of measuring such wealth and, while I'm a realist enough to know it's impressive, it's not why I'm here. I'm here because I just lost my mother, who happened to be the only parent I ever had. She disappointed me more than she ever made me proud, and I hate that I was never lucky enough—in my *entire* life—to have a conversation with her not weighted with resentment or necessity."

He was silent for a long moment. After clearing his throat, he said, "I'm sorry to hear about your mother."

"Thank you."

He sighed. "You're a smart girl."

"Smart enough to know that no amount of poverty or wealth erases a child's desire for a parent's approval, their friendship, and love. It takes effort, and one person's determination isn't always enough. Your son is one of the most resolute men I've ever met, but even he doesn't have the power to fix your relationship unless you want to fix it as well."

Both men wore expressions of discomfort and averted their gazes. She stood. "I'm suddenly tired. Why don't you stay and talk with your father for a bit while I lay down, Lucian?"

"Evelyn." Lucian's tone was laced with warning.

She kissed him and whispered, "I never had a dad. I'd like to know what that feels like."

His eyes narrowed and she turned away, quickly leaving the room. Her heart raced as she slid the doors closed, waiting for him to storm after her, but he never did. She paused on the other side of the door and listened as the rumblings of words finally came. Sighing with a smile, she turned and stilled.

A woman with dark black hair and striking eyes watched her from a few feet away. She asked something in French and Evelyn shook her head. "Sorry. I don't speak French."

"You are the woman who brought Lucian here?"

"Yes. I'm Evelyn."

She held out her dainty hand. *"Bonjour,* Evelyn. I am Tibet."

Ah, the mistress. She shook her hand. "Thank you for letting us stay."

"Christos's children are always welcome here, although they never come. It is a surprise to see Lucian twice in only a few months. He spoke to me about you during his last visit."

That took her by surprise. "He . . . he did?"

She gestured to a door and Evelyn followed her. It was a room completely made of glass. The garden blooms created a whimsical splash of color on the walls. "I told him I knew he was in love." They settled into wicker chairs cushioned with floral pillows. "He did not deny it. I told him not to waste time. His heart was clearly in the States."

Was that what sent him back to Folsom before the supposed thirty days had passed? "I'm glad you told him that."

"I also told him we fall in love with people who resemble our parents. I asked who you were most like, his mother or father."

"I never met Lucian's mother, and I only just met his father." It was a strange comparison to make, but she was suddenly curious of the answer.

Tibet smiled sadly. Her fingers laced over her crossed legs as her gaze drifted. "She was a lovely woman, the kind of woman who was difficult to look at, because she was always so perfectly put together. But most of her beauty was inside. She had a grace about her that could not be mimicked. She was serene, angelic, and delicate."

And this woman destroyed *that woman's* family. Evelyn imagined Lucian's mother and then looked at Tibet. She was dark, beautiful, and quietly dangerous, reminding Evelyn of a black widow spider, nothing like the description of Lucian's mom. On the other hand, neither was she.

"She doesn't sound like me."

She smiled. "Then you are like Christos."

Why did she have to be like either of them? "I don't think so."

"Really? Christos is brave. He has more fortitude in him than any person I know. No challenge is enough to make him quit without trying. Yet he is terrified of love. He resents having people close to him, because they become liabilities."

She was speechless. That was her. Was that what drew Lucian to her? Was she a supplement for the unattainable love of his father? She frowned. "I'm not all that brave."

Tibet tilted her head and studied her, a knowing smile on her painted red lips. "The tabloids can be quite harsh at times, but there is also some truth behind them. The media likes to paint the Patras family as better than everyone else. I know what it feels like to come up short in their comparisons."

She resented being put in the same category as the woman who broke up a family. "I don't waste my time with their assumptions."

"Eventually you will come out with a statement."

"Lucian says that's up to me."

"And what do you plan to say?"

This woman was indeed a spider. Evelyn didn't appreciate the sticky sense of being caught in a web. She stood. "I haven't decided yet. You read the tabloids. You'll have to wait with the rest of the gossipmongers."

Tibet stood and caught her arm. "I've offended you. I'm sorry. That wasn't my intention."

Evelyn stared down at the woman's hand curling softly around her wrist. Lucian loved his mother and that made it difficult to care for Tibet. They'd definitely gotten off on the wrong foot. She stepped back, cutting all physical contact.

"I think you want to protect Christos the same way I want to protect Lucian. If Christos considers the people he loves a liability, and sees Lucian as a threat, it only proves that he loves his son. I'm glad. But they both have to own their mistakes for anything to change. Your husband taught Lucian everything he knows about being cold and calculating. We won't stay long. He can either make this right or continue on the way things have always been. I asked Lucian to come here, but if I was wrong and he gets hurt, I'll never push him toward his father again."

A door slammed and they both winced. Tibet sighed. "Christos wants to love, but he doesn't know how."

"Does anyone? Excuse me."

Evelyn left the garden room and knocked softly on the doors that led to the den. "Yes?"

It was Christos. She slid the doors open and sighed at the sight of his haggard expression. Lucian was gone.

"I suspect you'll be leaving shortly," he said.

She entered the room and settled into a chair. "You fought?"

He sighed. "It's the only way we know."

"Why?"

"Because that is the way it's always been."

Looking down at her knees peeking past the hem of her dress, she thought. "You know, my entire life, I never heard my mother say she loved me. I wasn't quite sure what love was. I saw it as an obligation of attachment. When I met Lucian and, for the first time, actually fell in love, I hated it. It was inconvenient and messy and changed me in ways I wasn't comfortable with.

"I denied my feelings, but he insisted the absence of words didn't negate the truth of sentiment. I didn't come around until I thought I lost him." Her mind tracked back to those horrible nights she spent crying for him, hating how much he could hurt her. "He was right. I loved him. Saying so didn't make the feelings any more true, and bottling them up did nothing to diminish how I felt."

Christos watched her as she spoke. The resemblance between him and Lucian was perhaps what made her comfortable speaking to him so candidly. She went on.

"My mother was sick from the time I was born. Drugs. She was the only influence I ever had. There was plenty about her that I hated, but also plenty I adored. She taught me what not to be as much as she showed me how to survive. When you aren't given certain things, it's difficult to miss them. But after meeting Lucian, every time he told me he loved me, I realized, more than any object of value, that was what I wanted most. Love. I finally understood how starved I was for such tenderness. I wanted to hear those words from my mom, to just once know what it felt like to hear that she cared for me the way he did. I never did."

"I see why Lucian cares for you. You're a very intelligent young lady," Christos said, and she lowered her gaze to hide the heat rising under her cheeks. His voice grew soft, barely audible. "I was not a good father."

She gave him a moment for his words to settle in. There was no need to comment. The truth is what it is. She was glad when he went on.

"I'm proud of the man Lucian's become, but if I told him that, he'd make some snide comment, discrediting the truth of my words."

"We all have defense mechanisms. Nobody wants to be rejected, but love means putting yourself out there. Someone has to take the first step."

"I suppose that should be me," Christos commented, his dark eyes meeting hers.

"He loves you. I know he does. If he didn't, the distance between you wouldn't bother him so much. Hate does not negate love. Indifference is what you need to fear, but I promise you, Lucian is not indifferent toward you."

They were quiet for several long minutes. "Do you intend to marry my son?"

If she hadn't known Lucian as well as she did, she might have been put off by his father's bluntness. "He has to ask."

"I think," Christos said quietly, "it would be a novel experience having a daughter I can talk to."

She smiled. His compliment was simple and understated, but it gave her a great sense of accomplishment. She met his gaze as if there was an unspoken secret between them. "I think it would be nice to have the same in a parent."

"That won't be possible if Lucian forbids it."

He was right. She wouldn't speak to him if it meant hurting Lucian. Her first loyalty was to him. "You can make sure he doesn't."

They both turned as the door slid open. Lucian appraised the two of them, his eyes narrow and suspicious. "Evelyn. I ordered a car. We're leaving in a few minutes."

Her heart sunk. "You said we could stay the night."

Before he could answer, Christos stood. "I'd like to take the two of you to dinner. I know you made other plans, but . . . it would mean a lot to me."

Lucian's jaw ticked. She gave him a pleading look. "I'd like to stay."

His eyes shut and his expression looked pained. "Very well. We'll leave first thing in the morning."

Dinner was an experience. The cuisine was much like the fare served at the hotel, being that the head chef at Patras was Parisian. Tibet and Lucian were silent for most of the meal, while Christos and Evelyn held up the majority of the conversation.

Several times she caught Lucian watching them, a perplexed look on his face. They didn't talk about business. Rather, she spoke of their trip to Ireland and England and how much she loved the island off the coast of Florida.

Christos complimented her often and smiled with natural affection crinkling his eyes. It was a side, she believed, Lucian had never before seen in his father.

The ride home was filled with chatter. She often invited Lucian

into the conversation, but he only offered up one-word statements. Tibet also seemed to watch them with a sort of disbelief.

Evelyn saw signs of that stubborn, determined Patras mentality,
but compared to Lucian, Christos seemed like a big marshmallow.
It was so blatantly obvious to her that this man, like his son, was
desperate for the connections they'd denied themselves over the
years. She was happy to bridge the gap and took great pride in the
building connection she sensed between herself and Lucian's father.

When they returned to the house, she was still tipsy from dinner and gripped Christos's arm as their laughter echoed through
the foyer.

"She's a pistol, Lucian. Don't let her go," Christos laughed.

Lucian's expression remained blank. "I don't intend to." His
unaffected tone sobered them.

Evelyn turned to Christos and said, "Thank you for a lovely
evening."

He smiled, perhaps a bit sad to see it come to an end. "Any-
time, my dear."

She said good night and followed Lucian up to their room.
When she shut the door, the tension was palpable. "Are you
okay?"

He mumbled something and undid his tie. "You certainly won
over my father."

She stilled. "Does that aggravate you?"

"It will aggravate me when he does something typical and hurts
your feelings. I know him. This act he's putting on now isn't real."

"Why? Because it's incongruent with the man you knew ten
years ago? People change, Lucian."

"Not him."

She tossed her bag on the chair and stilled his hands over the
buttons of his shirt. "Your father loves you, Lucian. He's trying to
show you, and you aren't giving him the opportunity he needs."

"Why should I give him anything?"

"Because you love him too, and this void between the two of you hurts."

He sighed and shut his eyes. His forehead came to rest on hers. "How is it you see the parts of me I've spent my whole life successfully hiding?"

"Because I'm like you. Love is scary. But now that I know all the good things it can bring, I've changed my position and decided it's worth the risk. Your father is not the enemy anymore, Lucian. Stop fighting him. Give him a chance before he's gone. I'd hate to see you haunted with regret."

His head tilted, and soft lips traced over hers. "I should strangle him for flirting with you."

She drew back. "He was not flirting with me."

"Oh yes, he was. It was like you put him under a spell. I only allowed it to go on because it was pissing off Tibet."

She laughed. "I don't get her. She's . . . it's like she loves your dad, but he'll never love her back enough, not by her standards at least. And she knows it."

"She's got a lot to answer for. She'll never be more than the woman who hurt my mother. I can tolerate her, but I'll never see past that scarlet letter."

Her fingers traced down his throat. "What now?"

The zipper at her back was dragged down and her dress peeled away. "I'm done with the family stuff for a while. Tomorrow we'll have breakfast before we leave and I'll make an effort to play nice so long as you remember which Patras you belong to."

Her fingers brushed over the ridge in his pants. "Hmm, here I thought I belonged to myself. Maybe I need a lesson to remind me—"

His fist gripped her hair and tilted her head back. All words cut off as he pressed his lips to her jaw and nibbled the soft skin behind her ear. Looking in her eyes, his fingers tightened. "You're mine, Evelyn. *Mine*."

His mouth closed over her in a total act of possession. Her fingers pulled at his shirt until he had her pinned beneath him on the bed.

Her clothes were ripped from her body. He spread her thighs and his eyes dilated, going completely black. "You're soaked." He grinned wickedly.

She gazed down at his now-naked body, all sinew and strength. His cock swelled, and with one deep thrust he was driving into her.

That night he took her completely, irrevocably, and she cherished the sensation of being so thoroughly owned.

Breakfast was cordial. Lucian made an effort not to close himself off, and Christos delicately tried to incite conversation. It was sort of precious, seeing two intimidating men struggle to become more than enemies. It would take time, but Evelyn was glad they'd made the trip. This was a big step in the right direction.

When their car arrived, Christos hugged her. "Don't stay away too long, you hear?"

She patted his cheek. "You know you could come to Folsom too."

Christos looked at Lucian, who was doing a remarkable job of acting like he hadn't heard her suggestion. His father glanced back at her, "If we reach that point, I'd count it as a win."

"Time," she whispered and he nodded. "Thank you for having us."

"You're always welcome."

Saying good-bye to Tibet was sort of like petting a cactus. She could be soft, but she also had the proven ability to draw blood. She doubted the Patras children would ever fully accept her, but their tolerance of her presence in their father's life was perhaps enough.

As the car pulled away, Lucian rested his hand on her knee. "Do you think you'll hear from him soon?" she asked.

"I don't really know what I'd say if he called. This entire trip has been . . . a surprise."

"Maybe he finally realizes what he's been missing all those years away from you three."

"Maybe."

"Do you regret coming?" she asked, holding her breath.

"You know . . . I did, but now I'm not sure. It made me happy to see you two get along. My dad doesn't say much as far as praise, but, the way he looked at you, it made me proud. I think he, in a way, was proud of me too."

nineteen

COMING HOME

THE jet landed in New York. It was strange being in a city that was not Folsom. There were familiar structures and the same recognizable metropolitan pulse, but they were still very far from home. However, she wasn't homesick.

They stayed the night at Lucian's brownstone in Manhattan because he'd arranged an appointment with a doctor to remove his cast the following day. The narrow house was compact, but luxurious nonetheless. They'd dined at a renowned steak house, and on the way home Evelyn had a sort of epiphany.

Lucian had so many houses, but she wasn't sure which was his home. "Where do you live?" she asked as they climbed the steps to the brownstone.

"Pardon?"

"You have so many houses. Which one do you consider home?"

He tilted his head and unlocked the door. "I'm not sure. The estate is my home, but so is the hotel. I love Ireland, but I also love England."

She toed off her shoes and faced him. "Is one your favorite?"

"They're all different now," he said, shaking his head.

"Different how?"

"Whenever I think of Ireland, I'll think of you singing in the pub. And the ocean off the coast of Florida was never as beautiful as when your toes first touched the water. Artifacts and historic places of England I see with new appreciation, because of seeing them through your eyes. And even my condo in Folsom . . . that's always been my central home, but when you left it was nothing more than a cell. I think . . . you're home. Wherever you are is where I want to be."

She blinked as emotion snuck up on her. "I feel the same way," she whispered, going up on her toes to kiss him. "Make love to me, Lucian."

He led her up the stairs and together they stripped off their clothes. When their bodies came together it was a joining of souls. He was her shelter. He was her peace.

She had nothing to offer him other than herself, but that was all he ever seemed to truly want of her. Over the past weeks, she understood so much more about who he was, and for the first time, she saw herself.

She was no longer a girl, but a woman. No longer was she racing against all odds to find the security she'd always coveted. She had everything she needed right there in the arms of the man she loved.

Her body writhed beneath his weight as he filled her. For him, she was a vessel of surrender, and for her he was a tower of strength. She realized home, for either of them, did not come in the shape of walls, but in the sense of heart. He showed her how to love and she, somehow, taught him the same.

As they lay beneath the shadows of night, holding each other tightly, she thought of all her fears over the years. When would she eat? Where would she sleep? How would she stay warm? Lucian had become a safe harbor for her to always come back to, but he was so much more than the reliable security she assumed she wanted. He was her solace, her happiness, her reason for laughter, and her desire for so much more.

For the first time in her life, she was able to imagine a future without considering Pearl. She could go wherever she wanted, be whomever she chose. She was free, but held safe. Not out of obligation or because he had become a liability to her heart, but because she wanted him.

On the nightstand, she saw a felt-tip pen and paper. Lucian's fingers trailed over her breasts as the two of them gazed at the ceiling in contentment. She reached for the pen and sat up.

"What are you doing?" he said, grumbling that she interrupted their comfort.

"Give me your hand." He held out his right hand. "No, the other one."

His brow crinkled, but he gave her the hand covered in the cast. She looked down at the plaster bandage, remembering how frightened she'd been that day. Turning his wrist, she uncapped the pen with her teeth and pressed it to the scratchy surface. Her hand moved with practiced effort.

MARRY ME

Lucian looked at her inscription and stilled. His shoulders rose, as he seemed to let out a breath he'd been holding for far too long. When he gazed up at her, there were tears in his eyes, shimmering like dark puddles in the moonlight. He shook his head, a smile pulling at his lips.

A soft, gravelly laugh slipped past his throat. She didn't know what was so funny, then he leaned over to his side of the bed and produced a familiar box. It was her ring. "I've been lugging this thing around for months, waiting for the right moment, and you beat me to it."

Her face split with a grin as relief rushed through her veins. "I didn't know if you'd ever ask again."

"It's all I've wanted to ask." He opened the box. There was her favorite stone, polished into several fine pearls nestling the most beautiful diamond she'd ever seen in her life. He withdrew the ring. His voice was soft, full of emotion. "Evelyn, be my queen, protect me, stand by me, love me, and I promise to always do the same."

The ring slid on her finger and fit perfectly. She admired the way the stones and the diamond winked in the moonlight. Gazing back at Lucian, she whispered, "Yes."

Every night, every chill, every ache, suddenly fell into place. This was what she was meant for. In a world of uncertainty, she'd never before felt like she belonged as she did in that moment, in his arms. He was hers. And for the first time, a true sense of peace opened her heart. For he was the most valuable thing she'd ever owned.

mrs. lucian patras

epilogue
.....

six months later . . .

"*The wedding was an intimate affair. Mrs. Patras wore a couture gown, her hair hung in loose curls, as she made her vows to Folsom's most sought-after bachelor. Only a few close friends and family members attended the ceremony in the yard of Lucian Patras's mansion in the Hamptons.*

'*The mysterious Evelyn Keats, now Patras, was rumored to have been escorted down the aisle by none other than Christos Patras himself, who has been residing in Paris, France, since his son overtook Patras Industries over a decade ago. The engagement was kept secret for many months. Sources believe the couple was out of the country when the proposal was made.*

'*When spotted at a Manhattan bakery and asked about her past, Mrs. Patras simply stated, "Perhaps someday I'll write my own story, but until then, all you need to know is that I fell in love with an incredible man who showed me what home was."*

'*The couple has since returned from their honeymoon in Greece and they are now back in Folsom. While Patras remains*

the same unyielding financial king of Folsom, there is specula-
tion he is a different man behind the scenes. Family and friends
have remained tight-lipped regarding the newlyweds, but we
suspect Folsom will be welcoming a very young, new tycoon in
the coming year.'"

Evelyn closed the tabloid and stared at her mother's gravestone. "I wish you could have been there, Momma. It was so wonderful. We danced and feasted like royalty. Everything was perfect. Lucian even had a pair of sneakers made to match my dress for when my feet got tired." She shook her head, overwhelmed by how irrevocably she'd fallen for her husband.

Her hands patted the turned earth blanketing her mother. "We've started discussing children," she quietly confessed. "Lucian would like to try for a family, but I'm scared. He'd be a wonderful father. Our children would never want for anything. I just . . . sometimes I worry."

Evelyn never wanted to let her children down. She always wanted to be there for them, love them, and assure them of it every day.

She had grown used to letting Lucian make most of the difficult decisions. He was good at it, and she trusted him to choose what was best for them. She held on to her apartment until after the wedding, giving him the key as a wedding gift, a sign that she was ready.

He supported her decision to continue with her education, and there was something so priceless about seeing words and reading them herself. She would be getting her GED soon and wasn't sure what her future would bring. She'd convinced Lucian that she would work and he finally accepted the inevitable, proving his support the day he unveiled the art studio he built her, stocked to the rafters with sea glass and uncut metals. He'd even started discussing higher education with her, suggesting she might enjoy earning a degree in art in order to turn her skills into an independent business venture.

When it came to submission, they'd both learned a bit about sacrifice. Most of all, it never felt like sacrifice when a compromise was made for the one person they loved more than themselves. She continued to surrender to Lucian domestically, and he had learned to accept her independence outside of the home. She would never be socially submissive, and that was enough.

Trust.

She trusted him to decide for them, but he never overlooked the fact that she'd always be *her*. Evelyn Scout Keats Patras.

However, with the decision to start a family, he'd said it was her choice. He wanted a family and she wanted to give him one, but it would be her decision when that would actually happen, and she'd finally made up her mind.

Her eyes turned toward the house as the limo came into view. She scooped up her magazine and kissed her fingers, then placed them on the cool headstone. "I love you, Momma."

She quickly headed down the hill toward the house, racing to make it inside before Lucian. The grass crunched under her feet with each hurried step as the crisp January air chapped her cheeks. Lucy held the door for her as she bolted in the house, and the maid quickly took her coat.

Evelyn rushed up the steps and began stripping away her clothes. He'd find the trail before the servants did and would know where she was. When she made it to the bedroom, she dropped to her knees and rested her hands, palms up, over her thighs.

The sound of the front door opening had her pulse quickening. She breathed steadily as she awaited her husband. His steady footfalls imprinted on her heart. A low chuckle echoed in the quiet house, and she imagined he'd found her trail of clothing.

When the door slowly opened, he spotted her and stilled, her discarded clothes in his hands. His eyes bore into hers, crinkling with anticipation and curiosity. "Mrs. Patras," he said tossing the clothes aside and loosening his tie. "How was your day?"

She lifted her lashes and smiled. "Very nice, Mr. Patras. How was yours?"

"Long." He stepped into the room and quietly closed the door. "This is quite a welcome. May I ask what has provoked such a beautiful display of surrender?"

"I have a gift for you."

He toed off his shoes and removed his jacket, adding it to the pile of her items. He stepped closer. "A greater gift than finding my wife awaiting me in nothing but a smile?"

She nodded. "I saw Dr. Sheffield today."

He stilled. Lucian was usually aware of her every move, and the fact that she'd done so without his knowledge clearly took him by surprise. "And how did that go?"

A shaky breath filled her lungs. Courage. He'd once taught her that clothes were courage, but over time, she'd learned that there was nothing more courageous than laying yourself bare for the one you loved. "I want to have a baby."

His breath caught and he dropped to his knees. His hands found hers as he pressed his forehead into hers. "Are you sure?" he rasped.

"I'm sure."

His lips pressed to hers and emotion erupted between them. His gratitude for her gift came in the form of tight breaths and shimmering eyes. His hand tugged at her neck as he drew her close and kissed her passionately.

"When?" he asked.

"After my graduation this spring. I would like to have at least one year of my husband to myself, but then . . . then we can try."

He laughed softly and pulled her into a tight hug. "You will always have me, love. A child will only expand on the love we already share."

It was unfathomable, to love more than she already did. Intrepid excitement rolled through her. Her gaze found his, and a potent need unfurled at the look in his onyx eyes.

"Welcome home," she whispered, and he took her mouth, easing her to her back, claiming the haven of her surrender.

Safely tucked in the shelter of his body, the one home she'd learned she could always depend on, she sighed as his lips grazed her ear, his voice low and intense. "I love you, Scout."